All The Young Warriors

Copyright © 2012 Anthony Neil Smith

All rights reserved.

All the characters in this book are fictitious and any resemblance to actual persons, living or dead, is purely coincidental.

Cover design by JT Lindroos
Cover photos: Expert Infantry and Moriza

Published by Blasted Heath

ACKNOWLEDGMENTS

Special thanks to Ahmed Umur, Abdiqaalaq Ahmed, and Mary Ellen Daniloff-Merrill for their help with research for this novel.

Thanks to Allan Guthrie for the incredible enthusiasm and editorial help, and to Kyle MacRae for whatever it is he does.

ONE

Couple of cops watched a couple of black guys in a little Korean car slide all over the iced-up road in the middle of a blizzard. Poulson said, "Shit, I don't know if they're drunk or foreigners."

Holm didn't want to laugh but she couldn't help it sometimes. He phrased things just the right way. Missed his true calling—stand-up comedian. Audience full of white good-ol-boys and he'd bring the roof down.

Poulson had a point about drunk or foreign. Lots of students from overseas came here for some reason. From Nepal and Kenya, ending up in a farm town of about twelve-thousand in southwest Minnesota. How'd that happen? And then all the Somalians coming over from the Twin Cities, where there were a ton of them. These women in *hijabs* everywhere. Laundromats. Video stores. Wal-Mart. Working in the grocery stores. They wouldn't touch your pork or your booze, had to call someone over to ring it up.

Poulson had laughed about it. "I need to try that one day. Paperwork's against my religion."

"Lutherans are built on paperwork, remember? Nailed to the church door?"

"Not American Lutherans."

The car they were watching slid again while trying to stop at the light between the taco shop and the liquor store. Wiggled its tail.

"Didn't think he was going to make it. See that?"

Hard enough to see anything. A near whiteout, the snow blowing sideways, piling up against the sides of buildings and all the cars at the dealership, the trees heavy with snow on the west side, starting to bend. A few trucks on the road. The plows weren't out yet but they should've been.

Poulson and Holm had pretty much figured it would be a quiet shift. Holm had brought magazines, most of them about raising babies.

She was three months along and everyone in the department knew it, and they knew it was Ray Bleeker's kid, and they knew Ray Bleeker was twenty years older, unhappily married, and last year's bullshit was already carrying over into the first week of the new one. Still, they had decided to keep the baby and make a go of it. Didn't matter if Ray's wife was going to get half of everything, didn't matter that they worked together.

The light changed and the car spun its wheels trying to get traction. Finally did and shot forward. The driver hit the brakes and went sideways, pulling it back around before doing a full donut.

"I think we should light them up." Poulson reached for the shifter.

"No, I'm sure it's okay. Let them go."

"I'm just saying—"

Holm sighed, tossed the parenting tips into the backseat. "Maybe, I don't know, *follow* them a little. See that they get home okay. But do you really want to get out in this?"

"Cold air's good for the heart." He shifted into D and inched forward from their shelter on the East side of the abandoned Chinese buffet, shut down for health violations. Shame. Holm was craving their barbecued pork. Soon as they cleared the wall, it felt like a crowd of bodybuilders was pushing the squad car sideways.

Poulson eased in behind the car, kept a good thirty feet or so between them, but it wasn't like it was hard to tell what was up. Even on a blizzard-free day, they couldn't follow someone in New Pheasant Run without being seen. The town only had two main streets that criss-crossed right before downtown—College and Main. They were on College.

"Going to be okay, Cindy? Need a break?"

"Fine, fine. Keep going."

"When are you taking leave, anyway?"

"You in a hurry to get rid of me?"

Poulson blushed. "It'll be hard talking to myself. I don't think they can spare a replacement."

"I figure a couple of months."

"Don't I get one more run at you while you still can? God knows you've been teasing me." Smiling.

"That's enough, alright? Didn't we talk about you laying off on the flirting?"

"I didn't mean anything—"

"Ever been with a pregnant woman?"

"Yeah. I cheated on Jenn with one. She was showing as much as you. Jenn found out and put me in the hospital. I didn't wake up for a day, at least."

Holm rolled her eyes. Poulson had a great marriage in spite of the fact that both he and Jenn were rotten to the core. Holm would never let Polson take a shot at her, but it was a joke that killed time on patrol. Lately, she'd stopped feeling it so much, didn't want Poulson to get any ideas. But it had been fun to riff on before.

"Ever see *Cool Runnings*? The Jamaican bobsled team. That's who these guys remind me of. Look at them."

Sliding to the curb again, bypassing the stoplight at the corner by shortcutting through the parking lot of a video store. Barely able to make it out the other side because of the snow piling on the low curb.

"He's going to mess up his car."

Holm said, "Really? Do we have to?"

"You betcha. We can at least let them know we're not going to arrest them. Maybe then they'll go home and stop trying to ditch us."

Holm closed her eyes. The wind was the killer. Snow felt like needles with the Midwest Wind Machine cranked up like this. She could pretend like her back was hurting, or something about the baby, then Poulson would probably let her stay in the squad. The cozy and warm squad car. He would never ask, but if she were to even hint at it, he'd cave.

That wasn't fair. If she started crying for sympathy, well, it was bye-bye Cool Cindy and hello Bitchy Holm around the office. *Sure, they say they want equality, but when you get down to it...*

She snugged on her winter hat, earflaps brushing her ears, making her nearly deaf. Zipped up her coat, which didn't help much. Anything bulkier and they'd have trouble grabbing cuffs, pepper spray, gun.

Poulson did the same, gave her a wink before he hit the lights. "Baby's first traffic stop."

*

The car turned a corner, correctly using the blinker, before coming to a stop next to the empty, long-for-sale plot of land behind the Burger King, along a road that led to the small college campus. It was a no man's land between cookie cutter town houses and a rehab halfway house.

Holm had trouble opening the door. The wind grabbed it from her hands, slung it open farther than it should've. Snow already biting her face. She put on her gloves, climbed out, and fought to close the door again. Poulson was standing opposite, puffing out his chest and taking in deep breaths like this was his favorite time of year. Holm knew it wasn't. Poulson was more of an Autumn guy. So was nearly everybody. Ray Bleeker, though, he was a true winter guy. Ice fishing, deep woods hunting, snowmobiling. Cold was in Bleeker's blood. Holm was trying to share some of her Spring love with him—gardens and sunshine and birds, oh my.

The Korean car's brakelights were still flaming red. Holm had called in the tag number, got back a hit on a rental under the name Jimmy Quick, so that didn't help. Rented in Minneapolis. Not a local after all.

Holm eased up on the passenger side, a few steps behind Poulson's approach on the driver. He did his thing—easy-going, joking. No big deal.

"You guys having a little trouble with the ice?"

"Sorry. It's a new car. Still getting used to it."

She caught the passenger's face in the sideview. Young guy, trying to grow a beard. Not decked out like a gangsta, so that was good. Nervous blinking.

Poulson kept on, smiling. "Just so you know, it's not the same as racing a dune-buggy across the desert. One little patch of slick here, and you're gone."

He bent down closer to the driver. Sniffing for alcohol or weed, Holm knew. Trying to find some reason to haul these two guys in. She set her jaw. C'mon. That meant searching the car. That meant more time out in the wind, and she already couldn't see the closest buildings. Only their smudgy lights. Her teeth were starting to hurt. Another couple of minutes was all she could take.

"You guys been drinking tonight?"

"We don't drink."

"Nothing?"

"No sir. Nothing."

He thought about it for a minute. Nodded. "Okay, I can buy that. So what are you doing over here? You own this car?"

"No, I rented it."

"Good, good. So what's up?"

"I drove over to see a friend. We had dinner. I'm taking him home now."

"Looked to me like you were heading out of town. Where does your friend live?"

"It's not far."

"That's not what I asked, though. You weren't going to head out to Minneapolis in this, right? You'll get blown off the road."

Holm tapped on the passenger's window. He stiffened. Made eye contact. She motioned to roll the window down. He did, an inch, flinching at the snow.

"ID, please?"

He shrugged. "I left my wallet at home."

"Uh huh."

She finally got a better look at the driver. He was the one decked out in hip-hop, head to toe. A hoodie covering his head—in the car. The worst place to wear a hoodie, right? Couldn't see side to side. He turned to check what was going on with his passenger, and she saw the scars. Knife scar on one cheek up to his temple. The rest were acne. Eyes reminded her of a snake, the way he held them. Compared to him, the passenger was angelic, practically glowing.

Poulson said, "So, Mr. Quick, let's see a license and proof of insurance, to make it official."

"Please, no. Please don't arrest us."

"Hey, nobody said anything about arresting you. Still need to see a license, son."

"We didn't do anything. It's the car. Not good in the snow."

Poulson raised all five-foot-eleven of himself up to full height, glanced across at Holm. She knew he was feeling the tingle, same as her, the one they got when things were about to turn shaky on them. Poulson said, "Okay, step out of the vehicle. We need to talk some more."

"Please, sir, it's not far."

Holm caught movement. Why hadn't Poulson told the kid to keep his hands in sight? His right was down in his seat. He started to lift it, but the passenger grabbed his arm and seethed through his teeth, "Jibriil, god, no!"

Holm went for her pistol, started shouting, "Don't move! Don't move!" Fumbly with her gloves on. Goddamn it. She stepped backwards. "Don't move! Hands where I can see them! Now!"

Poulson still didn't quite get it. He'd stepped back and pulled his S&W, but hadn't picked up on why Holm freaked.

She said, "The driver's got a gun! The driver's got a gun!"

The driver yanked his arm free and Poulson's eyes went wide.

She fired. Caught her glove in the slide. Sliced right through. Bullet went *ting* off the top of the car, then through the window. Thinking, *My baby my baby my baby* as she stumbled and ended up on the ground. Gun in both hands. She couldn't do that. Needed one for her radio.

That fast—three seconds? Five? The shots. Six in a row. Poulson taking them standing until the last two punched through his skull. The pink and red mist bloomed and then raced off in the wind.

Holm grabbed for her radio, fingers numb. "Officer down! Officer down!" Location, unit, all that. Shouting. Keeping her sights trained on the spot that kid would show up if he stepped out of the car. Steady. Hand shaking. Steady.

Maybe they would leave. Come on. Take off already.

But then the driver's side door opened, and the driver's head rose into her line of fire, and she squeezed the trigger. Had no idea where the bullet went. She kept squeezing, but the kid was already crouched out of sight.

She heard screaming from the passenger. He had opened his door, but hadn't gotten out. Hands high. "No, no, let's go now! What are you doing? This is bad, man, it's bad."

Holm shifted her aim to the passenger, shouted, "Freeze! Out and down on the ground! Now!"

The passenger ducked into the car.

She turned to the driver.

But he'd already found a good angle and popped off three more.

They were hot shots where her skin had gone hard and cold. Burned. The only good being that they were probably nines, and probably full-jackets, cheap-ass target shooting shit, passing right on through instead of mushrooming, fragmenting, tearing holes like craters in her body.

But then she figured out where she'd been hit: Leg once. Leg twice. Guts. Guts as in womb.

She wailed, hand straight to her stomach. Where'd it go in? Where was the blood? Maybe it missed the baby. It had to miss. She felt nauseous. Bile coming up fast. She swallowed it back. Where were the sirens? It was a small town after all. How long had it been? A minute? More?

She tried to lift her gun. Couldn't even do that. If she strained enough, she could get it up there. Took a shot in the driver's direction. Like it did any good. She scooted back again and the pain turned up the volume. She tried to stand, failed. Tried to open her squad door. The wind took it and flung it, hitting her in the cheek and ripping away skin. Bruised her arm bad. The pistol went flying.

She picked up the mike and said "Officers down" and then there were a whole bunch of people suddenly. EMTs and officers and deputies, finishing off the kids in the car before turning to save Poulson's life, then Holm's. Then Ray was there, standing over her, holding her hand. Lots of "You'll be okay" and "Just in time" and "The baby's fine".

But then something jarred her leg, sending a shock all over. She opened her eyes. She'd been dreaming the rescue. Fading out and dreaming her own rescue.

The driver looked down on her, kicked her leg again. The passenger's voice in the background yelling, "Leave her alone, man. She didn't do anything. Why did you even have a gun?"

"Cause you never know where your enemies might find you."

"They were just cops! They were going to let us go!"

Still staring down at Holm, cheap Hi-Point nine in his grip. "You that stupid, college boy? They weren't going to do shit except take us to jail. We can't let them stop us now. Got to catch that plane."

"You didn't need a gun. We're dead now. All cops, everywhere. They're going to kill us."

Holm wanted to say something. Wanted to tell them it was hopeless. They would never get out of town. But something about the driver told her otherwise. He was going to get away with it. Killing Poulson, herself, the baby, and he was going to skate. So unfair.

Driver lifted his chin. "Ain't going to kill us tonight. Allah's got other plans."

Holm blinked. The nine was barely a foot away from her face.

She thought she heard the blast…

Then saw a beautiful baby girl, hair in barrettes, wearing a yellow and white spring dress. Taking her first steps in a field of green, her daddy helping her stand, mommy cheering her on. What a smile. The best smile she would ever see.

And then the sound of a Korean coupe driving away while sirens wailed closer. The snow scoured away the town's usual assy smell—cow manure, sugar beets, and soybean processing. The snow filled her open mouth. It tasted clean.

So much snow.

TWO

Only four people knew where to find Ray Bleeker when he went ice-fishing, and one of them was dead. His buddy Forrest, who he'd known since his Army days in the Nineties, had died last fall. Cancer. Guy was only forty-eight and had seen it coming for a year. Their last fishing trip, seven months before he died, Forrest told Bleeker it was going to happen. Hard to believe, the guy still in fighting shape by then, if a little more tired and a little more bald thanks to the chemo. He'd told Bleeker that he would like his ashes spread in the lake where they fished, but on the condition that he wait until it was frozen over.

So that's what Bleeker was up to the night of the blizzard. Forrest's widow was supposed to come with, but by then she'd already met a new guy and her kids were sick and, you know, "How about you take his ashes and do it yourself? I've had five months to mourn him, and it's time to move on."

Fine.

The lake was seventy miles northeast. The weather sucked, but Bleeker needed this. Needed to get away from the heat at home, still living with the wife he'd already asked for a divorce. He'd only told her about Cindy Holm and the baby not even a month ago. Cindy had kind of forced his hand. But if that's what it took, then there you go. He was ready to make a break and start over again.

He hooked up Forrest's ice-fishing shack, now his, to the back of his 1996 Buick Roadmaster. What a car. It could tow an elephant. He'd only put eighty-four thousand miles on it in fourteen years. Looked as clean as the day he'd bought it.

It was a bastard to fight the wind and whiteout for an hour until it slacked off closer to the lake. Then he drove on across the ice, past clumps of other shacks and big SUVs or 4X4s. A temporary city on the ice, every year, clearing off before the Spring melt as if it was never there. Bleeker drove on, ignoring the cracking noises beneath the car—it would hold, not a problem. He and Forrest had a secret spot. Or maybe it wasn't a secret. Maybe it was because they never caught much there and everyone else knew it. But catching fish wasn't the point. Boozing it up while watching a hole in the ice, talking about anything other than the stuff that mattered—that's why they did it.

Bleeker unhooked the ice shack, a red and white tin number that had a little kitchen space inside—a few cabinets and a counter barely enough for a toaster oven or microwave—but it was empty this trip. He opened one of the catch covers on the floor and worked at drilling the hole. He got hammered on Rum and Cokes while he drilled, forgot to hook up the generator for the lights and heat. At some point when it was too dark to see, he tried to get the plastic container of ashes opened, spilling some here and there before clumsily tipping it over the hole. Most of the dust fell into the lake and drifted along under the surface of the ice. The rest turned into mud and clogged the hole.

Bleeker mock-saluted and sat down hard on his canvas chair. He had left his cell phone and radio in the car. The wind was howling outside like souls in hell, snow piling on one side of the shack. Bleeker opened another bottle of rum, another bottle of pop, and sipped himself to sleep.

That's how Trish found him the next morning.

*

She said his name. Said it again, louder. Took it up a notch each time until he blinked his eyes and yawned. She wasn't about to go rustle him since he was gripping his .40 caliber pistol in one hand, an empty plastic cup in the other.

When Bleeker finally realized who it was, he turned away, let out a big sigh. He'd come here to get away from the never-ending fight. Seemed like Trish always had a new knife to stab him with, some old wounds ready to be reopened and poked. Jesus, why couldn't it be simple? Got tired of life with one woman. Pay her enough so she won't be left high and dry. Move on with new life, new partner, new possibilities. It's not like he was actively trying to hurt her. Shit, he was hoping she'd been thinking of her Plan B, too, since it had been obvious for at least the last eight or so years that the love had been sucked clean out of the relationship. So why go another ten years filling it back up with bile?

Bleeker looked back. She stood in the doorway of the shack, arms crossed, sun bright behind her. Just like a blizzard to sweep away all the clouds and blind you with clear blue big sky the next day. His face hurt from the cold, his jaw felt like someone was stabbing him—grinding his teeth all night—and his hands were numb. He squinted, realized why Trish was stand-offish, and put the gun into his jacket pocket. Dropped the cup by the empty bottles of Sailor Jerry's and store brand cola. The swishing in his head wasn't so bad, until he tried to stand up. Felt like the ice was breaking and he was going in.

Trish nodded at the hole in the ice. "You did it?"

The plastic box was upside down, and a lot of ash was still ringing the hole like margarita salt. Then there were smudges, bootprints. An embarrassing funeral.

"I could've used help, I guess. But it's done."

She didn't react much. Walked closer to the hole, took a look down, arms still crossed. Bleeker had a hard time seeing her like this—a puffy parka over a long sleeve t-shirt. Jeans and boots. Severe short hair, spiked on top. Frown lines etched in forever and forever. Rose-tinted eyeglasses with extra-thin gold frames. It wasn't that she looked *bad*, really, but more like she looked the same way she'd been acting for so long—bitter.

Bleeker didn't know what was important enough to get her up here. He didn't bother saying goodbye when he left the day before. Separate bedrooms, separate meals, separate schedules. They'd never had children, so that made it even easier, as easy as these things could be. Except for the one scare, the reason they got married in the first place. But she lost it inside of a month. They saved the date anyway. Grinded along until the gears had frozen. She wouldn't be here for the small stuff.

His cop instinct was tingling.

Trish said, "Something's happened."

His stomach dropped. Kept his footing. "Jesus, spit it out."

She shook her head. If it was anybody worth crying about, she'd done hers already and was through. Which made him think...no.

"Something happened last night. A shooting. I'm sorry."

"Cindy?"

She couldn't look him in the eye. "I'm sorry."

He reached back for his chair. Wasn't even close. Caught himself, then sank to the floor, cross-legged, face in his hands. He wasn't one to cry. Wasn't one to yell. What he felt was tight. All his nerves and tendons and muscles tight to the point of tearing. Teeth might explode. Throat closing up.

No idea how long he sat like that. Could've been ten seconds. Could've been an hour. Trish left him alone. Not a hug, not a pat on the shoulder. He looked up and she was back in the same spot near the door, arms crossed, looking across the lake at the other ice houses. Then she lit a cigarette.

He remembered the gun in his pocket. So did she, obviously. That's what it had come to.

Bleeker pushed himself off the ice. Cleared his throat. "Dead, right?"

Trish nodded. "And Erik Poulson, too."

"Who did it?"

"Couple of black guys. Probably Somali."

Fuck. It was a small town, small police department. Out of three detectives, he was the one who best knew how to deal with the Somalis

"Why don't you let me drive you back? You're in no condition."

He thought about it. A kind act on her part, no ulterior motive. But that was the problem. To go with her meant he would lose control of the situation. She wouldn't be the only one to give him a ride or babysit him at home.

Bleeker shook his head. "I can drive."

"Ray, come on."

"I said that's okay." A little too loud. "I'll follow you."

Her lips were tight, nostrils flared. She stomped out the fucking cigarette and walked out to her SUV.

Bleeker closed the shack door and walked over to the Roadmaster, got in, and followed Trish off the ice. He turned on talk radio to keep himself awake and focused. Was a time he'd bought all these guys' acts—the liberal and fag conspiracies, the Illuminati, the Mark of the Beast, the President being the Antichrist, the government with its disarmament squads and black helicopters. But at some point between the decent Somalis he'd met, and the way his Lutheran church had taken Trish's side, pretty much kicking him out, telling him to find God elsewhere, and Cindy's soft-heartedness, he'd started listening more carefully, not accepting the party line as easily.

Now the bozos were mostly noise to keep him awake on iced-up roads.

Just when he thought the world might be a better place than he'd believed, this had to happen. His love, his baby, Forrest, Poulson, his marriage, his peace of mind...

His cell phone rang. He picked it up, saw that there were a dozen messages waiting, starting at around three in the morning. His dash clock said it was seven fifty-one. Trish had been a real trooper, getting up that early to come tell him his mistress and unborn child were dead. Jesus.

Answered the phone. It was the Chief.

"Trish find you yet?"

"Yeah, just now. I'm heading back."

"I'm sorry, Ray. If we could've found you last night, you know. Trish left as soon as she could. It's shit. It's all shit."

"Thanks." What else could he say? "Yeah, thanks."

"Howie's already out talking to people. We'll get who did this." He was having a hard time even saying consoling things. All business, the Chief. "If you need time, I can give you plenty of time, if you need it."

Bleeker wouldn't know what to do with himself without something to take his mind off it. Paperwork. Small-time shit. "I'm good. I'd rather work."

"Really, a few days, then."

He could tell what the Chief was thinking. Last thing they needed was a cop with a gun set on revenge. If he didn't play it right, he'd end up on forced leave for a month, all paid, of course, just to get his ass out of the way. He said, "Maybe, okay. But not right now. Maybe after the funeral." Choked up saying that last word.

The Chief waited a moment while Bleeker cleared his throat. Then, "If you're up for it, there's, ah, something here. You can talk to a few people for us. A college kid is missing, a Somali from the Cities. His roommate doesn't know where he is, didn't come in last night. That's unusual for him. This is a very good student, very nice guy, not some whackdoodle muslim. Everybody agrees. Unless he's hiding it well."

That was how they got us every time. "So when was he last seen?"

"By the roommate, maybe eight or nine that night. A friend from Minneapolis came to visit, and they went out."

Bleeker had to white knuckle the steering wheel on a patch of unplowed road, thick with freeze, to keep all four wheels down. "That's not even a full night. What's the big deal?"

"This guy didn't have a car. His friend did. The way the roommate described it, we think it's the car Erik and Cindy stopped."

Bleeker's mouth went dry and he swallowed, got stuck, coughed. Heard the voice on talk radio say, "...losing what makes our country so great, and I don't want to live in that sort of America. I want it like it's always been."

It wasn't right. You didn't put the dead cop's lover on the case. You just didn't. Were they that hard up for people who knew how to talk to the Africans? Hell, Bleeker didn't even know the language except bits and pieces. He'd only learned the etiquette and culture by trouncing all over it, making every possible mistake until a Somali man who worked at a local soy processing plant had taken the time to explain it to him over a few weird dishes at a tiny Somali restaurant above an import shop downtown Bleeker had known nothing about. Since then, Bleeker had said the right things, showed the proper respect, and started getting some answers. And that made him the police department's "expert".

Bleeker told the Chief he'd check in after changing his clothes. Closed his phone. So they wanted him on this after all. Wanted him to go in shooting, it sounded like. Fine. He could live with that.

Bleeker started nodding his head along to the radio host, who was damn near crying talking about his ruined country like she was some sort of teenage whore who'd gotten knocked up. Not going to let 'em destroy what we all helped to raise!

What Bleeker was really thinking: God help that young man's soul if he

ALL THE YOUNG WARRIORS

was the one who pulled the trigger

THREE

Waves of super-heated air rising from the tarmac. Adem squinted his eyes, shielded them, too hot to see, it felt like. Jibriil shoved him from behind, off the last step of the plane. He'd been at it the whole trip, calling Adem pussy this and pussy that because he whined half the way back to Minneapolis about how the cops would get them, and how Jibriil should turn himself in, and the gun, the fucking gun, why did Jibriil bring a motherfucking gun with him to New Pheasant Run?

"Cause you never know. And now you do."

"We were supposed to disappear. You don't disappear when you kill police! We won't be able to come back. Just…just…"

Unspoken between them: As an eyewitness, now Adem couldn't go home again. He would never rat out Jibriil. But there it was, the reason they couldn't split up. The reason Jibriil wouldn't let them.

They ditched the rental outside of Redwood Falls, found another car. People on the farms left keys in, stuck in the visors or under the wheel wells. Took five tries. The weather made it feel like more. Their plane didn't leave until six thirty-five a.m., so they could afford to take their time. The car was a Pontiac Grand Am, red. Thousands and thousands of them on the road. The police couldn't stop all of them, could they? And the owner probably wouldn't realize until morning.

Adem had finally stopped complaining when he feared Jibriil might lose his temper. His friend had gone stone silent, hand so tight on the wheel it kept squeaking. The pinch in his stomach went tighter. Couldn't ask Jibriil to stop the car, not anymore. Had to hold it in until the plane.

This wasn't supposed to be about killing anyone yet. That would come later. Righteous killings. God's work. Not small town cops doing their jobs. Didn't matter if they were jerks and almost certainly stopping Adem and Jibriil because they were DWB—Driving While Black. There was no *reason* to kill them. So what if they were harassed for a while, ended up talking to that Dutch cop all the Somalis in town knew? So what? They would've missed their plane. It was all kind of a joke anyway. Adem never expected it to get this far.

This far being Somalia. K-50 Airport. Two more spoiled Americans about to join the good fight, redeem themselves before Allah.

They flew from Minneapolis to New York and from New York to London and from London to Nairobi and from Nairobi, finally, mercifully, a small plane took them to this airport south of Mogadishu. Adem was amazed at how Jibriil had pulled it off. Navigated the myriad flights perfectly. Not once were they ever stopped and questioned. Jibriil had the whole act down—forged passports, documents, US cash, a few credit cards that couldn't have been Jibriil's, no way. But they slipped through every time. Only once did Adem ask where the money had come from. Jibriil cut him off, said not to worry about it. They were being looked after.

On the ground, a constipated and dry-mouthed Adem fought to keep sand out of his eyes. "What's next?"

Jibriil pointed. "He's holding a sign. By that truck. That's him."

Adem squinted and made out a tall man, maybe not even thirty, in a military uniform, rank unknown, holding a sign with Somali, some form of Arabic, and English on it. All three languages, the same word: *Americans*.

Jibriil pulled at Adem's shirt. "Come on."

"What about our bags?"

"What about your carry-on?"

Adem lifted the backpack he'd brought along. "This isn't my clothes."

Jibriil pointed towards the back of the plane. "You mean those?"

Adem looked—more teenagers with guns grabbing bags, opening and going through them before tossing the scattered remains onto an ever-widening pile. Like a party more than a job. His shouts were drowned out by the prop engine winding down.

"You forget why we're here. It's not a vacation."

Like he could forget that. Adem knew exactly why he was here. Because Jibriil had wanted it more than anything now that he studied at the feet of some freaky Imam in the Cities. He sold it to Adem like an adventure. Like Fifty Cent on the streets of L.A. but with bigger stakes and God on their side.

"I need underwear."

Jibriil smiled. "Go commando."

Adem gave up and walked behind Jibriil to the man with the sign. His truck was plenty old, ramshackle. The sand had blasted it shiny in spots, holes beginning to show.

The truckbed was full of boys. Maybe the oldest was fifteen. Faces wrapped with scarves, covering all but their eyes or framing their faces.

Every one of them had guns, and a few had rocket launchers. Real fucking rocket launchers. They chattered so fast that Adem couldn't make out the accents at first—the language a blend of Arabic and Somali. He'd gotten used to English at the college, not like at home. But then it clicked and he understood they were dissing him. Laughing at him, pointing. He pretended not to notice.

Jibriil stumbled over whatever phrase he was supposed to tell the man. More laughter from the kids. He had a tougher time with Somali than Adem, whose family had come from the northern coast and were well-versed in English even before they left the homeland. He spoke up, saved Jibriil from further ridicule.

"We have come from the snow to fight in the desert."

The man spat on the ground beside him. "Are you sure you're in the right place? Would you like a nice Coca-Cola?"

The boys in the back: "With lots of ice." "Look at them. Rich boys." "They'll die quickly and we can take their shoes."

Jibriil laughed along with them. It was the right move. The man put the sign into the truck and greeted them each with a big hug. The boys in the back applauded. They reached out their hands to help Adem and Jibriil get in. They slung their backpacks over their shoulders and climbed aboard. The man got into the cab and cranked up.

The other boys handed them AK-47s. Adem only knew what they were because Jibriil told him. Adem sat with the gun straight up between his knees, one hand wrapped tight with the strap of his backpack, now in his lap. Eyes on him like they were waiting for something.

He said, "Where are we going?"

A boy near him, middle-school aged, leaned over and said, "Initiation. Football."

"Football?"

A wide smile. "Yes, football."

Adem turned back to Jibriil. "We're going to play football?"

"Aw, yeah. Righteous."

"I didn't think we would be playing football."

Shrugged. He checked over his rifle like a pro, pulling back on the slide and slamming a bullet into the chamber. "Got to have something to do in-between killings."

*

The ride to Mogidishu was dusty, crowded. Painful. Adem had thought the planes were uncomfortable, but they were bliss compared to this hard-bucking truck, the smell of unwashed soldier boys, death and gases, all of it getting to him. One of the boys offered him a sweaty bandana. Adem covered his nose and mouth with it. Still better than the actual air.

They passed another truck, slow-going with people in the bed and hanging onto the sides, growing like a giant tumor as it made its way into town. Many more people walking, no guns or rocket launchers. Just staffs or bags of food or bottles of water. At one point, the truck stopped and a couple of boys demanded the food and water from some women, vividly dressed and carrying the goods on their shoulders, only the most essential parts of their faces visible. The boys showed no respect. Instead, they were pissed that the women were angry for the soldiers taking the food from their children's mouths.

One boy said to them, "We're you're children! We are, too!" And then he took away the second bottle of water he was going to leave with them and poured it out on the road.

One of the boys told Adem and Jabriil that the woman was actually in business, trying to sell food and *khat*. Adem kind of knew what *khat* was. His dad and uncles had talked about it with smiles on their faces.

Adem wondered what they were fighting for, or against, if this was all it took to rile them up. Shoving. Pointing guns. A mother and daughter and two young sons, much younger than those in the truck. The sons made guns with their fingers, danced around. The boys in the truck laughed, urged them on. Adem turned to Jibriil, found him grinning. Adem coughed.

The boys climbed back into the truck, their stolen bread and lamb and water passed around like a prize. They'd also taken some *khat*. Raw leaves. Many of the boys grabbed at those and chewed. Adem lifted his bandana, took a sip of the tart, lukewarm water, and wished it was Mountain Dew.

*

In the city limits, the truck rattled along past piles of rubble and burned-out buildings. How some of them were still standing seemed physically impossible. Everything was broken. Most of the people the truck passed had guns. A handful were shooting blindly down streets. Everyone else ignored them. Some of the boys in the truck shouted to friends on the street. Smaller children in dusty clothes played soccer, and even some of them had laid their rifles to the side for a while.

What surprised Adem the most was the normalcy. People here were used to this. Guns and rocket launchers were a way of life. They still had to buy, sell, work, and play. They had to laugh, or what the hell else would they do but cry? And they cried a lot. Adem heard wails from blocks away. One growing louder as they passed the aftermath of a mortar attack. Blood seeping into the dust. Bodies barely covered by the fallen tarp. Sandaled dead feet peeking out.

Street vendors. Shelled businesses struggling to keep storefronts open. A lot of smoke and noise. Rifle-fire echoing from all over. And singing. Raw, tone-deaf singing. Adem was surprised. He knew the tune. The words were different, foreign. Still, something familiar finally, after thinking he was more of a stranger here, the homeland, than he was in America. Someone in the truck started singing along. Adem looked up. It was Jibriil. They'd sung together in the high school chorale group, Adem never really on key. But Jibriil had it down pat. A natural. Adem hadn't heard him sing in a couple of years. But he knew this song. Could hardly speak a couple of sentences in Somali without making a mistake, but he knew this song? When had he learned this song?

They twisted through the streets, avoiding rubble from the stone buildings, and crisp, still smoking debris from trucks, military jeeps and vehicles, and small cars. And then they were there. A massive stadium, rising from the ruins. It looked like a ruin itself—battered, cracked, and forgotten. The truck kept on through one of the tunnels, dark and cool for a blessed few moments, before bouncing hard and fast into the field. Adem ground his teeth together to keep from shouting. The stands were empty and sun-blasted. The field itself was dry but filled with desert scrub brush and trees. Like the Earth was reclaiming the space while hell burned all around outside the walls. There were men and boys and other trucks scattered inside the ring of growth. Maybe several hundred people. Babbling. Looking serious. No one was playing football.

The truck came to a stop and the boys jumped off. Adem stood and stretched. He'd been sitting with all his muscles tensed without realizing. The release was painful, but worth it. A full lungful of dry air made him cough. Jibriil shook his head and hopped onto the ground as if he was a veteran already.

Amongst the voices, Adem still getting used to the speed and rhythms after another full semester of American Midwestern accents, one was higher in pitch, reciting poetry. No, wait, she was praying. A woman.

Adem looked around. All male.

Then a voice over a bullhorn: "Come on over. It's time to begin. Come on."

A large group of the men had already gathered near one end of the stadium. The truck driver stepped over to Adem and Jibriil, urged them on.

"What's going on?"

The driver urged more, hands on their shoulders. "Justice."

Close and closer. A couple of men had shovels. The closer to the center of the circle, the younger the men, most carrying stones as large as their hands.

Adem's stomach sank like he was falling. He pressed his lips hard together, not wanting to throw up. Then, someone handed both of the newcomers stones. Adem rubbed the top of his with his thumb. Jagged.

At the center of the crowd, a clear area. Several feet around the main attraction: a middle-aged man and a teenage girl, both buried up to their waists. The girl was in a hijab, her head covered except for her face, praying calmly. Another man went over and crouched, told her to be quiet. The man was begging. Crying.

He said, "It was a demon. Momentary weakness. Please. It was not my fault."

Adem turned to the driver. "What...why? What did they do?"

The driver crossed his arms, leaned down and spoke low. "The girl, she accuses this man of raping her. He is a friend of her father. But the court says she allowed the situation to occur. She was alone with him in a car."

"How is that possible? She caused her own rape? Was she not dressed?"

That got Adem the stink eye from the driver. "Does not matter."

"Sure, it matters. How can it not matter?"

Jibriil nudged Adem. "It's just how it is. That's the law."

The driver nodded. "The law."

The driver pointed to a young man in the crowd. Grim-looking. Hard grip on a stone. "That is one of her brothers. Her father is here too."

Adem was about to say more, but Jibriil nudged him again, eyebrows knotted. Like, what are you doing? Stop asking questions.

The driver said, "God's law. We can't question it. We just have to fulfill it."

Another man on the edge of the crowd stood out. Wearing a white *koofiyad* on his head, with dark sunglasses, and a shawl over the shoulders of his western suit. Gray. White button-up shirt, no tie. Men stared at him with outright love. Crowded close. The man had a peaceful look on his face.

The driver nodded in his direction. Wouldn't point. Told Adem, "The Imam. He was the judge who ruled on this case."

His hands together, fingers clasped. He wouldn't get them dirty with a stone. That wasn't his place. But everything happened on his schedule, his word. The man with the bullhorn was paying close attention to the soft-spoken man, whose voice was lost in the rustling.

Adem looked at the girl in the ground. She was looking right at him. He blinked. Looked away. Then back. Still staring. Lips tight. No signs of tears, wet or dried. No fear at all. Anger, more like it. Adem thought he could read her mind: *This? My life for you, Allah, and I'm being killed for this? What he did to me?*

What could he say? Anything? He mouthed *I'm sorry*. Then felt foolish. Couldn't dare look at her anymore. He hoped no one saw what he'd done.

When it began, Adem was surprised. He wasn't standing in a blood-thirsty mob. These weren't hooligans flinging stones for fun. They took it seriously. They aimed. The man's screams, then the girl's, finally breaking down as the stones rained. Dull thuds. Stone on bone. Adem wondered if he could drop his and no one would notice. But there was the driver behind him, shoving him on the shoulder. "Go on! Now!"

More and more stones. Where were they all coming from? Arcing from the back of the crowd or fastballing in from closer. Larger than Adem's. Huge, jagged white things the size of footballs. Adem wrenched his arm back. The man. Aiming for the man. That made it better. The man was a rapist. He deserved it. Deserved to die. Horribly. Back in the States, they'd send him to prison. Back in the States the girl would be a victim, not a conspirator. Shit. What would his ethics professor think of him right about now?

Ready to let loose.

All for the cause, remember. Like Jibriil had said—if we don't win, then our homeland descends further into hell. It needs peace. It needs justice. It needs *God*.

Adem flung the rock. It sailed past the man and kept going. A good toss in baseball, a terrible one for a stoning.

Someone handed him another stone. They were pressing tight from all around. He flung that one, too, and missed again. The noise in the crowd was bubbling up. Each rock that connected unleashed another howl from the damned until they had no strength left in their lungs. Bloody. Bruised. Arms broken, fingers gnarled, heads starting to swell, shiny welts as the skin tightened. Adem watched the crowd instead. Barely noticed Jibriil had already thrown a few. He told Adem, "Watch how I do it." Much closer than when they had started. The girl, a rag doll. Jibriil lifted the stone over his head and brought it down, cracking her shoulder.

Adem closed his eyes before impact, but the *sound*. Louder than he had expected. Then he blinked, adjusted to the blinding sun, and saw that the man must have already been dead, as he was slumped over with half his skull caved in, thin blood spilling onto the ground below like a leaky faucet. Eyes still open.

The rain of stones ceased. Adem squinted, found the Imam. He had held up his hands. He ordered a couple of men to check the bodies. They wore stethoscopes. Doctors? Really? They did their duty, kneeling and checking the obviously dead man's vital signs, pulse, even a breath test with a small mirror. The doctors stood and nodded. On to the girl. They knelt, placed the stethoscope on her back. One shook his head.

"She's still alive."

Adem thought, so, does that mean she can go free? Or at least a little jail time? Did they even have prisons for women? Take her to the hospital?

He got his answer when the doctors backed out of the way and several of the boys in red scarves around their heads crowded closer. Adem grabbed Jibriil by the collar, got him to meet his eyes. Unsaid: *This is wrong.* As loudly as Adem could say it through his eyes alone.

Jibriil adjusted his neck, reached for Adem's hand and plucked it off his shirt like a bug. A hard look, lips on the verge of curling. Adem pushed away, forced his way through the maze of solider boys, so many of them tall and thin, towering over him like trees, to the back of the crowd. Broke free into the pitch. Open air. Hands on his hips, taking deep breaths like he'd run a marathon. What he hadn't counted on was how much louder the stones sounded back here, echoing across the empty stadium time and time again like the worst *déjà vu*. He wanted to cover his ears. He couldn't do that in front of this crowd. The men with shovels were still on standby. Adem didn't want to be next.

FOUR

The woman in charge of the International Student Program at the University had tired eyes. She sat forward in her chair, tense. But so tired. Ray Bleeker wondered if she had slept last night. God knew he sure as hell hadn't. Maybe sometime around four or five he'd dozed off, because that's when he saw Cindy alive and pregnant and happy. Not like the body he'd seen the night before—dead and cold and one eye blown clear out of her skull.

He seen Poulson, too. His chest and gut like a water balloon popped by several pins. Too cold to bleed. The doc said he was probably still alive when the bastards killed Cindy, listening but unable to do a damned thing, his lungs already half full of blood.

The ISP woman, Eileen Gromen, had short red hair and if she wasn't sitting like so, her feet wouldn't touch the floor. She also cursed a lot more than you'd expect from a college administrator.

"Fucking nerve, that's all. I've got enough problems with the Nepalese. They heard they can come over here, get visas, driver's licenses, get a bank account, and then move to the goddamned Cities. We take them in like, shit, like they're going to stay four years. All our efforts, all the recruiting, then they get here and screw us. Never had any problems with the Kenyans, the Somalis. Hell, none of our Somalis are even internationals anymore. All from Minneapolis. One's local, his family's been here, shit, like five, six years."

"How many Somali students attend the school?"

She shrugged. "Last I counted, maybe five."

He had to remember to stay on track, not wander off, not get preoccupied with thoughts of the funeral. Talking to her parents. Having to explain. "So, with Adem, you had no clue. Nothing to indicate that he had problems?"

"He was an angel. A fucking angel. Unless it was all an act. Isn't that the way it usually happens? They gain your trust, then bomb your ass. I would've sworn Adem wasn't like that."

She'd already heard the rumors. Spread fast in a small town on a small campus. Nothing he could do about that. He'd been pointed towards Gromen by the school's Security Officer, who said she'd spent a lot of time with these guys even if they weren't from overseas because they were friends with the internationals, came to their campus club's events—International Film Fest, Food Fest, Crafts Fair. A pretty tight group. The local white kids, maybe a few tried to broaden their horizons and get involved, but no more than that. The Nepalese and the Africans, they needed each other.

Bleeker had already spoken to Adem's roommate, a couple of classmates, and knew at some point today he'd have to deal with some ass from the Cities in order to talk with the kid's parents. Maybe even the FBI. In that case, he might as well sign off the whole thing and take the rest of the week off. But…to do what?

Eileen Gromen was riffing on how fucked the university's international recruiting was, getting farther off-track from the questions, but that was okay. She was easy on the eyes and kind of fun to watch get all wound up about stuff. Bleeker's phone rang. It was the office. He excused himself and stepped out into the cinderblock hallway, beige.

A sergeant with whom he'd sometimes shared a beer and a couple hours on the firing range. "You're not going to believe this."

Cindy's parents? Their lawyer? Cop shop head shrinker? "Kind of busy."

"No, listen. This one's, uh, yeah."

"Can't you just tell me?"

"I want to see the look on your face."

"Jesus, Lev."

Guy was laughing. "Okay, okay. I'll give you a hint. You ever heard of the Somali Hardcore Killahs?"

Fuckers had been all over Twin Cities news a few years before. Trouble for the sake of trouble. He'd talked to a few ex-members after some barfights in downtown New Pheasant.

"And?"

"Ray, please. Humor me."

*

Bleeker didn't need this shit. The sergeant told him a couple of officers had been keeping an eye on the missing kid's apartment, all police-taped, when this giant black guy goes right up, rips the tape off, and goes in like he owns the place. The cops ran their asses over and arrested him.

Turned out he was the missing student's father. "And, wouldn't you know, the former leader of the Killahs. Called himself Bahdoon. Never pinned anything on him. Guy was smart, like Capone. We can't even pin tax evasion on this one."

Bleeker said he wanted to meet this Bahdoon guy. The detective questioning him said that if he knew where his kid was, he sure wasn't saying.

"Take a break, get a coffee. Give me a half-hour."

He stepped into the meeting room, mostly a file closet but with a card table and some folding chairs crowding the far side of the room. A Somali man, still wearing his black North Face parka, hood up, melted snow on the ground all around him. He was slumped in the chair, fingers clasped together, resting on his stomach. He didn't stand, didn't reach out to shake Bleeker's hand, but maybe that was because Bleeker had a legal pad in one hand and a can of Mr. Pibb in the other.

Bleeker said, "I can hang that coat up for you, you know."

He shrugged and made a noise in his throat like a dog. Cleared it. "It's aw-ight."

Definitely some leftover Somali accent, but it was ninety percent gangsta.

"We know who you are, Mister, uh, Bahdon. Bah-Doon?"

"Yeah, uh, I don't go by that. I'm Mustafa."

"What, you changed it?"

"Bahdoon is my grandfather's name. I'm Mustafa Abdi Bahdoon. I don't mind telling you. Ain't nothing on me."

"Well, you broke into a crime scene."

"My son's apartment is a crime scene?" A weak laugh. "Shit, that's good. His momma called me at work, told me to drive over, see if I could figure out where he went. This is not like him at all."

Bleeker nodded slowly, didn't realize he was doing it until he blinked and imagined the gun in Bahdoon's hand, shooting Cindy in the face. Might as well have been. He took a seat caddy-corner to the Somali gangster. Now he could see the guy was older than he acted, probably in his early forties, still sticking to the street thug routine. But Bleeker saw he was wearing a Target pullover polo under the coat. Worked at Target. Okay. "So you don't know?"

Another shrug. "Man, is this all necessary? Can I pay the fine and keep looking?"

Bleeker set his pad and drink down, slumped onto his elbows and ran his hand through his hair. Greasy. He hadn't showered since the morning before he set off for the lake. He'd need to do that soon. "There's no need, really. We'll do the best we can to find him. If you answered some questions for us...um...how did you hear so quickly? I hadn't even had time to give you a call."

"My wife, she called him. No answer. Like I said, this is not like Adem." Then a pause, a look down at the knuckles he was kneading. "Look, okay, I *think* I know where he is."

Bleeker sat straight. "Right now?"

"For real."

Round up a squad. Go in guns blazing. Shoot first, ask questions later. Or were they in the Cities? Why would this punk be here if so? Protecting him? Or maybe they were already across state lines.

What the fuck, right?

Mustafa made the dog noise again.

Bleeker said, "Are you alright?"

Mustafa waved him off, cleared his throat.

"Can you tell me where your son is? Because he's in big trouble."

The Somali man looked puzzled—vulnerable, even. Almost no doubt he was responsible for plenty of murders over in the metro. Bleeker was supposed to offer him the same respect he would anyone else with a missing kid?

Mustafa said, "How is he in trouble? He disappeared. That's not a crime."

Bleeker stood. "I don't think I should tell you anything about the charges until you tell me where he is. Fair trade, right?"

"In trouble with you?"

Killer. Killer. Killer. A killer with a killer for a father. A family of killers.

"Let's say…let's…" Sigh. "I need to talk to him. Him and his friend. We need to go find him. So if you go ahead and tell me—"

"I can't." Mustafa stood, too. About five inches taller than Bleeker.

"You just said, though. Don't get in our way, here. It's bad enough already. I don't need a, a, a fucking incident here, arresting you for whatever the word is … impeding?"

"I know. That's not what I meant. But tell me about this trouble first."

Bleeker didn't think he could take the guy without cheating. Right in the balls. Or right in the throat. That would come after he doubled over. "Non-negotiable."

Those eyes. Getting serious. Was Bleeker staring at the killer or the dad?

Finally Mustafa closed his eyes for a moment, shook his head. "It's okay. It's not like you could…it's okay."

"Tell me where I can find him."

"You can't find him."

"Why? You hide him somewhere? This is only getting worse for you, man."

Mustafa squeezed his fingers into a fist. Unfolded them. Angry dents where the edges had nearly broken the skin. Tough hands. Mustafa sat down again.

"He's in Somalia. Fighting in a war."

Bleeker felt empty. His whole reason for going on the last twenty-four hours, sure to find these dumbass Sammies with their gangsta gat, bang bang, killing cops like it was some music video. And now the gangsta daddy, Jesus. Fuck.

He reached for his Mr. Pibb, took a sip. Hand shook. Spilled some on his beard. Mustafa was up again, helping Bleeker find his seat. Bleeker slapped him away.

"I'm fine. I'm fine, goddamn it."

Splats of Mr. Pibb on the legal pad. He set it dead center.

Mustafa said, "I'm sorry. I hate what he has done."

Bleeker closed his eyes and gritted his teeth. Then said, "Your boy killed my girlfriend, my baby, and one of my friends."

Mustafa winced. He knelt beside Bleeker, inches apart. Both in their own worlds. Until the goddamned *gangsta killah* raised his head and said, "No, man, not Adem. He didn't do it."

Bleeker's world went strobe light. Red. Wanted to kill the motherfucker.

And then it got real bad.

*

Scratches on Mustafa's neck. Bandages not long enough to cover them. Mustafa had said that Adem hadn't killed the man's woman and child. Of course he hadn't.

Bleeker erupted, grabbed Mustafa around the neck like he was going to choke him. Pushed him to the ground. The back of his head popped the floor hard enough to make a welt. But Mustafa had plenty of experience with street fighting. He pulled the detective's hands off his throat, which is how he got the scratches, as some other cops came in to pull Bleeker off, drag him across the room. They helped Mustafa to his feet. Asked what happened.

Like it wasn't already obvious. Lucky they didn't suspend Bleeker right then. Mustafa's blood under his fingernails. Another cop got a paper towel and some peroxide for Mustafa. Not serious wounds, but plenty of sting to them.

Of course, right? You don't tell a man his one ray of hope is a dead end. Mustafa tried to explain, even after that. He wanted Bleeker to understand. It was the friend. Someone named "Jibriil." Mustafa said it over and over. Another couple of cops led Bleeker from the room, stowed him in the Captain's office to cool down.

*

His colleagues started the apologies, hoping to avoid a lawsuit, obviously. They didn't care for the interloper no more than Bleeker had. But this guy saying his son was in Somalia, they needed him. Asked if they could talk to him in the morning, put him up in a hotel. They'd already searched Adem's apartment, couldn't find his computer. Couldn't find his backpack. Spaces in the small bookshelf in his bedroom, but none of the remaining books were provocative. Mostly texts for school. PS3 in the front room, rented games spread on the floor. The roommate had been questioned, released, and was headed home to Minneapolis for the weekend.

The captain came in, ignored Bleeker, sat behind his desk. Still looking down, he said, "He's not pressing charges. Said he understands, you know, because of what happened."

Bleeker nodded.

The captain let out a sigh. "This isn't going to work, you on this, if it's connected."

"Let's not…not yet."

"What am I supposed to do, then? You're lucky. You need to take some time off."

"And do what, spend time with Trish?"

The captain stood, finally looked over. Eyebrows scrunched. "Go apologize to the guy, all right?"

Mustafa was sitting at a table out in the main area, elbows on the table, leaning forward. He supposed he should make the sort of an apology that had been "legaled" to death, covering all asses. He looked up at Mustafa, said, "You should watch your mouth."

Mustafa slouched again. Laughed. "Aw, fuck this." He got up. The other detective told him they'd paid for a room, told him there was a small Somali restaurant downtown above the ethnic grocery store. Mustafa said he wanted some ribs instead.

Bleeker said, "No, really. Check it out. Good goat."

Mustafa gave him a curt nod. "Tomorrow? When I'm back here? You stay away from me."

"Sleep tight, asshole."

*

Instead of driving home, Bleeker drove by the budget hotel where they'd set up Mustafa. He didn't know why. Kept thinking maybe he should talk to the guy again without all the other cops around. But then it would turn into another fight, wouldn't it? Bleeker felt punchy. Banged the roof of his car. No matter how many times he hit the roof or the steering wheel, he still felt full of it, whatever it was.

Only a handful of cars in the lot, one of them the hotel van. Bleeker guessed the yellow import with the big spoiler and the shiny rims belonged to Mustafa. Bahdoon. Whatever. After he'd left, Bleeker looked him up on the internet. Some brushes with cops all over the cities, kind of a minor celebrity among the hip hop crowd, but then he disappeared. As of about eight, nine years back, no more articles, no more arrest reports. None of it. So maybe he'd gone legit. Or maybe he'd become even more like Capone, insulated himself even better. The Somali gangs were small and scattered, but growing in strength. They had their hands in drugs, sex trafficking, guns, all that. And they were vicious.

Bleeker didn't want to go home. To either one of them—the place he still sometimes shared with Trish until they figured this all out, or the apartment out in a small farm town about eight miles west of NPR. It was cheap, it was nearly empty, and it was full of empty rum bottles. So he parked in the parking lot of the Goodwill store next to the hotel and waited. For what, he wasn't sure. Just a hunch.

Sundown, barely four o'clock. He kept waiting. Listening to talk radio descend into noise. Politics gave way to conspiracy gave way to sports. And then, out of the corner of his eye, Bleeker saw Mustafa pushing through the hotel doors and walking over to, yep, the yellow car. Got in. Drove out of the parking lot. Once he had made a left at the light, Bleeker followed.

The snow was starting to blow harder. Tough wind. Lots of people heading home from work, slow going. A few cars separated Bleeker from Mustafa. But it was a small town. Maybe twelve thousand, but it never felt like it. So many people knew each other, so easy to get around, it was surprising to realize that a town this small could even hold that many people. And in this weather, most of them were staying home.

Followed him downtown, which was pretty much a four-block stretch of buildings built in the thirties, only half of them still in use for businesses, some with apartments on the second and third floors. There was a sign on top of one building, old letters held up by a steel grid, announcing HOTEL NEW PHEASANT RUN, but as long as Bleeker had lived here there'd been no such place.

They passed the store owned by the Somalis, the ones who kept the room upstairs as a restaurant, lucky to have more than one cover a night. After all, the Somalis could make everything on their menu at home, and the Minnesotans didn't want to take to the snow when there was a good ol' hot dish waiting for them. Mustafa took a left at a light. Bleeker followed. Only one car between them now. The gang leader pulled into a parking lot behind a block of businesses. Bleeker kept going forward and pulled into the drive of the utility company where he could see through the shrubs, their bare branches clogged with snow. He could still make out the yellow import parking outside a bar. Well, mostly a bar. It was a pretty popular hole called Chuck Wagon. Also a damned fine place for patty melts and fried walleye. But not for ribs. Didn't the guy say he wanted some ribs?

Mustafa climbed out, snugged on a wool cap, and trudged through two inches of snow to the back door, went inside.

Dinner. Bleeker was hungry too. Why not go in, join him, share a beer and burgers, see if he could talk more about the kid running off to Somalia? It had been big news lately, a bunch of Somali men in their late teens and early twenties from the Twin Cities disappearing, then turning up in Africa fighting for this terrorist army made up of young Muslims trying to impose Sharia Law on the country. This after years of civil war amongst the various tribes still coming to terms with being clumped together as countrymen. Mogadishu, already in ruins, was worse now as these boys with rocket launchers and machine guns did unholy things to anyone who didn't practice Islam like they did. All the horror stories Bleeker had heard from the Somalis in town, so much worse than what he had experienced in Iraq as a Ranger for the first Gulf War. And, shit, that had been brutal enough.

But he stayed in the car. Turned the motor off. He didn't mind the cold. Sometimes he felt more at home when the numbers dipped below zero. A year in the desert was all it took to make him appreciate this frozen hellscape so much more. He'd had enough hot-bloodedness. The cold wind kept him even. And Cindy's death had raised his core temperature to a boil that, if he wasn't careful, might lose him his job.

Fuck the job. But he needed it right now. Needed it to get the goddamned…to get…you know…just…shit. He picked up his pistol. Knew it was loaded. Checked the clip anyway, something to do. When this Bahdoon guy was finished eating, then, okay, then Bleeker would confront him. No buddy-buddy meal. Just a cop with a pistol in a wind-whipped parking lot telling him to come clean.

He tucked his arms and waited. He was good at waiting.

*

Bleeker heard the yellow car chirp, saw the lights flicker when Mustafa unlocked it via remote.

He had to hurry. He stepped out of the car. The wind so bad now, he didn't even have to close the door. Wind blew it shut for him. Tucked his gun behind his back and took the sidewalk. But before he could set foot on the lot proper, he saw them coming. Before Mustafa did, even. Three black guys, closing in from different directions.

"Hey, you!" From near the restaurant. He'd been hiding in the shadows, stepped out once Mustafa was past him. Startled the man. The voice was Somali. Hood pulled low over the guy's eyes. Thick parka, hands in his pockets.

Bleeker took a step back, ducked low behind a shrub.

From the other side, a tall one, wearing all black, a wool watch cap like Mustafa's.

The tall one: "Are you lost?"

Hooded man still coming. Maybe not even men. Teenagers. Bleeker knew the tall guy, local troublemaker. Never arrested or anything, but always around when something was happening—fights, carjackings, loud parties. The first one, no idea. The third one, he didn't think Mustafa even saw him yet, hiding.

He inched closer, keeping low, hiding behind a pick-up where he could hear them better.

Mustafa said, "It's cool, y'all. I'm in from the Cities, looking for my son. You know him? Adem? From the college?"

A town this small, where the natives know most of the people like family, the Somalis should be an even tighter group. Saying *Adem* and *college*. Should've gotten an instant response.

Instead, the men kept coming. Mustafa backed up. Stupid, Bleeker thought. He should get in the car. Once in, he would have the advantage. Could talk to these guys with the heater running and the window cracked barely an inch.

"Sure," the man in the parka said. "We can take you to him."

No they couldn't. Bleeker saw it now. These weren't guys hanging around outside a downtown saloon for kicks. They had followed Mustafa, same as he had. Tracked him. Waited for him to emerge. So why hadn't they seen Bleeker first?

"Just tell me where he is. I'll go to him. I'm his father."

"We know." The tall one. "He sent us. We're here to help."

Then the third one, creeping, gave himself away. Jacket rubbing against itself, that *shiff, shiff*. Bleeker pulled his gun out. He hoped it didn't come to him using it. No, couldn't do that. Hoped the sight of it would be enough to get rid of them. But first, he wanted to see if Mustafa could handle himself. Had to be something to his legend, right?

If the man was carrying a piece, he sure wasn't acting like it. Kept his coat zipped up. Kept his hands in front of him. He took another step back. But that's what they wanted, right? He turned his head. Couldn't see far enough behind him. Turned his body.

Come on, man. Fight, for fuck's sake. Bleeker wanted to shout from the sidelines. Cheer him on.

Too late. The tall one was on Mustafa, pinning his arms back. Then the third guy was out of his hiding spot, rushing towards Mustafa with a thick wooden dowel, ready to strike.

Thunked him right in the forehead. Mustafa let out a growl. He sagged but the tall one held him, kept him on his feet. The guy with the dowel thrust it into his stomach. Bleeker finally recognized him, another punk grief-magnet, but not a Somali. Light-skinned, moles scattered on his cheeks. Born and raised in NPR. Mustafa, gagging, blood and grease streaming from his mouth.

The first guy was back, close to Mustafa's ear. Bleeker couldn't hear everything he said, but he caught the last part: "Leave it alone."

Mustafa stopped coughing, tried swallowing the thick bile in his throat. Fought to get the words out: "Never. *Aabahaa was!*"

Good move. Bleeker knew that one. Mustafa had told the guy "Fuck your father".

A fist exploded on Mustafa's jaw. The tall one dropped Mustafa's arms, kicked him to the back of his car. Landed in a good four inches of snow. The dowel came down on his shoulder blades. A kick to his balls. Another to his arm. They shouted at him, called him *Qanees* and *Eey*. Enough. More than enough. He wasn't Batman after all. Bleeker stood and started towards the fight.

He finally saw Mustafa reaching for something. Guess he was packing after all. Tried to pull all three layers of clothes above the grip. The attackers saw it first. The light-skinned attacker bent down, slapped Mustafa's hand away and ripped the 9mm from its holster.

The others *ooh-ed* and *ahh-ed*. Guy dropped his dowel and held up the handgun like a trophy.

And they still hadn't noticed Bleeker, only a dozen feet away now.

Mustafa was shaking. The cold and the throb of swelling injuries rendered him mute. They were going to let him live. They were going to blackmail him with his own gun. They were going to own him. That was the plan.

Bleeker said, "You boys got a problem with this guy?"

The attackers stood still. Frozen. Even the one with Mustafa's gun. Yeah, that was Bleeker's reputation. He didn't take shit from the local Sammies, but he could be your best friend if you played fair with him.

The tall one spoke. "Sorry, sir. There is a misunderstanding. He is drunk. We were helping him."

"That right?"

The others mumbled. *Sure. Yessir, sir.*

Bleeker looked down at Mustafa, still curled up against his car. Bleeker winked at him.

"He didn't look drunk when he went inside. He didn't look drunk when he came out. And he didn't look drunk when you grabbed him and beat him with that stick." Bleeker pointed at the dowel on the ground, then stepped over and picked it up. Twirled it around lazily. Still coming closer and closer.

The one with Mustafa's gun, what was his name again? Something easy. Leon, right. He was gaining confidence. Restless with the grip on Mustafa's piece. Jittery. "You didn't see it right. Believe us. Have we lied to you before?"

"Barely said a word to me, that's the problem." Turned to the tall one. "Got Abdi Nadif over here. Dad's a good guy. Yeah, he really is. Thinks you're on the wrong track, though."

Abdi Nadif hung his head. "I try my best."

"Sorry to hear that. And then you," Nod to the light-skinned kid. "Leon. Raised by your aunt. Dad died when you were young. I know it's hard. But I thought you were doing well at the packing plant. Why are you here?"

No answer.

"Think you should give me that gun you're holding, maybe?"

Held out his hand. Leon didn't move. No matter. Bleeker didn't either. There was his outstretched hand, collecting snowflakes. One second, two. And then Leon let out a breath, mumbled something like *Shit, man*, and stepped over, laid the gun in his palm.

Bleeker turned his attention to the ringleader. "You, I don't know you."

No need to wait for an answer. Like lightning, he struck the man in the nose, chest, and forearm with the dowel. Kid tried to rush him, grab Bleeker around the neck. Another whack to the fingers. Loud crack. Guy grabbed his fingers and dropped to his knees.

Leon should've taken a hint. He launched towards Bleeker while his back was turned. Mustafa stuck out his leg, tripped him. Bleeker spun and knocked him upside the head.

Which left Abdi Nadif. On the run. He was built for it. Rounded the corner of the block in less than ten seconds.

Mustafa pushed himself up. Blood on the ground around him. Bleeker knelt beside the one in the parka, cuffed him, made sure to squeeze his probably broken fingers, then rifled through his pockets.

Mustafa, now on his feet again, breathing heavily and holding a sleeve to his nose, said "You *followed* me?"

Bleeker kept rifling. "You're welcome." He found what he was looking for—a cell phone. Flicked the cover off to the side and started pressing buttons. "Can you get up, or do you need an ambulance?"

"I'm fine" He held on for dear life to the yellow Mitsubishi's spoiler, then his legs started to buckle. Bleeker hurried over, lifted beneath his arm until he was supporting him.

"I'm pretty sure these jackasses didn't have a reason to follow you. No reason at all. Unless someone told them to."

"Yeah, that was…um…same as I thought." Going to black out. Must've had a concussion. He took another look at the wooden dowel, something anyone could pick up for a dollar at a hardware store or Wal-Mart.

Powerful weapon. The guy in the parka was still on his knees, face in the snow, muffling cries of pain.

Bleeker showed Mustafa the screen of the smart phone. A text message. He didn't know the sender—*IslamFlex1*—but figured it was sent from a temporary phone anyway unless these were idiots. Crossing his fingers. No, strike that. Even hurt to do it in his mind.

The text: Not home. Lving 4 NPR. U know peeps their?

"Wrong there," Bleeker said.

"I know. I can read, too."

"Everybody gets it wrong these days. Drives me nuts. Same with 'your'." He thumbed a button. "Next message, this one he sent."

Ys. Can do. Wht d U want us to do?

Thumbed again.

Hurt. Not more. Scare him quiet.

"Got the picture?"

Mustafa shook his head. Not a word.

Bleeker stepped over to the perp. "Want to tell me your name or should I find it in the phone?"

"Fuck you, fucking pig! I ain't saying shit."

Bleeker shrugged. Pressed a few more buttons. Definitely a nice phone, not a throwaway. This was one to be proud of. He said to Mustafa, "You got a phone on you?"

He nodded, pulled it out of his pocket.

"What's the number?"

Mustafa told him, and he dialed it with the attacker's phone. Asked Mustafa if a name was coming up.

"Yeah. Roble. It's Roble." Then, "You followed me? Really?"

Bleeker shrugged. "I had a feeling. Listen, how about we get someone to pick these two up and I'll take you to the ER."

Mustafa shook his head. "I'm fine. I'll be okay."

"No, we need something to hold against these idiots. Pictures, you in a neck brace, all that."

"You already tried that." Pointed to the bandage on his neck.

Bleeker sighed. "That? That was just a friendly 'Welcome'."

The wind whipped snow and blew it like baby tornadoes across the concrete. Bleeker thought Mustafa was still waiting for that elusive apology. Well, the best apology he was going to get was lying before him on the ground.

Bleeker pulled out his own cell phone, called it in. "Need a squad behind the Chuck Wagon downtown. You'll know us. Hurry it up, please."

After that, quiet all over except for the faint jukebox from the saloon, the grunting from the guy with the broken fingers, and Mustafa's whistling breath, finally blending with the rising siren. Blue lights. Bleeker led Mustafa to his car. "I thought you wanted ribs?"

Shook his head. "Why bother? We've got Scott Ja-mama's in the Cities."

Fucking city folks always had to one up them. "Never heard of it."

FIVE

Another girl screaming. Three days in country, and that was the sound that still got to Adem, an electric current through his body. Chills in the middle of this crazy heat. He'd hold his breath, pray for it to end.

The girl ran by the corner where he and Jibriil and two other boys sat, moving with a small strip of shade over the last half hour. Waiting for something to happen. Something to do. They'd moved the TV inside closer to the window, watched the news. The soldiers watched a lot of TV, a lot of football, even though they weren't supposed to like football. A lot of news. A lot of music.

Adem had learned to shoot the gun, barely. He'd learned to shoot the rocket launcher, and never wanted to again. That was it for "training". Nothing like what he'd seen on the internet—men in hoods on obstacle courses, one after the other, making themselves quicker, stronger, better. Not here. Too hot.

The girl covered her face. Cries trailing her. Adem thought *Acid*. Again. The first time, he'd seen the result—the young woman's cheek cracked, her eye gone white. The second, from afar, a man stepped from behind a car and threw it into a woman's face. Adem was in the truck, so it was a split second as they passed, then the scream, soon lost in engine noise.

This time, he just knew. The same scream. Three days, three women. Supposedly for adultery or some other sexual trespass. Sometimes for not covering themselves as fully as they should have. But honestly, the attackers were jilted boyfriends or unsuccessful suitors. If he couldn't have her, then no one else should want her.

One of the other soldiers said, "Shame."

Adem perked up. Here was a guy thinking like he was. You couldn't go around throwing acid on people, right? He was about to speak up when he realized the boy simply meant the girl herself. She was the one who should be ashamed. The soldier got up, went inside the building, and turned the volume up on the TV.

Jibriil must've known what Adem was thinking because he tapped Adem's boot with his own and shook his head. It had been like that the whole time, Jibriil instinctively getting how this world worked and helping Adem get through without making some fatal mistakes. So far this war was as boring as it was frightening. After training out in the desert, they came back to the Mogadishu streets to sit in the heat with guns waiting for…something. Adem didn't know what. People passed by, remarkably calm considering they lived in a war zone. Why were they still around? So many people had abandoned the city, so why did these survivors stay? Didn't they have anywhere to go at all?

Once or twice the gunfire sounded closer than usual and all of the soldiers—a mix of grizzled veterans in their twenties and young teens in football jerseys—had leapt up, heads low, rifles at the ready. But then nothing happened.

Still, Jibriil had made a name for himself already. Willing to do and say the craziest things. Any dare, any challenge. He took his shirt off and dared government snipers to take him out. Shouted at them: "God will protect me! Aim for my heart!"

While Adem looked on, he had tortured boys accused of treason or desertion before they were dragged off to be punished or killed. On the second day, he had been called out by an older man, either a cleric or commanding officer—so hard to tell—and sent away for most of the day. Adem had to sit still, make small talk, pretend to like the soccer on TV, and try to keep his fear bottled like pop, not let it shake him up. Seven hours later Jibriil returned with five others and three dead bodies, one being a government soldier. The body was handed off to the younger boys, who tied rope around the naked man's foot and drug him through the street, gathering a crowd running after. Jibriil had been covered in blood and dust, caking on his skin. When Adem asked what had happened, his friend had smiled, reclined in his bunk with his hands behind his head.

"I did what I was asked to do."

And that was that.

But Adem knew Jabriil had a restless night, same as he had. The stink and heat of the room where he slept, too small for the twenty soldiers who slept there, kept him half-aware, half-dreaming. At one point, he dreamt that Jibriil was talking to him, telling him they were headed for glorious deaths, glorious afterlives, and then Adem blinked awake. There was Jibriil standing above him. Eyes wide. Adem held his breath. Another long moment, a minute? More? The white of his eyes hideously bright. Jibriil turned, laid back on his bed. Adem held his body tight and waited for sunrise.

He tried to doze on the corner. But then the girl. Then the fear.

"I want to fight," one of the soldiers said. "When do we get to fight?"

Adem asked, "When was the last time?"

"Couple of days ago. That's the thing. Between battles, it's boring."

Sure. Boring. Five prayers a day. Scared of everyone because Adem didn't know the enemy from his own people—not that it mattered. They might kill him as easily as the opposition. So many things were forbidden by Sharia that Adem had to be careful not to offend by accident, even if the soldiers all seemed to look the other way when it came to football, the internet, TV, and American rap. Again, Jibriil was his guide. Funny, since Jibriil had been the one who ditched school after eleventh grade. Got a job. Got new friends. Turned out he was studying harder than Adem thought under this "Rockstar Muhammad". Strange nickname, since the Imam was in his fifties and no doubt hated rock and pop and hip-hop and all the other soul-destroying music his followers clung to.

Jibriil laughed. "Ready for action, Adem? Getting impatient?"

The others laughed too. Pantomimed Adem all wide-eyed, rushing into the firefight. Another one of the gang. Adem knew he hadn't made much of an impression, and Jibriil was doing all he could to bring his friend into the conversation, make him sound like a true warrior. But both of them understood words could only go so far.

Another said, "How about lunch?"

That got them stirring, talking, moving. "This corner can watch itself for a while."

*

They all sat on the ground outside around a rug, one of many, under a ragged tarp. They were on the edge of town, an HQ growing from rummage and junk found in the streets or burned-out buildings. But then there were the fine command tents, or the rooms in these buildings set up with modern media—cameras, internet on laptops, flat screens—run by generators. Where did the money for that come from? Or for the tanks, trucks, guns, rocket launchers, the *food*? Adem wanted to ask. He wasn't sure if it was forbidden. Jibriil never brought it up. Someone somewhere was supporting this threadbare army very well.

The temperature under the tarp wasn't much cooler than it had been in the shade on the corner, but Adem was already beginning to be able to tell the difference between one hundred twenty degrees and one hundred fifteen. For lunch, flatbread, some sort of stewed meat, and rice. Water, not cold but not bad. Mostly clean. Adem tucked in, a few bites of gamey meat, not able to place the taste under all the spice. Crazy spice. He'd gotten used to the bland cafeteria meals on campus. Coughed as he swallowed. The water didn't help put out the fire. Someone passed a glass of milk along to him.

"No, no, too hot for milk."

"It helps ease the tongue. For girls who can't take their spice."

More laughter at Adem's expense. He was starting to feel like the class clown, except he hadn't done anything other than act like his usual self. Even surrounded by other Somalis, he was the odd man out.

He sipped the milk. The odor made him pause, like smoke. Like char. And it was warm. He held the glass away. The milk dribbled down his chin, thin as water.

"Come on, drink your milk. Makes you grow strong! Like a man!"

The aftertaste was cheese and salt. Was this some sort of trick? More hazing? He pushed ahead, tired of being the butt of the joke. Another swig. Strong, warm, not like the milk back home. But the sting in his mouth faded. Kept drinking, even as he gagged. Downed the whole thing. Felt ill. Less laughter when he was done. Some "Well done" and "He's getting better".

Jibriil leaned over and said quietly, "Just so you know, that's camel milk."

Adem's esophagus reacted on its own, backing up as he tried to swallow, making it worse. He turned from the group, letting loose behind him. The burn of the spice came back. The warmth of the milk, the saltiness.

Cheers all around. Shouting. "Pussy American boy. Can't kill a man if you can't handle your milk."

Adem tightened every muscle in his body. Forced himself to swallow. Counted to ten. He wiped his mouth with the back of his hand, then turned to the other soldiers again. He motioned for another glass of milk.

One of the other boys, who they called Madoowbe, called for one of the women who had served them and refilled their glasses. One came with a pitcher, her *guntiino* striped orange, purple, and red that was almost pink. She reached out to pour. A long-sleeved t-shirt under the dress. Adem wondered how they could stand the heat. He'd seen Minnesota kids in winter wear shorts, so maybe it was the same idea. Plus the scarf wrapped around her head, revealing only her face.

And what a face. Must've been about his age. She wore thin wire-rimmed glasses. When she looked at him after pouring a full glass of the camel milk, it wasn't the shy, submissive look he'd gotten from most Somali women here the past three days. There was something different. Electric.

Adem picked up the glass, waved it around like giving the toast at a wedding, and then gulped it all down in one slow pull, the boys pushing him on. One of the younger teenagers, Abdi Erasto, took a photo with his cell phone. When Adem finished and slammed the empty glass back onto the rug, they waited just long enough to applaud him. He smiled. Winked at the girl who had poured the milk. "Thank you."

Her face lit up, a grin. Cheeks lifting. She left the table. Adem felt queasy but glad to be on everyone's good sides. "The server, she was my inspiration."

Quiet. Not the response he expected. A look at Jibriil, whose mouth was an "O", head subtly shaking. Adem turned to his food. He'd lost his appetite, even though he was starving. And he suspected that the mystery meat in the stew was also camel. He sat there drinking water, trying to chase the burn down his throat again.

A shout from across the room. A soldier standing, pointing at another. A man around the same age as Adem, but a hundred or more pounds heavier. He froze when the shouting started.

Two other soldiers approached the fat soldier, these in elaborate uniforms, Eyes visible but the rest of their faces hidden from view by scarves, red and white diamonds, twisted and wrapped around their heads tightly. AK-47s in their hands. So now the target began pleading, his voice pitched high.

"I didn't mean it. It was an accident. I didn't know." He began pulling flatbread from his pockets and from under his shirt, dropping them on the nearest rug. "I swear, I didn't."

"Don't swear." The soldiers closed. "Come with us."

"Please, no, it was a misunderstanding. I—"

One soldier lifted the butt of his rifle and slammed it into the fat guy's back. He scrunched, his shoulders contracting, but he stayed on his feet.

Adem said aloud before he could think about it, "What did he do? What's going on?"

No one answered.

"For nothing? They're taking him away for nothing?"

Madoowbe said, "Shut up. Don't get involved."

Adem thought about arguing, getting in deeper, when Jibriil said, "He stole that food. You saw how fat he was. He was taking food, stockpiling it for later. I'll bet he's done it before but happened to get caught this time."

"Didn't we have plenty of food? Was it really a big deal?"

"Everyone gets his fair share. He could've asked for more, though. Instead, he stole it. From the mouths of his own brothers. Can you imagine?"

Somber mood around the table. The others obviously either knew the thief or felt bad for him regardless.

"But…" Adem waved an arm at all of the rugs around them, overflowing with food. "There's more than enough."

"That's not the point." Madoowbe was pissed. Held a triangle of bread like a blade, shook it towards Adem. "We are modest. We await our reward in heaven instead of seeking momentary pleasure on Earth. And we don't *steal.*"

It took all of his strength to not bring up the women on the road, the food the soldiers took. Not to mention the very land they'd taken by force and were eating on right then. Instead, he stifled his American side. Took a deep breath. Said to Jibriil, "What's going to happen to him?"

A shrug. "A court. Then punishment." He stood. "Let me go see what I can find out. I'll be back."

He went the same way the soldiers had marched the fat man earlier, disappeared around the corner of another tent.

Adem drank the rest of his water, thought about calling the serving girl over again, but remembered Jibriil's expression and decided against it. "So, how often does something like that happen, anyway? I'd think it would only take one to—"

He stopped himself, seeing that all of his fellow soldiers were glaring at their rug, not eating, and sure as hell not interested in hearing anymore from the American.

Adem nodded. Killed time waiting for Jibriil by thinking of all the time the two had snowball fights in the streets outside their apartment building on snow days in Minneapolis. How if he tried really hard, he could feel the icy cannonballs explode against his skin, this time a blessing instead of a curse.

*

A while later, Jibriil reappeared. Adem had already gone back to his corner, this time only with one other boy, a real hardliner. Didn't say a word the whole time. Singing under his breath, praises to Allah, a bit of Wu-Tang, all that. Adem tried a couple of times—"Where are you from?" and "How long have you been here?"—but received clipped answers he couldn't even understand. So he gave up and reclined against the building while his partner squatted on the ground.

Adem stepped out to meet Jibriil in the middle of the street. "Where have you been? What was that all about?"

Jibriil looked around as if he hadn't heard. "Just you and Garaad here?"

"I don't know where everyone went. No one talks to me. This is…this isn't what I expected."

"I know, man, calm down. Easy." Jibriil patted a hand on Adem's shoulder. "It takes time. You've been spoiled. We both have."

"Yeah, but you're a natural. Look at you, already seen combat, they treat you like a hero."

Jibriil shook his head. "I do what I'm asked to do. That's all. It's not about me."

They stepped back to the corner, Jibriil and Garaad nodding at each other. Adem remembered that Garaad had been one of the soldiers who went along on Jibriil's mission the night before. They didn't speak either. Jibriil lifted the loose part of his scarf and wiped his forehead. Adem had thought of asking for one of the jungle hats he'd seen a few men wearing. His own scarf was beginning to stink.

Jibriil stared down the street, not so much at anything. "I think I can help you, but you've got to trust me."

"Sure, okay. What do I do?" Adem was thinking he could be back-up on another secret mission. Or that Jibriil might teach him the right words to say, the right posture.

"So, the fat son of a bitch at lunch today?"

"What happened to him?"

"Nothing yet. He's to be tried in the morning for thievery. Everyone gets a trial."

Adem thought back to the girl who had been stoned, the man who had raped her. She should've gotten lashes instead. He'd read enough to realize that, but the court had decided she was as much to blame. How could they do that? They weren't following Sharia law. They were *rewriting* it.

"He's obviously guilty."

"Oh yeah. But there must still be a trial. It has to be, you know, tight like that."

Adem flinched at far-off gunfire, but not much. Already desensitized, and that bothered him more than it should have. "What's going to happen to him?"

Jibriil, still staring. "They're going to chop off one of his hands. Most likely his best one."

Exactly. Adem got it then. He had to ask anyway. "How is that supposed to help me?"

Still staring far off into the distorted air, shimmering above the road. "You will be the one with the blade."

Garaad laughed. Adem turned to him. The soldier, bright-eyed and pointing at him, laughed louder.

Adem smiled. Thought to himself, *It's just a hand.* Then flexed his fingers.

SIX

Bleeker thought Mustafa could sure take an ass-kicking. He had that going for him. Wasn't very gracious, though. Once Bleeker had helped him into a bed at the cramped ER, Mustafa said, "You were there the whole time?"

"I had your back."

"Then why didn't you call for help earlier, like before they hit me?"

"You're welcome. It was nothing, really, me saving you from a hell of a lot worse."

"I'm saying, if you had an idea—"

"I didn't." Bleeker sat on the stool beside the bed, too low, brought him eye level with Mustafa. "Not about that. You could've known those guys. Damned if that was my business. The only reason I was on you was because I didn't want you tracking mud all over my city trying to play detective."

That got Mustafa grinning. Reminded him he was hurting, too, from the look on his face. But not so bad that a few bandages and painkillers wouldn't get him back to rights in a couple days.

The doctor came by, felt around. No broken bones ("Let's x-ray it to be sure"), no sprains. Some lacerations, one on his head that needed a handful of stitches. Otherwise, decent bill of health.

Bleeker checked out the others waiting for service. A fully covered Somali woman in a chair, a whimpering baby bouncing on her knee. Most of her family leaning against walls or pacing. A middle-aged guy, shaggy, holding his bloodied towel-wrapped hand in his lap, a policeman hovering nearby. The cop tipped his hat at Bleeker but didn't say a word. Awkward. But what could anyone say to a guy whose pregnant girlfriend had been gunned down barely three days ago? Mostly they did the stoic, Minnesotan-style repression, ask him about the weather, if he planned any more ice-fishing trips, and when the funeral was.

Mustafa said, "Thank you."

Bleeker turned back to him. "No problem."

"I made mistakes out there. They could've killed me."

"Would be a first for them. Worst that would've happened, I think, is that you'd have been spending a few nights here instead of walking out with me."

"Are you going to wait outside my hotel room door all night?"

Bleeker stood from the stool. His knees made popping noises. His back hurt worse than it had before his days in Iraq. Another glance at the cop in the waiting area. Sure, they could sympathize. They could rouse the anger over a fellow officer shot down, want some revenge. But Bleeker didn't think they really understood. Not the big picture, which would make some sort of wicked sense when he finally saw it.

But this guy, Mustafa Bahdoon, might get it.

He said, "You know what happened. Your son and another guy shot two cops. One of those cops was my girl. She was carrying my baby. I'm getting old, and here I had a chance to start over, nice and fresh. Cindy made me feel...different. Like I had taken too many wrong turns but didn't know I was lost until she—"

A tech showed up to take Mustafa for x-rays. Tired eyes, early thirties but already getting a preview of her forties. To her it was just a job. A dead end. She wore Jack-o-lantern scrubs even though it was January. Bleeker told her to give him a few more minutes. Soon as she left, he forgot where he'd left off, this shining image of Cindy's face in his mind. No words.

Mustafa said, "I swear to you, if Adem had some place in killing her, I will wash my hands of him. Whatever the courts say, I will abide. I swear. He is a good kid. A smart kid."

Bleeker gripped the bed rail with both hands. "But...let's say he really was involved. Let's say I'm there in front of him, and he's confessed and I have my gun."

Mustafa forced himself up on his elbows, straining, to give Bleeker the most hateful and serious look the man could muster. "I would kill you before you know what happened. That, I can promise you. Whether you saved my ass or not."

Bleeker smiled. Not that it was funny. He believed Mustafa was a stone cold killer who got real lucky when he quit the streets to work at a department store. But they were past that. Had Cindy shot an unarmed Adem, Bleeker wouldn't have hesitated to take out Mustafa had he come after his own justice.

Family, right? Fuck justice.

Bleeker said, "Tell me about his friend, the one you think did it."

The lines crinkled around Mustafa's eyes, lips tightened. "Always a wannabe. The shame of it? He could've gone on *American Idol*. He sings so well. But that wasn't what he wanted. He wanted to be a thug. The crazies prey on boys like Jibriil. Not only do they make the boys killers, but they make them feel righteous about it."

The Jack-o-latern tech came back. Hands on her hips. "I can't wait any longer. My shift's going to end."

She helped Mustafa off the bed and into a wheelchair.

"This is police business." Bleeker stepped in front of the wheelchair. "You can stay a few minutes after, can't you?"

She wrapped her fingers tighter around the handles of the wheelchair. The plastic squeaked. "It's not going to take that long. Grab a magazine for a bit. Geez."

Bleeker ignored her, knelt in front of the chair. "There's not much we can do, you think?"

Mustafa shrugged. "We can try."

"So tomorrow, you press charges on the guys who jumped you. Then tell our people the boys went off to fight in Africa. All that. I'll take some leave, which they want me to do anyway, and meet you in the cities after Cindy's funeral."

Mustafa looked away, slid his fingers together across his lap. "Then what?"

"Then we try to find them. Make sure this Jibriil character gets what's coming to him."

Shook his head. "If they're really there on the ground, fighting this war, then that's worse than anything Hell could serve up for them, let alone us."

SEVEN

It wasn't until he had been assigned the task that Adem began noticing other soldiers around the camp with one hand. He'd been told punishments such as these were supposed to be deterrents, used sparingly. But he counted four one-handed men before breakfast.

He grew tired of searching, but couldn't help himself. Turned his attention to finding the girl who had poured his milk yesterday. The way she'd looked at him. He wanted her to do it again. If he got another chance to look into her eyes, he would gladly drink a gallon of camel milk.

Ate what he could—more *laxoox*, the flatbread, with honey, and a strong tea. More to settle his growling stomach than because he was hungry. Throwing up something would be better than dry heaving. Jibriil was nowhere to be found, so Adem ate alone. Didn't look up from his plate. Acid in his throat.

If Jibriil began keeping his distance, Adem's days were numbered. All that talk about country and Allah, all of it sounding big and important until they were on the ground, and it seemed to Adem like a big high school clique. A gang like the one his dad had led, except with more prayer and no alcohol. Had to face it: he'd come along with Jibriil thinking they would be welcomed with open arms. He had hoped to reconnect with all of the culture Jibriil had told him they had both lost. That they had been lied to by their parents, their aunts and uncles, their older brothers and sisters. Brainwashed by Americans. Especially Adem, off in college. Jibriil telling him, "Son, you've changed. Like I don't even know you anymore."

Adem could've said the same thing, but when he looked around his small campus, out on the prairie, sitting next to farm kids who barely knew their own language while Adem already had three under his belt, and yet they looked at him when he spoke as if he was mentally challenged. It wasn't exactly like he'd hoped. His dad was dead set on him getting a degree, maybe even going to grad school. His dad, who used to run with the baddest gang on the streets, now, what, a wage slave?

While his family hadn't been the most fervent Muslims, Adem had steered even further away from faith until arriving on campus and realizing how little the white farm kids knew about Islam, and all the awful assumptions they made to fill the holes. Berated him for his treatment of women. What? "Not me," he would say. "Never." Or he'd get the talk radio Republicans—boys who got their politics from their dad and glorified DJs—wanting to debate him on terrorism, then not believe him when he told them he agreed with them. Then they would say "Islam is a religion of death. It's right there in the Quran. You can't deny it." But he would try, half-heartedly, to save face. Told them they hadn't read the Quran, and probably hadn't read the entire Bible they kept quoting either. Truth was that neither had Adem. As a child, sure, memorizing verses, all that. These days, he had the general gist of the story. Enough to get by on.

So when Jibriil told him about this trip—this *crusade*—he asked more questions. Kept getting deeper. At the very least, he thought the trip would set him straight about the importance of keeping his faith alive. But so far everything he'd seen in country had smashed what little was left into shards.

Adem heard his name being called. He looked up from his breakfast. Garaad was coming towards him, face not as wrapped as the day before. Crisscrossed with several nearly white scars on his lips and chin. He waved.

Adem stood. His stomach wasn't ready.

Garaad was talking and walking. "Come now. Let's get this over with."

Adem followed Garaad out of the tent and towards a crowd in an open area that used to be a town square, he'd been told, but was now barren, all the decoration removed by the soliders. Adem thought about the football field, the pitch overgrown with shrubs. Here, not one plant or tree. Only the crowd, a couple of goats, and a loud dog. Stone and dirt.

He asked, "Does this make sense to you? Losing a hand over, what, a little bread?"

Garaad, with his devil's smile, lifted his chin like *You've got to be kidding me*. "Tell me, in America. Someone who steals, say, a car? He goes to jail?"

"If he's caught, sure."

"And in jail, the prisoners tell him how to steal the next car without getting caught. And also, they take his manhood, make him a faggot. He starts on drugs. Maybe sells them when he gets out. His life is ruined."

"But not always. He has a chance to make himself better. He wouldn't want to go back again, right?"

"They do, though. Over and over. In jail, out, and in again." Garaad sniffed. "I'd rather lose a hand. Look at a stump every day and thank Allah for it."

"Okay."

"You?"

A minute ago it had been no contest. At least in America, losing your hand wasn't an option. "I don't know." Surprised to say it, but he really didn't. He wouldn't want either fate, but with a possible felony murder charge hanging over him in New Pheasant Run, prison was becoming a real possibility.

Even Sharia didn't whack off a hand for murder. They went straight to "Eye for an eye". Dead for dead. No appeals.

He and Garaad made their way through the crowd, weaving through unwashed soldiers, sweating townspeople, children. It was the hottest morning Adem had ever felt. Even a family vacation to the Badlands when he was younger, middle of a heat wave in South Dakota, hundred and ten by noon, easy. That was nothing compared to nine-thirty in Mogadishu.

The air was so hot it stung his nostrils. Squinted until his brow hurt. Several high-ranking men—two in combat uniforms, clean and pressed. The others in Somali robes, brightly colored, heavy, wearing white *taqiyat*—prayer hats. One of them, an old man with a white beard, held a machete. As Adem approached, the man with the machete presented it to him, a hand under the handle and the blade.

The man was praying. A chant. Adem didn't know if he should bow his head or close his eyes or put his hand over his heart. Still no sign of Jibriil, which was starting to freak him out. It was Jibriil's fault he was doing this. Were they going to give him a lesson in hand chopping? Was he expected to put on a show? The solemn faces of the leaders suggested not. He was to act as God's agent of Justice. He was to be blessed for it.

Crowd noise behind him. Adem turned to see the people make a path for the accused, looking shocked but not frantic. Almost like he'd been drugged. Leading him by his arm into the center of the square was Jibriil.

Following him were two men, one carrying a metal table like you'd find in a hospital. The other, a chair. In Jibriil's free hand, a plastic shopping bag. The men set up the table, the chair, and Jibriil led the convicted man over so he could sit down. Speaking softly in his ear, to which the man nodded, did as he was told. Adem could imagine what Jibriil was telling him: *It's alright. You'll be punished, won't feel a thing, then forgiven so you can get on with God's work.* What else could you tell a man about to lose his hand over a few extra pieces of bread?

As the guilty man was prepared, the holy man who had handed the machete to Adem placed his hand on his back, led him in slow steps to the table and chair. The crowd closed in, shrinking the circle. Jibriil backed away, revealing the thief's arm being tied off with a tourniquet. His hand rested palmside up on the table. One of the men assisting Jibriil took the bag from him, pulled a syringe from it, and held it up to the sun. Tapped his finger against the side, plunged just so a drop bubbled out and ran down the needle.

He wiped a cloth across the man's arm. The alcohol smell hit Adem's nose. The needle slipped into the man's arm near his wrist. He flexed his fingers. Small sounds coming from him, not quite crying, not quite whimpering. Pathetic. Much calmer than Adem would be if they switched places.

Time passed. No one in the crowd said a word. A surprise. Adem expected shouts, jeers, but it was much the same as the stoning. Silence. Respect. Then why did they bother to watch? It was a horror show. They claimed to be the more civilized religion, right? Not even the American devils used public punishment as a spectacle anymore. That had faded away at some point in the twentieth century. Prisoners had the right to accept their time behind thick walls, no prying eyes, or in antiseptic execution rooms with only a select few on the other side of the glass.

Here? Why did they flock to see this behanding instead of going to work, taking care of their homes, playing football, cooking, laughing, praying? Like an American car wreck. In spite of the suffering out in the open, it was hard not to watch.

Adem didn't understand the injection at first. What was the point? But as the men poked at the hand, testing for a response, he realized that they didn't want screams and blood. They didn't want carnage. They wanted to please Allah. So they found the least painful way they could to do this while still making sure the message got through. Never take bread without asking.

Jibriil held the man's numb right hand high, made sure all of the crowd got a good look, before he set it down again gently on the table.

Adem wasn't even going to get a practice swing.

Another of the clerics spoke into Adem's ear. "They will mark the best place to strike. You bring it up over your head, keep your eye on the mark, not the blade. Let it fall heavy with a little force behind it. Don't think too much. It has been sharpened so fine that a child could do this."

"But what if it doesn't come off?"

"Do what I said, and you won't have to worry. It's been taken care of."

Adem stepped up to the table. Glanced at Jibriil, who winked at him. Glanced at the convicted man. Head turned the other way. Eyes tight. Waiting.

Adem took a deep breath. Cleared his throat, gagged, placed his free hand over his mouth. Easy, easy. Just do it. Nothing to fear.

Once lifted, there was no turning back.

Adem arced the machete over his head. Held it a moment too long. Knew as he was coming down with it that he was off, pushing too hard. Flinched his shoulders. The blade landed with a clang, shaking the table. Adem had closed his eyes without realizing. He looked down.

Three fingertips, two on the table and the other on the ground flecked with sand.

The guilty man began breathing fast, heavy, wheezing. He'd looked too. Shit! Shit! Shit!

Adem lifted the blade again. Slung blood over his head. Came down again. A better blow, but only half a cut. The man tried to lift his hand. It wobbled, dangled. Adem grabbed his arm, pushed it back against the table, fit his blade against the remaining attached skin and muscle, and sawed his way through. The guilty man screaming the whole time. Shrill and painful.

Jibriil held the man in the chair by his shoulders. Leaned down and whispered in his ear some more. Whatever he said calmed the man immediately. Adem stepped back as the two attendants came forward and began bandaging the stump. Another look at the severed hand—a ragged cut, too much loose skin left over. Too much blood.

The clerics and military men turned back and forth between the guilty man and Adem. Animated talking. Shocked eyes. Then the man with the white beard raised his hand chin high, spoke loudly and got the others' attentions.

"He did as we asked. He did the best he could. No one can fault him." Turned to Adem, reached out.

Adem walked to him, dropped the blade along the way. The cleric took both of Adem's hands in his own, never mind the blood. Kissed him on each cheek.

"I'm sorry. I'm so sorry." Adem bowed his head to the holy man.

"No, no. It is I who am sorry. You did the right thing. Blessings on you, son."

Another embrace, Adem staining the man's robes with the blood.

The murmuring of the crowd raised in volume as they dispersed. They said things like, "Awful. Just awful" and "It's bad enough to take his hand, but to humiliate him like that..." and "Imagine if that had been someone's neck."

As the clerics took their leave, Adem turned to the men working with the convicted. The blood had flowed more, with a pool of it now on the table, spilling over into the dirt. Jibriil stood back, arms crossed. Adem walked over, stood at his side.

"What's wrong?"

Jibriil shrugged. "Maybe the heat. Maybe he's a hemophiliac. I don't know. But they can't stop him bleeding."

The men shouted, frantically waved at soldiers who were standing around like Adem and Jibriil. Finally, a truck rushed down the road towards them, parted the remaining crowd and screeched to a stop. The attendants grabbed a cot from the back, laid it on the ground, then forced the man out of the chair. He refused to lie down. He held his stump as the men fought to control the bleeding, making a bigger mess. They finally got him to stumble towards the back of the truck. Helped him into the bed. He started out by sitting up, but then slipped out of sight as if he'd fainted. The truck sped off, kicked up dirt clouds. Left Adem and Jibriil staring at the blood-covered chair and table, both of which had been knocked over, turning the dirt dark.

Jibriil clapped Adem on the shoulder. "Still, all in all it was a good job. You did what you needed to do."

"Is he going to die?"

A grin. "Some things are out of our hands. All we can do is—"

"Yeah, I know. God's plan, God's will, all that."

"Hey, it got us this far."

Adem wiped his hands on his pants. What had he done? How did he know this guy didn't have AIDS or Hep or worse? Like Ebola, all those crazy jungle bugs. Wiped some more. Seeping into his pores now. "Water. I need to wash the blood off."

"Okay, yeah. That's good. Let's do that."

They headed off. Adem wasn't certain, but it seemed as if the soldiers weren't laughing at him quite as much. At least today.

Jibriil said, "Good news. Thanks to that, you're coming along with me tomorrow."

"What's tomorrow? Where are we going?"

A smile. "You'll see. Try to get some time in on the gun today."

The gun. His AK. Struggled to keep the bullets from spraying like a crazy fountain at the water parks in the Dells. Jibriil telling him he needed it. Shit, he was heading into combat.

"What's it like?"

Jibriil stopped, glanced around. Then, "I can't tell you. Everyone feels it differently. I should have been afraid. Like, shit my pants afraid, right? But I wasn't. Not at all. It felt like the thing I was best in the world at."

Adem didn't say anything more as they made their way to a spigot on the side of what used to be a school. Until this week, he would have guessed the thing Jibriil was best at was singing. But he was sure singing wouldn't have gotten him so bloody.

EIGHT

Bleeker waited for Mustafa in the parking lot of the Super 8 in Golden Valley where he had checked in earlier that afternoon. It had been several days since the beating in NPR. Mustafa had done as Bleeker asked—went to the police, pressed charges on the assailants, and told the chief what he knew about his son and Jibriil, almost certainly in Somalia. Then headed home.

Bleeker climbed into the tiny yellow Mitsubishi with two cups of coffee from the Burger King next door. "Might be a bit cold by now. Didn't know when you'd get here."

Mustafa waved him off. "I don't drink coffee."

"More for me, then."

They started out. No drink holders in the Mitsubishi. They'd been removed to put in more electronics—Slick lights, speakers, switch for the nitrous. Bleeker kept shifting the full coffee in his left hand, drank the other with his right. Steam on the windows. Finally, Bleeker said, "Fuck" and winced and elbowed the window button. Rolled it down and tossed out the full cup. Mustafa said nothing, turned onto 394.

Bleeker didn't like the silence. "Where're we headed tonight?"

"I checked Roble out. He was with this gang, small gang, only about ten of them. Call themselves The Black Ice Boyz. Over in Little Mogadishu."

"Only ten?"

"Somali gangs are like that. Mostly small, more for fun than profit. These guys haven't stepped up yet, but I think they're trying."

"Like you did."

Sharp breath. "Don't."

"Look, it's fine if it helps—"

But Mustafa held up his hand, fingers straight and stiff like he wanted to slap the prairie detective. He calmed down, rested his hand on the wheel.

"These boys are not like me, no. You're right about that. My gang, if they saw me with you tonight, they would kill me. Out in this car—everybody knows my car—white man alongside. They'd think I was a threat. You don't know how careful I have to be everyday. How...*isolating* it all is. No such thing as just leaving. You end up becoming some sort of test, see if they can take you out."

Another sip of coffee. "Sorry."

"Tonight, no Clint Eastwood, please. No smart-ass remarks. They won't be scared of you like the Somalis in your town."

"Fuck, scared? They respect me, son. I worked long and hard to get their respect."

"I saw what I saw. You haven't worked hard enough yet."

"Says you."

"Okay, whatever. You mind some music?"

"Is it that rap shit?"

Mustafa let out a breath. Wasn't sure if he had the balls to say it or not, Bleeker could see it on his face. But then he did. "It's that rap shit your daughter is listening to when she's sucking a brother's dick."

There it was. Taking the piss. Testing him.

Bleeker said, "Be a shame to get blood all over these leather seats."

Mustafa laughed at that one. Couldn't hold it in. Bleeker stared out the window, didn't want him to see the smirk. Then Mustafa sniffed, got control, and said, "Yeah, I'm sorry, man. I didn't mean anything. You know, I don't even know your daughter. I was out of line."

"I don't have a daughter. I don't have any kids. Cindy's would've been my first."

Quiet. Two miles, then three.

Mustafa said, "How was the funeral?"

Bleeker *hmphed*. "It was sad. It was a funeral. The fuck you think it was?"

"I watched something on TV about New Orleans. They had happy funerals. Like, a celebration. Music and dancing."

"Lutherans don't dance."

"I didn't mean...I mean..."

"Forget it."

"I thought, sometimes, funerals can help heal wounds. Talking about the good times."

"It was a closed casket. The embalmer couldn't make her face look presentable. And now the ground's frozen, so she has to be kept in a fucking cooler until the ground thaws up in Stillwater. Get it? She's like a side of beef. So's my kid. I've got nothing to celebrate and that's why I didn't want to talk about it. Happy now? Do you enjoy hearing how bad my life sucks because your son wanted to go fight for Allah?"

Red-faced. Voice creeping louder until it broke. Balled up a fist. Finally pounded the dash so hard it cracked.

"Fine. wanted to sell this car anyway. Like, I want a Suburban, something like that. Trick the wheels out, put in big ass JL subwoofers. That'll be some sweet shit, man."

He took a Downtown exit and slowed down, ignored Bleeker, who was huffing and puffing.

Mustafa said, "Pay for my dash?"

Bleeker turned to him, jaw clenched. Teeth grinding. Bleeker winced, put his palm to his ear. "Yeah, fine."

Only a few more miles.

*

They skirted the U of M campus ended up on a busy street in Cedar-Riverside outside an African café, some rough-looking bars, and coffee houses. An "alternative" vibe, but there was something off-the-tracks about it.

Mustafa parked on the curb, turned off the car. "This place is like home. Back in the day, we liked it here. Did what we wanted, got left alone. Taunt the police, scare the college students heading to the clubs."

Bleeker reached to open his door. The dome light clicked on.

"No, wait. Not yet."

Bleeker closed his door again. "What, you see them?"

"No."

"Know where they are?"

"I don't."

"Then...what?"

Mustafa kept staring out the window, peeked in the rearview mirror, at the people on the sidewalk. Much of the remains from the storm earlier in the week had settled or been dozered away. Piles of snow on the curbs, shiny slicks of ice on the walkway. Not a thick crowd, but enough. Of course they would be out. They couldn't keep up a reputation by staying inside all winter. Mustafa picked up his cell phone from the console, flipped it open, and began texting.

Bleeker snapped his fingers a couple of times. "You awake over there?"

"Calm down. This is how we will find them."

"We're not doing anything."

"Yes we are. Soon, someone will come talk to me. They might even pull a gun on me. Keep an eye out."

"Jesus, man. What?" Bleeker's hand already searching for his pistol.

"They know my car. Most of my own gang still wants to kill me. The others, more or less. They all know I'm out, and that makes me a very valuable target. Anytime I wanted to roll on them, they're going down.

Killing me is one of the biggest prizes. A betting pool for who gets me first. Over five thousand, I've been told."

"So you're going to sit and let them shoot you?"

Mustafa smiled. "No one has killed me, though. Almost ten years, and no one has tried. They know the car, know where I live, but so far nothing. I think most of the men out here who know me think it's all a joke. That one day I'll come back to them. Or they think I'll go after all the other gangs and leave my own to do as they please."

"Do you?"

He turned to Bleeker. "I am not a criminal. What I used to be doesn't matter anymore. I chose this…bullshit, right, so that Adem wouldn't turn out like me."

"Yeah, how's that working out? Little fuck's not exactly a model citizen."

Bleeker could tell Mustafa wanted to grab his shirt at the throat and twist. He wanted to spill the hot coffee on Bleeker's privates. But the man had some restraint. That was good. More than Bleeker had. All it took in NPR for Bleeker to nearly strangle Mustafa was him mentioning the mere possibility that Adem was innocent.

Mustafa said, "You dare say that when you cheat on your wife? Fuck a fellow cop? Leave the woman you vowed to love over some hot new pussy?"

"Hey!"

"No, you 'hey'! I'm supposed to just take it? But you, so holy and clean in the eyes of God. Fuck you."

"I never killed anyone, Mohammed."

"That is *not* my name. You call me by my name or this is over now."

"I said I never killed anyone." Said it smug and slow, too.

"What is my name?"

The car windows had steamed up on Bleeker's side. He pretended Mustafa had said nothing at all, sitting there as if he was chief of police, chauffeured by a black man. There, that's diversity. That'll show the crackers out west.

Mustafa shook his head. He cranked the car.

"Wait. Fine. Bahdoon We're all friends here. I'm sorry for, whatever, taking the guy's name in vain."

"Nobody calls me Bahdoon anymore, I told you that. What is my name?"

Bleeker said "Fuck" and got out of the car. He lit a cigarette. Paced. Guy trying to teach him some touchy-feely civics lesson. Of course he knew the bastard's name. Mustafa. Mustafa. Sounded like some sort of Arab bread. But this guy thought he was some big shot down here? The fact that no one had approached them yet had Bleeker second-guessing how "wanted" the asshole was. Could be the price on his head had been canceled. He was just another worthless stockman at Target, no power to hurt anyone he used to run with.

And who else did he have helping him out?

Bleeker tossed his half-finished cigarette butt into the road and climbed back into the car. Shivering.

"Mustafa Your name is Mustafa."

Mustafa nodded. "Thank you."

"Welcome."

Someone tapped on Mustafa's window. It was a hard tap, metal on glass. Gun barrel. Mustafa said to Bleeker, "Time to work."

*

The kid with the gun, maybe sixteen, got into the back seat and played at being a badass by poking the gun behind Mustafa's ear, talking about his "traitor nigga ass", and asking Bleeker for his wife's number. "You can watch if you want, old man."

Old. Sure. To this kid they were both ancient. Easy to think old meant weak. Exactly what Mustafa was counting on.

The kid told them to drive. He had skinny wrists and the gun was pretty small—a big one would be too heavy for him. His bulky parka with a fur-trimmed hood hid how thin he was, but Bleeker could tell from the wrists, the cheeks, the voice

"Where to?"

"You go until I tell you to turn."

Mustafa took a hard right at the next corner.

The gun jammed against his ear again, scratching his scalp. "The fuck? I didn't say turn."

"You didn't not say it."

"I *told* you—"

"To drive until you said turn. So I was driving and felt like turning."

"Don't make me fuck you up."

Mustafa glanced in the rearview. It was obvious this kid wasn't going to shoot either of them.

"Get back on the road, right? Someone wants to know what you're doing out here tonight, peeping at us from your car. That ain't shit."

"Just give me the address. I know the roads better than you."

More pressure from the gun. "Smart nigga? How about you do what I say, huh?"

Bleeker's hand closed over the gun, yanked it clear of Mustafa's head. Gave the piece a little twist, and it was all Bleeker's. Turned it around on the kid.

He asked, "What's your name?"

"Shit, you ain't going to kill me, I know it. I didn't do nothing. Just playing, that's all."

"I've got to call you something."

"Call me a *lawyer*, man. I didn't do nothing. I've got witnesses."

He pressed himself far back in the seat, leaning left, eyes on the gun. His feet were working all over the floorboard.

Mustafa said, "His name's Tyrus. American born Somali. His mom's French, though. His older brother would be a good banger if he wasn't so high half the time. In jail right now, isn't he, Ty?"

Tyrus was wide-eyed. "How you know…yeah, Michael locked up for selling weed. Not even a lot of it. It's bullshit, man. You don't know me. I'm not saying anything."

Bleeker rolled his eyes, turned forward in his seat and set the gun in his lap. Some kind of snub-nose .38. Had to be a Taurus or Rossi. These kids usually didn't do revolvers. He had one like it on his ankle, a five-shot he'd bought for his wife to carry in her purse, but she never did so he took it back, wore it just in case.

Mustafa said, "Is that Mike's gun?"

"What part of 'I ain't talking' did you not understand?"

Bleeker, a bit too loud, said, "We're not arresting you, idiot. But we don't want you playing with this toy and hurting somebody. Where are we going?"

After another half-minute of whining, Tyrus gave up the address. An apartment about five minutes from where they were. Mustafa said, "I could've guessed that."

Mustafa got them headed in the right direction and floored it. Turned on the stereo—more to drown out Tyrus's bluster than anything else. Cranked electric guitars and funky beat. Thick base, wild lead, singer like he was preaching the gospel of rock and roll. A black rock band from the eighties.

Bleeker turned to Mustafa, brow creased. "Living Colour?"

Mustafa grinned. "Old school."

In the back, Tyrus covered his ears and shouted. "Sort of bullshit is this?"

Bleeker gave it a nod. "I can live with that."

NINE

He didn't make it. The thief. Adem took his hand and no one could stop the bleeding in time so he didn't make it. All over some bread.

What did they do to Adem? They blessed him for doing the will of God. They told him he had served well. And they sent him on a raid to an Ethiopian border town—his first time out in the field.

A caravan of trucks, driving all night. The soldiers sleeping as if the bumps and swaying were nothing—Abdi Erasto, Madoowbe, Garaad, others Adem didn't know. Even Jibriil, drooling on himself. Adem was crazy from lack of sleep, always drifting into microdreams that the next bump would rip him from. Not fair. His skin itched, his nose itched, his chest felt caved in, as if someone had run over him with a tank.

"Fear," Jibriil had told him earlier. "It's like an empty bowl. Once you fill up the bowl, by coming home alive, there's less and less of it each time. Until there's always a full bowl ready and waiting for you."

Adem didn't get it. But that was because he couldn't pay attention. The last time he had more than an hour of sleep, right before they started off, he kept thinking about the hand. How fake it looked once it was off. How it was all not what he expected. The hand. That was the worst. He didn't want to have to see his own hand lying on the ground like that, a grisly mannequin, all to make Allah feel like justice had been done.

He looked around the truck and wondered if any of these guys had the same thoughts when they first joined the rebels, or if living here through all of the wars had burned into their souls the need for such a harsh law from a demanding god. Would it ever burn into him?

When Adem was back at school, he felt that every day meant more work at "fitting in", like a puzzle piece that didn't quite snap into place. He had to file off the rough edges, the bad angles, make everything smaller—his heritage, his language, his dreams. The first few days of college, he thought there were no boundaries. He could study history, politics, sociology, science. He had wanted to be an advisor to legislators, governors, senators. But as the semesters ground on, he wondered if he'd be lucky to make manager at a chain store. Good in his classes, knew the material, could have great discussions with professors. Outside of the classroom, it was as if he was invisible.

Jibriil had told him no one would overlook him here. Allah had a plan for everyone and once Adem hit the ground with a rifle in his hand, he'd find his purpose. Smart guys like him were valuable for strategic planning. It all made perfect sense.

Except that so far, he'd been even more ignored than he was back in NPR except when the others were making fun of him. Jibriil had been dead wrong—smarts didn't matter. Instead, questioning less and showing a will to do more, no matter how awful, was what put you in the good graces of the higher powers. Jibriil was more likely to become a leader than Adem.

The truck rattled again, turned left and lurched and Adem fell from his bench and onto Garaad across from him.

"Idiot!" He kicked Adem, the dusty boot catching him in the shoulder. Adem fought to get back to his place, pummeled by more kicks. "You like this? You like getting kicked around?"

It took Jibriil to reach across, grab Garaad's leg, and say, "Enough!"

They listened to Jibriil, everyone there. Treated him like some prophetic warrior forsaking the pleasures of the world to do his duty. They loved him.

Adem just got in the way.

Soon after everyone had settled down again, the trucks stopped. The drivers got out, slapped the side of the vehicle, woke the sleepers. They all unwound and climbed to the ground, most of them sitting down again, the others stretching. It was very dark, only glimpses of moonlight, making everything indistinct and shiny.

The leader of the raid called over his top men, Jibriil being one of them. He hadn't told Adem of any promotion. Was that on purpose? Concerned about Adem's morale? He hated to admit it, but this was a reversal of their friendship in the Cities, where Adem had been the one who made the plans, decided what they were going to do and when. Jibriil always went along, at least until high school began to pull them apart, bit by bit.

After the huddle, Jibriil called over the men from his truck, explained their part in all this. "We want to destroy their supplies. Not steal, but decimate. We want to kill the men."

"The women? What about the women?"

Jibriil, no expression. "Whatever you want, as long as it doesn't get you killed."

The rest—partners, streets, escape route, time of operation, Adem absorbed without really paying attention. It sounded as if they didn't expect much resistance. The middle of the night, everyone asleep, far away from the frontline. Jibriil said they would split into pairs when they reached the village. Adem assumed Jibriil would keep him close, but instead teamed him with Madoowbe. It wasn't what Adem had hoped for, but it was better than being stuck with Garaad or the guy who wanted to rape the women.

Adem tightened his grip on the rifle as Jibriil kept on in hushed tones. The air was cleaner than it had been in the truck. He sneezed, tried to quiet it. His nerves were on edge like sandpaper, hard to touch anything. He scratched a bite on his leg and thought he might pass out.

Tonight he would have to kill someone. Not like he had with the thief, because no matter the intent, he had to accept that yes, he had already killed a man. This time, no accidents. No way around it. Adem would lift his gun and end the lives of men who were not expecting it. He was grateful for that part—not at all looking forward to the day the enemy was coming at him with their own guns.

He wasn't ready, but that was the point, right? Suffering through these long days of trial, waiting to hear the voice of the Prophet, when maybe it took action to open the doors. Taking the hand was the beginning, leading him to this. If that's what it took, okay. He would bind his fears and leave them waiting in the truck for when he returned. Hopefully, he wouldn't need them anymore.

Jibriil pointed the way, a half-mile walk west, and the crew followed, footsteps and darkness. Adem lagged behind.

*

An hour later he was running for his life behind two other soldiers, Jibriil behind them laying down gunfire at the pursuing men. Adem was sweating, cold, hot, out of breath, all at once. He'd dropped his rifle a long time ago. The Ethiopians had been waiting for them.

They all heard the gunfire, the first truckload of men being taken out by the waiting soldiers, before they'd even made it to town. Jibriil rushed ahead, told the others to stick to the plan and hurry up. He had to go see what had happened.

Adem and Madoowbe continued on, taking cover behind a makeshift hut, sneaking around to find it full of women and children. Awake. Afraid. Babies crying. More gunfire from behind. Adem and Madoowbe looked at each other. Reading thoughts—No way. Not me.

A shout from behind them. "Murderers!"

Three men running, dressed like shepherds, already lifting their rifles. Adem and his partner ran. Flinching as the shepherds' guns behind them popped with automatic fire. Shaking too bad to even think of firing their own. They ran fast. The soldiers behind them gave up, and the two ran towards another pair of their own, further along.

Before they could meet up, the gunfire rattled again. Flashes of light ahead like strobe. Two Somalis flailing in slo-mo, falling. One of them Adem recognized—Abdi Erasto, just fifteen, always happy. Shot down without a fight. Beyond them, more of their soldiers running like Adem had done. Another standing casually behind a stone hut, edging up and firing blindly around the corner, even into his own people.

The wall next to Adem and Madoowbe pinged several times, pieces of rock flying, cutting Madoowbe's face. He screamed, held his hand to his eye. Too dark for Adem to tell if there was blood. More pings and cracks around them. He grabbed his partner, pulled him down to the ground. Half a foot away from a pile of donkey shit. The cows and asses in town were freaked, braying and howling. More gunfire overhead on the wall. Shards of rock flying, slicing across their backs.

Then it was dark again. The gunfire stopped. Adem's vision was filled with bright specks, changing colors, and darkness. He blinked. Kept on. Couldn't get rid of the flashing ghosts. Finally caught a glimpse of men in sandals coming their way. Ethiopians shepherds.

One said, "A couple of prisoners?"

Another. "No, no, we hang their bodies in the square and desecrate them. Make sure God will not accept them in heaven."

Adem pushed himself to his knees, grabbed the other boy's shoulder, pulled him upright. Still pressing the heel of his hand against his eye. Adem couldn't find his own gun in the dark. He reached for Madoowbe's gun.

His hands were slapped away. "You can't have it!"

"Hey, we're going to die!"

"That's mine! Let me kill them."

Madoowbe pulled his hand from his eye, a sliced up bloody mess, already beginning to swell shut. He lifted the rifle and let loose. The bullets sprayed everywhere, like a fireman's hose, no control whatsoever. Lighting up the whole wall, probably not hitting a thing.

Then the shepherds fired back. Knew exactly where to aim. Precise. Right at Madoowbe's chest and head, ten, fifteen, twenty. Adem jumped back, scuttled on the ground like a crab to get away. His partner's body animated like a marionette for a moment before collapsing under the barrage.

Maybe they hadn't seen him. He felt around carefully, quietly for his own rifle. Nowhere to be found. He didn't have a pistol on him, not even grenades. He'd been afraid they would blow him up without warning. At that moment, he wished he hadn't been such a baby. Quick shallow breaths. Afraid he'd need to gasp and give away his position.

The shepherds had made it to Madoowbe's body, one reaching over to lay the guy out flat, search his pockets, take his gun. Another lashed a rope around his head, tied it into a noose.

The third was keeping watch around them. Adem lay flat on his stomach, trying not to breathe. He was close to a thatched fence and hoped it was throwing enough shadow to keep him covered. If only he had a pistol.

The shepherd looked directly at him. Squinted. Eased his rifle up. "Another one."

Oh, no, please, God, no, I'm so sorry, Mom, Dad. So Sorry.

The other two dropped the dead Somali. Turned. Rifles ready. The lookout pointed at the fence. Adem's exact location. "There, you see? He's trying to be still. See?"

One of them set off a flurry of shots. Puffed the ground in front of Adem, the fence behind. Grazed the backs of his legs. Stung like a bee. He gritted his teeth and tried to keep from calling out.

But he failed.

"Jibriil! Help, God, help me!"

More gunfire. Adem covered his head and rolled out of the way, through the donkey dung, wondering how he was not yet dead.

He looked up. More strobe. The shepherds turned and fired at someone else. Six or seven Somalis on the attack, running right towards the shepherds, one of them falling.

Someone grabbed Adem's shirt and began yanking hard, yelling, "Get up! Get up! Move!"

Jibriil's voice. Adem rolled onto his feet and followed Jibriil and two others out of the village. Jibriil turned, running backwards, firing until his clip ran out. The others—Garaad and a tall, caramel-skinned man from another unit. More Somalis sprinted away towards the other trucks as the last of the three shepherds fell, new men coming out of the darkness to replace them. Gunfire lit up the road behind them, zipping by or thudding into the ground all around.

Garraad, supposedly the baddest of the crew, ran fastest. Far ahead of the others, not looking back. Adem guessed that was how he had survived so long in this war—hit em hard and get out quickly. Just ahead of Adem, the tall man kept looking back, asking if Adem was alright. Checking on Jibriil, who had finally run out of ammo and was catching up fast, pistol in hand. Too dark to see how many followed, but bursts of rifle-fire lit up the black.

No way they were going to make it. No way. Adem's legs were way past cramping, now burning. The fire moving up his thighs into his chest. Garaad out of sight. The tall man still keeping pace with Adem, rifle strapped to his back. Surely he could run faster than this. But he was determined to make sure Adem and Jibriil made it.

Shouted, "We either all make it or none of us do!"

Jibriil shouted back, "No! You go! I'm in command now! Get Adem out of here!"

Jibriil in command? Then the leader was dead. The leader's right-hand man, dead. Jibriil now the highest ranking, holding it together. Adem could see what he was about to do. As soon as Adem and the other soldier were far enough along, he was going to turn and make a stand with his pistol. Total suicide. It was the only move they had left.

Adem wanted to slow down, talk Jibriil out of it. But he couldn't. He was on automatic pilot. Pumping those exhausted legs. Jibriil already slowing, giving them space. This wasn't the way it was supposed to be! They were going to fight together, discover what made them Somali to the core. Not this. A shit border town, an ambush, and a humiliating retreat.

Adem looked over his shoulder. Jibriil, still slowing, flashed him a smile and wink. Then Jibriil stopped, turned, and started firing.

Adem looked ahead on the road. Saw taillights heading for him fast. Way too fast, going to slam into him. He stopped, leapt to the side of the road as the truck screeched to a hard stop. It was their truck. Garaad leaned out the driver's window.

"Get up, you ass! Get in!"

Adem pushed himself off the ground and stumbled for the back gate. The tall soldier was already there, helped Adem inside. He fell on his shoulder. Hurt like hell. He hurried around and grabbed the soldier's hand as the truck lurched backwards again at high speed and made another jarring stop right before it hit Jibriil. He turned, tossed the pistol into the truck and grabbed their waiting hands. Bullets zipping by, slapping into the metal of the truck. All three inside, they shouted at Garaad to floor it.

He did, jerking forward, gaining speed. The Ethiopians were gaining, bullets exploding the side mirrors, back glass, barely over their heads. Jibriil grabbed Adem and they sank to the truckbed. Crowded together but alive. Jibriil and Adem breathing hard, staring at each other, before Jibriil's face lit up and he started laughing. Laughing as if he'd gotten off a roller coaster at Valley Fair, an amusement park back in the Cities.

The tall Somali joined in. Then Adem, not to be left out, but he didn't see what there was to laugh about. They had escaped, yes, but he didn't feel relieved. Instead, what was it? Terror. The sense that every day would be worse than the last. He would dream of strobelight silhouettes, bodies of boys he knew being dragged into the town square to be desecrated at that very moment as Jibriil and Adem were laughing on the way home.

When the sound of the gunfire faded, they sat up. Looked out in time to see another of their trucks beginning to pull away, not even half full. The third, beginning to fill, a young man climbing into the driver's seat.

Then the sky shook. The dark turned into fiery day, Adem having to squint to understand what was going on. His eyes playing tricks on him. The third truck had exploded, its frame on fire.

"Rocket launcher!" Jibriil crawled to the cracked window, yelled at Garaad. "Rocket launcher!"

Garaad began swerving. The truck behind them did the same. Sped up. They were in an open field. They needed trees, hills, anything. Too dark to see. Another blast behind both of the trucks, a miss.

Adem backed up against the front of the truckbed, pressing his back against the steel. Instinctually pushing, as if he could get away from the rockets by pure will.

"You've got to drive, man!"

"What do you think I'm doing?"

"Faster!"

"I drive as fucking fast as I can fucking drive, alright? Why didn't you bring a launcher?"

Another blast. This one sent the truck behind them spinning into the air, on fire, flipping over and over, throwing out flaming, screaming soldiers. A wave of heat washed over Adem, still pushing. Nothing behind them now but clear darkness.

"Ohmygodohmygodohmygod." In English. "No no no."

Jibriil clamped a hand down on his shoulder, shut him up. Leaned down to his ear. "Don't let it hurt when it happens. Go with it. Praise Allah and leave this all behind, my friend."

Adem wrapped his hands around Jibriil's arm. "Why like this? It's not supposed to be this way."

"Brace yourself."

The sound of the rocket screaming their way. Adem thought he saw the brief flash of flame from where they launched it. Squeezing Jibriil tighter, tighter.

Another blinding flash, another skyshaker, even worse this time. But they were still rolling. Still alive. The ground directly behind them on fire.

As they crested a hill Garaad turned on the speed. The wind whipped their ears, but the shouts of joy were obvious from the looks on their faces. Jibriil embraced Adem, held on for dear life, pounded his back hard. Tears streamed down Adem's cheeks, soaked into Jibriil's shirt. Miles and miles like that, it felt.

When they were far enough away, relatively safe within the Somali border, Jibriil said again, "The captain is dead. I led his men back across the village. I didn't know…"

He struggled, couldn't say it.

The tall soldier shook his head. "Are you sure? At the end there, when you wanted to be left behind—"

"You're saying I'm a traitor, Khalid?"

Held up his hands. "I'm not, no, just saying we have to investigate. You acted admirably. A true leader."

"Forget that right now. I did everything I could to tear up that village and get our men out alive. I'm no mole."

Kahlid dropped his eyes. "Forgive me. You're right. It makes no sense."

Adem asked, "Investigate what? I don't get it."

"Someone gave us up. They knew we were coming."

Adem pulled his knees to his chin, gripped his arms around his shins. He didn't want to think about it. All he wanted was to go home.

TEN

If they hadn't been packing guns, Bleeker would've twisted the ears of all these "Black Ice Boys" and made them stay after school for detention. Instead, he had to keep his mouth shut as he and Mustafa followed Tyrus into a sixth floor apartment in the center of Cedar-Riverside. The front room bare except for a couch, worn-recliner, and giant flat screen TV on a cheap stand. On the wall over the couch, a bronze-colored crucifix. Scattered all over the floor, wires leading from the TV to a video game console, and more wires leading to controls in two of the Boys' hands. Lots of "Aw, yeah, fuck that!" and "All you, Dub, all you."

On the TV, a split screen showing two tricked-out street racers, almost like a movie. But the boys were controlling the cars, flying past other cars, crashing into corners of buildings and other racers. Seemed tense, the guys gripping the controls tight and turning them as if real steering wheels. They also pumped their feet like there were real pedals on the floor.

They ignored Bleeker and Mustafa for a long while, Tyrus not announcing them. He drifted away into the kitchen, then came back with a red can of sugary pop and joined the guys watching the race. Mustafa watched too. He crossed his arms and waited. Bleeker didn't give a shit about a kids' game. Last time he played a video game, it was because he'd cut class and spent ten bucks worth of quarters on Defender at the Pizza Hut.

The apartment smelled like pot and stale beer, sure, but also like cheap citrus air freshener. A mother's touch. Bleeker thought he'd heard a woman's voice from somewhere in the back. He wondered what she thought of her home being HQ for children with guns.

Bleeker stepped over to Mustafa and mumbled, "How 'bout I jerk the plug out of the outlet?"

"Easy. Do that and the whole night was a waste of time."

"Kids, man. Squeeze them, they pop like pimples."

Mustafa wrenched his head around. "Well, thanks, Mister. I'll be sure to remember that when I'm working out in the country. Might even use a pitchfork."

Whatever he was going to say got lost in the outburst from the gangbangers. Hopping a good few inches off the couch cushions, and the guys on the floor doubled over, the ones standing up high-fiving. On the screen, massive explosions, Game Over for the bottom half of the screen. One of the guys with a control looked pissed, saying "Fuck that shit!" three, four, five times.

He looked over at Mustafa and Bleeker. One of those stupid gangsta snarls. Bleeker could never figure it out. To walk like a gangsta, to talk like one, to dress like one, that took a lot of effort. No one just *did* it. The whole shooting match, all of it an act. Of course, wasn't the whole Minnesota Nice thing about as bad?

No, not this bad. His jaw tightened. The pain behind his right molars ramped up. Not this bad.

The loser turned out to be the leader, it looked like. He got up, handed off the control to another one of his guys. A new game started, noisy and heavy. Made Bleeker's ears twinge.

The leader held his fist in one palm, looked them over like he'd probably seen some baddie in a movie look over the hero. Dumbass didn't remember that the hero always came out on top.

"Bahdoon. They fucked you up."

"Your guy? Roble? He gave it a shot. I'm still standing, but he's in jail."

A glance at Bleeker. "Big man, needed this cracker cop to help."

"He evened the odds. Made it two against three."

Bleeker noticed that the other bangers were deeply involved in the game, no one paying any attention to the conversation. Not even one guy backing up their leader.

He said, "So why don't you go back to playing with your toys and let us talk to whoever runs this little club of yours."

Mustafa went *Shhhh*. The iron-willed Black Ice Boy tried to look even meaner. Bleeker even expected some of that *You dissin' me?* bullshit. Then this Mustafa character, man oh man, went and ruined the play.

"Forget him. You know what it's like going from the farm to the city. He hasn't learned his manners."

Wanted to pull his pistol right there, arrest the whole room. The whole apartment. Even the mother, allowing this to go on so she could have a nice TV. Not like she ever got a chance to watch it. No father around to bring out the belt and discipline his sorry excuse for a son.

The Black Ice Boy stared down Bleeker, who gave it right back. On the tip of his tongue was *Life's not like a movie.*

The kid finally said, "How about we leave him here while you and I go talk to Teeth?"

Bleeker said, "Teeth?"

Mustafa said, "Sharp Teeth. He used to sharpen his canines until he went too far, hit a nerve. They pulled it. So now he's just Teeth."

"Ty!" The lieutenant called back at the kid. "You want to teach the Detective here—" To Bleeker, "What's your name?"

"Ray. The name I was born with, not some shit I made up."

Got a smile. "Probably cause you were Momma's little ray of sunshine." Then back to Ty. "Sit him down, let him play a while. Keep him company while we see Teeth."

"Alright, yeah."

Then the lieutenant held out his hand to Bleeker, who thought he wanted to shake. Then, "I'll need your piece. You can stay, but I'm not leaving you here strapped, you feel me?"

"Fuck you."

Mustafa didn't say anything. Hands in his jacket pockets.

"Not going to happen."

"Then Bahdoon here ain't going to see Teeth, and there's a good chance neither one of you will, uh, have a good night, if you know what I'm saying."

Bleeker took a step towards the kid. He wanted to make threats? But Mustafa held out his hand.

"Give it to me, then. I'll be right back."

Jesus, his jaw. Throbbing. He opened wide, closed. Opened wide again. This was supposed to help, but instead he felt the familiar clicking that he knew made it worse. Shit. He'd come this far, so why not trust Mustafa a little farther? He pulled out the piece, dropped the magazine, racked the slide and sent the chambered round flying. Caught it. Put the magazine and extra round in his pocket before setting the gun in Mustafa's palm. Mustafa slipped it into his waistband at his back.

"Good enough?"

Another curled lip, chin nod at Bleeker. "Ray's cool. Let him sit with y'all on the couch."

Fine. Bleeker held up surrender palms and stepped over wires and slid past gangbangers who didn't give way. The Black Ice Boys had cleared a space for him, dead center of the couch where the cushions met. He sat, sank deep. A couple of the guys sat by him, really squeezing him in. One handed him a control.

"Ever played one of these?"

He shook his head, looked towards the door as Mustafa and the lieutenant walked through and closed it behind them.

One of his guardians explained the buttons, thumbstick, triggers, and Bleeker nodded for all of it, didn't understand a word. He hoped the kids on the floor around his legs, leaning against the couch, wouldn't bump into him and feel his back-up revolver.

The game began and everyone laughed at how bad Bleeker was. Crashing, getting stuck, getting blown away by competitors. Always a big black thumb or finger reaching over to help him out. Steady, patient. Except the kid with the other controller, who at first was boastful of how bad he was beating Bleeker until the tide in the room turned and everyone *wanted* Bleeker to do better. They cheered him on, his opponent getting pissed, slapping Bleeker on the leg, telling him to get his ass straight. The play got more aggressive. Bleeker getting slapped around, squished between the bruisers, assaulted by the goddamned noise. No idea how long it was taking. A minute? Ten? Thirty?

When the game was over, he tried to hand the control off to another challenger. But it was placed gently back into his hands. "No, man. You up again."

About then he saw the woman he'd suspected had been here all along. Through the kitchen door, where Bleeker could see a nice stainless-steel fridge, couldn't have been too old. The son must've been a giving sort. The mother peeked around the corner at the action in the room, arms crossed. A long cigarette held between two fingers. She didn't look Somali. A bit plump, short, wearing sweatpants and a green t-shirt, the name of a church screened onto it, and beneath, "Spring Revival Days, 2006". Flip-flops. Big cheeks and a dull expression.

Bleeker started off the couch, had to rock himself up. His guards were up, hands on his shoulders gently pressing him back towards the couch. The music on the game looped, starting all over again. Waiting for someone to press Start.

"Excuse me, ma'am. I was wondering if I could talk to you while I'm waiting? Maybe you've got some coffee?"

Hands on his shoulders tighter now.

The woman didn't look at him. Stared at the TV instead, the cacophony of whatever the hell sort of hip-hop this was blaring from the stock speakers making Bleeker clench tighter.

The woman shook her head slightly. "None of my business." She disappeared back into the kitchen.

He was thrown back onto the couch. A controller thrown at him, almost striking him in the face before he made a grab, juggled it a sec. All the boys were standing now. One of them, in a plain white t-shirt that reached nearly to the middle of his thighs, said, "This time, you're going solo. Every time you die, you're gonna get bitch slapped, understand?"

"You little shitstain, you want to try it?" Itching for a fight now. Outnumbered, but by the time he'd put the weak ones out of commission with some simple Ranger moves, he could focus on the big boys. Might be fun.

Another one of them pulled out a gun from his jeans—nice one, too. Glock, 10MM. Powerful mojo. He turned it around in his hand, lifted and dropped it like a hammer. "Going to hurt, man. Better keep your eye on the road."

Bleeker had to get his revolver. Had to do something to distract them so he could make a grab. Hoped shooting the one kid in the shoulder might scare the rest into hitting the ground.

"Start the game, Five-oh."

He did his best to ignore them. What could he do that would get them all looking the other way?

"I said, *start* the *game*." One of those big hands reaching down, covering his, pressing his thumb down way too hard on the start button. Thought he heard something crack, hoped it was the plastic controller.

The countdown started onscreen—3, 2, 1, *GO!*

He drove. Slowly. Couldn't crash if he drove slowly. Inching along, taking his time at the first turn in the road. The Black Ice Boys erupted—laughs, jeers, "Motherfucker", "Aw no no no no".

"Come on, man, play it right."

Eyes on the screen. "I am playing it right. You didn't say I had to win. Just stay alive."

"We changing the rules. Drive faster."

"You can't do that." Eyes on the screen. Steady forward. Staying alive. "Rules are rules."

"Our place, our rules."

Bleeker kept his mouth shut. Eyes on the screen. Steady forward.

One of the bruisers called for the gun. "Hey, come slap this bitch."

"That's not what you said! You said not to die!"

"Man, fuck this." One of the guys grabbed the other controller. Paused it. All turned to Bleeker.

The one with the Glock tightened his grip, took a step and swung his arm, picking up speed and power.

Bleeker grabbed his wrist and held it steady like grabbing a tennis ball out of the air. Squeezed. Yanked that kid towards him. Face to face. Kid's face twisted in pain.

"Hey hey hey, I was just playin'! Let me go. Shit, let me go!"

"Drop the gun."

Kid dropped the gun onto the couch. Bleeker reached across and grabbed it before anyone made a move. Not yet, but he sensed it. All of

them tensing their muscles. Ready to rush him.
He tightened his grip on the kid's wrist. "The gun loaded?"
A nod.
"One in the chamber?"
"Just, just, just, like three bullets, man. All I got left."
That's when the apartment door opened, and in walked Mustafa followed by a new guy who made all the tensed-up Black Ice Boys relax. Must have been Teeth. A bit tubby, fat-necked. Coffee brown skin, some big moles on his cheeks, one right above his top lip. Wearing a soft leather hat, seventies style. His eyes went wide when he saw Bleeker, gun in hand, holding onto one of his gangstas.
"Shiiiit, Bahdoon, the fuck is this?"
Mustafa, maybe a bit amused. "Ray, you tell me."
How was he going to play it? Would Mustafa back his move? And one of their mothers in the kitchen. Teeth's mom? Could the music on this goddamn game get any more annoying?
Bleeker dropped the magazine from the Glock, shoved both into the couch cushions, then let go of the kid's wrist. Gave him a shove back. He fell on his ass.
"All I was doing was playing the game, buddy. Their game, their rules."
He stood from the couch, walked past the bangers and stood behind Mustafa.
Teeth grinned, huffed. Bit of a laugh hidden in it. "You alright."
Bleeker looked away. The door. He wanted out that door.
Teeth and Mustafa shook hands, slapped backs. The gang leader said, "Truce until you figure this out, man. I hope your boy's okay."
"Me too."
"We'll deal with Roble. Don't you mind."
"For real, Teeth. Thanks. I mean it."
He turned to Bleeker, nodded at the door. No need to tell him twice. He walked out into the hall. The lieutenant from earlier was there, leaning against the doorjamb across the hall, talking to someone through the door, opened a crack and secured by a thin chain. Talking low. Soon as they saw Bleeker, the door closed. The banger gave him another sneer.
Mustafa was out a second behind him, closing Teeth's door, then giving Bleeker a push. "Walk fast. Don't look back."
Down to the far end, turned a corner. They skipped the elevator and headed towards the stairwell, Mustafa picking up pace, passing the detective while pulling out his cell phone. Texted with one hand. Shoved the phone back into his pocket.
Bleeker yelled at Mustafa's back. "What the hell was that all about?"
Still moving on. "Stupid, man. Goddamned stupid."
"They played rough. I did what you told me, but I wasn't going to get

pistol whipped."

"You pull some Chuck Norris Texas Ranger on them, and now I'm not sure we're going to get out of the building alive."

"I was an *Army* Ranger."

"I know that. I get it. What I'm saying is that Teeth's a stone cold liar. He wants to collect on me. But he can't do it on his own. He doesn't touch the guns, no way he'd kill somebody directly. One of his boys will. And he's not going to be able to leash them now because of you."

"I swear, I did what you said to do."

Mustafa reached back beneath his jacket as they walked, pulled out Bleeker's pistol and handed it back to him, clumsily, wobbling it. Bleeker took hold. Pulled the magazine out of his pocket and slammed it home. Forget the Plus One round. He'd get the job done.

Bleeker said, "Did he even give you anything?"

"We need to talk to Al Jones. Not his real name, but he's going around recruiting gang kids for the holy war. Looking for real bad apples. Not sure how he found Jibriil, but somehow, they hooked up."

"They're going to warn him that we're looking for him."

"Last thing they want is to mess with extremists. Maybe the cops shine a flashlight looking for roaches, but the Feds shine a floodlight looking for rats."

Some doors along the hallway opened a crack, peeking. Others were wide open, people hanging out, glaring. Loud music, loud TV, none of it making sense. Bleeker heard some mumbling, like "Bahdoon thinks he's something, look at him," and "Come back here, the nerve, man," "Want me to take him? Get the prize?" Everywhere, the smell of smoke, and grease from fried food, and the spices he'd only ever smelled in Somali homes and stores back home.

No one came out and made a try for Mustafa. No one taunted the man to his face, always after they'd passed, low tones. Made Bleeker wonder how evil of a bastard this guy had been before his conversion. Like Saul of Tarsus, persecuting the Christians, then getting knocked on his ass with Jesus Love.

At the stairwell they started down, two steps at a time, Mustafa finally grabbing his own pistol. Bleeker hadn't realized he was strapped. Two floors. Three. Then they heard the noise above them. Scuffling, hurrying. Bleeker leaned over, looked up. Nothing.

"Let's go. No need to look."

Bleeker caught up. On the second floor, the hallway door banged open. Both men brought their guns up, ready to fire. Scared the hell out of some kids. Young teenagers, a boy and two girls. The girls, lip-glossed and eye-linered, and the boy in a parka too big for him.

The girls screamed. The boy's eyes went wide. Hands up. "No! I swear! I don't know nothing! Mr. Bahdoon, please, I didn't do anything!"

Mustafa let out a breath, eased up on the gun. "Go back home. Do not go outside."

He nodded, pushed the girls into the hallway. The door closed again, air-cushioning into place.

First floor. Stairwell to the outside was open, door off the hinges. Mustafa stopped on the second step. Bleeker was three behind him. Couldn't see why. Outside the door, a patch of light on a small patch of concrete.

Like Mustafa was frozen. It didn't make sense.

"They're coming fast, man. Let's go."

Mustafa glanced back over his shoulder. He nodded. But Bleeker could tell he did not want to go through that door. About to have his John Dillinger moment. Or what was the rapper who got shot? Nefarious F.A.T.? Like that sort of thing. Guts and glory.

Mustafa crept to the door, careful to keep to one side. He shoved his gun down his waistband. Bleeker's breath caught. He took aim dead center of the darkness beyond the door. What was this?

Mustafa called out, "Who's out there?"

Nothing.

Louder. "Who's out there?"

Some rustling. Some footsteps. A shadow on the concrete. Bleeker closed one eye. Two handed the gun like he was on the range. Center mass. The shadow grew, darkened. Then a man in the door.

A white man, jeans and a pea coat, wool hat. "Yeah, Bahdoon. I'm here."

Bleeker dropped his gun. Stupid. Was about to raise it up again, thinking, *Right, I just assume the first white man I see wouldn't kill us?*

Mustafa exhaled. Shoulders dropped. "Shit."

The white man looked at Bleeker, said, "It's cool. I know this guy. I heard he might be back here when he knows he shouldn't be."

Mustafa said, "All clear out there, Knuth?"

"Jimmy's holding down the squad. No one's doing anything."

Mustafa stood with his chin down. Eyes closed. "Okay."

"We'll get you back to your car. We checked. Some of their guys were keeping an eye on it, but we chased them off. You're good."

Bleeker, hands on hips. "I'm feeling left out over here."

Knuth reached his hand for a shake. "John Knuth, Sergeant, MPD. Let's say Mustafa and I have an understanding."

Mustafa's hands weren't so steady. He looked at Bleeker. "I'll tell you in the car. We have to go."

They stepped through the door into the darkness. Bleeker followed. Felt like a million eyes were on him. He couldn't see any one of them, but the hair on the back of his neck, on his ears, his arms, all let him know they were there. Watching. Aiming. Choosing.

The cop named Jimmy was a giant, filled up most of the front seat. Knuth asked for the banger's keys before Mustafa and Bleeker climbed into the back. Mustafa handed them over without thinking. Maybe Jimmy was going to take Bleeker back to the hotel or to grab a bite. He was starving. Something soft because his jaw was on fire. A burrito, maybe.

Mustafa didn't say a word. The squad took some corners, finally made it to the curb where Mustafa had left his car. The partner jumped out. Mustafa waited for him to open the door. But that wasn't happening.

He leaned back, spoke through the cage. "Sorry, man. Orders. I'm driving your car back to the station. Someone wants to have a talk with you guys."

Mustafa leaned forward, a tiger rushing the cage bars. "You piece of shit! It's not even funny. Let me out, Knuth. Now. This is bullshit."

Knuth shook his head. "What were you thinking tonight? Jesus, man."

"Let us out!"

"Don't worry about it. It's nothing."

He slammed the door as Mustafa shouted his name. Kept shouting.

Jimmy said, "Don't make me spray you."

Mustafa sat back, fell against the door. Knuth got into the yellow car, cranked up.

Bleeker tapped on the cage. "Hey, Jimmy, how about some drive-through? I'll buy you a couple of tacos."

"I'll think about it. Thanks."

Bleeker watched the street as they drove away, the clumps of kids trying to be bad. Trying. Some succeeding, but most doing what kids do—trying to grow up too fast. He'd never tell Mustafa, but he felt like shit. Would've broken some bones over a video game. Who the hell did he think he was?

ELEVEN

Jibriil. An officer. A *leader*. Only a few weeks in country. But after losing their commander the night before and somehow making it back from a raid that should have left them dead, Jibriil was promoted.

Madness. Utter madness.

Adem didn't even know why they'd been to Ethiopia. There was a lot more to the war than he originally understood. They were supposed to be defending Islam against a corrupt government who squashed religious expression and lived like kings while hundreds of thousands starved. Instead, he hadn't seen much sign of government outside of his own army. The soldiers and leaders were brutal to anyone who colored outside of their very narrow lines. They took what they needed in spite of how that would disrupt the lives of everyday Somalis, who were fleeing the city, the country even, as if it was a giant sinkhole, falling away at their heels.

Why Ethiopia? Because Ethiopians had invaded Somalia, occupied it, and killed indiscriminately. And they were *Christian*. Now they'd been chased back, but still attacked whenever they felt like it. Same with the Somalis, tit for tat. Mutual hatred. Nothing better to do.

They'd made it back in the early morning hours, bodies aching from the fight, the bumpy ride, the fear. Boys gathered around while Garaad regaled them with the story, told all the young warriors how Jibriil had picked up the mantle when their leader fell in the ambush. Everything was going wrong. They'd been sold out!

"But," Garaad said, his timing perfect. Could've been an actor. "While we struggled to find God's will in this, Jibriil knew. He gathered us together, an unstoppable force, and led us across the town. Devils, hiding their true selves behind shepherd's clothing, firing at us. But onward we swept, picking up our brothers as we fought."

He left out the part about running ahead of everyone else.

But he wasn't going to bring it up because Jibriil wasn't. In fact, whenever the boys would look back at Jibriil, who was resting against the truck tire, to confirm some wild sounding part of Garaad's story, he would shrug it off, say, "We all did our parts. Especially you. You saved my life."

That sort of leader. Yeah. How the hell did that happen? In less than a week, Jibriil had grown from a boy with ADD to a respected man above men right in front of Adem's eyes. No one event or moment. The entire experience seemed to lift him. He was made for this.

Adem sure as hell wasn't. He had to get out of there.

Especially because when Garaad turned the story to the mysterious rat, the soldiers grew quiet, some flicking their eyes towards Adem. The outcast. He must be the one, then. Garaad didn't exactly say that Adem must be the rat, but he did warn the boys that a traitor was among them, watching their every move. "Who knows? Maybe he'll get you next as you pray."

Jibriil broke in, reassured the crowd that the rat most likely stayed behind, played dead, so he could give the enemy intelligence. "He would be crazy to come back here now. Absolutely crazy."

But that didn't stop them from glaring at Adem, whispering when he was near. Half a day of this as he tried to find a place to escape the baking sun, the sand, the smell of goat over the fire for lunch. It usually made him hungry, but today his stomach lurched. Mainly, he wanted to be alone. That was the hardest thing to find here—solitude. There was always someone...*judging* him all the time. Making sure he played by the rules. An entire army built on that. He'd heard that in the American military, despite the cause or the goal of whatever combat they engaged in, the soldiers fought on for each other. Bringing their brothers in arms back home alive was what drove them. Here, among these soldiers for God, the cause outweighed the individual. There was always someone to take the place of the fallen, who had gone on to whatever afterlife they deserved.

He found a scant patch of shade under a Qudhac tree not far from the mess tents. He had to huddle tight beneath the low branches, nearly made him invisible. He watched the women preparing lunch, tried to pick out the one with the brave eyes who had poured his camel's milk. But the flurry of colorful dresses made it impossible to tell who was who. After a while, as soldiers passed by without a glance, Adem began to think he was perfectly camouflaged. He wouldn't mind sitting out the rest of his stay like this. There's a question he hadn't bothered to ask Jibriil lately. Before they left the States, he'd told Adem that it would probably be a month or two. That people were coming and going all the time. But since then he'd heard stories of deserters being flogged, beheaded, and dragged through the streets. No one got out early unless God willed it to be so—by death.

"Adem?"

He looked up. Jibriil stood above him, face obscured by the limbs. He turned his head back towards the mess tents. "It's nice under here."

"Mind if I join you?"

Adem shrugged. No camouflage. He was unimportant, until it came time to pin the blame on their mysterious rat.

Jibriil put his rifle down, crawled under the branches and sat beside Adem against the trunk. Quiet for a few moments, listening to the calamity in the tents, clanging and arguing, sizzling and shouting.

"You okay?"

Sigh. "You know I'm not a rat."

"Don't worry about that. Not a problem."

"This isn't working out for me. I shouldn't have come."

Jibriil rocked into his friend's shoulder. "Man, come on. You're doing great, I'm telling you. The fear will fade. Would you ever have been in a firefight like last night back home?"

Adem looked down at his filthy shirt, still reeking of donkey dung. All he remembered about the night before was darkness, the corpse of Abdi Erasto, and a tent full of frightened but defiant women and children.

"Hey, you were under some serious fire last night and held it together. That's good soldiering. I need men like you who can keep their shit. Not like Garaad over there. Him coming back? I'll bet he was more worried about his head than about us."

Despite the heat, Adem shivered. "So close. Those grenades."

Jibriil eased up on his cheer. Hummed part of an old riff from a song Adem didn't recognize. "I promise, it's only going to get better. Today, they promote me. I'm in charge now. All you have to do is keep proving yourself worthy and I can help you climb out of this. Imagine, you and me commanding thousands of soldiers."

"I can't imagine that." Adem picked at the cuticle of his thumb. It started bleeding. "That's your dream. I wanted, I don't know, to understand what it's all about. Being Somali, right? Instead of just feeling Minnesotan. But I don't think this is the same thing."

"It's not. It's Islam. It's the Truth. That's more important."

"Than what?"

Shrug. "Than anything." Jibriil rose onto one knee, pushed himself against the tree trunk. "Come on, let's eat. We can talk about a plan for you."

"I'm not hungry. I like it here."

"Seriously." He reached down for Adem's arm, lifted. Adem kept it stiff. Jibriil was really trying, too. It started to hurt.

Adem said, "Please, leave me alone. For a little while. Please, man."

Jibriil let go, but he looked worried, glanced around. He said, "Okay, but not too long. I'll save you some."

He climbed out from under the branches, picked up his rifle. Shuffled, turning his head left and right. Twitchy. Then, without looking at Adem, said, "Stay where I can see you, though. Can you do me that favor? Don't go wandering off. I mean it."

Adem wished he was part of the tree. He'd seen a movie last year about a cursed pirate who became a part of the ship as he grew older, eventually unable to act on his own. A living slab of wood, watching but silent. That would be perfect. Because Jibriil had told him without telling him that the others were after him. Garaad must've been working overtime to convince the soldiers that Adem was the spy. And spies lost more than a hand or foot.

*

He found another shirt—dark green fatigues, not his, a bit big—and wrapped his head in a red and white-striped scarf to blend in with the many other soldiers whose faces he had never seen, names he had never known. Didn't matter how hot it was. He had to brave through it and start walking. Move and not look back. Hold his rifle like he'd shoot anyone he pleased until he found someone who could help.

He passed loitering groups of boys standing around, laughing, hanging off the sides of trucks, caressing their rifles the way Americans might their IPhones or exotic bottles of spring water. No one paid him any mind.

The scarf cut off some of his peripheral vision, and it made him feel like he was breathing in a steam room—heavy, humid air. It stank of him, the dung, the dead. He turned down another street, found three poles shoved into the ground, a bloated, picked-apart man's head on each one. He winced. These were not traitors. He'd heard about what happened from Abdi Erasto—a father and his two sons helped their young sisters, ages eleven and thirteen, escape because several soldiers demanded that the father hand over the girls for marriage.

The girls made it out, so he'd heard. Adem wished he could ask those men how they did it so he could, too.

He kept on. Abandoned streets. Occasional trios or quartets of soldiers. Occasional businessmen standing outside their shops, looking numb. Stunned to still be in business, maybe. A cell phone rang and he watched a businessman pull it from his pocket. Lots of phones in the city, Adem saw. Flew thousands of miles, and still people needed their cell phones. Except him. His had been taken as soon as he got to camp. He imagined the bill waiting for him back home.

More businesses, more people in the streets pretending to live normal lives amidst the end of their world. They had been doing it for years, skirting the harsh brand of Sharia law pushed by this crazy bunch of boys trying to run the country.

Adem was fine to leave them to it. Whatever was left of Somali culture sure as hell wasn't here. He looked back at the man on the phone, who was staring at Adem as he talked. They had a reason to be afraid. Didn't even matter if you were a strict Muslim who prayed five times a day and followed the diet and dress code. If the boys wanted you dead, you were going to die.

Adem turned back to the road ahead, kept on. He didn't have that much time. Jibriil would notice he was gone. Better him than one of the others. But even then, it wasn't good. Jibriil would never let him out of his sight again. The longer he walked, the more likely this wasn't going to work.

Where were the aid trucks? The only people stupid enough to keep driving in, getting hijacked almost every time unless the UN blue hats felt like fighting, which they didn't most of the time. He'd been told that some trucks carrying water had been jacked only a few days before he had arrived, and that it was time to send it back, empty, along with a couple of the aid workers. They'd been beaten, robbed, and threatened, of course. Sport for the soldiers. But now they had to go.

He took a few more blocks, then made his way down a narrow street, mostly rubble, some smoke here and there from fires, people trying to cook a goat, it smelled like. All of them gave him looks as if he were a strange creature, walking alone amongst them. Not backed by a gang. Just a man with a gun and a covered face.

He glanced down a side street and caught a glimpse. A white truck, maybe. He went back. It was two blocks over, definitely white but filthy. Mud and dust. He tracked down the street, one where the shadows kept everything cool, dark. He passed what he thought was a sleeping man. But then the smell hit him, the buzzing of flies. Didn't even want to take another look, but saw part of his leg. The man's skin looked like tight paper that had been ripped by a knife. Discolored, lighter than it should be. Not any of his business. He held his breath until the next block.

This was it. Had to be. The directions he'd been given were sketchy but got him here, barely. He stepped out onto the street. Two of them, flatbeds with large cabs, old but workable. Some flag draped across the front, nearly falling off. Letters in Arabic—something about peaceful and legal. Bored soldiers, most dressed more like him than the usual mix and match of street clothes and military fatigues, stood around, hands hanging off the weapons strapped around their necks. A Somali man in a black but faded Jay-Z concert t-shirt stood in front of one of the trucks. He was with a white woman, wearing a *hijab* but also short sleeves, capri pants. Another man with them, half-Chinese at first glance, had a bandage across the top of his head and another wrapped around his left forearm. He was lucky to still have both hands. He wondered if the woman had been beaten.

He stepped up to another soldier. "They're the ones? They're leaving?"

"Not fast enough. They're waiting for a friend. He's late."

"Why's he late?"

The soldier shook his head. "He's not coming, really. But they don't know that. He's dead."

Anywhere else, this would be a big problem. The soldier sounded like he was amused by it.

"Something he ate. He shat himself dead. But we're not telling them."

"They're going to wait?"

"If they don't leave soon, we'll start making noise. They'll get moving."

"I want to talk to them."

"No."

"For a moment. My captain wants me to question the girl."

The soldier pulled his scarf down so his whole face showed. Looked at Adem for a long moment. "She is shameful. She is of no use."

"But it's important."

"Then tell your captain to come speak with her himself."

Adem had had enough. No more time. He grabbed the solider's shirt and twisted, pulled him closer. "You think you're superior to my captain? Would you tell yours the same thing? You ass!"

Shoved him. The soldier held his ground. Eyes burning. Breathing hard through his nose. This was a guy who could crush Adem. Easily.

"Yes?"

The soldier finally nodded. "Go on."

Adem hid the relief. Waited until he was walking towards the trio of aid workers before letting out a deep, aching breath. As he approached, the woman of the group stepped out to meet him, speaking exaggerated, slow English with a German accent.

"Our friend, is he coming? Do you *know*..." She pointed to her temple. "About our...um..." She pointed at the other two. "Friend? Another man? Do you know?"

Adem thought she should be careful. Almost like she was asking if the soldiers were planning to shoot her companions in the head. He pretended to not understand her, took her by the arm and led her back to the other two. She tried to pull away, but not so hard. Like Adem, ready to go home. Let God forsake the whole country, which He seemed intent on doing anyway.

Huddled with the others, he pulled his scarf from his nose and mouth. Dripping sweat. He wiped it off with the back of his hand. "You all speak English, right?"

The Chinese man blinked, looked around. Adem thought, No, don't make it look any more suspicious than it already is. The aid worker said, "You're American?"

Not only that, but his accent was as American as all the TV shows Adem was missing. "Yes, yes, I am. You are?"

They shook hands. "Wayne. I'm from Oregon, man. What the hell are you doing here?"

"I made a mistake. I need a ride out of here. You're heading home, right?"

"Once they bring our friend back, we're gone. I had no idea it was this bad, man. This is hell."

"You're lucky they're letting you go at all. But we've got to hurry."

The German girl said, "But what about Jeff? We have to wait."

Adem shook his head, pulled his scarf back into place. "When I tell you this, don't look shocked. Don't cry. Don't faint. Please. Get in the truck and go."

The Somali man screwed up his face. "No, it can't be. No."

"What? Isaac, tell me." The woman, looking from face to face. "What is this?"

"He's not coming. Jeff's dead."

Her eyes went big. The Somali man put his hands on her arms, pulled her closer. "No, Greta, don't. Cry later. Now, let's go. Come on."

She swallowed hard. Isaac helped her into the cab of the first truck from the driver's side. He climbed in behind her. As Adem and Wayne walked back to the other truck, the first one's engine came to life. Rattled and grumbled as Adem turned in a slow circle, rifle ready, to check on the soldiers. They were watching closely, but not moving to stop the trucks. About ten of them, Adem counted. All of their faces were covered, obscured, turned—couldn't tell if he knew any of them.

Wayne opened the door of the truck. "How many Americans are over here? Are you, like, a CIA guy?"

"Hurry, get in. I'll tell you on the way." Adem kept his eyes on the soldiers. Once he climbed into the truck on the other side, what would they think? What would they do? His heart was thumping so hard in his chest that he worried it might spring a leak. A few blocks behind them, one of the troop transport pickup trucks turned onto their street, coming their way.

God, no.

"Get in! Get in!" Adem pushed Wayne into the driver's seat. Closed the door. The first aid truck lurched ahead, eased up to speed. Soldiers got out of the way, let it drive past. Score one point. Adem breathed a sigh of relief. But the other truck, soldiers dangling off the sides, packed like sardines, guns at the ready, was gaining fast. Spewing dust behind it. As it got closer, he heard a voice over the engine.

"Stop him! Stop him! Don't let him get away!"

The soldiers on the ground hopped into action. Rushing towards Adem. He ran around to the passenger door, yanked it open and climbed in.

"Hurry! Fuck, hurry!"

Wayne was cranking it, but the truck wouldn't turn over. That terrible noise, *Ru-ru-ru-ru-ru*. Almost, almost, almost.

Soldiers now at both doors, pointing guns, slapping the metal. The pickup truck had skidded to a stop. More soldiers jumped off and joined the mob.

"Now! Go!"

Wayne cranked harder, stomped the gas pedal. "I'm fucking doing it! Damnit! I'm doing it! It's flooded!"

More slapping. Gun barrels now clinking against the windows.

Ru-ru-ru-ru-ru…

The butt of a rifle slammed into the driver's window. Glass exploded, pebbles all over. Wayne scooted in Adem's direction. A hand scrabbled in, cleared off remaining glass, unlocked the door. More hands grabbed at Wayne's legs, began pulling him out.

"Shit! No, no, no, I'm going home! I didn't do anything!" Crying, too. Kicking at the hands. Kicking. He was sliding.

One shot. Pistol. Wayne screamed, reached for his foot. It was shredded, bleeding. More hands. Wayne slid from the truck, banged his head against the frame on the way down to the street.

Adem launched for the driver's side. Tried the key again. Nothing but clicking. Soldiers now grabbed for his arm. Adem brought the rifle around in his right hand, turned it. Squeezed the trigger.

Loud like lots of little bombs. Ringing ears. Spent jackets burned his face as they were ejected. Someone outside grabbed the barrel and gave it a hard tug. Adem let it go, too disoriented to stop them.

And he was next, thrown to the ground. He saw legs and dust and the shape of a man who might have been Wayne, middle of the street, surrounded by soldiers. Screams.

A boot at his face. Cracked Adem's nose. Another shot followed it. Then another. More boots, all over his body. Balls, back, knees, chest, fingers. One kick after another. Cries of "Rat!" and "Deserter!" and "Traitor!" and "American Bastard!"

Adem couldn't answer. His lip had been split, mouth full of blood he kept spitting. He shook badly. He wanted it to be over. He wanted to be sent home or allowed to die.

Two soldiers grabbed Adem under his armpits, pulled him to his knees. Everything was pain. Waves of it. He tried to think about Lake Superior, the waves rolling in. But they turned to storm waves, angry and dark. He felt one crash against him. Opened his eyes. Still in Somalia. A solider had thrown water on his face, now reached down and rubbed the dirt and blood away. It was the one Adem had grabbed by the shirt. Looked at his filthy hand and gave it a shake. Mud and water flung back onto Adem's face. The soldiers holding him dragged him to the circle of soldiers, let him through. Someone was going on and on, reading from the Quran. Loud and on edge.

Wayne was on his knees, being held in place. Several younger soldiers stood behind him. They faced a boy with a handheld video camera.

Adem was too weak to put up a fight. More waves of shocking pain. One eye swollen shut. A hand slapped his cheek. "Stay awake. Watch what happens because of you."

The boy reading from the Quran kept on. Another solider pulled a knife from his belt, wiped it on his pants. He took over from the one holding Wayne. Grabbed him by the hair and forced him to his stomach. Wayne fought and kicked. Shouting for help. A soldier stepped forward, grabbed his legs. The boy with the knife knelt on Wayne's shoulder blades.

Adem tried to turn away. He knew what was next. He was slapped again, then his face pushed until he had no choice but to look. Tried to close his good eye. His minder forced it open with two fingers.

By then, Wayne's shouting had stopped. They'd already started on him, sliced right through his throat. Geysers of blood when he hit the arteries. Wayne's face like a Halloween mask. The boy with the knife kept sawing. The knife tore through gristle, hit bone. More sawing as the boy sliced around the entire neck. He stepped back. Another solider grabbed Wayne's head two-handed, lifted it easy, like a melon. Blood dripped from the neck. Oozed from the body, the hard ground soaking it up.

They brought the head to Adem, who was gagging, trying not to throw up. They held Wayne's head in front of his face. "This is what you did. And Allah will have your head next. You're next."

Wayne's face. It was like Wayne was saying it. Eyes closed, lips tight, but Wayne's voice: "Look at what you did."

"No, God, no, I want to go home. I just want to go home."

A hard blow to the back of his skull. The two men holding him let him go. He flopped to the ground face first. Still heard the reading of the Quran, like background noise. Another voice on top of it: "This is what happens to traitors and deserters. Adem came telling us he was a brother, one of us. He spoke with the Devil's tongue. All lies. This is what happens to liars!"

He was on his way to oblivion and sweet dreams of home as someone grabbed his hair and lifted his face. Lake Superior. He'd gone there one or two summers, once with the high school chorus. He could stare at the Lake forever. Something magical about it. Too cold to swim in, full of stories of lost lives, lost ships. But maybe the most peaceful place Adem had ever been.

His own voice echoed in his head: You won't feel a thing. Not one thing.

TWELVE

"Short leash."

That was the phrase the police captain had used several times after hearing their story. Which was much better than what he'd started with, aimed squarely at Mustafa: "Prison. Finally get to throw your ass in prison."

Bleeker took most of the blame. He'd come too far to let Mustafa take the fall. Said he had bullied Mustafa into taking him along, a sad guy who'd lost his woman, his child, and his sense of right and wrong.

"Really, I shouldn't have. I should've come to you guys for assistance, instead, but, well..." and a shy shrug to finish it out.

Another half-hour of battering from the captain and one of the Gang Task Force officers who couldn't stand the sight of Mustafa. Burning a hole through him, crossing his arms. Pretty typical posturing. Maybe if they'd ease up on the hate and realize what a true convert they had in Mustafa, he might help them really make a dent in the gangs around here. At least, Bleeker thought the guy was a convert. Saved his ass once already when it would've been easier to let the wolves have him.

Bleeker held them off. He was used to talking his way back to shore. Told them they'd learned nothing from Teeth. Nothing. Bleeker mimed washing his hands.

He knew Mustafa was ready to tell them, too. It was Bleeker who stepped on his words, pushed ahead with, "Guy was playing big shot with us. I think he liked having Bahdoon come calling on him. Showed how important he was."

So it came down to "You tried, you didn't get what you needed, so that's it." The captain slouched deep in his office chair, elbow on the armrest, palm holding up his chin. Made it hard to understand him. "I'm really sorry, Detective. Terrible what happened, my God, really terrible. Wish I could bend the rules for you, but, well, rules are rules to keep us safe, you know."

"It's hard, a guy like me, sitting on the sidelines."

"Oh yeah, absolutely. Geez, I hear you. We'll keep you updated, of course. I'm hoping Mr. Bahdoon is wrong about the boys ending up in Somalia. I thought that had stopped some time ago, but we'll look into it. Anything we can do, we will."

Bleeker stood and reached across the desk. The captain took his time creaking out of the chair, like he had bad knees already and hadn't hit fifty. Shook the man's hand. He gave Mustafa, still seated, a *We're not done* look. It wasn't going to be pretty.

But then Bleeker clamped a hand on Mustafa's shoulder. Said, "I think I owe my friend here breakfast before I head home. Even though we came up blank, he did a good job of getting us in and out safely, no drama."

The captain, all smiles. The gang cop rolled his eyes and left the room without another word.

"Sure, sure. Really redeemed himself, I tell you."

Like Mustafa wasn't even in the room.

Outside, Mustafa pulled his cap over his ears. Told Bleeker, "I'm not hungry."

Bleeker could read his face. Enough of hanging with this cracker cop. Gonna fuck it up for me.

"Neither am I. But I will be after five cups of coffee. Come on."

Couple of minutes, Mustafa looking left, right, tapping his foot. Then, "Fine. I know a place."

*

They ended up right back in Seward, closer to the University, at Pizza Luce. Beer for Bleeker, water for Mustafa, a baked potato pizza instead of breakfast. Going to close the place, it looked like. Al Jones would have to wait another day. But it wasn't so bad. Bleeker had downshifted out of his take-charge attitude, at least after the first beer, which he drained in under a minute. Ordered another.

As Mustafa sipped, Bleeker said, "Not a drinker, then. Religious?"

He nodded. "I'm trying. It's hard sometimes here, so much to distract you."

"That's got to be better than being over there."

"Most of the Somalis in Minneapolis now, yes, they still follow Islam. It's part of who they are. But so many things they would never dream of doing in the homeland, here it is nothing. Women have so many more options. So much more worldly shit." A smile. "Guess my language could use some work, but like I said, it's hard. You heard about Somali cabbies here? They won't pick you up if you're carrying alcohol."

"You kidding?"

"It was a big deal. They flat out refused."

"Because of their religion?"

Mustafa grinned. "What I think? It's to fuck with white people."

They both laughed. The pizza arrived. They each grabbed three slices. The booze had Bleeker starving, but it had eased his jaw pain. Chewing through these slices, though, it would be right back, worse than ever.

Mustafa downed half a slice in a bite, then asked, "Please, don't take this the wrong way—"

"Well now there's no other way I can take it."

"—No, wait, I'm just asking, how did you become the expert on Somalis in New Pheasant Run? Seems to me you don't know as much as I would expect."

"Or hope?"

Shrug. "Was it something you wanted? Or did it somehow...*happen*?"

Bleeker kicked out one of the empty chairs at their table, propped his boot on the edge of it. "I was in Iraq for the first war. Army Rangers."

"That's a long way from Somalia."

"But not from Muslims. Lots of day-to-day dealing with them, learning the body language, how they argued, how they expressed themselves, you know? What the rules were. I had to break a hell of a lot of them to learn, though." A long swig of beer, like he had to consider what he said next. "It's not like I accept it or believe any of their bullshit. Sorry, your bullshit, I guess."

"Forget it."

"We were killers, not regular infantry. Biggest disappointment was sitting around waiting to do stuff, doing patrols where some guy stole another guy's goat."

"A goat?" Mustafa pushed air through his teeth. "That's pretty serious, a goat."

"Now you're messing with me."

"Really, a goat is currency. It's milk and cheese and all that. Yeah, it's like stealing a car."

"Maybe not a car, but I get it now." Bleeker took a couple of bites. "How about you? Were you there? In the middle of the Somali war?"

"Not this one."

"But you were there for something?"

Mustafa shook his head. "We left before I was five. Moved all over. I was in Kenya for seven, eight years. Then we moved to Minneapolis. That's the way it was with a lot of us. Move before the boys turn five."

"What's that about?"

"Because when you're five, you're old enough to hold a gun, and they come for you. They want you young."

Nothing else to say. Around them, a handful of quiet hipster conversations as the college kids waited out the wait staff, having not decided exactly who to take back to their dorm rooms yet. A good life, if they could get back without getting mugged.

Mustafa pointed at the students. "I wish Adem was at one of those tables, even if it meant being dreadlocked or wearing nerd glasses. I would have given him a hard time about it, but I would've been proud too. So much better than going back to the homeland."

Bleeker nodded, said, "So I get back from Iraq, I rotate through a couple of jobs. Sugar beet plant. Farm co-op. But I liked watching shows like *NYPD Blue*, *Law & Order*. I liked that, what those guys were doing. It was romantic. So I took a chance, rose through the ranks. See, at least having a little Muslim experience helped at first, and then I stumbled through Somali customs the same as I did the Iraqis. I'm not the smartest at it, I know. But I'm willing. It's easier for me than the other detectives. That's all."

"Fate, then."

"More like an accident. I wish I had a better story for you, I do. But that's all there is." He felt the eyes of the wait staff, the cooks, some already pouring themselves beers, waiting patiently to head off to whatever late-night bars would have them after 3AM. "I'm sure you've got a better one. Bad ass gangsta turned honorable citizen."

"This again?"

Bleeker looked at the empty beer glass in his hand. Odds were it wasn't getting a refill. "You don't seem like an asshole or anything. But you're one of these hip-hop guys. Carrying a Glock. Putting caps in asses. Three dead by your hand, that's the rumor."

Mustafa pointed to Bleeker's propped foot. "Cowboy boots in the snow? You one of those cowboys? Pick-up truck and big hat? Redneck?"

"What happened to you?"

"I guess I grew up. Here I was, married with a little boy, playing gangstas. Drugs, and I didn't even do that shit. Then, like, why should I give a shit if some guy from another gang comes on my turf? Just wants to go buy some shoes, eat some pizza. Why should I care, go off and shoot his ass? Watched how easy it would be for Adem and that idiot Jibriil to get sucked in like I had. I don't want him to become like I was. And then...they started dealing with women. Trafficking, for sex. Good Somali women, girls. I mean..." Shook his head. Closed his eyes.

"Could have turned yourself in. Done your time."

Mustafa grinned, a sad one. "Having his father in jail would've been as glamorous to the boy as if I was still banging. In jail, I would've ruled, man. Instead, I got a job. Being working class, that's worse than death."

Bleeker grinned too. Waved his hand towards the server, who rolled her eyes on the way over. Bleeker asked for the check, then called her back, told her to split it. Owed Mustafa breakfast, sure, right.

Waiting to get their cards back, Bleeker asked, "So tomorrow night? Al Jones?"

Mustafa sighed. "You heard the captain. I can't afford to."

"Then I'll go find him on my own. I'm still a pretty good detective even if I'm not on my home field."

"Listen, Jones will already have been tipped off. We're not getting to him by knocking on the door. It's going to take some negotiation."

"And I can't do that."

"You have to know people, and how to smooth things over. It's about respect."

They got their receipts, signed their names, and pocketed their cards. On the way out, Bleeker zipped up his jacket, got in front of Mustafa and stopped him.

"I'm not going home to sit and think about my dead girlfriend. I won't do it. Especially in the same house as the wife I cheated on. Call me heartless or a coward or whatever. I want someone to tell me why this kid shot her. Someone who really knows."

Mustafa kept his eyes on the ground. "It won't make you feel any better."

"Don't care."

Students from another table brushed past them in the doorway, out into the snow, paired up, ready to ride out the rest of the night, sleep until noon, drink coffee together and then pretend it never happened.

Mustafa said, "Yeah, Adem should've been here, arm around the pretty thin brown-haired girl with the green-framed glasses and hoop earrings. Talking about movies, you know. Music." He cleared his throat, sniffed. "I think I know how to get to Al Jones."

Bleeker opened the door, held it for Mustafa. "Tomorrow night, then?"

"Your car this time."

Outside, Bleeker called a cab. He shook hands with Mustafa, who headed for his car, parked a block away. Bleeker wondered what it was like—like someone had a bead on you every step, every day. He flinched a little, waiting for the shot, waiting for Mustafa to fall dead in the street. It never came. Maybe it would happen somewhere down the line. But that night, he got in his yellow car and drove away.

THIRTEEN

The heat didn't make sense. The lake he stood on was frozen. He looked down at mittens, a thick parka. Ears were covered. Breath billowing out in thick clouds. But he was hot. Sweating. Looked around for a source. Not a soul. Not a heater. Not a fire. Above, the sun was barely there, obscured by fast-moving clouds.

Adem couldn't take it. He clawed at the zipper on his parka, not dealing well with his mittens. Since when did he wear mittens? Maybe as a kid, but it had been a long time. The fingers inside felt like one big flipper. He struggled with the zipper, felt as if some invisible hand was fighting back. Over there, almost to the horizon, was something man-shaped. His father, had to be. Big man. He ran across the ice, farther and farther until he couldn't see shore. Kept yanking at the zipper until it caught near the bottom, open enough so that he could free his arms, push it down his legs and step out. A sweater underneath. He pulled that off too. Then his undershirt. Bare-skinned in the cold. But it wasn't cold at all. Tried to get his mittens off but they wouldn't come loose. Again, the invisible hand fought him. His dad was still as far away as before.

He sat down on the ice. Laid down. His chest and face against the slick, cloudy surface. Should be painful. Glorious shivering pain. But there was nothing. Only the dull throb of his head, growing worse every moment. The sweat. The heat. He wanted to scream. Instead he closed his eyes.

And opened them again in bed, staring at a mosquito net, a curtain beyond that, open enough to show him a long room full of curtained off beds. He thought he caught sight of a bare concrete wall past the foot of his bed.

And it was hot. No ice.

Sitting at his bedside was a woman, watching him as if she was expecting him to wake up. A familiar face. The eyes. The lips, almost like Mona Lisa's smile. The girl who poured his camel's milk.

"You're back with us?"

In English. Flawless, with a British accent. Was he still in Africa?

The throbbing was coming from all over. Aches like he was still being punched. Raised his left hand to his head. Three fingers were wrapped together in tape. The other hand, his pinkie and fourth finger bound together. Felt his head. Bandages around his temple, across his nose. A broken nose. Damn. He creaked his neck until he could see the rest of himself. Lifted the sheet. Bandages everywhere, bruises spilling out from the edges.

"Can you hear me, Adem?"

He nodded at her. Tried to talk, but his mouth was dry. "Um…water?"

She held up a glass with a straw. He sipped, and his body took over, craving more and more. He hit bottom and kept on sucking, the woman having to pry the straw from his teeth.

"I'll go and tell them you're awake." She turned, swept through the net and curtain.

"Wait." He brushed her arm before she could get away. She stopped, turned back. "I don't know your name. How can I thank you?"

A moment. She looked over her shoulder, then side to side, then whispered to him. "Sufia."

Adem closed his eyes. "Okay. Thank you, Sufia. Can I ask you something else?"

"Hurry. I'm supposed to tell your superior as soon as you wake."

"Promise me you'll come back. Come back and talk to me."

Her eyes told him she wanted to, he was pretty sure. But her mouth, the lines around them, showed something else. "If I'm asked to help you again, I will."

She dropped the curtain, pulled it together so he couldn't see out anymore. He sensed men in the beds around him. From somewhere far off, he heard babies crying. Then Sufia's voice, in Somali again, calling for Jibriil.

It should have eased his worry, knowing his friend had been waiting for him. The last thing he remembered, his head being held up to look into the video camera as a punk kid, face hidden under a red scarf, held a knife to his neck. He reached his free finger from his right hand to his neck. Another bandage, right where the knife had been held. Only a second or two from losing his head. What had happened?

Bootsteps. Two men. Then Jibriil swept through the curtain followed by the old man who had handed him the machete for taking the convicted soldier's hand. A holy man, someone who had great influence among the ragtag boy army. Same gray suit. Same white hat.

The tent filled with Jibriil's odor and the dust from his boots. He was smiling. "Back like new, yeah? Like your old self?" Spoken in Somali, Adem supposed as respect to the cleric.

"I thought I was going to die. I thought I was dead."

"Almost. But I stopped them."

He wasn't even there. How did he stop the mob?

Jibriil gestured to the old man, who stood peacefully, hands clasped together.

"We did it. I heard what was going on, and I was with the Sheikh at the time, and pled your case. He made the call to stop your execution."

Seconds from having his head sawed off. A humiliating, unearned death, much like Wayne's. Wayne's dead face.

Adem blinked, lifted his eyes to the old man. "Thank you, Sheikh. I humble myself before you."

The Sheikh nodded. "You are special, your friend tells me. I trust his word. But you were also trying to escape, correct?"

To admit it would mean a death sentence. He'd escaped one, so why would they expect...but he noticed Jibriil's expression, urging him to say yes. To apologize.

Adem said, "I don't belong here. I only get in the way of God's will. I have failed, and I should be sent home."

"A brave young man. You lived through a firefight. You took this beating. You attempted to escape when the odds were against you. No, I don't consider you a failure at all."

Adem couldn't help himself. He started crying. Mercy. He chopped off a man's hand for less than what he had tried, and this man was showing him mercy. He cried and said *Thank you* over and over even though it made him feel sick.

The holy man moved closer, took Adem's hand, said blessings for him until his tears dried. The Sheikh embraced Jibriil and then left through the curtains. Adem heard more footsteps follow as he walked away. Bodyguards. In case Adem tried some sort of craziness, he realized. Under Jibriil's command. Becoming more and more clear.

Jibriil settled beside his friend, pulled one boot up onto his knee. Big grin. Adem wondered how many bodyguards remained outside waiting for their commander.

"Why, Adem? You could've come to me. Could've said something." In English.

"I did. I tried. But what can you do? What is so hard about sending me home?"

Jibriil shook his head. "I can't."

"Why not?"

Jibriil crossed his arms, yawned. "It's...complicated. You tried to escape. If I were to send you back to the States now, they would see me as weak. They would see you as worse. Everything bad about the West. And they can't let you go."

Adem pushed himself up onto his elbows. Every nerve shocked him with pain. He said through strained teeth, "*They tried to cut my head off!*"

Jibriil was on his feet. Slapped Adem hard across his cheek. "And you tried to leave like a coward! You tried to kill our brothers! Because, what, you miss the snow? The food? Cow's milk?"

Adem didn't have an answer. Plenty he wanted to shout—I almost died in Ethiopia. The soldiers think I'm a traitor. A pussy. A target. I hate the heat and the dust and the smells and…what they've done to Islam.

Let it slip out. "This war. It's not about God."

Jibriil leaned closer to his face. "It will be when we win."

His friend's odor, days now without a shower. Intense. Jibriil believed what he'd just said. Without question.

Jibriil sat down again as Adem turned on his side away from him.

Jibriil spoke again as if nothing had happened. "They caught the traitor, though. They don't think it's you anymore."

"Who was it?"

"I can't hear you when you mumble like—"

"Who was it?"

"Okay. Okay. I guess he had an Ethiopian wife. You don't know him. He was in another truck that night. So, like I had said, he stayed behind. But I guess he didn't give them enough intelligence. He showed up again this morning, telling us how he escaped and hid and walked all these miles."

"You didn't believe him?"

"He looked in perfect health. Not a scratch on him, well fed, in good spirits. I sent out patrols. We found his motorbike hidden in a burned-out home on the edge of town."

Adem curled tighter. "How'd you know it was his?"

"I told him we'd found his bike. Told him there was a note from his wife in the storage compartment behind the seat. He broke down. Pleaded with me. I told him we could track down his wife now, sneak in tonight and grab her, let her suffer for both their crimes."

"He didn't know about the note? She'd snuck it onto the bike?"

"There was no note. I made a guess."

Adem went quiet. How had Jibriil become so smart so quickly? A week ago, he'd shot two cops for no reason. Now he was Sherlock Holmes, flushing out spies. Commanding an army. Right-hand man of the Sheikh.

"No one blames you anymore. You took your beating well. It was the bravest they'd ever seen you."

"Sure, thank them for me. I don't think I'll ever walk normally again."

A laugh. That was funny?

"Seriously, Jibriil. I'm a wreck. I can't fight anymore."

"You'll heal up. In the meantime, maybe you can train the new recruits.

'How to Survive'. Something like that."

"Stop already. It's not a joke." He pointed to the bandage on his neck. "They'd already started to cut. Would you have laughed if I'd died?"

Jibriil let out a sigh. Adem turned his head towards him. He was staring away, at the mosquito net, at nothing. More of the baby's cry. Another man's breathing ramping up nearby. He began moaning, then screaming for help. The pain. The fires of hell. Help. Unbearable. Crows screeching.

Jibriil peeked through the slit in the curtains. "He was burned in an explosion fighting government troops. Yesterday."

"Where am I?"

"This is where we heal our wounded."

"A hospital?"

Jibriil shrugged. "Our guys already bombed the hospitals. Weakens the resistance of the city. We'll control this place soon, you know. The whole city. All of southern Somalia. Our own government. Our own land. No more fighting."

"I don't see it happening."

"Whatever. I do. All of the blood will be worth it when everyone sees what we can do on our own."

Adem laughed, but coughed, swallowed hard. He shook his head. Rattled out, "Not a chance. You don't get it."

Jibriil stood, reached down to grip his friend's leg below the knee. A shock of pain nearly took Adem's breath away, but he held his tongue. "Get some rest. I'll be back as soon as I can and we'll talk about what to do with you."

"What *are* you going to do with me?"

"Sleep. Relax. We'll talk later."

He swept out, humming to himself. Barked a few commands at his guards. They answered, a clipped simultaneous reply. Bootsteps leaving quickly. Adem was alone again. But not really. He saw the shadow of the guard Jibriil had ordered to stay behind. Keep an eye on him. No more escapes.

*

He'd lost count of time. Lost count of sleeping versus waking, except that his dreams made more sense than when he was awake hearing labored breathing, screams, gunfire, muffled explosions, babies. A long dream, continual between fits of thrashing and pain. Adem was at an airport. An American airport, all the signs in English but he couldn't read them. He could never read anything in dreams no matter how hard he tried. The letters shifted before his eyes. He knew he was supposed to catch a flight to Paris. No idea why. But it seemed he kept missing flights, or he'd get lost, or he'd get to the plane and fly to a connecting airport but not remember the flight. One airport after another, always lost, always running late.

He woke after flying somewhere…Chicago maybe? Detroit? Next to a girl from school he liked. One of the RA's. They would never be more than friends, though. She'd made it clear, no matter how many times they'd kissed or she'd draped herself on him or spent time in her room listening to music.

Tried to close his eyes again to recapture the flight. Let me talk to her again. Let's take a trip together.

But he couldn't. Eyes wide. It was darker, setting sun making everything orange and shadowed. Someone beside him again. He didn't wait for his eyes to adjust. Reached his hand for whoever it was.

Soft fingers took his, moved his hand back across his body, laid it on his chest.

"Sufia?"

She blinked. Became clearer. She lifted a glass of water, held the straw to his mouth again.

When he'd had enough, she said, "You're lucky. The others here, if they don't improve, they'll be taken away soon. But you, lucky warrior, are protected."

"You've met my friend? Jibriil?"

"Your *commander*. Yes. I have. He asked me to take care of you."

That dog. Adem smiled.

"Sorry, but your English is perfect. How did you…where?"

"I studied in London. Lived there for several years before coming home."

"Really? And you came back?"

A look on her face like Adem was stupid. "Home is home."

Adem thought *Yes it is*. "Right now, where I'm from, there's two feet of snow on the ground."

"Sounds terrible." She lifted a cloth from a bowl of water. Wrung it out, then folded it. She wiped Adem's forehead and cheeks, careful around his bandages.

"No, not terrible at all. In fact, it's beautiful."

Like you.

No, not yet. That wasn't the way things were done around here.

She shook her head. "When I was in London, I used to dream of home. The trees, the colors, the food. It's pretty bad here right now, I know, but there are still all of those. And we owe Allah the praise for it."

A believer. Like Jibriil. All about God's will. Doing their part.

He changed the subject. "When we were in school, Jibriil and I were singers. He's a great singer."

She scrunched her eyebrows. "Singing?"

"Like show tunes."

Sufia laughed. Good, he could make her laugh.

"Really? Show tunes? Like West End?"

"Broadway."

"Those are forbidden."

Adem smiled. Cracked lips split wider, but it was worth it. "Yeah, maybe that's not a bad idea."

She laughed again. It was darker outside. She said she had to leave soon, but would be back tomorrow. That was okay, Adem told her.

When she was gone, he thought about her. He was feeling better. Even the pain felt sweet.

FOURTEEN

People back in New Pheasant Run were looking for Bleeker. Calling him day and night. He only returned one or two calls, told them he was ice fishing and to leave him the hell alone.

He worked out in the hotel gym. He was alone because it was after four in the morning and he couldn't sleep. More and more of those nights. It hurt but pain wasn't something you tried to get rid of. It was something you used to get you back to good. He needed pain, goddamn it, or he wouldn't know which direction to go. Cindy had been brutally cut down. To end that pain, Bleeker needed to see her killer's body on a slab.

He got tired of the weight machine, just bricks on wires. Not the same rush of free weights. He moved to the stairclimber. Would've been happy to take a run outside, but the wind was blowing like hell and the snow was coming down again. Didn't bother him out in New Pheasant, but here he was a fish out of water. Too much slick ice, too many cars. So he pushed himself up the fake stairs on the hardest setting, pumping, pumping. Gritting his teeth. Bring on the searing jaw pain. He'd push through that shit, too.

Mustafa. On his mind. Not what he expected. The gangsta mannerisms of that first meeting had slacked off. That shit was even infecting the Somali kids out west. Whatever video they'd seen, whatever music had been spewing from the speakers. A collage of it all, pasted all over these kids' fashions, language, attitudes. And the baddest of them all, supposedly, had turned a new leaf.

It wasn't the most comfortable feeling, pairing up with this guy, but the one thing he trusted was that Mustafa wanted his boy back safe and sound. And that he hated the cop-killing fuck Jibriil. God, a bit naïve, thinking Adem was clean like spring water, but Bleeker would go along for now, see where it led.

After punishing himself on the stairs, legs like overcooked pasta, he walked across to the hotel pool, dove into the cool water, blew out as much breath as he could and did a few laps underwater until he was burning all over, the water around him going to boil if he kept it up. Then exploded up from the middle of the pool and sucked in as much of the room's air as his lungs could take. Stood shoulder deep, slicked his hair back. Finally noticed a housekeeper, middle-aged woman, Hispanic, watching him. Holding towels, hypnotized. They eyed each other a long time. She looked like she had worked so hard all her life that each hour had etched itself onto her skin, but she carried it with pride and a lot of eye make-up. She looked nice.

Bleeker swam to the ladder at the deep end, climbed out, and motioned to her to throw him a towel. "Please?"

He imagined her dropping the entire stack, stripping to her bra and panties, and diving in with him. Chasing each other, finally tiring, and floating together, wrapped arm in arm, kissing her lips, neck, shoulders.

But she looked weird instead. She didn't give him a towel. He stepped over, took one off the top, and said, "Thanks, yeah."

She nodded. Walked away. Placed the stack of towels on the rack near the door, and pushed through into the hallway. He kept watching as she went down the hall past the long windows lining the wall. Once she was out of sight, Bleeker felt cold. Stupid fantasy. Weeks since he'd been with Cindy, at his house while Trish was at work. Now she was dead. Hard to connect that.

He looked at the hot tub. Good long soak might finally relax him, let him sleep so he could be ready for the night's work. See if Al Jones could confirm that Adem and Jibriil had been sent to Somalia. Yeah, turn on the whirlpool and close his eyes. Maybe go back to the room, keep on thinking about the housekeeper, about taking her on the bed, stretching her toned worker's legs and hard scrabble feet for him. Jack off, fall asleep. Doze until dinnertime.

Instead, he dropped the towel and dove into the cool water, colder still now, for more breathless laps.

*

Mustafa knocked on his door after ten. By then the snow had piled at least six inches. Bleeker had slept maybe thirty minutes since parting ways with the city cop outside the pizza place. He chose not to pursue the housekeeper in his mind, keeping himself wound tight. Fell asleep mid-afternoon watching a butchered 80's flick on AMC. All the cursing dubbed over. All the violence de-fanged. A joke. How the fuck did all those changes make it any more classic?

Now up, two pots of hotel room coffee in him, another two large Burger King pops. Pissing all evening waiting, but awake, ready, and willing.

"You think anyone's tailing you?"

Mustafa shrugged. "If they are, we'll lose them later."

Bleeker didn't invite him into the room. Mustafa acted as if he didn't want to come in anyway, leaning against the opposite wall of the hallway. Bleeker slipped on his jacket, hunter's cap, and closed the door behind him. "Let's go."

Outside, the temperature drop was like stepping onto another planet. They climbed into Bleeker's Roadmaster, cranked up and waited for the engine to heat up. Five minutes. Ten. Warm air began to flow through the vents. Bleeker pulled out of the spot and slowly made his way through the lot, down the service road, and down the on-ramp to the interstate.

Mustafa said, "Eden Prairie."

Bleeker laughed. "You're kidding. Come on."

"Serious. Took a lot of work, so let's go."

"Are we expected?"

Mustafa rubbed his gloves together. "I hope not."

Eden Prairie was a suburb down in the Southwest metro, closer to Bloomington and the Mall of America than to the city proper. Bleeker drove through it every time he came and went, usually stopping at their mall to shop and their fast food joints to eat because it was less crowded, easier to navigate.

The drive was slow, the plows not out yet. Slippery roads. Not a lot of traffic on the way out. Mustafa brought along a Tom Tom he'd borrowed, the computer pointing the way, except it wasn't updated and got confused the closer they got.

Mustafa said, "A couple of sources, plus a couple more guys from my old posse confirmed this. They'd left the gang about the same time I did, got married, grew up. Both still Islam, but not the extreme kind."

"No offense, but it seems they're all extreme to me."

"Thanks, real helpful."

The machine told them to go straight and stay right.

Bleeker said, "Sorry, but, okay…keep going."

"So there's an Imam, like a pastor—"

"I know, remember? I'm the Somali guy. I know the lingo."

Mustafa sighed. Bleeker cringed inside. Couldn't help himself. It wasn't that he was trying to disrespect Mustafa, but it seemed so goddamned easy to do. He was touchy. Guy gets away with killing some punks, and now he's noble or some shit. Still, Bleeker knew better than to burn a bridge while standing on it.

"I didn't mean…" Trailed off. Bleeker shrugged.

Mustafa started again, quietly. "This Imam, the kids call him Rockstar Muhammad. He revels in it. Anything to increase the flock. He's smart. He uses the language of the streets when necessary. Knows hip-hop lyrics.

Hates them but knows them. So he ends up looking like he understands these young men when all he really wants is for them to be exactly what he wants them to be—Warriors for Allah. He wants them to either go and fight in Somalia, or head to Europe and Africa and all across the states and proselytize, keep building, until they can attack."

"Like Nine Eleven?"

"Not as flashy, but pretty much. Bombs, fires, mayhem, times a hundred. Also, sneaking themselves onto city councils, state legislatures, all the things Americans are scared silly of. Except, you know what they really want?"

Mustafa glanced over, hint of a grin. Held Bleeker's eyes.

"What's that?"

"White. Converts. Undercover Islam. Totally unsuspected."

"Like tonight?"

"No, no, not tonight. All Somali tonight. Rockstar travels around to the homes of donors, brings in new recruits, and pretty much tells them their lives are shit. All the violence, all the bling, all the drugs. Meaningless."

"And how's that go over?"

"Let's say there's thirty, forty there tonight? He'll get maybe ten, fifteen who want to join him. They'll play militant for a week or two, then fade back into what they were doing before."

"Because they don't like being told what to do."

"Exactly. He'll push them hard, too. Weed out the lazy, the rebellious, and the proud. Until there's one left."

"Like Jibriil."

"Just like Jibriil. But the Imam doesn't do all the legwork. He's very subtle. He's a preacher, that's all. A religious teacher. He has a small mosque in Roseville. Nothing fancy, very modest. From the outside, almost like a storefront. I think it used to be a pet shop. Behind the façade, he's building an army."

"And Al Jones is the one doing all the heavy lifting."

"You got it."

They didn't say anything else the rest of the drive.

*

For three blocks around the house, cars stretched in all directions. Lots of them tricked out imports like Mustafa's, some old Chevys and Lincolns from the 90's, mom and dad's old cars getting a second life. All of them dark, empty, the snow not yet covering them completely, but coating the windshields. Footprints converging on the two-story suburban cookie cutter in a development built maybe ten years ago.

Mustafa said, "The family who lives here owns two Super America stations. They're doing pretty well. It's their son who put this together. He's not a banger, but he knows plenty of them. And they got carried away by Al Jones singing the Rockstar's praises."

"What do we do?"

Mustafa smiled, pushed the car door open. "This."

He got out. Bleeker followed. Mustafa was striding, not a care in the world. Bleeker was starting to worry, though. So two uninvited guests show up at a private recruiting party. One obviously a white cop. Everyone will face the wall and wait to be handcuffed, sure, exactly.

"Seriously, what do we do?"

Mustafa kept on walking. "Ring the doorbell."

"You have no idea."

Mustafa stopped, turned. Middle of the street. "Got something better?"

"I'm not walking in on a bunch of gangbangers and terrorists if you've got no plan."

"Do you have one? I can't call for back-up. How about you?"

"This is crazy."

"Nobody is going to do anything." Mustafa reached over, gave Bleeker a couple of pats on the arm. "Keep cool."

Up the walkway, which had been plowed, shoveled and salted, only a sheen of frost and clumps of wet snow on the concrete. Bleeker wondered if he should have his shield ready, but then decided against it. He was going to shove his hands deep into his jacket pockets and not say a word unless someone asked him a question.

Mustafa rang the doorbell.

Moments later, a tall Somali woman opened the door. Hard to tell her age with skin that smooth, but Bleeker guessed around forty. The elaborately patterned yellow and violet hijab covered her head and neck, framed a face that immediately recognized Bleeker as police. The rest of her was clothed like an American. Slacks and a loose silk blouse. Maybe flaunting her freedom in front of Rockstar, or maybe he was the type that turned a blind eye.

She said, "I'm sorry officers, is there a problem?"

Mustafa said, "You have a lot of cars out here."

"I'm sure we can move some if they're in the way."

"What's going on here tonight?"

She knew they knew. Something about the tight lips, the posture. "A private party. For our...church."

Mustafa nodded. "May we come in?"

She backed away from the door. "Please remove your shoes, coats, and hats. Don't drip on the hardwood."

They stepped inside the foyer, tiled, that opened into a sitting room, obviously not used all that much. They had taken great care with the décor—much to remind the visitor of the family's Somali heritage, art and pottery, alongside a contemporary American leather couch and glass and wood tables, very pricey. Dim table lamps barely lit the room, throwing amber light and creating fuzzy shadows. The lady of the house took their coats, hung them in the entryway closet. A man came from the hallway at the back corner of the room, gray slacks and a blue button-down shirt, your typical middle-class manager ensemble. Clean-shaven, rich brown skin. Obviously the husband, and probably ten years older than his wife.

He said, "Late arrivals?"

Mustafa didn't wait for the wife to warn him. He stepped out of his shoes—slip ons. Smart. Bleeker was still untying his boots. Reached out for the husband's hand. "Mr. Hassan? Nice to meet you. I'm Mustafa Bahdoon."

Hassan's cheeks sank, eyes widened. If the wife hadn't recognized him, the husband sure did. "Bahdoon. You are here to see…here for…?"

"Please, tell me what's going on tonight."

He glanced at his wife. Smirched his mouth. Bleeker checked her out. Talking with her eyes. Looking down at the floor. The basement. They were all in the basement.

"It's nothing." Hassan spoke low. "A sermon, my son's friends. He's a good boy."

"Sermon?"

Hassan motioned. "I'll show you. Downstairs. Please don't interrupt, though. I'm sure the Imam will talk to you after."

"I'm not really interested in him."

They stepped out of Bleeker's sight. He yanked off the boot, dropped it. It bounced off the tile onto the hardwood, the gorgeous rug laid out in the room. Melted snow splattered and Hassan's wife let out a sharp breath.

"Sorry." He stumbled, pushed himself up with a hand on the wall, and followed the men.

They had gone through the kitchen, still talking softly, and turned at the stairs to the basement. Bleeker saw trays of crumbs. Spices in the air, more than one, swirling and combining and releasing. Made him hungry. He'd need a Smashburger later.

He caught up with the men on the carpeted stairs. They'd ceased talking. Below, a voice in Arabic, louder than conversation, not quite shouting, then another loud voice right behind the first, in heavily accented English. "When Jay Z tells us it is a hard knock life, we accept it to be so. We accept whatever we are told. We think the government hands us our rules. The government judges whether it's *hard knock* or not! Does that make any sense to you?" Then more Arabic.

Mustafa and Hassan stood at the bottom of the stairs, watched. Bleeker made it down, looked out at the very American den with the large flatscreen

TV, entertainment center, sectional sofa, La-z-Boy recliner. Nearly every square foot of floor space covered with young men in hip hop jeans, T-shirts and polos, their shoes lined-up in a utility room to the left. Riveted. Before them, a man sitting crosslegged on top of a big wooden box set in front of the TV. He looked old but vital. Salt and pepper beard. Chubby. A white robe, white prayer hat, very dark skin. He was the one speaking Arabic.

Where there had once been a bar, Bleeker supposed, was now what looked like a place to pray. Several rugs on the floor. A woven wallhanging, more Arabic. The flag of Somalia beside it, a creamy blue with a single white star in the center.

Too busy noticing all that to notice the bottom step. He missed it, flung out his arms, grabbed Mustafa and Hassan before falling on his face, slammed his feet hard onto the floor. Plenty of bangers turning to look, creased brows, angry eyes. The Imam stopped mid-sentence. The translator stood. Somali guy in a fine business suit, fine silk tie, spread collar shirt. Balled his fists. Like he was going to beat the shit out of whoever dared interfere. Then he saw Mustafa.

Fists loosened into fingers again.

Mustafa wrapped an arm around Bleeker's waist, pushed him towards the utility room while Hassan apologized, begged them to "Please continue. Please. Don't mind us."

But there was nothing else to come. The Imam began speaking again—in English this time—blessing the boys and telling them there would be time to talk again later. A rumble in the room, disappointed *Aw, man* all over the room. *This is bullshit, scared of the police same as any bitch* and *Shit, Bahdoon just shut him down, man. That's cold.*

In the washroom, Mustafa shoved Bleeker against the washer, turned him around and grabbed him two-handed at his collar. Boiling eyes, red veined.

"Let go."

"How the hell can you be an expert on us? You step on us like dog shit!"

"I said let go."

Mustafa let go. The gangbangers had to come in to retrieve their shoes on their way up the stairs, getting a glimpse of their hero. Like an idol, the way these guys looked at him. More reverence than they showed Rockstar Muhammad, even.

Bleeker said, "I missed a step. Anyone could've."

Hissing. "Anyone would've been more careful. Like handling a beehive."

"I'm sorry, okay?"

Hands on his hips. A step left, one right. Head down. What was the deal?

Hassan waited at the door. Bleeker was about to leave, wash his hands of the whole damned mess, when the thick black man in the suit shoved Hussan and Bleeker out of the way, headed right for Mustafa. Mustafa shouted and smacked the man on the side of his head, over and over. Didn't phase him. Punched Mustafa in the face, sent him reeling into the wall, knocking over detergent, fabric softener, and a bag full of lint. Mustafa went down. The translator picked him up like a rag doll. Grains of detergent in Mustafa's hair, stuck to his face. The translator held him up, arm over his shoulder, and drug him from the room. With his free hand the translator gave Bleeker a hard shove that knocked the wind out of him.

Bleeker, wheezing on his hands and knees, got the picture. That translator was the "Al Jones" they'd been looking for.

He heard the big man's voice booming. "The Big Bad Bahdoon thinks he can interrupt our teacher? Thinks he can tromp his traitor ass all around, drag this *infidel* along with him?"

Bleeker made it to his feet. Pulled out his pistol.

The scene: Rockstar Muhammad hadn't moved. Still serene on his pedestal. Al Jones stood over Mustafa, writhing in the middle of the floor, hand on his back. From this angle Bleeker saw more of the room, the steps and door that led to the backyard, where some of the gangbangers had surely escaped. A handful of rough and tumble guys in identical North Face parkas stood sentry over there, AR-15s in their hands. Shit.

They noticed Bleeker's pistol, took aim, started barking at him. "Drop the gun! Drop it! Drop it now!"

Al Jones turned his head, pointed a thick finger at Bleeker. "Drop it or I stomp his skull."

He lifted his foot, set his bare heel on Mustafa's head, pressed down.

Instinct. Not like on TV. Not so easy to give up his gun. Not so easy to fire, but easier to do that to solve a problem than make them both helpless.

Bleeker fired from the hip. Powerfully loud, everyone ducking, covering ears, squinching eyes. Bleeker had missed badly, way right, busting up a rack of DVDs. A burst from someone's AR-15. Bleeker dove behind the couch. Hassan, back near the stairs, grabbed his guts and dropped dead. His head flipped back when a late round got him, dead eyes and surprised, bloody mouth staring at Bleeker. The cop peeked over the back of the couch at the action.

Al Jones, screaming and waving his arms. Still standing with his foot on Mustafa. Mustafa grabbed the foot, pushed and twisted hard. Kept at it while Jones hopped with his other foot and tried to shake Mustafa off.

Bleeker was up again, took quick aim. Fired two shots in the direction of the sentries. One flinched, went down. Another dropped his gun, grit his teeth. The other two stepped ahead and started in, bursts of fire into the sofa. Bleeker dove flat on the ground, covered his head. No fucking way they could miss him. No fucking way. The rounds thudded into the wall behind him, all around. No fucking way.

Then the gunfire stopped. They run out of ammo? Were they waiting for him to pop up again? He could hear that Al Jones was still struggling with Mustafa, but then another voice, the Imam's, rose above it. In English again.

"Now is not the time! Not now!"

Bleeker raised up on his elbows, crawled to the edge of the couch where he still had cover from the end table. Sentries, guns down, helping the other two. Neither one dead. Jones still struggling with Mustafa, until Mustafa gave the man's ankle a mighty twist, the guy's knee going with it, toppling to the floor. Mustafa got up, not going for his pistol, backed away. When he saw that Bleeker was okay, he stood his ground, stared down Rockstar Muhammad, who was now standing on the box, head and shoulders hunched to avoid the dropdown ceiling.

Bleeker rose to his knees, kept the gun trained on the sentries. It didn't matter how much of a badass he'd been in Iraq. Didn't matter how intimidating he was to the Somalis over in New Pheasant Run. Here, he was scared. Trapped. Not sure how any of this was going to end. He took charge, marched over to the sentries while they were distracted, gun in their face, took their rifles, slung three over his shoulder and reached one back to Mustafa. He took it, but let it hang loose in his hand rather than covering the rest of the room.

Bleeker said, "Someone must've heard that. Cops'll be here soon."

Mustafa looked around. "Pretty soundproof room."

"Think, man! Automatic weapons fire!"

Shrugged. "A movie. Look at the set-up here."

Bleeker was about to say something else, something with lots of "fucks" and "shits" but not "niggers" because he was surrounded by black men and he hadn't said "nigger" in months and months, thanks to Cindy, but by God, it was on the tip of his tongue right then and he had to bite it back, bite it off.

The lightning crack of a handgun and the pain blacked him out. Reeling on his feet. The pain radiating up his arm, like hot lava across his back. He grabbed at the fire on his right arm. Split skin across his upper bicep, on through to his upper back. Not so bad. It would heal up with a few stitches. Still hurt like all hell. He sucked in a deep breath and turned. Hassan's wife, eyes wild, stood at the base of the stairs over her husband's body holding a pistol. Another crack, bullet went wide.

Mustafa lifted his auto and let loose, cut her down right across the middle.

Then it was quiet.

Al Jones grunted, pulled himself up onto Rockstar's box. "Look what you've done."

Mustafa, still staring at the wife. Like he was in shock. "We...wanted to talk."

"A peaceful gathering. The police can't accept that, can they? Have to make us all out to be murdering lunatics."

"But you are," Bleeker said. His arm was dripping red, filtering through the fingers clamped over the skin. "Tell them, Mustafa. Tell them why we're here."

Al Jones, sitting on the box, rubbing his ankle. "Oh, I know why. We heard you coming miles away."

Mustafa said, "Why? A couple of stupid kids. You sent them to fucking die?"

"To fight. To bring glory to themselves in the next life."

"I need to know who. How'd they get there? Where are they?"

Rockstar sat down again, tapped Jones's arm, and leaned forward, speaking low into his ear. Jones nodded.

"Come on. Where are they?"

Al Jones said, "Are the Imam and I under arrest? I think it's important we understand our rights."

Bleeker said, "Yes, goddamn it, of course you're under arrest."

Mustafa said, "No. Where are they?"

"Wait." Bleeker stepped over to Mustafa. "Yes. I'm arresting them."

"We can't do that. This was a home invasion. A Somali gang hitting the Hassans because of something their son did."

Unbelievable. "The hell are you talking about?"

"They tell us where Adem and Jibriil are, and how to get them back, and then we get out of here. They're on their own."

Bleeker, the feel of the blood all over him making him sick, trembled. So pissed. "This isn't your fucking *gang* we're talking about here. You're on my team. Get used to it."

"Is it going to help us get Adem back? No, all it does is make us killers."

"Makes us *heroes!*"

"Is that what you want? Because all I want is my son!" Mustafa's face stretched and furious. Right in Bleeker's. Stabbing his finger into the man's chest. "You started this! I would've talked to them and we would have left. But you started shooting. You wanted to kill. Not them. You."

"I did what I was supposed to."

Mustafa looked tired. Screwed up his face. "Fuck you, man. We need to get you an ambulance."

"Excuse me." Rockstar Muhammad raised his hand. Didn't wait to be recognized. "I have not done anything illegal. I do not understand, this ... this ..." He spoke to Al Jones in Arabic.

Bleeker couldn't figure it out. Too fast, and he wasn't concentrating. Mustafa bobbed his head, answered. Rockstar's eyes lit up. That set them both off in Arabic. Bleeker's arm and back hurt more listening to them babble, shut out of the loop. He stepped aside while the Arabic flew over his head, pulled out his cell phone and called 911.

Told the dispatcher, "Detective Ray Bleeker, out in Eden Prairie. We've got a problem."

"I'm sorry, you're a Detective in Eden Prairie?"

"No, no, but yeah. Look, We need an ambulance. We need some back-up."

"Why didn't you call—"

"Listen, no time. I'm bleeding. How about 'off-duty officer needs assistance'? Can you put that out there?"

She told him okay and started typing, and he told her the address. Was about to tell her the situation when he heard Mustafa's gun rattle to the ground. He glanced over his shoulder. The three standing sentries now had goddamned Glocks, covering Mustafa. Al Jones helped Rockstar off the box, started for the back stairs.

Bleeker closed his phone, stepped forward. "No, no no no. You're staying here."

"Let them go." Mustafa, disarmed, standing like a dead tree.

"The police are on the way." Bleeker chased Al Jones, who escorted the Rockstar like he was James Brown. Hand on Jones' shoulder. A sentry stepped up, shoved the Glock against the side of Bleeker's nose. He blinked, looked away. Finally held up his hands. "All right, all right."

Up the stairs, into the night. Jones and Rockstar were gone. One by one, the sentries backed up the stairs, the seriously injured man helped out first. Bleeker was sure they were going to fire. Last two witnesses, no need to keep them alive. But then…nothing. Mustafa and Bleeker stood alone except for the bodies of the Hassan's wife crumpled over the husband, his expression even more alarming when Bleeker took a second look.

Mustafa let out a long breath, looked at Bleeker's arm. "How bad?"

"Flesh wound. I couldn't even get shot in Iraq, but here, Jesus."

Mustafa shook his head, sat on the couch. Knees wide, held his head in his hands. "Damn it, Ray. Listen, when they get here—"

"How about I take care of that?"

"No, you don't see it at all. You can't tell them about Jones. Not a word about Rockstar."

"This isn't a game, man. What happened is what happened, and that's what we've got to tell the cops."

"Then they'll die!" Mustafa's head lifted. Face bright with tears. "If you tell them what really happened, Jones is going to make a call, and Adem and Jibriil will die. Their own guys will cut their heads off, and they'll send me the videotape. But you'd like that. You want to see them dead. Justice, right? What they deserve, right?"

Sirens, closing.

"That's what he told you?"

"I didn't make it up! He said...he can't tell me exactly where they are, whose command they're under, but he knows they made it. Alive. And they're still alive. *He's* alive. One call, and that's it."

"Shit." Bleeker closed his eyes. True, if Mustafa was telling the truth about Jibriil, then watching him die would be sweet justice. Dying in the worst possible way, having his head sawed off in some godforsaken alien landscape. But if Adem was innocent, even if there was the tiniest whiff of doubt about his part in Cindy's murder, was it worth it?

Less than a few minutes to decide.

"You swear to me Adem didn't take any shots that night. Didn't egg on Jibriil, didn't have any idea the son of a bitch would do it, right?"

Mustafa, exhausted and limp, swiveled his head. The heel of his hands press into his eyes. "I'd stake my life on it. I'm already done. When these police arrive, I'm in big trouble here no matter what. My whole family. And the best we can hope for is that Adem finds a way to survive without his own men killing him because of something I said."

"You're giving up."

"It's the only way to make sure he's safe."

Bleeker knelt beside Mustafa, but then fell off his knees to the floor. Grabbed the Somali's knee to steady himself. Weak from blood loss, shock, fear, whatever. About to piss himself, but too tired to stand again and stumble around looking for a toilet.

Sirens louder still. Fever pitch, then they stopped. Then voices, chatter, footsteps above them in the house.

Shit.

Bleeker tightened his grip on Mustafa's knee. "Hey?"

Mustafa looked up.

"Get lost. Go." Bleeker nodded. "Okay? You were never here."

Shook his head. "I can't. I ... you can't."

"I'm a fucking cop. I sure as hell can. Get out of here. Now."

When Mustafa didn't move, Bleeker got up and grabbed Mustafa's shirt, dragged him to his feet, and threw him towards the stairs. "*Now.* Forget about me. Get out of here."

Another moment of hesitation, then there were footsteps on the basement stairs. Bleeker huffed and bit his lip, and he was gone. Up and out.

Radio noise. The footsteps stopped, a cop at the bottom of the stairs saying, "Uffda! Look at this shit."

Bleeker thought, Yeah, fucking uffda indeed.

FIFTEEN

The baby eventually stopped crying. Adem wasn't sure if it had gotten well or if it had died. Didn't know if it was a he or a she. He didn't ask. Otherwise, day and night came and he stayed in bed and then day and night would come again. When he first awoke, he'd thought he was only a day or two away from a full recovery. But as the drugs ebbed and flowed and he tried to get out of bed when no one was paying attention—but it seemed someone always was, like the ever-present guard outside his tented bed—Adem discovered that the beating had been almost as bad as stepping on a mine. He hadn't lost his limbs or his eyes or his genitals, but another minute of boot stompings would've done the trick.

Legs, bruised up and down, his left fibula broken in two places, some bones in his feet crushed. Broken right arm. Broken fingers on both hands. Possible bone spurs along his spine. One testicle, badly swollen. Broken nose. Lacerations all over his face and scalp. A few cracked ribs. And a knife wound across his neck.

He had his eyes, his mouth, despite split lips, and his mind. Enough to survive. Enough to keep him afraid that at any moment, someone would come and pass more judgment on him, finish where his would-be executioner had failed. He slept lightly through the nights, only relaxing once the morning came and Sufia arrived to take care of him.

He'd asked Jibriil more about her on his next visit. Was she a nurse? A soldier's wife? A visiting crusader like they were? His friend had smiled. "Are you getting ahead of yourself a little? Falling in love?"

"I just...it's nice to have someone to talk to."

"Someone who looks that good, too."

"Come on, not like that." But it was and they both knew it.

Jibriil had lowered his voice. "Adem, be careful, though. It's different here. Talk to her, but keep it casual. You want to rub one out thinking of her, fine. Don't let the guard find out. Be *careful*. Don't lose yourself."

"I wasn't going to—"

"Yes, I know you say that but then feelings get complicated. What if she really does like you? You going to take her out? A nice Italian joint? Sure, a night on the town. I'm sure her fathers and brothers and all of these teenage boys around here who hate you and can't fuck her will be fine with it."

Adem promised nothing would happen. Nothing. He wouldn't risk her like that. But he asked that Jibriil make sure she would keep taking care of him. It was helping him grow stronger every day. With a wink, Jibriil left. Sufia kept coming around, maybe a little more shy than before. She was harder to engage in conversation. Kept flicking her eyes around as if someone was always watching. But Adem kept trying, anything to keep his mind off the pain. And sometimes he would hit a subject—books, music, cooking—that would open her eyes wider, make her spill more animated giggles, show her teeth. And that was reason enough for Adem to keep fighting the depression, the boredom, and the fear. He would do it. He would build his strength and go back to his patrol, standing tall amongst the men who had beaten him and wanted his head on a pike.

He'd be fine. All he had to do was think of Sufia.

*

Seven, eight days in bed. Nine, ten. He wondered how far away from the camp he was. If this wasn't the hospital proper, then where had they set this up? Hidden from government troops, what few there were anymore. The building didn't shake so much when the artillery shells exploded. Like thunder and lightning, counting between the flash and the rumble.

Another boring afternoon. Adem had a Quran and a four month old South African newspaper that Jibriil sneaked to him, which Adem then had to hide under his mattress. The leaders found so much to be "un-Islamic", like football, music, movies, books, newspapers, a list that grew longer everyday, including the rules for how men and women should and shouldn't interact—mostly, how they shouldn't interact at all. The boys in the army seemed to have a problem with women especially, as if blaming them for the lack of Islamic discipline amongst the citizens.

Adem was surprised that Sufia was allowed to tend him, although it was only for mundane things. When it came to bedpans, changing bandages, a wet cloth to wipe down his skin, there were men to do that. Even once his colleague Garaad, not someone Adem had expected or hoped to see. He came to help clean his "brother", grabbed him by the hair above his bandage and pulled, wiped his face, his chest, his feet. Smiling as he did it. Regaling Adem with all the great battles he was missing. All the punishments doled out to the traitors. "But you feel sorry for them, no? Even though you killed a man for stealing bread."

"I didn't mean to—"

A hard yank on his scalp. "You did. That's all that matters."

When he was done, Garaad peeled back the bandage from Adem's neck. Adem slapped at Garaad's hand, but the soldier easily grasped Adem's wrapped fingers, squeezed, sent a river of pain through Adem's arm, shoulder, neck. Garrad examined the neck wound with a slightly open mouth, almost titillated by it.

"It would have been a deep cut. Right through half your neck. He knew what he was doing."

Garaad poked the wound. Adem seethed.

The soldier slapped the bandage back into place and stood. "Lucky man. Blessed, even. Or one might say 'privileged'? One might say."

Adem caught on. Didn't answer. Some of the boys must have thought it was only because of Jibriil that Adem was recovering in such luxury. Or that he was recovering at all instead of his body being paraded up and down the streets as a cautionary lesson to other traitors.

On his way out, Garaad made a finger gun and went "Pow, Cowboy," in English. Then he swept through and was gone, laughing.

Adem closed his eyes and wondered what his friends at college were doing as the snow piled higher outside their dorms. He wished he could give them a call.

*

More days passed. A crutch, some practice, and he was up and around. The room wasn't as long as he'd thought, his bed being at the far end instead of floating in the middle of a sea of them. Adem never saw any doctors around. The closest was when Jibriil visited, which was less often as he improved, and asked what he needed. Like asking a surgery patient to guide the scalpel. But whatever he asked for—pain meds, clean bandages, antibiotics—showed up almost as soon as Jibriil had gone.

Adem began chewing *khat*. It gave him a boost of energy, helped with the pain. Spit green out the windows. Loved to stand there, looking out while chewing, walking from window to window. Some afternoons, he saw children playing football in the lot behind the building.

Sufia found him one afternoon, chewing, spitting, watching. She watched with him, didn't say anything.

Adem said, "Isn't it dangerous for them to play that? Won't they get lashes?"

"Since when do boys care about that? If they get caught, they'll run."

"They're crazy for it. Willing to risk their hides for it."

"What do you expect? It's football." Something else to make her laugh. A nice smile as she looked out the window. "As long as they're having fun.

There's not supposed to be much of that anymore."

He turned to her. "Then why are you here? We're working for the side that hates fun."

"I can ask you the same thing."

"I didn't know."

Sufia turned her face to the floor. "What a terrible answer." She began to walk away.

Adem hobbled behind. "I should have, you're right. Just another ignorant American. But please, why you?"

"Let's not discuss this. It's not right." Busied herself, taking sheets from beds, balling them up.

"Okay, okay, but, let's talk." Finally caught up, tried to get in front of her. "It helps me feel better."

"Sure it does."

"Do you like soccer?"

Sufia stopped, rolled her eyes. "I thought it was bad here, I had no idea. In London, you'd think the college boys were on the team, the way they talked. '*We* won. Look at us.' Is that a better obsession than the word of Allah? The will of the prophet? It's only a ball."

"I know, right? The whole sport, so boring. I mean, you know, back in the states we really like basketball. That's got some speed to it, always moving, always taking a shot. Got to think quick, move quick."

"I've seen it." Wrinkled her nose.

"Really? You didn't like it?"

She balled up the next sheet more fierce. "Sweaty boys in, in, baggy shorts. They're not shorts! They look like they're wearing a dress. At least the footballers are manly. That's how sinners are supposed to look."

"Seen any American football?"

She barked a laugh. Adem looked around. His guard was now at the window where they'd just been, watching the kids play until Sufia let that noise fly. Now he watched them both with angry eyebrows.

"Isn't it time for you to get back to bed?" She said, still the hint of a smile there, fading into the gracefulness of her smooth, caramel skin.

Adem wanted to reach out, touch her cheek. Maybe even lean in for a kiss. Simple things. Natural things. All the things the God of this army said he should never ever do. He didn't understand.

"One day you can tell me more about London. I've never been."

"Maybe that's a good thing." She carried her sheets away. He stood watching her go. Turned back to the guard. Still staring. Still had angry eyebrows. Adem winked at him and eased his way back to bed, all thirty-three excruciating steps.

*

Sufia finally told him about London. Whispered about it one morning when Adem ventured down the stairs and outside for the first time in nearly a month. She said it seemed the whole world could live there together and be perfectly fine. She had to be careful. It was so easy to get caught up in the world—the clubs, the shopping, the indulgent food, the books and movies.

"Like my father told me when he called me home. He said, 'The devil throws everything he has at us because all we have is the Word. He knows what we've hidden and shines a light on it.'"

They were slowly walking along the road in front of the building. Still in Mogadishu, but an area where the buildings weren't mostly rubble, the pavement wasn't broken, and where Adem thought he heard the ocean. Could be they were near the shore, sure. He would love to see it, would have to ask Sufia if it was a possibility.

"Then why? If you had all that, what was it that made you come back here?"

"Weren't you listening? All that was taking me further from what I had been taught. I wanted to see the country again. I want to see it beautiful again." Her face gave away something sad, though. "I thought…I mean, I still think one day…I thought it would be different, that's all."

"Less hell, more heaven?"

A nod. "I know war is ugly. Necessary, but…maybe you soldiers should remember that we're all on the same side."

"Hey, don't blame me."

"You know what I mean."

Jibriil had found Adem some clothes, regular T-shirts and pants and sandals. They fit a bit loose, which was more than fine. Adem wondered if they were taken off dead soldiers. Any other place but here, he would not have worn them, but for the moment they were a blessing. His toes didn't send spikes of pain when he took a step. His nose bandage was down to a minimum. The cuts on his head, mostly healed. Only his leg held him up, and then the pain along his spine, the bone spurs. But when he was with Sufia, despite the looks of men and women and soldiers all around them, he felt as good as before the beating.

Adem asked, "Would you ever think of leaving, though? For good? It's okay to love your country from far away."

"It's not the same."

"Think about it, though. London again? Or Dubai? Or, out on a limb here, the States?"

Whatever rhythm they'd had froze over. Adem felt the chill. Sufia stopped walking. Adem nearly fell over trying to stop himself. He worked his way around until he was standing in front of her. Very close.

"I'm sorry," he said. "I didn't know we couldn't say—"
"I think it would be better if I left. I can go back to the camp and cook."
"Come on, don't do that."
"You are the one who's doing. This is very inappropriate."

It was a strange feeling, looking into her eyes and knowing that every word she was saying, no matter how sharp and forceful, didn't express how she really felt. She wanted to say *Yes, please, I'd love to see the States*. She was curious like that. Sufia deserved to see the world, not told her "proper" place in it.

He glanced over her shoulder. No one paying attention. Something so innocent, really. He took one more hobble towards her, took her arm in his free hand gently, leaned in for a kiss. At first she pulled back, but not so much. If she'd truly wanted away, all it would have taken was a step backwards. But she stayed. He kept on. A tiny, dry peck on the lips.

He pulled away. Her eyes, wide open. She shivered beneath his touch. Blinked one two three four—

Then cupped his face with her hand and kissed him for real. Bold, hard. He fought to keep his balance on his crutch. Wanted it to go on and on. But a few seconds later, she backed away, five feet. Held her hands together tightly. As if he was a stranger. What had he done? Adem felt as if every eye in Somalia was on him. Nothing was innocent. He should've fought the urge. Fighting urges was the whole point, now he realized. Oh God. How could he accept anything less than more after that kiss?

"I have to go."
"I'm sorry," Adem said.
"Me too."
"Can't we talk about—"
"I have to go." She shook her head. Her whole body was in denial, like he was a stranger to her.

When she was gone, he leaned against the wall. There was no place to sit except the ground. If he did that he would never get up again.

Maybe that would be okay.

*

He didn't see her again over the next few days. An older woman took over his care, didn't look him in the eye, didn't say much at all. The shadow of his ever present guard appeared closer, darker. He asked Jibriil about Sufia.

"I told you, forget it. So forget it."
"At least tell me, is she okay? She's doing well?"
Jibriil sighed. "Of course. Absolutely. But she's lucky."
He didn't explain why.

Then she was back, one morning, unexpected, there as he was opening his eyes. As vivid as ever. She startled him. He sat up and wanted to shout out her name

Sufia put a finger to her lips. Went about her business, then left without another word.

Maybe it was a weird relationship from then on, but he could live with it. Being close to her, that was worth it. There were a few shared glances, smiles, touches. But all of them subtle.

A week of it. Then another. Small talk between them building each morning. More newspapers delivered from Jibriil. Still distant sounds of war, none of them encroaching their building. It was boring, but it gave him time to think. Whatever reasons Sufia had for wanting to return, for being loyal to her faith and family, sounded a hell of a lot better than whatever Jibriil was chasing. It didn't feel like the same thing. The army of young men, zealots who got off on killing and finding a way to bend the rules so that they could kill and kill again no matter what their holy book said.

They talked about their battles, their ambushes, their assassination of prisoners, all while laughing, smiling. Nothing about those boys reminded him of the beauty of a call to prayer. Or of the beaches, which Sufia and his guard finally took him to see. Or how the women, modest in dress, expressed themselves in brightly colored hijabs. What was it, then? Was Islam what the soldiers said it was, or what Sufia showed him just by being who she was?

He sat on the beach in the afternoon, watched the waves, and thought that he would be more than happy to help Sufia's dreams about Somalia come true, as long as he didn't have to carry a gun any more.

*

Another week. Adem only used the bed for sleeping, but he was sleeping more than usual. It felt good. He could walk without the crutch, but with a limp. The better he felt, the less Sufia was around. To fill the void, he began talking to the other soldiers here, some burned badly, some shot, one or two with AIDS, nearing their end. Adem was surprised to find a couple of boys slightly younger than him, both from elsewhere like himself—Australia and Sweden. They could talk about TV shows they missed, music, movie stars. Quietly, of course. And the stars had to be pretty big for all three to connect—Jay Z, okay. Will Smith, okay. Beyonce, okay. ?uestlove, not so much.

The Swede, adopted before he could walk, had really come back to find his father. Turned out Dad had died by way of the Ethiopians, which was enough for Hirsi to sign up. His truck had been attacked fighting the government. He was stuck inside while it burned. Half his face was cracked, crisp, his eyelid burned away. Scalp so thin in parts, Adem thought he could see skull.

The Australian, Yusef, had lost an arm after being shot in a battle with Uni African forces. He seemed proud of it. He asked Adem if he'd met any of the American white guys over here. "So weird. One was from Carolina. Like, South Carolina. He had a drawl and everything."

"White Islam? Really?"

"There's a few. Weird."

They told him stories. Crazy stuff. Soldiers who whipped women for wearing bras. Grand schemes to terrorize Israel, a handful of martyrs at a time. More stonings for adultery, theft, and blasphemy, which could be nearly anything.

Just when he thought he'd found some guys who understood where he was coming from, they began talking about rejoining the fight. Doing whatever it took to prove they weren't weak in the eyes of Allah. Hirsi told Adem, "Yes, they are going to send me home. But it's so I can plan an attack. I'll lie in wait, one year, and then trust me, you'll hear about it. It'll be great."

Adem made some excuses—pain, needed to exercise—and got out of there. Down the stairs, outside, walked right past Sufia without a word. She would've seen it on his face. He didn't want to risk hearing that she agreed with those guys. Hirsi, still cringing in pain, his face half a deathmask for the rest of his life, taking it out on the people who rescued him from this hell before he could even walk. Giddy about it.

He made his way several blocks to the beach, fast as he could. Walked all the way out to the water. In up to his shins. Felt good. He thought about swimming. Then about swimming for it. Freedom. How far along the coast would he need to swim before finding a town not controlled by this army? How far before he gave up and drowned? He stared as far as he could, the sunlight popping off the water like a million flashbulbs.

Then there were the sharks. Both in the water and on land watching. He wouldn't make it far. Didn't matter how free it looked. The ocean was as much a prison as his hospital bed. So instead, he sat on the sand right beyond where the waves could reach.

That was where they found him.

*

He heard them first. Turned, made out four, the heat blurring them. Jibriil was always recognizable to Adem, no matter what. The way he walked, the swagger. With him, someone at least two feet taller, and then two more men, officers. Something about them said officers. As the blur cleared, it was clear that they were all wearing uniforms. Jibriil's was new, dark green, maybe his first time to wear it. The *keffiyeh*, the white scarf, around his head was blinding. The tall man wore a double-breasted suit, a wide floral tie, and a green beret on his head, ones that their enemies, the UA, wore. That didn't make any sense. The other two men were obviously higher-ups, their scarves sitting on top of their heads, flowing in the breeze behind them. No doubt they'd come looking for Adem.

By the looks on their faces, the sharks suddenly seemed a better fate.

"Look who can walk all the way to the beach by himself now. See? He's in good shape." Jibriil, finally breaking into a smile, helped Adem from the sand. Adem was only a little taller than Jibriil, but next to the giant in the suit, both seemed like children.

One of the older officers, fully bearded with more of an Arab look, said, "And not running away this time. That's good."

No one introduced themselves. They acted as if they all knew Adem's story already. He didn't know if he should drop to his knees or fear for his life. Jibriil would've told him, he was sure. So he stood there. Not a word.

His friend now motioned to the tall man. "Go ahead. Really."

Now that they were closer, Adem saw that the green beret had a bullet hole in it and was stained by blood. The tall man's blood? Or had he taken the hat as a prize?

He'd been used to the mix of Arabic, English, and Somali he'd heard, but when the tall man began speaking, it was different. He immediately understood—this was Northern Somali. The "official" version, slightly different in dialect from the Mogadishu version. "I am Farah. And yes, I took this beret from the head of my enemy."

Adem didn't realize he'd been staring at it. Farah took it from his head. "Shot him by my own hand, back when I did that sort of thing. Next time I'll aim lower and keep the hat clean."

"I'm sorry, I didn't mean...I wanted to ask."

"Absolutely. Tell me, your family is originally from the eastern coast?" Switching over to Arabic.

"Yes, north of Mogadishu. I've never been there, though. I might have some uncles and cousins there. I wouldn't know them."

"Shame, then. You came so far to be so close and still not know. Are they Muslim?" This time switching to Af Maay Maay, a Southern dialect, almost a different language. It was like watching a bad Minneapolis comedian doing a Texas twang. Was this a test? Adem's father knew Maay, taught Adem a lot about it while he was in high school.

"Yes. We all are. I'm pretty sure."

Farah glanced at Jibriil and the others. Nods, raised eyebrows.

Then, in very mannered, rough English, "But this language, this is your bread and butter, is it not? An American college boy. You grew up speaking English. More than that, you know how Westerners think. You know when they mean what they say."

Back at him, in English, "What's going on here?"

In French: "Can you tell when an American is lying?"

"About as well as I can tell when Jibriil is."

Laughs all around. One of the officers slapped Jibriil on the back. But Jibriil did not look amused. Pain was creeping down Adem's leg again. He hoped they'd let him sit down again soon.

Farah said something else, something Adem couldn't translate. But he recognized it. "I don't know Dutch. Or Swedish. It's one of those, isn't it?"

Farah waved it off. In English again, rough indeed. "No matter. I need someone like you. We have importance...ah....importance for you. A job for you."

"One that involves talking to foreigners?"

"Can you tell where an American is from on accent alone like you can a Somali?"

Adem shrugged. "Sometimes. But a lot of people grow up watching TV now, so they're losing some of the differences."

In Minneapolis he'd hardly heard the typical Minnesota accent everyone laughed at and imitated. Then he moved out west for college and discovered many of the adults honked like that every day. The kids his own age, though, could've been from anywhere. He missed that sound—the flat, neutered English of his friends.

The men laughed the way older men do. Adem wasn't sure what was funny. Jibriil said, "Shall we go back now?"

They began walking the road to the hospital, all of them patient with Adem's limp, as if he was the most important among them. Jibriil and Farah flanked him.

"You're perfect for this. It's going to be great." Jibriil wrapped Adem up with an arm around the shoulder, a big squeeze, knocking Adem off-balance. They waited for him to get his rhythm back, started again. "They need a translator."

"Who are they?"

A shrug. "Kind of like the navy."

Farah said, "When enemy states send their tankers and cruise ships into our waters as if they are immune simply because they are not on the frontlines, then we act. They take our fish, they poison our water. And we make those states pay for their transgressions."

It took a moment to click in Adem's head. He turned to Jibriil. "You mean—"

"Yes, exactly. Pirates."

"Pirates?"

This was when Adem expected to wake up. It was bizarre enough to be where he was and to have seen what he had seen. But then there were pirates?

He didn't wake up. He was still limping towards a building he wished he'd never have to sleep in again, full of seriously wounded young men still dreaming of martyrdom. A woman he couldn't fall in love with even though he already had. A handful of newspapers he'd read forty times apiece.

But he'd rather sleep there than be a pirate.

"I can't be a pirate. Look at me! Just because I have a limp doesn't mean it's a wooden leg."

Jibriil laughed. The others didn't. Jibriil explained the thing about the leg, and one of the men said, "Oh, Johnny Depp. Pirates."

Adem hadn't meant to be funny, leaned in to tell Jibriil, "I can barely walk. I'm in a world of pain. This is ridiculous—"

Jibriil shut him up with a curled lip. No jokes.

Farah said, "You can come to Bosaso with me, and you will help me talk to the companies who own the ships. You will be my mouth. But they will know that you are an independent....ah....contractor, I think is how you say it. So if they were to arrest you or threaten you, it would not deter us. You will have no inside information. You will only know what we tell you."

Adem couldn't believe it. Bosaso. Like, a real city. Modern, growing, free. It was on the northern coast, near the horn, Puntland. Mostly untouched by his army. He was surprised to hear they had any presence there at all.

One of the other officers picked up again. "We have trained some of their men. They recruit from us. In exchange, we have been rewarded very well. A vital source of help to wage our campaign."

"So I don't have to be on the ship?"

Farah said, "No, no. To put you there would be pointless. I need you on land, in meetings with me, talking to moneymen and politicians. They won't see you the same way they see us. We dress like them, talk like them. We will give you a place to live, on your own. When your job is done for the day, you will be free to move about the city. And you will be given money to cover your living expenses, and a small portion of any ransom you help negotiate."

Another glance at Jibriil. Grinning, made his scar look more frightening. "You're perfect for this, Adem. It's what you've been studying for. It's business, politics, world affairs, all balled up into one."

It hadn't come out of the blue. That was obvious. Jibriil must have used his rank to ask around, find a way out for Adem. Not a real way out. As the man had told him, he would be "free to move about the city", but he left unsaid, *but not to leave it.*

"I don't know," Adem said. "I need to think about it."

Farah looked down on him, a sour look on his face. "I don't have time."

Jibriil pulled Adem aside, spoke softly. "What are you doing?"

"There's a big difference between fighting a war and becoming a criminal."

"Not really. Not here. Look, to kill a man, for the glory of God even, is still killing a man. What will you be doing for these men instead? Talking. Just talking. Not killing. Some of us are called to fight. But you're special. You are not a fighter. But goddamn, can you talk."

Adem shook his head. "Too fast."

"You've been here over a month now. How much more time do you need? I've been trying to help you, and now I can. Please, take the job. You'll be like an ambassador. Adem, please."

He was right. It was better than what he had expected. Lying awake at night, waiting for his guard to tell him it was time to go back to the camp, gear up for another fight. Or worse, for the guard to take him out back, put Adem on his knees, and finish the job the mob had started. This limbo was nice—Sufia, the beach, the quiet. But once it was over, there would be no plane back to the States. Farah's offer was the best chance he had.

He said, "Okay. Okay, I'm ready."

Jibriil let out a deep breath. Smile coming to his face. "Thank God."

They rejoined the men in the middle of the street, Jibriil about to start talking when Adem said, "I'd like to make one request, if that's okay with you, sir."

Farah narrowed his eyes, but it wasn't anger. More like he was amused by the weak American standing up to him like that. He told the other officers in Arabic, "What kind of monster have we created here?"

Laughter. Then, "Hear him out, at least. He's already started negotiating hasn't he?"

Did they think he didn't know Arabic? Hadn't they tested him, like, two minutes ago? Adem said, "Please, it's not much to ask."

More laughter from the officers, but Farah wasn't so happy this time. Adem continued in Arabic. "I would like an assistant, especially since I'm still not completely healthy yet. There's a woman who helps me here, Sufia, and I could really make use of her kindness until I'm fully recovered."

No one was laughing anymore. Farah stared into Adem's face. Taking it apart in his mind? The tall man finally said, "Absolutely not."

Jibriil leaned towards Adem. "It's not the way—"

"I'm sick of that answer. I know it's not what they do here. But it's what I want, and I can at least ask."

"You asked, he said no. There."

Adem turned back to Farah, Jibriil's hand wrapping around his bicep. "Why not?"

Not used to being talked to like this. The tall man let out a breath, probably dismissing the little bastard. There was always combat if that's what he preferred. Farah said, "We can give you a nurse. We can give you an assistant. There's no need—"

"Tell me, you can give me a cook, someone to change my bandages, someone to help with my schedule. But you can't give me a woman who speaks English better than I do. One who was educated in London. I don't need an assistant. I need her. If she's in a meeting, maybe she sees or hears something I miss. Body language. Tone. I don't know. But believe me, you want both of us for this."

Farah couldn't help but grin as Adem pled Sufia's case. He turned to the other officers. "A born negotiator. I'm glad he's on our side. Otherwise, I would kill him where he stands."

Adem flinched. But held his ground and his tongue. Nothing else to say.

One of the other officers motioned to Jibriil. "You know the girl he's talking about?"

"Yes, she's helped his recovery greatly."

Nods all around.

Farah finally stuck out his hand. "Deal. But you pay her out of your cut. You find her a place to stay. Not with you."

Adem shook it. He wondered what else he could've gotten—more money? Two weeks vacation? But Sufia was worth more than any of that. The others began walking back to the hospital. Adem didn't have anything to pack. He wondered if they would let him keep his rifle. He hadn't seen it since being dragged from the truck, so it was probably lost forever, in the hands of some twelve-year-old ready to take on the infidels. Let him have it. Adem preferred a shower, a bed, and some time alone with Sufia.

Jibriil told Farah, "I'd also like to send along a bodyguard, if that's okay. I know you might have plenty of men for this, but I can send a man with combat experience, someone vested in keeping Adem away from danger at all costs."

Not a bodyguard, Adem thought. A babysitter. Maybe the guard who had been watching him his entire time here, never got his name. Whatever. If he wanted to stand in the hall with his gun and look bored, fine.

At the hospital, a jeep awaited Farah, his driver very much looking like a pirate—sleeveless shirt, bandana around his head. Scars on his arms, face. Staring daggers. Farah told one of the officers to find Sufia. Jibriil called out to one of his soldiers, but Adem missed exactly what he said. The soldier rushed off.

Jibriil slapped a hand on Adem's back, pride spilling out of him. "Trust me, this job is important. I even think it can help you make it home."

"Really?"

"No promises. If this goes well, there are high hopes for you."

"For what? I don't get it. If I get them a good ransom, I'm set free? Is that the deal you made?"

"Better than that. Much better." Wide smile.

"Cut it out. Tell me already." He'd been standing too long. Shifted from foot to foot and again and again.

Jibriil said, "If you prove yourself, then they will see you are perfect to lead crusades back home. A long one, where you will plan and guide our people towards a strike against the Cities. One big target. You understand?"

Adem first thought he meant Target Center, the arena in Minneapolis where the Timberwolves played basketball, and where many pop artists held concerts. Adem had been there several times to see games and shows. He saw Jamie Foxx in concert there last summer. But then he realized, the prize, the one big symbolic strike that would really hit at the heart of American indifference and consumerism.

"The Mall."

"Now you see. The Mall."

The Mall of America in Bloomington, south of the Metro. Adem hadn't gone there much, but of course he'd gone. Everyone had to go at least once. Huge, so much stuff to buy. Filled at all times of the day or night. Some tourists came from out of town to shop there—that was the whole vacation. A bus from your hotel would drop you off at the mall, pick you up. It was like a city. You could practically live there if you played your cards right and had some money in your pocket. To hear Jibriil say it this way, excited, hopeful, even, chilled Adem. He remembered hanging out there with Jibriil, meeting up with girls, talking about all the clothes and watches and sunglasses they couldn't afford.

Adem couldn't imagine how he would react if a suicide bomber detonated himself while he was there buying some sneakers. Four, five, six bombers at once, strategically placed. More, even. The scary part was that he could pull it off, easily. His stomach twisted. His sweat felt colder.

A soldier arrived with Sufia behind him. She looked confused but placid. Nothing about Farah intimidated her, either. Made Adem feel all puffed up. Wanted to say, *That's my girl.*

Farah said, "Adem has been given an important assignment in Bosaso. He'll be working with us. You will come along to assist him."

"Sir?"

"He requested you. You'll help him."

Shouldn't she be smiling? Or at least trying to hide it? Adem said, "You've been so helpful, I thought...anyway...."

She nodded. Still no sign of gratitude. "I have work here, caring for the soldiers, preparing food, so much to do."

Farah, loudly, "There's always someone else for that. We've already decided. Your needs will be provided for. We're ready to go."

Finally a glance from Sufia. Those eyes. Adem raised his eyebrows. *Great, yeah? Isn't it?* But what he got back from her made him feel like hiding. Such a contemptuous stare. A frown. Adem looked at the ground to escape it.

And then a young soldier joined them, stopping his run, kicking up dust. Out of breath. Adem kept looking down. His boots.

"You wanted me, sir?"

The voice got Adem's attention. The last one he wanted to hear. Raised his chin. This wasn't his guard at all. It was Garaad. Good ol' Garaad, ready to take off Adem's head in a second. An idiot full of bloodlust. No, please, not this, Jibriil. Anything but this.

Jibriil pointed towards Adem, then Farah. "My friend here is going to Bosaso to do some important work. He needs you to watch over him, protect him. It is very important you keep him safe."

Garaad was nodding the entire time, hands on his hips while he caught his breath. "Yes sir. I will, sir. You can count on me."

Adem's heart sank. Even more when Garaad saw Sufia and said, "What's this one doing here? What's her problem?"

Adem stepped up. "She's coming with me. My assistant. My rules, understand? You keep me safe, but we play this my way."

A round of *ohs* and *ahs* from the crowd, applauding the American's balls, standing up to an obviously much stronger, tougher, and deadlier soldier. But even standing toe to toe, Garaad smirking, looking down on Adem like he could crush him in one go, all Adem could remember was Garaad running away from the gunmen in Ethiopia, passing all his brothers-in-arms as if they were stumps. Somewhere deep in those muscles lurked a coward.

Farah placed his hand on Adem's shoulder. "No. *My* rules. Are we clear?"

Adem sucked his cheeks tight against his teeth. "Yes."

"Excellent." The tall man in the suit started for the jeep. "Shall we?"

Jibriil embraced Adem one more time, a hard hug, one that hinted that Jibriil knew this might be it. "Be safe, brother. Don't give them a reason to kill you. Do it right. For me."

"You stay safe, too. Come see me. We can get you off the battlefield, you know."

Jibriil let go. "Why would I want to leave? I love it here."

Then Jibriil embraced Garaad, a fine, undeserved send-off. The silent guard was looking to be a good choice right about then, but Adem didn't dare mention it. He knew exactly why Garaad was the one Jibriil wanted. He was the one who wouldn't put up with any bullshit Adem tried to throw at the pirates. He might say all those kind things, call Adem his brother, but all of it was nothing compared to his distrust.

Sufia sat in the front seat of the jeep, since to put her in back would have her rubbing up against two men. Adem thought it was a place of honor, but the others he knew considered it shameful that she was coming along alone. If any other soldiers happened to see this, they might drag her off the jeep and stone her immediately, no trial.

But they made it down the road, Farah between the two men in the back. Bumpy road, traveling too fast. Not much was said. Adem wanted to ask many questions—what boat? How many hostages? What's the hold up with negotiations? Has there already been talk between them? What's my job, really? But he had already guessed that Farah was not a man who liked questions. He preferred giving orders. So Adem kept quiet, bumping along until they came to a clearing where a helicopter waited for them, blades already whirring. No wasting time.

They held onto their scarves to keep them from whipping around as they ran from the jeep to the chopper. Sufia struggled the most, her *hijab* threatening to fly clean off her head. Adem helped her up into the chopper, climbed in after, and there they were, finally, sitting next to each other.

He said to her, "Trust me, this is going to be better for both of us."

She didn't answer. Didn't even look at him. He couldn't understand why this wasn't okay. Why was she giving him the cold shoulder? Maybe it felt like a demand—Adem turning into one of the other men, always demanding but never thinking to ask what she had wanted.

He turned to the windows, watched the chopper lift from the ground. His first chopper ride. His stomach knotted tighter as they moved forward, the land and the beach and then they were over the open water, leaving purgatory for a lesser kind of hell.

SIXTEEN

It was better to be cold and alone. By his third week back from Minneapolis, now suspended pending trial for ... well, for whatever the hell happened in that basement, Bleeker should have been looking for an apartment, but he retreated to the ice shack instead. He brought along a toaster oven, a space heater, plenty of gas for the generator, and plenty of rum and coke. He set up the fishing line but set free everything he caught. He drank, slept, and dreamed. His dreams confused the massacre in Eden Prairie with the missions he'd had in Iraq. Gangsta thugs in street clothes kicking up the sand as they crossed the dunes, swords held high. Hell, that wasn't even Iraq. That was *Lawrence of Arabia* or some shit.

Another three weeks. When he had enough of the ice shack, he'd roll back into town, stop by and talk to his boss. Not much to talk about. Not when you've got an ex-Army Ranger showing up in a basement full of dead people, swearing he just happened on it, following up on a tip about the missing college student. Self defense. He had the wound to prove it. But there had to be someone else. Forensics told them that. "Just me," was all Bleeker had to say. "Got lucky."

So he floated, sneaking back home when Trish was gone. A cheap hotel when he wanted to sleep and shower. Driving, aimlessly, the whole time thinking he should've turned Mustafa in rather than letting him slip away through the door. He should've ratted out Rockstar and Al Jones. If it meant those two kids ended up dead, then fine. At least one of them shot Cindy. Let the universe work out the blame.

But he couldn't do it. The look on Mustafa's face, the weakness in his voice. The tough guy gang leader crumbling like stale bread. Bleeker kept his mouth shut. It was killing him. So he got drunk a lot. A whole lot. Got drunk and let the fish go and curled tightly in his sleeping bag, dreading the coming thaw when he'd have to face the world again. Some said it was due earlier this year. He hoped not. If so, he would stay until he felt the ice crack beneath him. Maybe even go down with the shack, all the way to the bottom of the lake.

Day after day of waiting for whatever it was that would make him stop waiting.

Like a knock on the ice shack's door.

Gun out. One in the chamber for weeks now. When they came for him, there would be a lot, but he'd get off a whole magazine first. Kill at least three or four. Make it hard for the survivors to get to him. Might even save one shot for himself to spite them.

Another knock. "Yo, Ray, man. Come on."

Mustafa's voice.

Not good enough. Bleeker sat up, aimed for the door. Breathing calm. Center mass. Focus.

A fist slamming the wall. "I know you're in there, alright? Don't fuck with me."

Bleeker cleared his throat. He hadn't spoken in days. "Door....door's open."

A click. The door swung open. Mustafa, in his parka and wool cap, stepped inside. His face, though—bags under his eyes. Unshaven. Didn't even blink at the gun leveled at him. In one hand, a bottle of pop. In the other, a jug of Bacardi.

"Thirsty?"

Bleeker's gun hand shook. He dropped it to his lap. "I thought you didn't drink."

"Not the rum. But I'm up for the Coke."

Bleeker pushed himself off the floor, kicked his sleeping bag to the side. Sweatpants and socks, a filthy undershirt. His uniform for a week now. He grabbed the two folding chairs, handed one to Mustafa.

"How'd you find me?"

"Your wife. Didn't want to tell me at first, but I guess you'd told her about me. Soon as I said my name, she wrote down the directions."

Yeah, he had told her. It was too late to reconcile, too late to keep living at home, so he went to her parents' house, sat her down in the kitchen and told her what happened. The only person he'd told the truth to. As much as she hated him, she had never betrayed his trust, something she'd take to her grave. Payback for Cindy.

Bleeker and Mustafa sat. Nothing to say for a long time. Five minutes. More.

Mustafa nodded at the line in the water. "Catching anything?"

"Plenty. I throw it all back."

"Didn't think you had it in you. Remember? 'I go after someone, I get them'?

Shrug. "People, not fish."

"You doing alright?" His voice rougher than usual.

Bleeker inhaled, let it go. "I sleep. When I'm awake, all I want to do is get back to sleep. I don't want to think. I don't want to do anything. Your son's life depends on me, and all I have to do is forget what I saw and move on. But I can't. It's not fair."

Mustafa picked up one of the plastic cups that littered the floor. Sniffed it. He poured some Coke. "Got ice?"

"You're welcome to chip yourself some off the lake."

"Never mind." Mustafa took a sip.

Bleeker stared at the rum Mustafa had handed him. Badly wanted to unscrew it, drink it straight from the bottle. Let the heat of it warm his breath, his lungs, his blood. But he couldn't do it. Instead, he tightened up, sniffed back tears.

Mustafa didn't say anything. Shifted in his chair.

Bleeker set the bottle on the floor. "How are you doing?"

"Better than you. I went home. I went to bed. I didn't get up for a week, wife yelling at me about my job. Sure enough, I got fired. So I've been praying. Crossing my fingers." Cleared his throat. "I owe you. For making me leave, you know."

Bleeker wanted to say "It was nothing" or something like that. Didn't want to open the flood gates. But they began to crack.

"Look, I know I made a promise to you, but when I see Cindy in my dreams, alive again except she's always in her uniform, it's like she's telling me to call down fire. I'm sorry, man, but I still might. I know how much you love Adem and all, but, goddamn it. It's not fair. War or no war, as long as they're alive, they're laughing in my face."

Mustafa nodded. Sniffed. Bleeker noticed the banger's eyes were a little moist. He rubbed them out with thumb and index finger. "You up for a ride? There's something I want to show you."

*

Bleeker drove, Mustafa riding shotgun with a laptop. The closest real town was twenty miles north, so they drove on with the talk radio bubbling low so that they couldn't make out the words, just the anger. The sky threatened snow. An inch or two a day for the last eight days, more on the way. Bleeker wouldn't have minded being buried in it. But a switch in his head wouldn't let him go that easily. No headshot, no pills, no drunken forays into the snow. If he was going to kill himself, it would be a long torturous fade, and there was nothing he could do about it.

He should've taken a shot at Mustafa back at the shack. A miss, of course. Wide right. But something to get the gangsta shooting back at him. End it like that. Because he already knew the script—the police were going to find a soft way to retire him off the force, and his few friends might come help him move out of the house, and he'd have enough of a pension to cover a studio apartment and several hours a day at the bar.

Day after day. Years. Maybe one day someone would find him, tell him Jibriil got his guts cut out and his corpse dragged through the streets of Mogadishu. He'd lift his Bacardi and Coke in salute and down it, then go right back to numb.

Once in town, Mustafa asked Bleeker to find a place with a good wireless signal. They pulled into a hotel parking lot. The signal wasn't strong enough. They tried another, closer to the front door. Better, but not enough for whatever it was Mustafa was trying to show him.

"Can't you just tell me?"

"You need to see it to understand."

Bleeker sighed, reversed out of the spot and got back on the road. "I'll buy you some coffee."

"Decaf."

"Shut up."

Bleeker took them to a bagel shop with free wi-fi. They got inside as the snow started falling. Bleeker bought them coffee, some rolls, and sat at a booth by the window while Mustafa tried to get the page up. The place was mostly empty, but Mustafa got a few hard looks from the other patrons, like they expected him to pull out a sawed-off and steal everyone's wallets. Right. Even in Mustafa's gang days, robbing a bagel shop would've been baby stuff. Not even on his radar screen.

It was taking a long time. Mustafa hadn't touched his coffee. Bleeker said, "What are you doing, looking at porn?"

"It takes time to download. But…wait…here it comes."

He turned the screen around. Bleeker pulled the computer closer. The language wasn't English, wasn't Arabic or Somali. Looked like some sort of news site.

"This is Dutch?"

"Yeah. Someone sent it to me yesterday. I've watched it a hundred times."

A video clip below a headline that Bleeker was able to figure out from one word: "Piraat".

Bleeker hit play.

Obviously from some sort of television broadcast. A woman newsreader. A picture over her shoulder of a freighter, "Piraat" across it. Bleeker picked up a few words that sounded like English, but it was all too fast for him. Then, they cut to the man on the scene, standing on a street with plenty of Somalis walking past on either side. They all looked pretty content, the town around them bustling, intact, not like what Bleeker had seen on TV about the capital. A word across the bottom of the screen.

"Bosaso."

"It's a big city on the Northern Coast. Lots of ships in and out. More like, you know, Duluth."

"Like Duluth?"

"Sunnier."

Bleeker looked back at the screen. Footage of happy Somali pirates, footage of a Dutch freighter, some of its relieved crewmen.

"So, the Dutch paid a ransom?"

"Watch."

"I don't...It's in Dutch."

"Okay, easy. Not the Dutch, but the owner of the ship. The corporation. But, you're missing it. Go back about ten seconds."

Bleeker pretended like he was going to do something with the touchpad. Shit, he could do e-mail, play Minesweeper, find some dirty pictures, but he didn't know how to roll back a video. Said, "How do you...Is that...Shit, Mustafa, I can't—"

Mustafa took it back, did something that took all of five seconds, then turned it back. "Hit play again. Watch this time, no questions."

He had to watch the man on the scene again, shirt-sleeves rolled up, extra button undone. Then the pirates, the ship, the crew. And then back to the man on the scene. And then...a familiar Somali face, young with a freshly shaved head, dressed up in an expensive suit, wearing wire-rimmed glasses, speaking in really good English: "We are pleased with the outcome, the safe return of the vessel to the rightful owners, and the good health of the crew. As always this—" And then the Dutch translation, which obscured the rest. So familiar.

"Show me that picture from your wallet again—"

Mustafa already had it out, holding it up to the screen. Adem. With hair, no glasses.

"Did he wear glasses? Contacts?"

Mustafa shook his head. "But it's him."

"That's a big problem, though. He's got glasses."

Mustafa pushed the photo closer. "You know how many times I asked myself that? I *know* my own son, damn it! It has to be. His voice, his eyes, his mouth, his nose. That's him."

"The fuck is he doing in Bosaso? What's that have to do with the war? Is he working for the Dutch?"

Mustafa took the computer back, started working on something else. "No, no, not that. I tried to find other stories about this, finally got one in English. He's calling himself Mr. Mohammed. What he does, he's an interpreter."

"Okay."

"But also like an agent. He can help with negotiations because he can speak English and Somali, all the different dialects. He's a smart kid, you know his grades. They tell him what they want, and he tries to get it for them like a businessman. No blood, no threats."

"He's been doing this the whole time?"

"He's suddenly shown up the past couple of weeks. This Dutch thing was his first, but he's moved on to a Canadian ship. He must be doing well. They're letting him negotiate on his own sometimes."

"This in the news?"

"Some, but not here. Americans don't realize how many ships are taken. Only when it's a cruise ship does it make the news."

"Jesus." Bleeker shook his head.

Mustafa turned the computer around again. This time it was a story in English through the BBC website. Another mention of Mr. Mohammed, translator for the pirates. He dressed in nice Western suits and held meetings in hotels. He always had bodyguards and a secretary with him.

"Why don't they arrest him?"

"No, man, they're not going to do that. In almost every case, the pirates release the ship once the ransom is paid. No harm to the hostages. So, you know, better to pay and keep the law out. Let the navy do their job once the boat's in the clear."

"You think he's being forced to do it?"

"I don't know what to think." Mustafa got louder. Antsy. "Just…look at him. He's okay. My son! He's alive!"

He pulled the computer back one more time. "I didn't know if he would be. Someone sent me a link to this. I mean, it's hard to tell, but…"

One more pass to Bleeker. YouTube. A mob scene. The camera was jittery. But a man was on his knees, someone next to him reciting from the Quran. Another put a blade to his neck. About to slice right through, enough of a cut to make blood run down, and then, more yelling. Someone from off camera. The man with the blade pulled the knife away and let his intended victim drop to the ground.

"And?"

"That was Adem. The one they cut. I swear."

In the booth ahead of them, a woman looked over her shoulder. Mustafa covered his mouth with his hand, breathing heavy through his nose. Blinking away tears.

"Okay, it's okay." Bleeker grabbed Mustafa's other wrist. "He's okay. That's good. They almost killed him, but stopped. That's a good thing. But doesn't this show he's still working for terrorists?"

Mustafa wiped his face. "I don't care. He's alright. We're all good if he's alright."

"No sign of Jibriil, then."

"If he's there, I haven't found him. Just like him to get shot down already." Mustafa raising a finger gun. "Pow, like he even lasted a week. My boy's still going strong, though."

"Do you mind?" The lady from the booth ahead. Voice sharp like a dog's teeth.

Bleeker said, "Sorry about that. It's okay."

"If you can't…control him, maybe you should leave."

Bleeker leaned back, close to her ear. "How about you shut the fuck up and eat your bagel? Guy's a little excited is all."

"Oh my god!" She was out of her seat in a flash. "My god! I'm going to find the manager."

Off she went, a loud "Excuse me, excuse me" to the people behind the counter.

Mustafa was staring out the window. Bleeker looked down at the story on the screen again. No mention of Jibriil, unless that bodyguard they talked about…it would take proof. Real honest to God proof that the murdering punk was dead.

The woman showed up at the table again, right behind a man who didn't look like the manager. More like a cook, beefy, in his fifties, thinking he was tougher than he really was. Arms folded. "You two are done. Get out."

Bleeker felt the blood flowing again. Oh yeah. Drop this guy with a shot to the kneecap. Bang his head on the tile until he's got no nose left.

He rose from the booth, got in the cook's face. The cook stepped back, loosened his arms. Held them at the ready. "We're going to call the police, but that doesn't mean I can't defend myself first."

Bleeker laughed, dug in his jacket pocket. Hoped it was still there, and it was, nearly frozen. He pulled out his shield. "Hey, look, I'm a cop, too. How about that? So what was it you were planning to do again?"

The cook backed off farther. "Hey, we're just saying, you understand. Our customers are trying to—"

"This bitch assaulted me. I can sell that story. Threatened me, too. Racial slurs against my friend here."

The woman gasped, then said, "I *never*, not at all. I would never say something like that."

Mustafa finally pushed out of the booth, closed his laptop and tucked it under his arm. "Ray, let's go."

"Didn't you hear the way she talked about you?"

"Let's go. Now. We need to roll." Mustafa reached into his jeans pocket, brought out some folded up cash. He flicked a couple of twenties from the center, tossed them on the table. "I'm buying that lady another bagel if she wants it. Come on Ray."

Bleeker waited another minute, eye to eye with the cook, who was withering. Good. He liked when they did that. Had forgotten how it felt. Until he remembered it was all his fault and the guy didn't deserve it. He dropped his gaze and caught up with Mustafa, who was already pushing his way through the door.

*

They didn't talk on the ride back to the shack. Mustafa switched from talk radio to FM and found some oldies. The Commodores. Followed by The Doors, so Mustafa turned it off. "I hate that organ. Like fingernails on a chalkboard."

Once out on the ice again, parked, sitting there in the car, Bleeker said, "I stood up for you."

"I didn't ask."

"Didn't have to."

"Man, you messed up. That was some sort of crazy you pulled. If you can't hold it together…shit, I don't know."

"What? What are you talking about?"

"Never mind. You need to take care of yourself. Just thought you'd like to know Adem's alright, that's all."

He opened the door, set a foot on the ice, then, "Listen, you've been cool with me, and I respect that. Did me a solid back in the Cities. It's a shame to see you like this. Wish I could help. Say the word."

Bleeker held onto the steering wheel, staring straight ahead. Not a word.

"Stay up, Ray." Mustafa climbed out, closed the door. Bleeker flicked his eyes over. The little yellow car. Mustafa opened the trunk, put his laptop into a bag, then closed it. Dropped into the driver's seat, cranked up, and made a slow circle until he was headed towards the dock.

Engine noise faded. Snow building on the windshield, smearing across with the wipers. Bleeker didn't move. The coffee had left a bad taste in his mouth and Mustafa wouldn't let him smoke in the car. That whole thing with the cook and the woman. Wondered if they'd have spoken up if he'd been with a white guy. Or if he'd been dressed in more than sweatpants and a t-shirt under his jacket. The shit he used to take for granted. People weren't *really* like that, were they?

Didn't matter. He rubbed his aching jaw.

Mustafa played it cool. For Bleeker's sake more than his own, now he could see that. And coming all this way, only to take off quick like that?

Bleeker slammed the Buick into drive and spun around. Had to catch up. Dangerously fast, slipping all over. Mustafa couldn't have been more than a half-mile ahead, not yet off the ice. Bleeker gained on him. Flashed his headlights. Finally got his attention. The little yellow car's brakelights flamed on, and Bleeker had to swerve. Slid off to the side, then started a one-eighty. Got control and ended up in front of Mustafa, facing him.

Bleeker got out, walked over to Mustafa. The car window eased down a couple of inches. "What, you crazy, man?"

"What did you come here to ask me? I want to know."

Mustafa shook his head. Heat poured from the window. Snow melted as it hit the glass. "Aw, man, you don't worry yourself about that."

Bleeker pounded his palm on top of the car. "Tell me! You want to go over there and get him, don't you? That's what you're here for. You want me to help you."

"It's okay. Don't even think about it."

"That's it. I know it is. You want me to go with you and bring him back."

Mustafa opened his mouth. Closed it. Let out a breath. Bleeker brushed snow off his head. Not going anywhere until he got an answer.

A long wait, but Mustafa finally said, "Would you go if I asked?"

"To get Adem? Not Jibriil?"

Shrugged. "Don't even know where that boy is, man."

"But maybe Adem knows."

"Alright, so maybe he knows. As long as it doesn't fuck with getting Adem back home safely, you can ask whatever you want."

Bleeked nodded. Snow collecting all over him, but he felt warm. "And when he's back here? Are you going to hide him, or make him talk to the police?"

"Hey, he's going to tell them the truth. Even if that means we've got to fight in court, cut him a deal, whatever. He's got to own up. But I'm thinking we've got to recognize that Jibriil talked him into this shit with lies, and once he was over there, he was forced to do what they told him."

Sounded good. Sounded right. If Mustafa would stick with that, it was all good. "He's got to testify about Jibriil killing Cindy. If your boy fired one shot—"

"Don't push it. Don't even."

Okay. Okay. Thinking. "Just the two of us?"

"I still have family over there. Battle-hardened men. We'll have help."

He didn't need to hear any more. "I'm in."

Mustafa rolled the window down more. "For real? Look at you, can't even dress yourself."

"A bad month, that's all. Deal me in."

Mustafa looked out across the ice, hand dangling over the top of his steering wheel. The snow blew right in on him. He didn't flinch.

Then, "Let's get you back to the shack. Fuck those bagels, man. I want some McDonald's. Then we've got to book some tickets."

Bleeker said alright and went back to his car. He climbed in, started back towards the ice shack. More snow. Heavier and heavier. But so what? He finally felt like he was thawing out. Turned on the radio. Oldies. "Dancing in the Streets". Bleeker hated that song. Didn't matter. He tapped out the rhythm on the wheel and realized he hated ice fishing almost as much as anything in the world.

SEVENTEEN

Air conditioning. Six weeks without it, Adem would never take it for granted again. He'd also never live anywhere this hot as soon as this job was done. The suits fit nicely, the shirts very soft, fine. The shoes, Italian leather. He had silk ties but only wore them when he knew there would be cameras.

Like today. The negotiators for the Canadians had asked for a break. Farah had let Adem handle the meeting on his own for the first time, and he could tell the men on the other side were a little uncomfortable with that. Maybe they believed he was softer than Farah. Maybe the whole break was meant to throw him off his game. Adem and Sufia stayed behind in the hotel meeting room as it emptied out, leaving only the two of them and their pirate bodyguards. Not Garaad, though, since he always seemed to be out of sight except when Adem wanted him that way.

He kept smiling at simple things. The pitchers of clean water around the table for anyone to drink at any time. The easy internet access—although he never had much time to look at it and Garaad was always right there in case Adem were to write emails back home. No, he knew what that would mean. He had to be careful.

Adem leaned towards Sufia. "What did you think?"

She looked at her notes. "They're stalling, obviously. Hoping the Americans will help, give them a cheaper way out."

Although she'd been forced to take the job, she was coming to relish it. Adem treated her as an equal and let her talk in meetings. He'd given her more than she had expected from his own payments so she could buy nice clothes and afford a good room. She was staying a block away from his condo, the home of an older couple with two rooms to rent since their children had left home. An ideal situation.

He nodded at her assessment. "I think Farah can be convinced that he should look to end this before the US sticks its nose in. He knows the hostages are worth a lot, but not that much."

"They've only ever come shooting after the cruise ship. Never for a freighter. And the President isn't looking for another war."

"How far do they want to push? If we come down in price a few hundred thousand—"

Sufia covered her mouth with her hand. He knew what she was hiding.

"What?"

"Nothing."

"You're laughing at me."

She sighed. "You've done this twice now. Always ready to cut the price."

Was she calling him a coward? He didn't like it, but he liked it. Showing a side of herself that would have been unheard of—punishable, even—back in Mogadishu. Sufia was playing the devil's advocate, teasing him.

"The first time was nerves. This time, it's reality. If the Canadians think the Americans will swoop down and rescue them—"

"More likely with money than manpower. We will get the number we want." She didn't need to say *Because that's good for our own pocketbooks, too.*

Adem lifted his water glass. Condensation made it slippery. He gripped tighter, took a drink. A small piece of ice washed into his mouth. He crunched it, liked the cold on his tongue. The simple things. Ice on his tongue. He'd missed ice.

Sufia closed her notes, stacked her papers. Adem never carried his own. Hands always free to shake or embrace as needed.

He said, "Hungry?"

Another of her *You don't get it* looks. "Please, Adem."

"We're partners. It's a business lunch. Come on."

The wheels turned. Always turning. She'd already played the social game once in London, so why was she so guarded now? A few more seconds of stacking, arranging, and she said, "Okay, just lunch."

That was good enough. He rose from the chair, buttoned his suit coat, and escorted her out of the air-conditioned conference room into the lobby, and then to the hotel's restaurant.

*

The condo, lush. The only problem was that Garaad lived with him. Garadd was too loud, too selfish. He hogged the television. He wanted to know what Adem was doing every moment they were in the condo together. Garaad also held onto Adem's cell phone. Adem had to ask to use it. Humiliating. He wondered if any of these people would ever trust him.

But the nights, oh the nights. A queen-sized bed all to himself. Fine sheets, several pillows. Adem opened the windows every night and listened to the ocean. Garaad also had a bedroom, but mostly he ended up falling asleep on the couch in front of the TV, volume up to wall-shaking. The couch had been pristine when they arrived. Now it was covered with boot stains, dirt stains, sweat. Never mind, there were plenty of other chairs in the place, and Adem made sure not to allow Garaad into his room. Even had a lock and key.

And an honest-to-Allah bathroom. A shower! A sink! Adem's shower that first day took nearly an hour, half of the time standing under the hot water, crying. As for Garaad, he didn't seem as enthused about it. Their first fight was over Garaad taking a shower, since he didn't want to but Adem kept pushing, more and more angry, how important these people were, the ones they had to meet. Businessmen. Power brokers. If they sensed weakness, rusticity, simple-mindedness, then all hope for a successful negotiation was gone. Adem also ordered him to dump the battlefield clothes for something that made more sense. Some khakis, perhaps. A loose shirt to help hide handguns.

Even though the car wasn't his, it was still a Mercedes SUV with a private driver at his call, any time, day or night. He and Sufia saw the city from the back of the car, ate in as many of the restaurants as they could, shopped. Garaad was always lurking, but Adem had learned the limits pretty quickly—no phones, no travel outside of the city, no long conversations that were not related to the job.

He'd only met the Captain of these particular pirates once, the first day, as the helicopter landed on the huge Dutch ship before taking them to their new digs. It was impressive, so small on the horizon, surrounded by nothing but water for miles, a few small surveillance ships and small pirate boats, light and fast. But as they closed in, the ship was like a city block, maybe two. Adem had only seen them at a distance from the Lake Superior shore. No idea they were this humongous. How did they stay afloat?

They'd landed, the pad on the center of the wheelhouse's roof. Outside, the deck stretched on forever ahead of them. Farah had ordered Sufia to stay in the chopper, but Adem wanted her along.

A wicked smile on Farah's face. "Dangling meat in front of starving dogs?"

So she stayed. Adem's heart in his throat every moment away, so sure they would fly her away and he would be stuck here at the whims of pirates. An elaborate trick—let the pirates cut him up and throw him overboard instead of having to let Jibriil make that hard decision. Later, they would tell the young leader that Adem had died at the hands of government forces. Something like that.

Didn't happen. Adem was taken to meet "Captain" Mahmood, in the wheelhouse with the Dutch captain, who was filthy, unshaven, and humiliated, but in otherwise good health. Mahmood was a living skeleton, some sort of freakishly tall, bony, immortal. Sunken eyes. Hard to age him, but Adem guessed in his late-thirties, but he'd had a rough time getting there. Scars on his forehead and right eye like he'd been raked by pitbull claws. In the captain's chair, he was slumped low, his knees as tall as his head. But when Farah entered, the man sat straighter. Adem easily picked up on who had the upper hand.

Mahmood spoke in Arabic, accented heavily with Somali overtones. A thick stew. "You? You're our mouth?"

Farah said, "He's very smart, this one. Very bright young man."

Mahmood raised his ass from the seat, his voice a growl. "I was talking to the boy! He is my mouth, then he has to talk! Talk, boy, talk in English!"

The odors of the wheelhouse, the heat and sweat and unwashed men, made Adem choke. Held a hand over his mouth. Not a good time to lose it. He cleared his throat, breathed through his mouth. "You can call me Adem."

A big laugh. Rolling. "The first man! Yes! He says it like, ah, Clint Eastwood. A, ah..." Chewed on the word in English. "*Cowboy*."

"I'm from Minnesota. The cowboys are from next door, in South Dakota."

Mahmood leaned forward, his knees moving ever higher. "You've seen real cowboys?"

"Some. They're not like in the movies."

"No, I bet they're better. Movies clean up all the good stuff. I'll bet they're cold hearted killers, aren't they?"

Why the hell not? "They can be, if someone gets in their way."

Mahmood loved it, clapped his hands and laughed. Looked at the Dutch captain, called him Jacob. "He's a real American, Jacob! Look at what we have. You'll be home in no time."

A worn-out grin from the Dutchman. "Sure, sure. No time."

Adem had been briefed. The hostages had been there seventy-four days. The captain and sixteen others. Three had died—during the initial raid, trying to escape, and from a heart attack. The question Adem wondered: Once your spirit was broken down so small, what kept you alive?

Maybe he would have found out had they not plucked him from the hospital.

That made him feel better. His wounds were not his whole world anymore.

Mahmood tuned his attention to Garaad, who had been very quiet. He lurked behind Farah. Adem wondered if the pirate captain intimidated the soldier. Mahmood looked him over.

Farah stepped forward, whispered, "Bodyguard."

Mahmood pursed his lips, nodded. He'd seen plenty of tough young punks, right? But Americans, not so much. He said something to Farah that Adem didn't catch. But they laughed together. Garaad seemed to shrink farther back into the wall.

Adem asked Mahmood in Arabic, "What do you want, and what have they told you?"

He shrugged. "Five million American dollars."

Adem looked around at the faces, all waiting for him. "Is that normal?"

Mahmood, either enraged or overjoyed gave him a wide-eyed look that Adem had only seen on circus clowns. His raked eye was cloudy, red. "It's not that bad, even to you, eh? Is it?"

Another roar. The laughter was frightening.

Adem took a wild guess. "They don't want to give you anything."

Mahmood shrugged. So did Jacob, who spoke up for the first time. "Maybe they never will. Please, whatever it takes. It's just money."

Mahmood was out of his seat, at the Dutchman's side. Slung an arm over his shoulder. Jacob didn't look at him. Down and away.

Another round of tortured English. "This man, this is a good man. An infidel, but a good man. He's no hero. There are times to be a different sort of hero. That's what he is being. I would love to have him as one of mine, except that I'd be afraid he'd surrender too fast!"

More laughter, echoing back at them. Farah looked annoyed with it. It was becoming more clear who was the real brain here, with Mahmood a Blackbeard-style figurehead. It was Farah who spoke to him on the way back to the chopper after Mahmood had more fun talking about American movies—*Predator! Unforgiven! Star Wars!*—and playing the role of Han Solo instead of answering Adem's questions. Garaad stepped up to Adem's side, said softly, "He's lost his mind. The most dangerous sort of man."

Mahmood swung Adem's way once more and grabbed his jaw, scaring Garaad back five paces. Looked at his teeth. Nodded.

"Good teeth. I'd like my mouth to have good teeth. And good clothes, not these. He's American, man! Make him look like one."

And that was that. It was Farah from then on. Back to the deck, chopper blades starting to whirl. Farah told him, "The idea will be to get three million. Fight hard for five. Make it seem like Mahmood is a crazy man."

"I can do that."

"Don't write things down that will leave a trail. Some notes if you need to, yes, but something that a stranger or policeman would not be able to interpret. Everything else is word of mouth. A handshake."

"And all of the details? The names of the company and the banks and the government officials?"

Farah pulled a thin manila folder from his coat. It had been folded longways, and he must have been carrying it for weeks, from the looks. "When you've memorized everything in this, burn it."

He lifted the cover, but Farah held a hand over it. Motioned for Adem and Garaad to get back on the helicopter. Farah wasn't coming along this time. "Wait until you're there. Don't let anyone else read it. You choose what to tell your partners. And, when we meet again, don't use your real name. Think of something…important."

Adem nodded at all this, then climbed aboard beside Sufia, still as he left her. Garaad sat across from them. The chopper lifted off the pad and everything large became small again.

Except for Adem, growing taller by the minute. He reach over, patted Sufia's hand, right in front of Garaad, too, and told her, "We're in business."

She looked at him, his retreating hand, then said, "With devils."

Devils or not, he'd do the job. Didn't mean he had become one of them, did it? He looked back at the shrinking ship. No skull and crossbones. Just business.

*

Lunch, at a fancy table, inside. Water and hot tea instead of camel's milk. Clean silverware. Adem had gained a few pounds back. He looked forward to meals more than anything. Most of them alone. Sufia would come along between meetings like this, but he had yet to get her alone for dinner. She always declined, took meals with her landlords. Fine, fine. She'd come around, he hoped. They had time. As much time as there were ships that dared sail through pirate-infested waters and companies that would rather pay a tiny fraction of their profits to get the ship and crew back than risk starting World War III.

Sufia didn't say much. Polite, but not like when they were talking business. That was when she came alive—she had the figures down cold, and she knew the players better than Adem did. She fed him and Farah the intel she picked up. Who reacted to what, who was getting notes passed to them from outside the room, who wasn't paying attention. Beautifully smooth. She was mostly ignored in the room except for the Western men wondering what she looked like without her *hijab* and modest dresses.

"I swear, it's like I'm back home." Adem lifted a forkful of chicken, cooked over a wood grill. Wonderful kebabs. He avoided the camel meat, but they always had chicken, beef, goat, a never-ending supply, it seemed. He didn't mind eating alone, because with each bite he could pretend he was home in Minneapolis, a restaurant in a strip mall with his parents and grandmother enjoying a night out. His cousins, his older sister, all there, warm on a frosty March evening.

Sufia had made herself small, ate barely a third of her lunch. She said, "Do you always order so much?"

"I didn't have much to eat at the hospital."

"But it was enough."

He pushed spicy chunks of chicken around on his plate. Not hungry anymore. "What have I done to offend you? I thought...you and me..."

She took a sip of water and then went right to, "When we resume, I think you should be cautious with the American." She flipped through her notes, but Adem knew she didn't need to. All the names were committed to memory, same as with him. "Derrick Iles. We still don't know why he is in the room, but he's been receiving notes and calls today, quite a few."

He didn't want to talk business. Tired of business. He had expected a break between ships, but it seemed as if only a handful of hours after the Dutch ship was released, Mahmood leapt onto the Canadian boat and Farah put him back to work. "Listen, truly, I want us to be friends."

A strained smile. "We are, Adem."

"I know you have ways of doing things different from me, I understand that. But then let me do things the proper way. Tell me what it takes."

"I don't think this is the time."

"It never is. It never will be. Is there some reason you are closing the door on me?"

"You assume I had opened one?"

"Well...if not, then I apologize. It was never my intention—"

"It was. Don't lie. Not now. You've been as honest as a man can be until now. I knew it wouldn't last forever." She dabbed her lips with the linen napkin. "You make a big leap and expect me to follow. You *forced* me to come with you. I had no choice. You asked for me and they handed me over. What made you think—"

"Are you telling me you don't love every minute of it?" He had raised his voice. Caught the attention of other diners, even a couple of Canadians from the negotiation room. He brought it down, eased his chair closer to hers. "This sort of work, you're great at it. Whenever we talk about the work, I've never seen you more alive, more vital!"

"The *work*. Not how I got here. You expect me to throw myself at you like an American whore. Like all of us are really American whores at heart, and that's the last thing we are. We are jewels! We are valuable! Allah has made it so. It is men like yourselves, dirty in your hearts, who mess up the will of God. Especially you. Americans. The light of the world. Freedom above all else. That's what you believe. God follows the flag, not the other way around."

The words, the heat behind them, took their toll on Adem. He loosened his tie, unbuttoned his collar. Throat bulging. "I...I really didn't know. I...it seemed...."

What to say?

"I thought you were different, but I was wary. Good thing. Of all people, I thought you would *ask* me. Not send a soldier, force me onto a jeep."

"I didn't have a choice, either. Did you think about that? I had to choose, right then. Go or not. If I had chosen not, then my fate was in the air. I *had* to, and I chose you. If I could've told you face to face, don't you think I would have?"

She pushed her chair from the table. Adem began to rise as she did, but a cut of her eyes sent him down again. "I don't know. This way you got to be my hero. How does that feel now?"

He looked around, raised his hand. "Please, sit. Please. Where would you go?"

Sufia huffed, but she sat. Adem was about to pour out his heart, every contrite thing he could think of to bleed at her feet. Make her see the real Adem. No, he knew better. The Adem he wanted to be for her. The man he wanted to be from then on.

But he looked up and saw Garaad weaving through the tables, approaching fast. Adem wondered if he'd seen any of the fight, especially Sufia trying to run off. But Garaad was oblivious, a sheen of sweat all over him, his new lightweight button-up silk shirt and thin linen pants sticking to his skin in spots. The obvious bulge of gun and the tip of his knife. Not subtle, but better than the whole camo get-up.

He took a seat without asking, reached over for an empty water glass, filled it from the pitcher. Downed the whole glass. Slammed the empty on the table, let out a loud belch. More attention from the diners. Great.

"I did what she told me." He never spoke to Sufia directly unless it was an order. "I followed Iles."

Adem hadn't known about this. Yes, the American had become more active after a couple of days when he had seemed some sort of government token player, never saying a word or even paying close attention. Today, though, it was as if he was the center of attention, all unspoken. The Canadians would stop speaking when a text message buzzed, or when someone handed him a slip of paper. He would take a look, and either nod to have the speaker continue, or he would leave the room, coming back minutes later with either a head shake or wink. Three hours of that today. At least ten times.

Adem said, "What did you find?"

"He goes back to his hotel. I pay a girl on staff to tell me what it's like. He makes a lot of requests—laundry, room service, extra pillows and towels. He's not carrying a weapon. He is constantly on the cell phone, never raises his voice. Definitely some rich asshole."

Adem thought he could've figured that out without paying anyone. "What else?"

"Lots of men in and out. Some of the Canadians. Some Americans who haven't been in the room. Some of these men, all pretty tough. They are armed. I don't know how. I don't know if they are military. Maybe CIA."

"Why would the CIA care about a Canadian freighter?" Adem said it aloud before realizing it. Garaad glared.

Sufia said, "Unless it's an undercover operation. Not really what it appears to be."

"Maybe so. Which is also why they are treating us this way. Lazy negotiating. No movement. I thought it was a strategy. Maybe they're waiting for something, though."

"For us?"

"No. But we can push the agenda. I need to talk to Farah, explain."

Garaad pointed at the leftover food. "You done?"

Adem waved the plate away. Garaad took both his and Sufia's. The sound she made, she must've still been hungry. But not a word. She watched Garaad devour the food. Adem picked up his phone, said to her, "Why don't you take a break? Make sure your mobile is on. I'll see you back in there."

Maybe she was tired of him ordering her around, but the relief at being sent away from the table was obvious all over her. Once she was gone, Garaad made a rude noise. Eyes on Adem. Then: "Don't worry. She'll be eating out of your hand again soon."

"Excuse me?"

Garaad smiled. It stung whenever he did. Something so smug about it. "Lover's spat. But you grab her by the neck, she'll fall in line."

Adem shoved his chair back, nearly knocked it over. Gripped his phone tightly, like he might crack it. "I have a call to make."

"You already paid the bill, right?"

Adem ignored the guy, shoveling in food without taking a breath. He walked out and called Farah, told him Mahmood needed to go batshit crazy on cue. "Sometime around two this afternoon would work."

Closed the phone. Found a cozy chair in the lobby. He rubbed his temples with his fingers and closed his eyes. Repeated in his mind, *You will go home again, she will go with you, You will go home again, she will...*

EIGHTEEN

By the time Bleeker and Mustafa stepped off the boat in Bosaso, Bleeker was in awe of how two American teenagers had managed to make it even farther. It had taken a day or two of planning the trip, trying not to draw attention to where they were ultimately headed. They needed to leave separately, different airports, different destinations. Then, once there (New York and Toronto), book flights to London. Same airport, but still not ready to travel together. Two more flights, one to Prague, one to Northern Italy. Bleeker traveled by train from Prague to meet up with Mustafa at a mountain villa, where they began laying down plans for the rest of the trip.

It had cost Bleeker all of his savings, plus a quickie loan from the local bank, where he had a few longtime friends. One of the vice presidents had gone to school with him in the Eighties. Sure, Ray could have twenty grand if he really needed it. Everyone had heard how tragic his loss had been, how he needed a new place to live. He was good for it.

Not anymore.

They packed like tourists—lots of clothes, cameras, toiletries, all the stuff Americans were afraid they couldn't get overseas. Once in Milan, they dumped most in order to travel light the rest of the way. They needed lightweight clothes for the African heat, something to cover their skin. Bleeker was at a disadvantage. He could never blend in with his wintertime Minnesota skin like milk. They could lay on the fake tan pretty heavy, make him as brown as possible. Darker, but not dark enough. So they would have to say he was a writer, like a reporter, paying them to let him tag along. They could say he was Canadian.

Guns. They couldn't bring their own. Bleeker hoped they wouldn't need to use any at all, but just in case. Bosaso was a modern growing city, but Bleeker couldn't escape the feeling that it would feel like the Wild West. Mustafa said his people would take care of the guns. No worries. Sure, that was something easy to shove onto the back burner. Right.

Next, Kenya, where Mustafa's cousins and uncles lived. The country had been a refuge for Somalis escaping the war in the early years. Many moved on from there to other countries in Africa, then Europe, then America. Minneapolis, for some reason. It was a quiet welcome. A friendly meal, some prayers, and then the guns, both of them given cheap but reliable 9mm pistols. They looked like they'd seen plenty of action. From Croatia, the uncle said. Good guns. Bleeker wanted more stopping power, but he took what was given.

Bleeker's attention drifted with a cigarette dangling from his lips, sitting with his back against the wall, looking out a window as the sun set, listening to Mustafa and his uncle talk in their native tongue. He could only pick up a few words here and there. But Mustafa had already told him what they would be discussing—how to get themselves into Somalia without anyone knowing about it.

One of the words he kept picking up: "Boat". From Kenya, south of Somalia, all the way past the horn, to Bosaso, without being noticed.

Bleeker thought he was laughing a little, right on the edge of dreaming. They'd come so far to be so close to bet it all on a crapshoot.

*

"That's a pirate boat, right?" Bleeker was going to point but Mustafa slapped his hand down. Not even to the halfway mark, early morning, and they were seeing the small fast wooden boats packed with skinny men armed to the teeth. If they had wanted Mustafa's cousin's boat—another long skinny skiff almost like the pirates—it was an easy target. But somehow they skated past. Nothing to see here.

"They're not a tourist attraction. Don't point." Even looking at them was a no-no.

"Shit."

A couple of cousins looked on, laughing. Altogether, there were seven of them. All black except Bleeker. They covered him up as much as they could—big sunglasses, a hat, shirt buttoned up all the way, a bandana around his neck, covering his nose and mouth. But those hands. No way to hide those hands. The heat was impossible, the gleam off the water as painful as needles in Bleeker's eyes. He would sweat pools of orange. That's why he had to wear darker colors, long sleeves. Mustafa and his people were in T-shirts and polos. He was obviously the odd man out.

"We're going to get caught."

"They've been up and down the coast for years. They know what to do."

"Did you ever go with them when you were younger?"

Mustafa shook his head, glanced at his cousins, then back at Bleeker. "Last time I saw Warfaa, there," he nodded towards the man manning the outboard, "we were both, I think, four, five. We left at about the same time. Our families had tried so hard to stay out of it, the war, and then our grandfather, Bahdoon, was killed when he refused to turn his sons over to one of the warlords, a man named Ibrahim. A military man. It wasn't like *Arabian Nights* with swords and genies. He had soldiers and guns and trucks. He stole food meant for starving people. He shot anyone who got in his way. The Americans were here, but they were useless. So my grandmother got us out. She died after the trip, but along the way, she was our rock. It was her sister in Kenya who helped us come to America.

"I was too young. I remember being told not to look when we passed the dead or soldiers or fires. I remember my father and uncles sleeping all day, only coming out of hiding at night to take over from our mom and aunts. Otherwise, they might be drafted into the army. So I don't know these men anymore, but we all went through the same thing. They won't let us down."

Bleeker didn't know what to say. "You know, Cindy's partner, Poulson? The one Jibriil shot first? He was in Somalia back then. In the Marines."

"Yeah?"

"Oh yeah. He talked about it with me. Guess it was his only time out of the country. But he said it was dull. They weren't allowed to do anything. He was there when Blackhawk happened, and still, what could they do? They pulled everybody out right after. As far as I know, he spent the whole time checking in equipment."

"No action? He didn't see the riots? The dead?"

Bleeker shook his head. "He was a guy with a clipboard. But still, even with all I saw in Iraq, and even with me supposedly being good with the Somalis in town, I'm thinking he understood you guys better than I did. He had a chip on his shoulder."

"Too bad."

"Not like he hated them. More like, I don't know, he made a lot of jokes. He liked to laugh with the local Somalis, even if they didn't get it. Or they did, and knew he was making fun of them. That's the sort of guy he was."

"He underestimated Jibriil."

Another pirate boat. Warfaa said something to Mustafa, who nodded. "If they stop us, you've got to be cool. They'll notice you eventually, but don't give them a reason to."

A nod. Then, "Did you underestimate Jibriil, back when he was friends with Adem in high school?"

Mustafa was keeping an eye on the pirates, who were too close for comfort. Warfaa waved. The pirates circled the boat, one lap, then waved back, went on their way.

He said, "Back then? He was nothing. A wannabe. Tried to join up with

my old gang all the time, and I kept telling them to push him away. There was no way I was going to let one of Adem's friends drag him into that."
"What if you had? You know, what if you had let him?"
Shook his head. "Boy would be dead. He would've gotten tough with the wrong man, got himself shot. It would be all my fault."
"Then he wouldn't have gotten wrapped up with the Muslims."
"One of those things, like, it was fate. If I went back in time, right? Tried to do it different? There'd always be something happen to make sure we ended up right here. Never going to change." Mustafa handed over a bottle of water, already warm. "Get yourself full. It's still a long trip."

*

They pulled up to a concrete pier jutting out from a shore of giant rocks, a large cargo ship nearby while many smaller boats came and went around it. Bleeker saw lots of these piers along the way, the deep blue water stopping against the rocks. Machine noise all around. Past the rocks farther ashore, Bleeker saw the arms of cranes, bright yellow, moving back and forth. Cargo containers, bundles from the farm, wooden crates.

One of the cousins tied the boat around a post sticking up from the concrete. They all steadied the boat, pulled it against the pier. Couple of scrapes, then Warfaa pulled himself onto the dock and reached down to help Bleeker and Mustafa out. Then the cousins, except for two who had to take care of the boat and would meet them later. And there they were. Bosaso.

Even after being on the boat for so long, surrounded by the deep and watching the land grow closer, the view from land was even better. Bleeker thought about the lakes back home, how he'd been sleeping on a frozen one that stretched for miles and miles only a few days before, and how now he'd spent most of the day on the Indian Ocean. Cindy would've loved it. They might have traveled one day, when the child was old enough. They would've taken her to Disney World. They would've left her with grandma and taken a trip to India.

Hard to keep his mind on the job at hand with a view like that. Mustafa laid a hand on his shoulder, gave it a shake. Bleeker swallowed, took a deep breath, and said, "Okay, I'm ready. Okay."

On down the pier to a dirt road, the left leading to other piers, other boats, and the right leading over to the larger docks. Warfaa spoke with Mustafa, pointing, nodding, and they started off. Thicker crowds along the way, and Bleeker began to feel self-conscious—all covered-up, face hidden from view. Yeah, he got looks. More and more. He thought a Muslim woman's burka might be a better choice, no skin at all and a slit for the eyes.

Mustafa led. Bleeker caught up.

"Are we heading straight there?"

"Not yet. First, Warfaa wants to get a look at the place. It's a hotel. He can get a lay of the land and we can draw it up. I'm hoping we can do this without a fight. Find him when he's alone and just go."

"After we ask about Jibriil."

"Risky."

"That was the deal."

"No, it wasn't."

Bleeker stopped, grabbed Mustafa's arm, pulling him back. "Wait a minute, are you trying—"

"The deal was that Adem testifies. He answers all questions. We always said it was about Adem."

"If Jibriil is here, we go after him, too!"

Through gritted teeth. "*That* will take a fight. On foreign soil, far outnumbered."

"Sure, fine. I'm ready. I told you."

Mustafa shook his head. "I didn't come here to watch you commit suicide. Stupid! I knew I should've never…So stupid."

He left Bleeker behind, the cousins following. Bleeker caught his breath, sea-salty and wet. The deal had been Jibriil. Of course it had. Adem was Mustafa's problem. Bleeker wanted Jibriil's throat in his hands. A confession right before the life was choked out of him. Even if it meant neither one would make it out of Somalia alive.

A minute or two of standing there, then he realized people were staring back. Talking about him. Who is that? The man with the pale hands?

He sped up as the dock faded and a busy city street opened up a block away, but the cousins were splitting. Fast, left and right, leaving Mustafa alone as a couple of white men who had gotten out of a sedan with blacked-out windows came right for him. The fuck was this? Had his "family" sold them out? Bleeker hurried. Mustafa stopped when he realized, looked back, saw Bleeker reaching for his pistol. Mustafa sliced the air with his hand down low.

Good thing. The white guys, sunglasses, slacks, oversized golf shirts with the tails hanging out, had to be packing too. One was reaching same as Bleeker, but his partner barked, got him to back down. They slowed next to Mustafa, asked him a question. Mustafa shook his head. Bleeker was still a good twenty feet away. The partner started towards him, his hand out. "Settle down, everything's good, Detective. No problem."

They were both tough guys—biceps, big trunks, thick necks. The one with Mustafa was a bit on the older side, Ex-Marine, maybe. The young one, shit, Bleeker couldn't make heads or tails of it. He'd covered his tracks pretty well, he thought. If someone was going to find him, he expected it to be later, not five minutes after they docked.

Bleeker didn't raise his hands, didn't say a word. The young tough guy inched closer, finally reaching out and taking off Bleeker's shades. The light off the white buildings pretty much blinded him. He squinted, tried to get a clear picture.

"If you could ride with us, we'll explain everything. Come along."

The young guy let Bleeker lead, put a hand on the back of his shoulder once he'd taken a few steps. What, the kid was going to catch him if he tried to run? The Marine was doing the same with Mustafa, but all it took was one roll of his shoulder for the tough guy's hand to let go like it had been bitten by electricity.

Opened the sedan's back door. Mustafa went in. A few moments later, Bleeker dropped in beside him. Door closed. Cool and quiet in the car. Bleeker was about to say something—about the cousins, about someone ratting them out—when the two toughs climbed in front, shutting him up.

The younger one drove. The Marine turned in his seat, elbow on the back. "I appreciate you cooperating. You are not in any danger, I promise."

"Are we getting sent back?"

"I don't know anything. You'll have to talk with Mr. Iles."

"What, CIA? FBI? We need their help."

Mustafa nudged Bleeker. Felt like *Shut up already*.

The Marine had this barely-there grin, like he was a bit too proud of how easy it was to grab his marks. "Hot out there, Detective Bleeker. Maybe you'd like to roll up your sleeves."

Bleeker looked at Mustafa. "Sold out."

"I ain't saying anything."

The air conditioner ran full on. Goosebumps on Bleeker's skin. He hadn't minded the way Bosaso looked with his shades on, but he hated the way it looked through these tinted windows, all the bright white buildings muddled, all the people shadows.

NINETEEN

They would take a step forward, then two back. Almost as if the Canadian negotiators forgot each day's progress and came back exactly where they'd been before. It was ridiculous. Even when Mahmood dangled a handful of crew off the side of the boat by their wrists, all Adem got was lip service. Farah held off his pirate's growing bloodlust—he'd wanted to gut a crewman and use him to catch a shark—by telling them that would pull in the American Navy, and those guys never paid. Never will.

Adem fought to hold his tongue when the exec across the table said, "We don't understand why all of our good faith is being stepped on. The offer of three hundred and sixty-eight thousand makes perfect sense."

It was a number they'd spit out a few days back. It was a joke. Farah had explained that, calmly, as if he was talking to a class of kindergartners. It was funny, the way he'd actually started to explain extortion as a simple economic transaction. Adem was beginning to believe it. In the same conversation, Farah said that they would begin with a number of six million American dollars, and that they would work it down until everyone was satisfied.

And here was Three Six Eight again. The main negotiator was too embarrassed to say it, Adem guessed. That's why he uncaged the barking puppy to fight for a while.

He looked at Sufia, taking her coded notes. She didn't look up. He needed her to. He was at a loss, except to say it was a stalling tactic. Maybe she was reading something more. But she kept to herself today, steady hand. Invisible. Adem poured more water. He could barely hold onto his glass already, thick with condensation. He had asked that the air conditioner in the room be turned low. After all, these were Canadian businessmen, not used to the heat. But neither was Adem, born and raised in Minnesota. He hoped his time in the desert would win out.

"Gentlemen," Adem said, speaking loudly as if to an auditorium. "We seem to have a problem with our communications. I have already expressed that particular offer to the Captain, and we have seen his response. The blade's edge is at the neck of these men, understand? I say that in all modesty as an intermediary working for the best interest of both parties."

He heard the older exec sigh and mumble *My ass you are*. The younger kept on, "He's crazy. This Captain can't expect to act like a two-year-old and get handed a bank for it. It has to stop."

"It will, with the death of your crew. That is not a threat. It is simply the truth if we cannot find a way to appease the Captain, all of us, working together. I implore you, reconsider."

The younger one shook his head. "Three sixty-eight. He's making a mistake."

Adem felt the room slipping away. The heat? The situation? His water glass slipped through his palm, landed on the table, a two-inch drop and thump, splashing all over. He caught the lip, a tsunami of water soaking his sleeve.

Sufia cleared her throat, barely audible. Adem looked over. Did she want to speak? He gestured at her, nodded.

She said, "Two point one million. That is the number. It is the only number any more."

What was she doing? If she shut this down by taking a hard stance, they were dead. Shark chum, same as that crew. What the hell?

He used her code name, "Miss Leyla, please—"

"A moment more. I am not speaking for the Captain or for Mr. Mohammed. I am simply setting the bottom line, which Mr. Mohammed has so far been kind enough to refrain from."

The execs looked shocked. The younger one, eyes wide for a moment, recovered and said, "Well, Miss Leyla, I had no idea you had the authority to speak on this matter." To Adem. "Does she? What's the game here?"

"There is no game other than the one you are playing." Think, Adem, think. "Time is running out. We should take a short break to allow time to consider—"

"I don't think they need any more time." Sufia again. Where had this come from? Was she working for someone else now? "I believe it's now or nothing."

The older exec sat forward in his chair, the first time he hadn't looked bored all session. He was about to say something, Adem was sure, but then he looked back over his shoulder at the line of secretaries and other hangers-on seated in chairs against the wall. He nodded at the one named Derrick Iles, who launched from his chair and stepped to the exec's side. Braced one hand on the table, his other arm on the back of the man's chair. Not quite whispering, not quite talking. But Iles shook his head several times. The exec finally said, "Are you sure?" Iles said something else, and the exec lifted his eyes to Adem. It was sudden, unexpected, and the exec looked away again quickly.

What did they know?

"Maybe the break is unnecessary," Adem said, interrupting Iles and the executive. "But I would like one just the same. Perhaps we can ask about the air in this room."

He turned to Sufia, his back to the other side of the table. "What was that?"

"Not in front of the Canadians."

He was speechless. He wanted to take her hand, drag her to the empty conference room next door, and beg her to tell him. But they had to be careful, not let any more of their hand show. As if it wasn't obvious that Sufia had surprised the hell out of him. Farah surely hadn't given her permission to negotiate, had he? And not told Adem?

They walked through the corridors, through the lobby, outside into the early evening, still hot enough to stick their clothes to their backs. They strolled easily, as if not at all wanting to scream at each other.

She went first. "They were stalling. They've been stalling. We need an advantage. It's like they're waiting for something."

"You could've passed me a note."

"Idiot. They expect it from you. They don't know me. When I spoke, all of those eyes were riveted, confused, and panicked. He called Iles over, did you see?"

What, was he blind now? "Of course I did. I think he said something about me."

"*Of course* he did." She shot the same tone right back at him. "You're the one. It's still your game. But you were playing it to tie, not to win."

"If I do that, it makes me one of them."

"Them? Businessmen? Or them, pirates? You are afraid of the pirates? At least they don't lie about their intentions or motives."

Adem laughed as if she'd told a joke. "Neither do I. But no one needs to die. No one at all."

"Everyone dies. Better to die for something."

"Die because someone else wants money?"

She stopped. The expression was definitely not one he would expect from a secretary. There was her superior curled lip, the long blink. "How high-minded. As if the shipping companies don't risk lives for money all the time."

Adem crossed his arms. He wanted to retreat within himself, avoid the manic pace of the street, the chatter, the dust. "I'll call Farah. We'll see."

"Do that. He'll agree with me."

"I'm not saying he won't. Why now? What have I done to make you so mad?"

"You don't even listen! Not one word."

"Sufia..." He reached for her hand.

She pulled away. "Go back in and make the deal. They're up to something. We have to cut them off before they can make it happen."

Same thing Adem saw. She was right, absolutely. But the company was a lot closer to being ready with whatever scheme they were planning than they were to handing over two point one million. She turned away. Adem pulled out his mobile, was about to ring Farah when a hotel bellboy walked up to him. Stood there quietly. Adem lowered his phone. "You need something?"

The bellboy held out a folded scrap of paper. Adem took it, opened it. Handwritten: "Hotel International. Room 14. Now."

He looked up. The bellboy was still standing there. "Who sent this?"

"Iles. Mr. Iles."

"Iles?"

"He sent me to find you, give you this. Alright, sir? Thank you sir." He nodded, took a few steps backwards, then turned and jogged away.

Adem turned back to Sufia, her eyebrows squinched. "Iles? Derrick Iles?"

"So we should have been paying more attention to him."

"You don't know that yet. Let's go meet him."

Adem shook his head. "I want Garaad to come along. You need to stay here in case something happens. You can step in for me."

She was a whirlwind, the loose end of her hijab flying as she waved in the air like she was backhanding him. Inches away. "He would not have asked for you had I not spoken!"

"You don't know that."

"Then why now? I deserve to be there. I am as much a part of this negotiation as you are."

"Yes, you are." How could he deny her? He had given her the opportunity, but the more awake she became, the more she was pulling away from him. "Yes. But we can't risk it. You can't go there alone. And we need someone here. And I need someone with a gun."

She tossed the end of her hijab over her shoulder. Looked off down the street, all the people walking, a few cars coming and going from the hotel. "I understand."

"Please. This will be over soon, somehow. Let me try to end this as quietly as I can. I can get them to pay. But they have to be convinced it's the only way."

"The only way?"

"A failed raid makes them look stupid, reckless. A successful raid means the pirates will be nastier the next time around. The only way, then, is to pay."

"Yes, yes, I know what you mean. I know. But the true *only* way here is for them to fear us. Fear what we can do to them."

Spoken like a true pirate. Adem sucked in his top lip. Bit lightly. He lifted the phone again, eyes on Sufia as he pressed a button, held it to his ear. Several rings.

"Garaad? I need you. Bring two pistols." He closed the phone, put it back in his pocket.

Sufia brushed past him, headed back into the hotel, making Adem regret the day he'd ever met her.

*

The driver took Adem and Garaad to the hotel, one of the newest in town. While white like so many of the other buildings in Bosaso, almost a Mediterranean feel, this hotel immediately felt phony. Prefab rather than organic. Adem was sure there would be a lot more of that, as he'd seen back home, with strip malls around Minneapolis going up in miraculous amounts of time while abandoned buildings sat collecting graffiti and broken windows. How long before that split was obvious in Bosaso?

Very busy, lots of fancy cars, much like their own. Europeans on holiday, mostly. Adem was forgetting the shock of Mogadishu here, so much growth so quickly that he felt swept up in it, no longer afraid like in those first days when he went to sleep in his locked condo thinking Garaad would let in a brigade of young soldiers to drag him back into the desert.

Garaad had turned out to be less awful to live with as time went on. He seemed to enjoy his new wardrobe, especially the straw fedora. As both bodyguard and their own private eye, Garaad was finding his niche. Still had no manners, still thought Adem was a pussy, but he was becoming, well, civilized. Adem hated to use the word, but what else was there? Whichever of Garaad's Muslim beliefs had caused him to sign up to fight for Sharia, they were taking a backseat as he relished his new role.

The driver pulled up in front of the doors. "Sir?"

"Take the block, park somewhere. I'll call you when we're ready."

They got out of the SUV, Garaad already looking conspicuous to the doorman and porter. Like the bulges weren't obvious. Adem had forgotten to take one of the guns, so there was Garaad like a Wild West gunslinger, sure to get them confiscated. While on the way over, Garaad had told him who this Iles guy really was. Took nearly an entire day of digging into it.

"Private security."

"What, like, bodyguards?"

"No, bigger than that. Have you heard about the American mercenaries in Iraq? An entire company hired by the government to be soldiers, but not playing by the rules. Iles is one of those. He runs a company you can hire if you want a private army."

It made sense then. This was worse than if the Americans got involved. In a sense they already were, just with Iles instead of the official armed forces. A private army, accountable to no one, preparing to raid the Canadian ship.

It had sent Adem reeling, trying to sit there quietly and hide the panic. Would they blame him if this went bad? What would happen to the three of them, sent off to do a mission and end up causing a secret war? Garaad kept talking, details about who Iles met, how many men were at his disposal, how much he was getting paid, and how he had this entire city under his thumb. Throw a little money around here and there, and everyone was on Iles's side.

"It is not as bad as it sounds." Garaad, that wicked grin. "They shoot under cover of darkness, yes, but not if it costs them money."

"Good to know."

Adem walked several feet behind Garaad as they approached the big double doors, surrounded on all sides by landscaped tropical plants, palm trees, like the Garden of Eden. If the doorman grabbed Garaad for the guns, Adem wanted to be able to slip inside anyway, act like he didn't know this thug. Instead, the doorman smiled as they both approached, even said, "We've been expecting you, Mr. Mohammed."

Great.

He opened his door with a flourish, and the cool air from inside brushed over them like an ocean wave, instantly chilling, even a little painful. A white man stood inside, hands clasped in front of him. Definitely bodyguard material, wearing a golf shirt that squeezed tightly against his upper arms and chest, but was loose at his waistband. He nodded at Adem. "Would you gentlemen come with me, please?"

The lobby was immaculate, like a theme park version of Africa but with lots of wasted water—fountains everywhere. Tile, stone. A recreation of a grand and stately culture, one for kings. And weren't all of the visitors royalty? Wasn't their need to be pampered the way they were back home the reason the people of Bosaso had these new, less backbreaking jobs? Adem caught touches of gold trim, marble, and ivory. Only the best and the rarest, damn the elephants.

There were only three stories, no real need for an elevator, but here it was, gleaming steel, with a TV monitor inside showing scenes of the tropical shore, the wild animals, the sand, the jungle, whatever else a tourist hopes Africa is supposed to be. Tribal music, cleaned up and digitized, cliché. It was only once they were in the elevator that the guard, so cordial up until then, whipped out his pistol and held it like a pro, not far from Garaad's nose. Garaad's hands went up. Up up up. Like a dance.

"Sir, I ask that you hand over your firearms while guests of Mr. Iles."

Garaad was trying the little bit of English he knew. "Please, I don't do anything. Don't kill me. It's good, eh? Eh? No kill?"

Adem translated, calmly, and the wicked grin slid up Garaad's face again. In Somali, he said, "Sure, sure. Tell him I'll hand them over. Just tools. We've got plenty of tools back at the flat."

Garaad reached for his waistband. The guard pushed the gun into his face, stepped forward. "I'll do it! Tell him I'll do it! Keep his hands up."

The guard yanked the first gun out of Garaad's pants. Then turned him around, grabbed the second. Garaad winced. The guard shoved the guns into his own waistband, front and back. He looked at Adem. "Two guns?"

"One was for me."

"When we get up top, someone will check you."

A digital chime rang, and the doors slid open. A couple of similarly dressed men were waiting. The one in the elevator kept the pistol on Garaad while he handed out the other two guns. Said to his partners, "I'll finish with this one. You guys take the negotiator."

It wasn't so much that Garaad got rough treatment. These were the same as any American cops Adem had ever run into—and they *were* Americans, which was weird enough—but exceptionally polite. It was that when it came to Adem, they were even more polite. They brought him off the elevator with a guiding hand on his arm, and that was it for contact.

"Would you mind holding up your jacket? I do apologize. It'll only take a second."

So he did, and he rotated left and right, and they told him it was alright. They asked if he was comfortable seeing Mr. Iles alone. "He would prefer it. We can keep your friend company."

Splitting them up. Could they do this? Make the negotiator disappear? At least until after the raid.

"Garaad is sworn to protect me. He can't do that from outside the room."

"Scout's honor, you won't need protecting. Neither will he. A nice friendly talk is all."

Garaad looked pissed, like it was Adem's fault he couldn't come along. He wasn't afraid of these men like he was of the Ethiopians, though. It was a sign. Or an omen. Whatever. Adem had to go it alone.

One of the guards, hardly able to tell them apart in their golf shirts and slacks, led Adem down the hall to a hotel room door, partially open. A couple of quick knocks, and the guard announced "Mr. Mohammed."

A cheery voice inside. "Great, great, send him in."

The guard motioned towards the door and stepped back. Adem waited a moment. "This is Mr. Iles?"

The guard motioned again. "Please." Turned and walked back towards the checkpoint at the elevator. Garaad and two of the guards were already going in the other direction, maybe to his room, maybe to the stairwell, no idea. Adem flexed his fingers a few times. He'd had them balled tightly without noticing. Aching.

He pushed into the room, a suite. The front room was dim, a couple of amber-tinted safari-themed lamps glowing. A couch. A couple of chairs. A television, a wet bar, a coffee table full of papers next to a laptop. Derrick Iles was on his feet, closing his cell phone. Confident steps, pocketed the phone, reached out to shake Adem's hand. All smiles. "Good to see you, so good. Glad you could make it."

"Sure, sure." Adem started to close the door.

"Whoa, leave that open, okay? I've got a thing about closed doors. Like a cat. Ever had a cat do that? Open a door just to make sure it's open. They hate closed doors."

Adem left it open. Even better for him, so no problem. "I've never had a cat. Some fish, though."

"Hey, good English. Where'd you pick up the American accent?"

"America." Mess with him some. "I've been there a time or two."

Iles let go of Adem's hand, said, "Please, sit. Sit." Offered one of the chairs as he sat on the edge of the couch, knees bouncing. He wore cargo shorts and a green pullover Polo. A trim guy, clothes fit snugly. Boat shoes, no socks. Some kind of preppie.

Adem crossed one leg over the other, the way he'd seen other important men in suits do. Wrapped his fingers around his knee. "I have to say, I was surprised to receive the invitation. I'm not sure we've met before." Keep playing along. Act as if he was a minor player in the room, unnoticed.

Nothing could get the man's mood down, though. The easy-going nature didn't feel like an act. "Sorry about that. I'm more like a consultant. You've been doing a great job, I wanted to tell you. These guys were smart to hire you on. Otherwise the whole incident could've gone to hell pretty quickly."

Iles was on his feet again. Not exactly pacing. The door to the bedroom was closed, and Adem wondered why that one wasn't left open, too, or if the room was full of men ready to rush him and wire him up to a car battery.

"You want a drink?"

Adem waved it off.

"Or water? If you're a Muslim, you wouldn't drink. Sorry, about that. Do you mind if I...?" Iles held up a bottle of wine. "South African. Good stuff."

"We'll need to get back to the table soon." Adem looked at his watch. "Is there something I can help you with?"

Iles poured his glass of wine, deep violet. He swirled it around the glass, legs thick as syrup. "Right, okay, right. I don't mean to hold you up or anything. Still, if you don't mind me asking, how'd they find you? An ad in the paper? Friend of a friend?"

Adem's legs twitched. He wanted to kick like the doctor was testing his reflexes. "Again, I appreciate the chance to, um…get to know you better. But I must insist. The gentlemen will be waiting for us."

Still standing, leaning against the wet bar. Still swirling. "That's not a problem. They won't meet unless I tell them it's okay. It's already taken care of. We can talk as long as you'd like."

Adem's leg shot out, banged the coffee table. He reeled it in. Breathing quicker. Shit. This man, shit, he was the one, shit. He was the shit. The one in charge.

"Good to know. What would you like to talk about?"

Iles reached down for the laptop, one-handed it to Adem. "Take a look. Tell me if you know these guys."

As Iles handed it off, before he saw the screen, Adem expected to see Jibriil and other soldiers, hung by the neck. Or Garaad on his knees, blindfolded. He thought he had prepared himself for whatever it was so he wouldn't react. He had to keep his cool.

Then he saw the screen.

The whine that escaped his lips was a dead giveaway. Arms weak. The computer dropped onto his lap.

A photo of two men, one white, one black. The black man was his dad, Mustafa Abdi Bahdoon. Holy shit. Both were alive, in a room much like the one they were in now. Same paint on the walls. Sitting on a bed, it looked like.

"Does that mean you know them?"

"No, I'm sorry." Adem cleared his throat. "I don't know these men."

Iles's grin turned funny, furrowed brow. "Really? Is it a bad photo? You should look again."

Adem looked. He didn't want to, but he was busy thinking, wondering if his dad was in the bedroom. Wondering what he was even doing here. Was Iles powerful enough to grab his father from the States, bring him over? And who *was* this man in front of him?

The blanks were filling themselves in. Not Iles's fault. Dad must have come over on his own. The white man had to be helping him somehow, like a guide. Not doing a very good job.

Adem closed the laptop. "I'm sorry."

"That's a shame. How long has it been since you've seen your dad, then?"

Adem uncrossed his legs before another spasm hit. He stood, smoothed his suit jacket. "I don't understand what that has to do—"

"Look, Adem, I deal in information. I know a lot of things. So I'll stop kidding around if you will. Very soon, we're taking the ship back. It's going to be messy and a lot of people might die, even the hostages. No one wants that, but that's the way it is. The company would rather pay me than give one dime to the fucking pirates."

"Please, don't."

"It's my job. But we never go rushing in guns blazing. That's the cool thing about information. If we have enough, we can achieve the objective without all the dirty work. My men still get paid. I still get paid. It's pretty sweet." Iles finally took a sip of the wine, made a bitter face. "Gah, I've had better."

Adem decided to take a chance. He walked past the couch and over to the bedroom door and flung it open.

Empty. Not even a back-up guard. A rumpled bed, some empty wine glasses, and his most recent suit, tossed on the mattress.

Iles came up behind him. "Yeah, no. I'm not that stupid. It was easy to catch them, too. Soon as you showed up on the scene, I had some people start digging. Turns out you and your buddy left a bit of a mess back home. Then these two turn up. The mourning cop and the crazy gangbanger daddy. I knew about it when they caught the plane over. I knew when they tried to zig zag, go off the grid. And I knew when their boat landed here. We were there to pick them up."

Adem tried laughing. So fake. "This is ridiculous. Obviously, there is a misunderstanding."

Iles squeezed past him, sat on the bed. "Sure, you need to do this, I get it. Part of the script or whatever. Here's what we do. You get Farah to give up the boat. I know he's the real pirate captain here. Get his people off, leave the crew on-board and safe. Not one drop of blood. Get them off. We're not out to make some symbolic strike against piracy, god no. We want the ship back. Period. If you convince him to do that, I'll give you twenty grand and let your pop go. You two can get the hell out of the country or whatever. If you can't do it and I have to go ahead with my raid, Daddy and his buddy aren't going to make it. Sorry. Some sort of boating accident."

Adem braced himself on the doorframe. What had happened to him? Where was the smooth? Come on, Adem, talk him down or up or something. "Twenty grand?"

"Well, I'm not a Bond villain." Another sip of wine. Another grimace. "I'm a businessman, and I know money is a better incentive than almost anything. You try, you fail? Your dad dies, and you tell yourself it was inevitable. But toss some cash in? You try, and you try, and you fucking try, man. From what I know about you, this sort of lifestyle suits you. Condo near the beach, nice suits, chauffer, good food. Easy money."

"You don't know me. I do what I do for our cause."

"You didn't believe in that cause until six weeks ago. Come on. I saw the video online." Iles drug a finger across his neck. "Almost lost your head. Goddamn, that was nasty. You pissed off a lot of crazy people, then you pop up here. That's not for the cause. That's someone saving your ass."

Adem stood up straight. "I'm not sure why you insist on this...*mistake*. What if I were to persuade Mahmood—"

"Farah. Fuck Mahmood. What sort of movie did he climb out of?"

"Fine, Farah, then, to accept your original offer? Three sixty-eight. Or let's round it up to an even four. I'm sure—"

"Wrong!" Iles slapped the glass onto the bedside table, sloshing his wine over the rim. "Not even that. Not anymore. This is no longer about the pirates. They get nothing. They either get nothing and live, or they get nothing and die. Their choice. I'm guessing they'll muddle on, survive, and will probably not hire you to work for them anymore."

He stood, came right up to Adem, inches from his chest.

"This is about you," Iles poked Adem right over his heart. "And me. Don't tell your partner or your bodyguard. Don't tell the pirate leader. This has to feel like it's coming from you. Farah's a smart one. He'll understand. This is our little secret. Drop by after they jump ship, collect your fee and your old man, then we're done."

Adem's cheek itched. He wanted to scratch it. Instead, he backed up a step into the other room. He didn't like Iles's body wash and sweat, too sweet and sour. His breath was like rotting vegetables. Adem swallowed hard to keep from throwing up.

"You're not ready for the raid. I know this. We have our own sources."

Iles nodded. "Good, I like that. Maybe *I'll* hire you after all this. But the price on your head after you accept my offer will probably screw up the insurance costs, so forget it."

"If the Captain moves the ship now, we can stretch this out for days."

"No. Nice idea, but no. The boat moves, Daddy dies. Easy. Didn't I tell you this is the end? It's not another negotiation. This is, like, the whole enchilada. You like enchiladas?"

Adem breathed through his nose, barely got out. "How long?"

Iles grinned, sat on the couch reclined, his feet on the edge of the coffee table. "Four hours? No, three. Do it in three. I'll set up the press conference. Three hours, the pirates are off the boat and we win. You can even announce it, act like a hero. Let's plan on it."

How did this asshole get to decide the endgame? How did that happen? Adem found some dignity, put it into his stance. "I'll call you."

He headed for the door. Down the hall. Loosened his tie. Too hot. The guards. Which one of these rooms was his dad in, with, what, a cop? Working together? That didn't seem like something Bahdoon would've done. Maybe Mustafa, the kinder gentler man Adem was embarrassed to realize his own father had become for him. Every day a struggle, working for clowns, following orders, all because he wanted to be a role model for Adem. Admirable. Ridiculous.

The guards saw him coming, and one went back down the hall to another room. Knocked, said something Adem couldn't hear. A moment later, Garaad came out of the doorway. The guard followed him back to the elevator to meet up with Adem, pressed the down button.

Garaad, not a mark on him, as tough as always. To the main guard, "My guns, please?"

The guard shook his head. "What guns? Guess you lost them on the way up. Better find new ones."

Garaad glared. "Yeah, I will. I always do."

The door slid open. They stepped in. No guards following them this time. Adem pressed "L". The door slid closed and the guard said, "You gentlemen have a good evening."

One floor down, Adem pulled at his tie. Again and again until it was off. He turned to the back corner, hands against the wall, and gagged. Not enough in him to vomit, but he dry heaved, a trail of spit and acid from his mouth to the floor. Over and over. Garaad watching from the other end of the elevator. One more ding and they would be on the ground floor. Adem wiped his mouth with his sleeve. He sniffed. Stood.

The door slid open. Garrad didn't move. "Was it a bad meeting?"

Adem walked off, beeline for the front door and the waiting Mercedes. "It stunk in that room. That's all."

TWENTY

A European sedan, a fancy hotel, men with sunglasses and earpieces and guns escorting them, treating them like dignitaries or rock stars instead of prisoners, which neither was sure they were anymore. Bleeker had his suspicions. CIA.

Once in the hotel, they were escorted to a room on the second floor, right off the elevator bank, where more golf-shirted guards kept watch. No one manhandled them. Didn't even touch them. The guard-in-charge politely asked for their cell phones, and they didn't resist. That would have been rude. Another guard opened the room, held the door open, and let them in. It was a plain room, two double beds, almost American except for the African décor and lack of a truly cold a/c.

Mustafa went to the windows immediately, opened the curtains. He tested the glass, tried to open it. The guard didn't stop him. He looked at Bleeker. "It's been welded shut."

Bleeker picked up the phone, dialed the operator. The guard didn't stop him.

"Yes?"

"I need an outside line."

"I'm sorry sir, but it has been requested that you not be allowed to make calls while guests of the company."

"What company?"

"I'm sorry sir, but I can't tell you that either."

He hung up. He'd figure out a way around the phone, give him a few hours. He wondered if the guard would stop him then.

Not long after, the ex-Marine came in, relieved the guard. The older man closed the door, motioned for Bleeker and Mustafa to sit on one of the beds while he grabbed the other chair in the room, like something out of Pier One Imports, and straddled it, arms resting on top of the back.

"Thanks for cooperating. You need anything, open the door and ask for

Carl. That's me."

Bleeker said, "Thanks Carl. I need to leave now."

Got a laugh. "Relax. I'm sure Mr. Iles will come and speak to you soon."

"Who's he?"

"My boss. I'm sure it's going to be fine." He pulled a small digital camera out of his pants pocket. "You mind? I'm supposed to take your picture."

As he lifted the camera, Mustafa reached out and grabbed his wrist. "That's what they do to hostages."

Held on tight.

Carl pulled his arm back, slowly applying pressure. The expression on his face didn't change. Mustafa's arm stretched. He held his breath, held on tighter. He was coming off the bed, dragged towards Carl. Mustafa blew out all his breath and let go, flopped back onto the bed.

Once he sat up again, Carl snapped the photo, then pushed himself off the chair. "Sit still. Watch TV. Don't try anything."

He left the room. Mustafa launched off the bed to the window. Pushing, shouldering, pulling the handle. Tracing his fingers along the edges. Turned to Bleeker. "You going to help?"

Bleeker got up and went over, took a look. "Nothing we can do."

"We can break it."

"With what? And how many whacks before the guards come in? Fifty? Sixty?" Bleeker thumped the window. "We're not going out that way."

Mustafa slapped it with the heel of his hand. He walked away, a tiger pacing the cage. "This isn't the plan. How'd they know us? We don't know them?"

Bleeker went back to the phone, picked it up. Nothing special. He looked on the bottom of it. Set it back down. Maybe it was as simple as pushing "9" for an outside line. Maybe he could keep hitting zero. He picked up the handset, waited for a dial tone. There was none. He clicked the button in the cradle over and over. Nothing.

"They cut off the phone now."

Mustafa stopped pacing and nodded. "Then we call Carl back, take him out quickly. Get a look at the hall, make a run for it. Anyone in our way gets dead."

"With what? Our incredible fists?"

"Adem is here. We know that now."

"Maybe he's the one who sent these guys after us."

Mustafa shook his head, but his eyes were closed tight like he was keeping that thought from getting inside. "No, no, that can't be. That's…it doesn't make sense."

"Your son making deals for pirates doesn't make much sense either. I mean, come on, man."

Mustafa got in his face. "They're making him! It's not his decision!"

"How are you so sure?"

"I know!"

Bleeker looked past Mustafa's face, out the window, now smudged with their sweat and oil. "I don't think you do. Not any more. What you know is what you *wish* Adem was. He could've shot Cindy and Poulson. He could've fought with these assholes. He might be working for pirates because he believes in their cause. Same way that mommy thinks her little angel couldn't possibly have done anything wrong."

Bleeker was off his feet, Mustafa grabbing his shirt in his fists and twisting and tossing Bleeker onto the bed like he was a sack of garbage. Bleeker went heels over head, bounced off onto the other side, crouching, ready to spring.

Mustafa stood, shoulders high, ready, huffing. "Say it again. Say it, motherfucker."

"That's a good Muslim mouth you've got there. Sounds more like Bahdoon to me."

Mustafa flexed his fingers. Pops loud like firecrackers. "Never said I was one or the other."

"Then what makes you think Adem is?"

"You can shut your fucking mouth, trying to judge him. You ain't nothing."

"Least I'm not all talk like you."

Bleeker saw the switch flick behind Mustafa's eyes. From Banner to Hulk, snap of the fingers. He was going to trap Bleeker in that corner between bed and wall and pummel him. Bleeker was looking forward to it. Show the Big Bad Bahdoon what an old Army Ranger could do. Fuck up his day.

Just as some young guy in shorts and a green polo walked it. Boat shoes, no socks. Carefully casual. He took a look at the scene and smirked. "Am I interrupting something?"

Mustafa acted on reflex, reaching for the guy, ready to drag him to the bed and throttle him. But the youngster was quick, hopping back as Mustafa barreled forward, giving him an elbow on the back as he went flying by. Right to the floor. The guy was good, confident. Maybe too much. Mustafa swept his leg, got the kid off balance. He lurched forward, face first to the carpet. Bleeker was on him, wrenched the guy's arm halfway up his back.

But then thick arms wrapped around Bleeker from behind, wrenched him away. The ex-marine. He looked over to see Mustafa on the floor, head pinched between the door and the wall as another golf-shirted guard held a pistol on him. Carl didn't try anything on Bleeker, held him rock steady while the preppie got off the floor, giddy. Clapped his hands. He waved off the guy guarding Mustafa, eased his foot off the door, still holding the banger's head in place. Mustafa sat up, dazed, hands on his ears.

"Okay, Carl, let him go." The guy shook out his arm, rubbed his shoulder. "He's not a killer anymore. Not like the old days. Even that thing in Minneapolis, what, six weeks ago?"

Carl let go of Bleeker. He felt small. "You know about us?"

"Just now you should've broken my neck. Should've been paying attention to Carl and Jim here, waiting outside the door. So, no, not the Army Ranger I was warned about."

A test? A dare? Let this guy think what he wanted, but Carl was too much for him. The others, easy.

"Take a seat, would you?" The preppie sat in the same seat Carl had earlier, hiked an ankle on top of his knee, jiggled his foot. Mustafa pushed himself off the floor, still looking pained. Bleeker sat on the bed, and Mustafa joined him a moment later on the other side.

"So, introductions. I'm Derrick Iles, the boss. These guys work for me. I know who you are, Detective Bleeker. And Mustafa Abdi Bahdoon, formerly one of Minneapolis's most wanted. But then you disappeared from the public record. It took some digging to find you, rising slowly up the ladder at the Target warehouse. Hiding from the police in plain sight. That's cool."

Mustafa sniffed. "They never proved one thing they say I did."

"Shit, no proof? There's all sorts of proof. I've got better detectives, and they don't need warrants."

Bleeker was racking his brains. Thinking about Iraq, not the war he was in, but the second. About the mercenaries. He'd seen this Iles guy before on TV, back when some of the soldiers of fortune got a bit trigger happy with no authority. Mowed down civilians, teenagers, guys goofing around.

He snapped his fingers. "I thought I knew you. Private security. What was it, ah, Liberty Shield Security, right?"

"Winner, winner, chicken dinner. Give him a cigar, Carl."

Didn't expect it, but Carl handed Bleeker a real cigar. Shit.

Mustafa said, "They're not with the government, then?"

Iles shrugged. "Sometimes they hire us, and it's good money. They don't even expect results, I'm starting to think. They're desperate for people who want to be over there, either Iraq or Afghanistan. Then sometimes private companies need protection overseas. Or sometimes some pussy-shit pirates hijack a big boat and the company would rather throw the money at us than the assholes."

"Hard to tell the difference," Bleeker said.

"You telling me you really didn't think about looking for a job with us or the other guys after your tour? We've got plenty of you. Carl here, see?"

The thick Marine nodded.

Bleeker said, "Fuck no. I was done. I was really done. I went home, became a cop. Didn't feel like war, but it felt…natural, like when the chill wears off after you've been out in the snow a while."

"I don't know how you guys live up there in the cold. I'm from Arizona, and it's perfect. The deserts here? Just like home. But look, we know who you are, and I think I know why you're here."

Mustafa blurted it out: "You know Adem?"

Iles did the *kinda* thing with his hand. "Know thine enemy. He's not really an enemy, but he plays for the other team. He's a good guy, actually. Business is a lot like the Art of War, have you ever heard that? Now, I'm getting paid to resolve this. If I do it by shooting a bunch of pirates, okay. Extra paperwork for me, but we'll survive. We've learned how to kill people all over the world and get away with it."

He stood. Bleeker thought he was restless, overcaffienated. Thought that Iles thought he was smarter than everyone in the room. "Most of the time, though, I've got resources that help us solve the problem without shooting anybody. Which would be good right now."

Mustafa stood. The guards got antsy. Iles sat there like he was watching a play.

"I want to see him."

"Fuck no. Sit down. I'm not done."

Mustafa didn't sit. Kept an eye on the guard who had covered him.

Iles said it again. "Sit. Down."

Nothing.

Iles sighed, dropped his eyes, and said, "Okay."

The guard whipped out a gun and fired and Mustafa was off the bed, on the floor, but there was no bang. Some buzzing. Some grunting. Bleeker got up, saw Mustafa rolling, shaking, some wires trailing from his shirt back to the guard's hands, a Taser.

"Enough."

Iles said, "I think a little more."

"Like fuck you will."

Carl clamped a hand on Bleeker's shoulder while the guard gave Mustafa another shot of juice.

"Stop it!"

The guard stopped again. Iles sat, crossed his legs, and bounced his foot again. "You've got leadership potential."

"He wants to see Adem, talk to him, so if you can make that happen—"

"If I can? Hey, I can, but I won't until I'm ready. And you can take him home or to prison or dump him off the side of the boat if you want. But not until I say so."

Mustafa was curled into a fetal position on the floor. The guard stepped over and pulled the Taser's metal prongs out of his shirt and skin, then knelt down to help him up. Mustafa's teeth chattered. His fingers were curled tight.

"You guys take it easy in here, take a nap, watch some TV. You want room service? I can get you some food up here. What do you like? Some of everything?"

Bleeker watched as Mustafa rose from the floor like he was racked with arthritis. He sat on the bed again, head hung low except for a quick look at Bleeker. A wink.

"How long?"

Iles hemmed and hawed, told Carl to check the schedule. He left the room, and Iles looked around, avoiding Bleeker and Mustafa. He said, "I know you just got here, but this is really a beautiful area. All of Puntland. When this is done, you guys should take some time, see the sights."

"I'll keep that in mind."

"It's either that or snow drifts, buddy."

Carl came back in with a smart phone, held it out to Iles, who looked at the screen and mumbled a few questions to Carl, who either nodded or shook his head, depending. Iles handed the phone back to him, said, "Tell them to wait. I haven't had dinner yet."

Then to Bleeker and Mustafa, "I'm hoping you'll be here less than six hours. Might be twelve. Either way, no worries. It could be a lot worse. Try this sort of shit in Mogadishu." He laughed. "What a hellhole. You might wake up without a head, not to mention *terrible* food."

On his feet, reached out his hand to Bleeker, who took it automatically. Funny how you don't think sometimes when there's a hand right there waiting to be shook. Iles did the same to Mustafa, who didn't give him anything. Not a look, a shake. Didn't move.

Iles gave Mustafa a squeeze on the shoulder. "No hard feelings."

Out of the room, Carl following, the other guard manning the door. Closed behind them. Just Bleeker and Mustafa, alone. Quiet.

"You alright?"

Mustafa nodded. "I've been tazed before."

"You're kidding?"

"Shit, you cops love that thing. Almost always justified. Cop stopped us, said we were drinking and driving. I didn't blow one drop. No bottles or cans in the car. Still wanted to search. I said no, and out comes the lightning gun. I was prone on the sidewalk after, handcuffs on, blinking away bright spots, while they searched."

"They ever apologize?"

Mustafa grinned. "You for real? I'm lucky they let me keep the car. One thing I knew, these cops can do almost anything if they stop your car. No one takes my ride. No drugs, no booze, no guns. My ride is sacred."

"Good policy."

"Worked for me." He stretched his neck, grunted a little. "So, that's

Iles."

"Guess so."

"Ready to get moving?"

Bleeker stepped to the window. Darkness pushing down the red and orange and yellow into the ocean. A few lights coming on in the buildings and on the street. "I told you. We can't break the window."

"No need."

Bleeker turned back as Mustafa shoved his hand down the front of his pants, looked like he was tugging on his balls. Then he pulled his hand out again, holding a cell phone.

"They might pretend to check my crotch, but not really. They won't grab my balls." He flipped it open, started texting. "I'm going to tell Warfaa where we are."

After, not even a minute for it to buzz. Mustafa opened it, looked at the screen, and his face lit up.

"So, what do we do?"

Mustafa slapped the phone closed, looked around for the TV remote, reached over to get it, and clicked the set on. He reclined on the bed, hands behind his head. "You heard Mr. Iles. We relax and watch TV."

On the screen, more soccer. Bleeker sighed. Goddamn, what was it about soccer?

TWENTY-ONE

Adem had left Garaad without a word as soon as they made it back to their hotel. He found the farthest restroom, not wanting his bodyguard to stand over him, and finished what he'd started in the elevator. Angry dry heaves. Sweat. Weak. When he closed his eyes, he saw heads on stakes. He saw a mob surrounding him. He saw rockets exploding only a few feet away from him.

"Oh God." A moan before the next wave passed through his stomach. He couldn't figure it out. How could he blow the negotiations without the pirates gutting him? Maybe Dad was already dead. There were no guarantees. And what if he warned the pirates about the raid? Couldn't they move the ship? Make it harder for the mercenaries?

No guarantees there, either. Iles was a businessman, not a murderer. Maybe he didn't have his dad and the cop. Maybe it was all a bluff. If he called the bluff and the pirates retaliated against the company, that could cause a breakdown, get the execs loading bagfuls of cash for the ransom with their own manicured hands.

When he was able to swallow again without retching, Adem left the stall, turned on the faucet and cupped the not-cold-enough water in his hands, splashed his face. Instead of making him feel better, the water was like slime on his skin. He reached for a towel but there wasn't one. He rubbed his hands on his pants, wiped his face with his jacket sleeve.

Took a long look at himself in the mirror. Fine suit, shaved head, the beginnings of a mustache. This wasn't him. This was a character. Crazy to even think he could keep this up.

Who was more dangerous? The pirates or Iles? Who was more willing to take someone's head off? It had to be a bluff.

Kept looking at himself, leaned on the sink. His own eyes. Coward? Wouldn't anyone be in the same situation?

No time to think about it anymore. He would have to decide at the table. He straightened his shirt, his jacket, and stood straight.

*

Before entering the room, Adem heard her voice. Loud, demanding. The usual. No, more than the usual, because she wasn't saying it to *him*, but to another. Adem rounded the corner in time to see her shaking her hands in the air, Garaad getting the brunt of her tirade. She was speaking fast, echoing in the empty meeting room. Adem heard "Stupid to let him…" and "Never let him out of your…" and "Ruined! You are an idiot!"

Garaad took it all with his usual inane grin, hands in his pockets, hat tilted forward just so. But when he struck, it was like a cobra. His expression was flat, didn't change. Grabbed her arm with his left hand, pulled her close, backhanded her across the face with his right. She let out a yelp and he hit her again.

Adem rushed out of the hall, into the room. "Hey!"

Garaad turned. Still no expression. Daring Adem to come closer. The provocation he'd wanted all along.

But Adem stayed put. Not putting his best foot forward. Garaad, still gripping Sufia's arm. She pulled back from him but the bodyguard wouldn't budge. Staring down Adem. Waiting for the right moment.

"She works for me!" Adem was loud but shaky. "Never hit her! Never! Do you understand?"

Garaad. Solid as a rock, eyes peeking out from the brim of the hat like ice. Sufia tried to wrench his fingers off with her free hand. Garaad swatted them down without looking.

"Let her go."

Nothing.

Adem stepped further into the room. Flinching. If he was going to get his ass kicked again, it might as well be over Sufia. Here where she could see him taking a stand for her. Closer and closer. Fists tight.

"I said let her go." Adem reached for Garaad's arm. Got swatted away, too. So he reached again. Latched on, the three of them linked together. Garaad's muscles rock-hard and no end in sight. Adem turned to Sufia. "Are you alright?"

Seething through her teeth. "He's hurting me."

Adem stepped even closer, putting himself between Sufia and Garrad, touching both, nose to nose with his supposed protector. The grin, like a worm, curled Garaad's lips again. He let go of Sufia's arm. Adem still held firm. Garaad looked at the arm, then Adem, then back at the arm.

Adem let go. Garaad nodded slowly, then walked backwards out of the room. Quietly, gently.

Adem turned to Sufia, put his hands on her shoulders. "Are you okay?

Let me see where he hurt you." He lifted her arm, was about to push her sleeve back when she yanked it away, rubbed it.

"I'm fine." Her cheek was swelling. "You shouldn't have spoken to Mr. Iles on your own. Garaad should have been there."

"Forget that. He's history. I'll call Farah for another guard and get rid of this creep."

"He should have been there! Why are you not listening to me? What did the man have to say? What made you so ill?"

Garaad must've enjoyed telling her that part.

"They're not going to pay." He touched her cheek. "We should get some ice for this."

"What do you mean they're not going to pay?"

"Let's go back to my condo."

"I don't think so."

"I'll tell you all about it there. Please, you can't sit at the table looking like this." He put everything he had into that line. Whatever it took to make her see it his way. Pleading eyes. A tender voice. "Please, Sufia."

She dropped her eyes. Nodded.

He led her out through the lobby, out of the hotel, and hailed a cab. He didn't need the driver keeping tabs on him. He told the driver where to go, received a long look from his eyes the rearview.

"Did you hear me? Hurry!"

The driver pulled away from the curb. Adem hoped he would never be back at that hotel again. Whatever happened next, his life as a negotiator was finished.

*

At the apartment, Adem had Sufia sit on the couch while he wrapped ice in a wet cloth. Garaad wasn't there. Adem would call him, send him on some errand to keep him away. But later. Right now, it was all about Sufia. He brought her the ice and she held it to her cheek. He crouched in front of her.

"You'll be safe here. I'll make sure Garaad doesn't come back."

Sitting there, she relaxed, but that soon turned to tears. Not out and out crying. She tried hard to keep from showing how she felt. Tight lips. Hard chin.

"It's okay, really."

"He did what he had to do. I should have kept my voice down."

Adem placed his hand on her knee. "You did nothing wrong. A man should never treat a woman like that, I don't care what god he thinks justifies it."

"He was right to do it. I deserved it."

"How can you say that? You deserve the best. I can give you the best. Give me a couple of hours, I promise, we can leave. You can go back to London. I can go with you. Or Kenya, or even Minneapolis. We can do it."

She shushed him. Then, a hard whisper: "Foolish talk!"

He took his hand away, sat back on his haunches. "I don't understand. What have I done? What have I said?"

She took the ice from her face, shielded her eyes. "How can I leave again? I came back, I honored my father's wishes, I am doing what I think is right, or was, until you dragged me into this."

"You can always come back once this war is over, when it's time to rebuild and make a new country. Even I would come back for that. But for now, we need to run. Please, come with me." He grabbed her hand. Her fingers remained limp in his grip. "If you really want to leave once we're safe, I'll buy you the ticket myself."

She shook her head, laughed. Bitter and sharp. "Why don't you slap me and get it over with? At least Garaad was being honest when he did that. Once you get me out of the country, I know what will happen."

Sufia pushed herself from the couch. Adem collapsed onto his rear, stayed seated on the floor, peering up like he was worshiping her. He didn't understand her at all. A strong woman, one with an independent mind and heart but who was loyal to a tyrannical father and an army of female-hating thugs.

She kept on. "You'll swear I'm free to choose, but you'll say the time isn't right. That I should stay another few weeks. Then you will keep pushing me to act more like them. To wear what they wear. To go to pubs like they do. Brainwashing me, that's what you'll do."

"I swear I won't."

"See? Already with the swearing." She crossed her arms. "You think you know what's best for me, but you do not."

Adem climbed up from the floor. He pointed to the cloth full of ice, and Sufia lifted it to her cheek again.

He said, "Then we'll do it your way. We need to get away from here, away from Garaad and the pirates and Derrick Iles, but you tell me where we can go. I'll follow you anywhere."

"Anywhere?"

She had him. Would he go back to Mogadishu for her? Rejoin the cause?

He said, "Anywhere safe."

Adem expected the withering laugh again. A sneer. Anything. But instead he saw a flicker of fear in her eyes. Of what? Of failure? Running away?

She said, "Egypt."

"Yeah?"

"We can go to Cairo. Would you go to Cairo with me?"

He nodded. "Yes, yes, I would. We can do that."

"From there, maybe Dubai. Maybe. I don't know. I have to think."

Adem's heart beat harder, faster. He could do this. He could save his dad and Sufia and and and...not the crew of the ship, though. This would kill them. But they knew the risks. They knew. They were on their own. Adem needed to get the money, get his dad, and get some plane tickets. And he needed to keep Garaad as far away from here as possible.

Cell phone already in his hand as he headed for the door, Adem said, "Keep the door locked. Garaad won't be coming, but if anyone does, pretend you're not here. If they break in, you can step out onto the walkway out the bedroom window. Just, please, be careful. I'll be back in two hours."

"What if you're not? What will I do?"

Hand on the doorknob. He tried to find an answer. "You go to Derrick Iles, tell him I tried, and tell him you want to go to Cairo."

Out the door, into the hall, phone up to his ear.

First, Garaad: "I need you to watch Iles. Don't let him out of your sight until I call you again. It's vital." Which should keep him out of the condo all night.

Then, Farah: "We need to meet. Send a chopper. I'm coming to the boat."

*

The ship at night was like an ancient ruin, dark and haunted. The pirates were hiding in the shadows, in plain sight, keeping an eye on the waters around them. He wondered if any of them had an inkling about Iles's soliders, somewhere out there waiting for the order. Watching the watchers.

The smell of diesel and sweat and whatever produce was rotting on deck, a portion of the goods being shipped, now worthless, was sweetly sickening. Adem's stomach was already touchy. Each step made his nausea worse. But he had to hold it together. Had to make this work.

Farah led him to the wheelhouse, dark except for a small lantern set on the floor. The windows had been mostly covered with plastic, wood, cardboard, whatever worked. Protection from snipers and night vision. But still Mahmood kept the lights off. Adem thought it was because he was paranoid. One sliver of light, and the magic bullet would find his head.

The Captain was draped across his chair, a leg dangling over the armrest. A pistol in his hand, which he was rotating, over and over. There were a few others with him, half-asleep or either experts at being still. Better trained than he had imagined. The ship's regular captain was nowhere to be seen, not like the Dutch Captain. Adem wondered if that was by choice or if Mahmood banished him. Or worse, maybe the man was sick, or maybe they'd killed him. Adem doubted that, since they really wanted the money. The pirates were good to their word—pay them, everyone lives. If they say they're going to kill someone, they do. Simple.

Mahmood looked sleepy. Did they have to wake him for this meeting? Like he had a say in this? The man's mood ran between manic and foul. Tonight, his eyes were slits. Didn't even try some American movie quote on him. Not a good sign.

Farah took a seat, nodded at Adem.

Adem pulled himself together, fingers interlaced behind his back. "It's time to abandon ship. They are not going to pay. If you do not give up the ship, they will attack. They're ready. We don't have much time."

That got the Captain's eyes open. He sat up, leaned forward, very much like an old-timey pirate. Farah's face was stone.

"What do you *mean*? Your job is to make it happen. You didn't make it happen?"

"Sir…I tried. I even tried talking them back into their first offer. But this time they have mercenaries. An army of them. And they don't care if the crew lives or dies. You'll all die and be dumped over the side before morning. It would be like this never happened."

"No! You go back and tell them I start killing the crew! Within the hour! You tell them! We are Clint Eastwood, remember? We are Blackbeard!"

Adem shook his head. Flicked his eyes towards Farah, who covered his mouth with his hand. He was the one to convince. "We are outnumbered. There are other ships. Let them have this one."

Mahmood pounded the butt of his pistol on the armrest. Adem saw that his finger was wrapped around the trigger. Lucky it hadn't gone off.

"What happened to you?"

Adem's jaw tightened. Thinking: Don't let it become about me. This is not my trial. He said, "I don't think they care about the crew. If you make threats now, if you slice off their heads, if you scream and yell for the cameras, no matter what you do, you will not get any money. You will have the world after you. They will find you and kill you and it won't even make the news."

He'd not finished when Mahmood bolted from the chair, pistol in Adem's face. Adem clenched. Blinked over and over.

"This is treachery! You…it's all planned, isn't it? They promised you a reward. You want to jump ship!"

Adem held his ground, still blinking, the gun barrel now on his lips. "I've done all I can! It's them, not me! Not us! They've called our hand. Now, is it a bluff or not?"

Mahmood tapped the gun against Adem's face. "I never bluff. It's never a bluff."

"If that's so, then you will lose with the best hand. That's how it works sometimes. Right, Farah?"

Mahmood growled, retreated to his chair, barked out something to his henchmen. Looked to Farah, who nodded ever so slightly. Adem caught it too late. And they were on him, one pinning his arms behind his back, the other punching him in the gut.

He doubled over and lost his breath and coughed, the hacking hurting worse than the punch. The pirate at his back kneed him upright again. The bruiser in front of him took another shot, same spot. More clenching, more hacking, strings of saliva dripping from Adem's mouth.

Mahmood was laughing. Farah was not. More punches, measured, the attacker taking his time between each one. Mahmood bellowed, "Not his face! His pretty face! He can't go back to the table with a broken face!"

Adem tried to talk between punches, finally got a lungful and shouted, "There is no more table! They will not negotiate!"

Mahmood waved off his pirates. Adem, spaghetti-legged, lumbered against the wall behind him, held himself up, barely. The Captain approached, bent at the waist, eye to eye.

"You call them. They will come back to the table for you. They will. We will tell them I surrender, but with terms, and once at the table, you announce I'm going to kill the crew, desecrate the bodies, and sink the ship."

Adem's eyes widened. He couldn't believe it. How did such a crazy bastard become Captain? Was it on some sort of dare? "They are done. They don't care anymore. It's a write-off."

Mahmood shouted for Farah, made Adem flinch and blink more. His guts were melting like candle wax. Farah handed Mahmood a cell phone, a throwaway, and the Captain handed it to Adem. "You call. They will listen to you. Unless you need more motivation."

Adem took the phone without thinking. "I don't know…I don't know the number."

Mahmood slapped the phone from his hand. "Idiot!" Spun around to Farah. "This is who you bring me? An idiot? A traitor?"

Farah shook his head. "Give him a chance."

"Oh, I am. I am absolutely giving him a chance. The same way you gave me one." Mahmood lifted the gun, not even a second's hesitation. Blew a hole in Farah's face, his left eye. Splatter all over the Captain's chair. Farah fell into a heap. Silence. Adem was frozen in place, crouched against the back wall, shivering in the heat. Mahmood stepped over the body, told his pirates to get rid of the asshole. And to find some bleach. He swiped the blood, brain and skull off his chair, then sat down. It was like he'd forgotten Adem was even in the room. The two pirates each grabbed one of Farah's legs and dragged him out of the wheelhouse, Mahmood screwing up his face and shouting after them, "Make sure you mop it all up!"

A couple of minutes passed. Adem strained against his aching gut, used his hand on the wall to guide him towards the door. Almost out when Mahmood said, "So now, I'm the boss. You go back, call them. Tell them what I said."

Adem nodded, stifled the yelp in his throat before speaking. "Yes, yes, I will. I'm sorry. I will call them." He didn't plan on doing that at all.

On the deck, he saw Farah's blood trail head the opposite way from his path to the chopper. He sucked in air, slowly made his way to the landing pad. The pilot saw him and started up. Adem climbed in. When they lifted off, the boat looked like that dark, haunted ruin again, no clue to anyone of the lunatic inside making life and death decisions on a whim.

Adem closed his eyes for the rest of the ride back to Bosaso.

*

Once there, he had the driver take him to the condo. He wanted to get Sufia and go see Derrick Iles right away. Make the deal. Iles would help. Where Mahmood would shoot his own superior without thinking, Iles liked to appear the hero without thinking. Made him feel good. That was his weakness.

The SUV pulled up to the curb outside the condo, and Adem nearly fell out, hit the ground running, fumbling his keys. Up the stairs, down the corridor, key in hand. He missed the lock a couple of times, then finally stabbed the key inside, turned the bolt, clicked the handle, and...

Garaad sat on the couch where he'd left Sufia only a couple of hours earlier. Garraad, hat tipped just right, his arms spread across the back of the couch, legs stretched in front of him, crossed at the ankles.

They stared at each other until Garaad's grin unnerved Adem and he shouted "Sufia!" and began checking the apartment. Checked his room, checked Garaad's room, checked the closets, the kitchen, the bathroom, outside the windows. She was nowhere. She was gone.

Adem stood before Garaad, still reclined, still grinning.

"What have you done with her? Where is she?"

He shrugged. "I didn't do anything."

"Liar! What did you do?" Hyperventilating.

"Calm down. Relax. Sit down." Garaad patted the cushion beside him. "Let's talk about your next meeting."

Adem kicked Garaad's boot off his other one. Garaad pushed himself off the couch, slapped Adem across the face. It stung with enough force to take him down, but he kept standing, straightened, and lifted his hand to return the favor. Garaad caught it in mid-flight. Shoved Adem all the way to the wall, crashing into it. Adem's back pulsed with pain. Garaad's forearm was pressing into his throat.

"Listen." The bodyguard's foul breath made Adem hold his. "They took her. Our people. They took her back to Mogadishu, where she belongs. She was a distraction to your work. Now it's just you and me. We'll do what needs to be done to get the bastards back to the table."

Adem tried to answer, couldn't.

"If you need more convincing, let me call your friend Jibriil. Do you want me to do that? Will that help?"

Adem nodded, best he could with Garaad's arm crushing his throat. Garaad let go, stepped back, and whipped out his mobile. Slid it open and punched a number. Adem limped away towards the window, rubbing his throat. The raised scar. What would they do with Sufia? Why would Jibriil do this?

Garaad said, "Hey."

Adem turned around. Garaad was holding out the phone. "For you."

He didn't want to take it at first. Didn't want to know the answers anymore because he wouldn't like them. He would be helpless again, like he was back in the desert. But the phone was hanging there, Garaad gripping it, his hand bouncing.

Adem took it. "Hello?"

Jibriil so loud the phone's speaker sound like it was ripped all over. "Idiot! What were you thinking? I was trying to help you! Why, Adem, why?"

"Um...I don't know...what you are talking—"

"*You sold us out!* You think we don't know? You met with the enemy, then you come to the boat and say there's no money. You bring Sufia to your own condo! You've lost your mind. You brought it on yourself."

"Brought what? Are you crazy? Farah's dead now. What can I do? That crazy bastard shot Farah!"

"Of course he did. I told him to. He was as bad as you, more interested in money than the cause."

A long silence. How out of the loop was he, really? "Where's Sufia? I need her for the meetings. What have you done with her?"

A laugh. "You don't *need* her for anything other than fucking. That's what you wanted. I should've known. I should've said no, but I gave you some room. I thought you'd see it my way."

"Where is she?" Anger rising in his voice. "What have you done?"

"Shut up. How dare you."

Shouting now. "Jibriil! I'll find you! I swear, if anything happens to her!"

"If anything happens, it's your own fault. Remember that. You listen. I don't know how to punish her, but I'll figure it out. And it's all because of you. You couldn't live without her, could you? And now...well, she's got a mouth on her, sure enough. That's the key, I think. Keeping her quiet. Agreed?"

"She hasn't done anything wrong. Don't kill her. Please, don't kill her. I'm begging you."

A sigh. "Oh, Adem, Adem, Adem. You're down to begging now? I'll have to think about this. It's not an easy decision."

"I swear, you fucking, you...I will find you. Touch her and I'll come after you."

Nothing for a moment. Then, "I hope you do."

Then a click.

"Jibriil? Jibriil?"

Nothing.

Adem's hand dropped to his side. Garaad stepped over, took the phone away and slid it closed. He said, "So are you ready for the next meeting?"

Maybe he nodded. He wasn't really paying attention, staring out the window and wondering what awful things were happening to Sufia somewhere out there. And how long it would be before they came after him, too.

TWENTY-TWO

If they hadn't been prisoners guarded by guys in golf shirts with Glocks, then Bleeker would've thought he was in the lap of luxury. He took a steaming shower to get rid of the thick layer of sweat dried on him like a molting snakeskin, and it was as fine an experience as he'd had in any American hotel. He stood there until the hot water ran out. Fuck Mustafa. If he wanted a shower, he could chatter his teeth under the ice-cold spray.

Closed his eyes. Saw Cindy. Saw her in her uniform. Saw her out of it, hand on her stomach, beginning to show. He wondered what sort of father he would be. If he'd been any good at all, maybe Trish would've wanted to have kids with him. But she'd let it go on so long. It never felt the right time to talk about it. He just always assumed this was the life they chose, and that was enough. Until it wasn't. Getting Cindy pregnant was an accident. And maybe that was all it took. You don't plan. You just either become a father or you don't. And when fate ripped away a kid the way it had with his unborn child, odds were that his first instinct had been correct and the universe had ways of fixing mistakes. God, Bleeker as someone's dad? God.

He had promised himself to be a better father than his own dad had been to him. Not that it was a bad childhood or anything. But his dad was the typical too-quiet, too-interested-in-the-game stereotype that rural men slipped into as easy as a warm bath. If Cindy hadn't been killed, if the little guy or girl—pretty sure it would've been a girl, going to call her Linda, like his mom—had been born with ten fingers and toes and her face on right, then Bleeker was going to be different, spend more time with her. Be someone worth loving.

His last chance to do that was to get out of this hotel, rescue Mustafa's dumbass kid, and go strangle the life out of Ja-brill or Gerbil or however you said it. He tried it a few times, mumbling as the water thundered onto his shoulders.

"Ja-brill. Jibree-ell. Jibriil. Jibriil."

Mustafa had called Warfaa earlier, found out the cousins had all split, knew they had some eyes on them, but were able to lose themselves in the sidestreets and meet back up later once the pursuers gave up. One of them had discovered which hotel housed the meetings between Adem and the shipping company. Now they were waiting for someone to show up.

"So, we...what? Go wait with them?"

Mustafa said, "If we do that, they'll know where to look. When Warfaa wants us, he'll call."

"Is that when we ask Carl to please let us go sightseeing?"

A smile. "Relax, man. We got this."

More soccer on TV.

After ten minutes of that, Bleeker had headed to the shower.

The water turned cold. Bleeker let it cool him, braced himself for it to get even colder. Wanted to remind himself of what it was like in New Pheasant Run right then while the sun baked the city outside. He wondered if anyone was looking for him anymore. And once he was back, provided no one threw him in jail, what would he do next? Time to face the fact that he was done as a cop. As soon as he'd heard Cindy had been killed, the law never crossed his mind. None of that "seeing justice served" crap. Every day, hoping he would find the asshole before the authorities or an enemy bullet did so he could make sure the man died badly.

After living with that for this long, and now so close to realizing it, there was no way he could do what was expected of him anymore. He was even tempted by Iles's offer. Jesus, how low did that make him feel?

He climbed out of the shower, toweled off, and wiped the steam off the mirror. Leaned in for a close look. Bags under his eyes. The beard, so much gray in it, shaved down to look more like a Muslim's. Gray in his hair, too. Cracked lips. Wrinkles around the eyes cut deep. All this time he'd thought the Minnesota winters had been preserving him, but he'd been fooling himself.

He put his damp clothes back on, clammy now. Took a deep breath and stepped out into the room, where Mustafa was pulling the leg off the wicker chair.

"What the hell? Where am I going to sit?"

Mustafa shrugged. "Floor. Doesn't matter, we won't be here long. Warfaa called. Looks like some of the players are arriving at the hotel. Soon as Adem shows up, we can get out of here."

Bleeker shrugged. He checked the clock. They'd been in the room seven hours. One of the guards had delivered room service. Decent stuff, club sandwiches, would make you think you weren't in Africa. It was like they'd done everything they could to make it look African while stripping it of the real tastes, textures, and air. Another guard had checked on them from time to time, asked if they needed anything. Lucky the phone didn't buzz. Lucky they hadn't come in when Mustafa was tearing up the furniture. That would get him another round of electricity.

Bleeker said, "Sounds like you didn't need me for this at all."

"Sure we did. Couldn't have made it without you." He pulled the leg free, hefted it and gave it a few swings. It was a front leg, so when he righted the chair and set it back under the desk, Bleeker couldn't tell it had been amputated.

"Can I have one?"

Mustafa tossed it under the side of the bed against the far wall, then reclined on the mattress, one hand behind his head and the other taking the remote control.

This time, no soccer on TV. Looked like a news report, mostly noise except for a handful of Somali sounds he recognized, and some English sprinkled in every now and then. Mustafa turned the sound up until it was nearly unbearable.

Bleeker understood, came around the bed and knelt, turned his ear to Mustafa's mouth.

"They'll come check this out. Make out like you're hard of hearing. We'll turn it down some. Soon as we get the call, we'll turn it up again."

Bleeker stood. Mustafa handed him the remote, but kept a hand on it. Sure enough, a guard came in the room, no knocking. Mustafa yanked the remote and started turning the sound down.

"You crazy? That's too loud!"

The guard said, "What's going on?"

"Tell 'em. I ain't putting up with it."

The guard looked at Bleeker. Waited.

"Iraq. I need the TV loud."

"You're not here on vacation."

Bleeker shrugged. "But I can't hear it, man."

The guard looked about to yell. Cheeks went red. He calmed down, took a deep breath, and said, "Do I have to take you to another room? One not as nice as this? With a blindfold?"

Bleeker held up surrender palms and shook his head. "Sorry."

The guard pointed his index finger. First at Bleeker, then Mustafa. "No bullshit, we clear?"

They mumbled stuff and the guard retreated, slammed the door. Bleeker started laughing. Couldn't help it. Mustafa shushing him, but he was about to crack up, too. They shushed each other, tears streaming. It was…funny. The whole thing. People had died, and there were Americans holding them hostage, and somewhere out there was a bunch of pirates. Just funny. What could he do but laugh? Laugh until he cried. Laugh until he fell to his knees, holding it in but laughing still and then the big, bellowing, breathless sobs. He looked up at Mustafa, mouth wide open, and shook his head.

Goddamn, he was going to make some noise and he couldn't hold it in any more and the guards could come running because he hadn't cried yet. He'd talked himself out of it so many times, drunk himself out of it.

Mustafa must've seen it coming. His eyes went wide. He glanced towards the door, then back to Bleeker. He lurched forward, grabbed Bleeker's head, held it to his torso.

"It's okay. You can do it. Okay."

Bleeker let go. A long tortured moan, muffled by Mustafa's body. Upping the volume and rage, pouring it out. More, more, more, until he ran out of breath and his muscles ached and that was that. Mustafa loosened his grip, patted Bleeker's shoulder.

"You okay? Gonna be okay?"

Bleeker sat back against the wall, wiped his eyes and nose with his sleeve. Said, "Yeah" between sniffles. Said it a few times. He felt his body crawling back down into the cold, the familiar restraint of a true Minnesotan. It was an eruption, that was all. Pushed to the surface, ejected, then turned to stone.

Mustafa again. "You alright?"

"I said I am."

"Come on, man, take a break. Lie down for a while." Mustafa got off the bed, reached down for Bleeker's arm. Bleeker pulled it away.

"Said I'm fine."

"Cool, cool."

Mustafa's pocket buzzed. He pulled out the phone, checked the number, and answered. "Yes?"

Listened for a bit, nodding, answering, "Hm" and "Um hm". Some Somali that Bleeker knew. "Okay". Then a grin. "Okay. He's fine? He looks good?" A sigh. "That's good."

Bleeker rolled to his knees, got off the floor with the help of the wall and desk. It sounded like they were about to make their move.

The conversation got more complicated, so Bleeker tuned out. He hoped Adem would lead them to Jibriil. He hoped to get through this without having Mustafa on his bad side. But if Adem was lying or holding out, Bleeker wouldn't hesitate. Kid deserved as much punishment as his friend in that case.

His sweat on the clothes and the smell of the soap mixed into something like dying flowers. He took in a deep breath. Going to kill somebody soon, that was all there was to it.

Mustafa closed the phone behind him. "Adem's arrived. He had some sort of bodyguard with him, but Warfaa doesn't know Jibriil. Could be him."

"Most likely."

"We'll find out. He says Adem looks okay. Nothing wrong from his point of view."

"Okay. Well...let's do it."

"One more thing."

Bleeker raised his eyebrows, turned around.

"Iles is there, too."

*

TV: loud as it could go.

Mustafa: shouting as loud as he could, tucked around the corner so the guard wouldn't be able to see him when he came through the door. Holding his chair leg.

Bleeker: standing in front of Mustafa so the guard could see him. Giving as good as he got. Barking.

The guard, through the door fast, this time with Carl in tow. Ready to kick ass.

Bleeker grabbed the first guard by the hair and yanked hard, dragged the bastard all the way to the bed. He shouted, "Carl!"

Mustafa got it, already had the chair leg swinging before the ex-Marine got past the corner. A shot to the mouth. Lips split, blood flowing. Carl had to stop in his tracks. Mustafa aimed the next one for his nose.

Connected. Carl went down. Mustafa was on him, kicking his head, then reaching down, pulling out the Taser while Carl's hand flopped around, trying to find it. Mustafa searched more. Shouted, "Just the Taser, nothing else!"

Same thing from Bleeker. He'd already wrapped the guard's hands with phone cord, hit him on the head with the phone to make him stop squirming. Searched all over and came up with the Taser. That was it. "Where's your gun?"

Guard shook his head.

"You're a fucking mercenary! Where's your gun?"

"No, no, really. No guns on guard duty. Tasers only!"

Bleeker heard the buzz before he realized that Mustafa had pumped some volts through Carl. Payback. But it left them with one less gun.

Bleeker ran to the hallway. His guard was already screaming for help. Another couple of guys out in the hall. One on his radio already. Shit.

He heard the chair leg back at work, Mustafa telling the guard on the bed to shut up as he gave him a few knocks.

If these guys in the halls only had Tasers, too.

One went for it. Bleeker gave him the juice. Dropped him to his knees. Bleeker rushed forward, kept the juice up till he was right on the guy, kicked him forward, lifted his shirt and grabbed the Taser.

He got himself turned around in time for the radio guard's prongs to catch on and slap him like a lightning strike. Holy *shit* it burned. Made his hands tighten on the Taser, had to be sure not to pull the trigger. He needed that gun. His other hand, fingers curled, nails biting into his skin. Teeth biting his tongue.

The radio guard's gaze went past Bleeker, then the burn stopped. Guard was backing up, trying to fire his Taser again. Mustafa ran past Bleeker, chair leg ready. The guard fired. But Mustafa swiped at the air in front of him, wrapped up the barbs and the wire with the bat, slung it aside, and kept on towards the guard, grabbed him by his shirt and threw him down hard on the floor beside Bleeker. Held out his hand. Bleeker's Taser. He handed it over.

He shot the guard in the ass. The *tik tik tik tik* noise giving way to the man's high-pitched whine, grinding teeth.

Mustafa said, "These things got three charges on them. Get his and you'll have a shot left."

Bleeker picked the barbs off his shirt. One had broken his skin, made him bleed. He made his way to the Taser on aching hands and knees, finally got it, cleared the wires, and tried to stand up.

Mustafa was behind him a second later, lifting him to his feet. "The stairs."

"He called on the radio. They're already headed up."

"Don't care. We've got to try."

There was a stairwell at the far end of the hall, and they slammed through the doors, ready to shock anyone waiting. No one yet, but they heard noise below.

Bleeker said, "Didn't we just do this back in the Cities?"

Mustafa didn't answer. Checked over the railing. Pulled his head back quickly. "They're going to be coming from both sides, elevator and stairs."

More noise below.

They looked at each other, nodded. Headed back into the hall. The elevator was dinging. They got there in time for the doors to open and see four golf-shirted guards with guns ready. Before they could say a word, Bleeker and Mustafa let the Tasers go to work, then hopped one on each side of the doors. Lots of clamoring and yelling in the elevator and the *tik tik tik tik tik tik* of the electricity. The doors began to slide shut. Mustafa shouldered them open, fell in, Bleeker behind him, grabbing heads and slamming them against the walls of the elevator. The doors slid closed again. Two of the guards were still in shock, while the other fought hard. Bleeker grabbed a wrist, pushed the barrel of the pistol out of his face. Mustafa had grabbed one from a shocked guard.

The elevator lurched and Bleeker found the panel. All the buttons were lit. They were going up before going back down. No way. No fucking way.

Bleeker's guy clamped his free hand around Bleeker's neck. Squeezing tight. He couldn't take much more. He pulled his head back, broke the grip. Slammed his head forward, forehead to forehead. The guard dropped his gun. It clattered to the floor. Bleeker dove for it. Someone was grabbing his collar, nearly ripping the shirt off his back. Someone stepped on the back of his hand. He kicked at a leg or a face or—

The elevator dinged. Third floor. The doors opened. Bleeker turned to see more guards try to rush in. Everyone got slammed against the back wall. Mustafa got one of the stunned guards up on his knees, then standing, sort of, and shoved him against the new wave. They parted and the guy fell to the floor. Bleeker got wise, stood, his foot on the gun, and pushed another one to the doors, almost off. He caught his hands inside on both sides, tried to stay in. Mustafa was kicking, Bleeker was prying the fingers off. A guard behind Bleeker was biting his leg, trying to get the gun from under his feet.

A shot went off. Everyone flinched and pulled tight into themselves. Ricochet. The guard on the floor screamed. "Mu fuwing jhaw, da it, it hi' mu fuwing jhaw!"

He was on his hands and knees, blood dripping off his jaw all over the gun. Bleeker snatched it up, shook the blood off. All the guards had recoiled from the shot, stood back a good foot or two, all aiming for the elevator. Doing their, "Don't move!" and "Step into the hallway!" and "Get on your knees!" even though Bleeker and Mustafa had the same guns as the guards, waving them back and forth, a screaming guard on his knees behind them. But only one. They'd cleared the others out.

The doors dinged, started to close. One of the guards leapt forward to hold them open, but Bleeker shot him in the arm and he fell back. Mustafa was stabbing the Close Doors button. They finally slid shut. The elevator lurched. Skipped the second floor. Ground floor next.

"They'll be there. Maybe they'll start firing this time. Not even give us a chance."

Mustafa made a deep noise, looked down at the wounded guard, now on his ass holding his jaw. He looked weak. Blood drooling. Still moaning.

Mustafa reached down, a hand beneath his arm, and lifted him. Bleeker did the same on the other side. An arm over each shoulder. He'd lost blood, but he'd live. Maybe a doctor could put his jaw back together. Maybe not.

Mustafa said, "Follow my lead, okay? Whatever you do, keep moving."

The doors dinged open. Lots of guards. Lots. All of them aiming.

It was like Mustafa didn't even see them. Rushed straight out of the elevator shouting, "Man down! I need a doctor! Now! He's been shot! Hurry!"

Kept right on forward, all three of them. Shouting Mustafa, shouting guards, moaning guard, onward. What were they going to do, shoot at one of their own? Or shoot at Mustafa or Bleeker and risk them dropping the poor bastard?

"Ambulance! Hospital! We need to get him there quickly. Now. Come on." Mustafa pointed at some guards. "You, you, and you, come on. Get the doors."

If Derrick Iles had been there, he would've ordered his mercenaries to kill all three of them. But he was busy and this was a fellow guard and the mercs, all Americans, weren't going to have a shootout unless they got paid for it.

Two of the guards got the doors. Another came and took over for Mustafa, shouldering the weight.

"We'll get this. You need to stay put." Another right behind Bleeker. "I'll take it from here. You two can't leave. Stay here."

Then he whistled, said to the other guards, "Hey, come get these guys, cuff them or something."

But momentum carried them right out the doors, the guards, Bleeker, Mustafa. Outside, there were a handful of cars—guests, taxis, shuttles—but one beat-up red taxi began making a lot of noise. Horn blaring. Engine revving. Mustafa said, "Let's go!"

He and Bleeker ran for it, ducking low as the guards got wind and started firing. Opened the back door right as bullets slammed into it, came out the other side, barely missing both men. Warfaa in the driver's seat, already rolling even before they'd climbed inside. First Mustafa, then he turned, grabbed Bleeker's arms and pulled him in while his feet tried to keep up with the speed. Then off the ground, inside, slammed the door shut, and went rigid all over as the window beside him shattered, bullet blowing the stuffing out of the passenger seat. Another round cracked the back window. A tire exploded, rocked the car violently. But Warfaa kept going.

He said, "Who needs wheels? I got this!"

They ground along, the shrill metallic scrape making Bleeker cover his ears with his hands. He smelled the blood on his hands from the guard. Swallowed. Plenty of time to throw up on the plane home.

Mustafa pounded him on the back. "You ready?"

"Right now?"

"Has to be. We've got another car. Time's up."

They rounded a corner, then another. It felt as if they were going to flip and roll. But Warfaa kept control. A few minutes later, they pulled up behind a white Range Rover, one of the cousins standing outside. Warfaa slammed the car into park and nearly gave them all whiplash. He was out on the road while Bleeker was still fumbling for the handle. Jesus, here he thought that even after twenty years, all the Ranger training would have prepared him. Now he saw this was a whole new ballgame. He was an old man getting dragged along by young men who knew the rules had changed.

Out on the street, he stretched his back. People were staring at him. He was a white man with a torn shirt hanging off him, a pistol in his hand, drenched in blood. Made him grin. He walked to the Rover, climbed inside, and told the others—Mustafa, Warfaa, and two cousins—what his Rangers used to say to each other, even if they didn't mean it: "Let's go have some fun."

TWENTY-THREE

Might as well have a machete to his neck. Might as well chain him up. The fancy suit felt like chains. Garaad on his heels. Out of the car, into the lobby of the hotel. This one had attracted media. Someone had leaked, said this was the big one. The reporters called him by name.

"Mr. Mohammed, is this the final meeting? Have you reached an agreement?" "Are they really going to pay the ransom?" "What about rumors of the crew being murdered? Mr. Mohammed? A body was seen being dumped—" "Are you really American?"

The last one made him turn his head towards the woman, a famous correspondent for CNN. Had she been demoted? Or was this story actually big news in the States now? He wanted to stop and ask, but Garaad was there, guiding hand shoving him along. Adem resisted, but Garaad shoved harder. Kept walking. Adem looked over his shoulder at the CNN camera.

Inside, more media, local police and more of Iles's guards, easy to spot now that he knew the uniform. Golf shirts, but this time under blazers. To hide bigger guns, probably. One of them seemed eager, coming directly to Adem, taking his elbow, and saying, "This way, sir. Come on."

The urgency sent off Adem's mental alarm. What had happened? Why was the meeting room now set up for a press conference? It was supposed to be that he came in, said what he had to say, and then went to find Sufia. That had been the plan. It was coming together. Forget Iles. He wasn't a murderer. He had no authority over Mustafa and the cop. This could be even better, though. All Adem had to do was deliver Captain Mahmood's message and demands, tell the cameras that Iles was holding his father hostage, and get out. The money didn't mean anything. The money had been a means to an end, but only if he had Sufia with him. If they would take him back to her, he would go with empty pockets.

Several of the company's negotiators were on the dais behind a thick bank of microphones from a variety of news outlets bundled together, some digital recorders wedged in among them. Whispering to each other. Lawyer, exec, middleman. They gave him the stink eye as he ascended, stood off to the side. Garaad stood at the base of the steps, arms crossed. Adem moved as far back as he could, not wanting any attention until it was time for him to drop the bomb.

No luck.

Derrick Iles was already headed straight for him. Rushing, shouldering reporters out of the way, eyes on Adem. Up the steps past Garaad, hand already extended for a shake. All friendly like. Adem took it. Iles pulled him close, ear to ear, and seethed, "*You're a dead man.*"

Adem opened his mouth. What was he going to say to that? How do these people know what he's going to say before he says it?

"*A dead man!*" Clenched teeth this time.

"Wait," Adem, stammering. "What about our agreement? What about my father?"

Iles didn't even bother with the pretense of cordiality anymore. Stabbing his finger into Adem's chest. "Fuck that. Fuck your dad, fuck the money. We're taking that boat. Say whatever you fucking want now. The ship will be ours before we're done here."

No no no. Had he read the man wrong? Was he really nuts? Stall, Adem, stall! "Wait, we agreed. I spoke to the Captain. I don't understand."

Iles shook his head. "It's fucking off, man. You're dead, the pirates are dead, and your father can burn in Hell."

One final stab of his finger, and he was gone, off the dais and out of the room. Adem had thought it was all going to work out somehow. Not the best for everyone, but Mahmood didn't deserve a fairy tale ending. None of the pirates did. Let the Canadians take care of their own. But the rest was supposed to work out. Unless Iles had been lying. Unless Jibriil was lying. Adem was beginning to wish for a bullet in the back of the head. Something to chill his bones, send him back to the shore of Lake Superior from his dreams.

So many thoughts tumbling in his mind, bricks in a washing machine, as the conference was called to order and the main lawyer for the shipping company, Kyle Gabriel, took to the mikes like slipping into an old comfy housecoat, a disaffected rambling of legality and thanks to people who didn't matter and sentences that didn't mean anything, finally leading up to his introducing one of the company execs. Reporters shouted questions at Gabriel—Ransom? Crew? Safety? Agreement? Rumors of an attack?—who couldn't help himself, answering them by saying he wasn't going to answer them, but saying it in the most long-winded way possible, the exec looking impatient but not about to interrupt the one guy who kept their asses out of even more trouble.

Once Gabriel passed over to the exec, Adem was even less interested.

He remembered that Iles didn't say Dad was dead. Said he'd burn in Hell, but not that he was dead. Literally, figuratively, whatever. He wondered about Sufia, too. It could be that she was the one who chose to leave. She could've called Jibriil, told him that Adem had lost his nerve, wanted to escape with her. What if she was a plant? This whole time, setting him up to fall for her in the hospital, then to have her come along. One to play the bad cop—Garaad—and one to play the good.

He couldn't believe it. But it fit. Fit perfectly. Goddamn it.

He lifted his head when the salt-and-pepper-haired Canadian mentioned his name. The exec with an extended arm, gesturing to him.

"—Mr. Mohammed, who generously dedicated his time to brokering this agreement. He was able to speak with the Captain on the ship, helping us reach a reasonable end to this so that no one comes away harmed. I don't condone the actions of those who took our ship, but they have been negotiating in good faith."

All eyes on Adem for a moment. He gave them a curt nod.

And then the police barged in.

Two black men in short-sleeved blue shirts, official badges sewed onto their sleeves, blue berets. Almost like UN troops, but those usually identified themselves with armbands with UN in big white block letters. These men didn't have that, but they had AR-15s. A third man behind them wore a suit and tie, and was calling for calm. He held a badge and ID wallet open and high, showed the room.

"Attention, and please keep calm. I am Detective Inspector Reno of Interpol. Please, no cause for alarm. Please do not leave the room."

More pleas for calm as he and his men made it to the front of the room, stood at the foot of the dais. Reno said to the exec, "Mr. Mohammed? Where is he?"

The man turned his head to Adem. The cop's head followed, and the men in blue shirts climbed the steps, one on each side of Adem.

Reno said, "We're taking you into custody on suspicion of conspiracy, murder, and terrorism. Please, come with us."

Adem took a step back. Was this Iles's nasty surprise? He found Garaad at the foot of the steps. Tried to tell him with a facial expression *Shoot them! Help me! Do something!*

But Garaad was already slinking his way through the crowd for the back door.

"Garaad! Come back!"

He took off, a dead run.

Reno, now on the platform in front of Adem. "Please, come with us."

Adem shook his head. "I didn't do anything wrong. I didn't do those things you said. Whatever he told you, I didn't—no, I didn't."

"We'll explain later. But for now, let's hurry."

Adem glanced around. All the cameras on him. The platform was clearing. Adem found the lawyer, shouted for him.

"You! Gabriel! I need a lawyer! Help me!"

The company lawyer ignored the cries, sneaked glances at Adem on his way down and out of the room. One final look, a sad wince, then he was gone.

The blue shirts wrapped their hands around Adem's arms. The Inspector grabbed the side of his neck at the shoulder, a good firm grip. "Let's go. We'll work this out."

Flashbulbs. Reporters shouting questions. "No comment" from Reno. The only thing he said. Adem thought of turning to the cameras and telling them Iles had kidnapped his dad. But how would that sound coming from a man being marched out by cops? Desperate? Probably wouldn't even make it into the report. Some crazy pirate/terrorist/American shouting about a conspiracy. Also, his mouth was dry like the desert he'd escaped, so he couldn't even get a word in. Stumbled along, nearly dragged by the cops. Reno led the way.

In the lobby, they were besieged. Pressing through. The cops one-arming the guns, trying to hold reporters back, slapping at their mikes and cameras with the rifles. Finally broke into free space and picked up the pace. Adem thought about what would happen next. Interpol, right? Not the locals. They had to treat him fairly. No beatings, nothing like what the pirates had put him through, his stomach still bruised and aching over it. None of that. Extradition? Maybe the Americans were waiting for him. A ride back home. But American prison? Guantanamo Bay? It all ended badly. He could strike a deal. Give up Jibriil and Iles and Rockstar Muhammad and the whole goddamned lot of them. He really had to pee. He was clutching. But he really had to go.

Some of Iles's guards were putting on a show, standing in front of the doorway with their pistols drawn, held down at their sides, trigger finger straight along the side of the frame. Why would they do that? But as Reno and his prisoner approached, they pushed the doors open. Always happy to assist the cause of law and order, of course. They were outside. Two vehicles waiting. The first, a white paneled minivan ahead, and Adem saw that Garaad was inside, his face pressed against the window of the passenger seat, almost like he was unconscious. A little closer, and Adem saw the pulped eye, nearly swollen shut. A fat lip. A missing tooth. Blood. More blue shirts climbing in, closing the door.

The second vehicle was a white Range Rover, two men in the back, one white. Yes, had to be an American. He would listen. He had to. Reno headed for the driver's side while the cops pushed him to the passenger side. Opened the door for him, laid a hand on his head and helped him in. But not before Adem got a half-decent look at the other man in the backseat.

"Dad?"

But then shouting from the hotel entrance, Derrick Iles running out the doors followed by his guards. "Stop! Don't let them leave! Fake cops! Fake fucking cops!"

This man Reno in the driver's seat said, "Get down!"

Adem was transfixed. He watched Iles, flailing, shouting, as his mercenaries lifted their pistols with military precision and took aim. Two of the blue shirts jumped onto the Rover's runners. At the last second, Adem ducked. Pistol shots. Windows cracking. The blue shirts returned fire. Engine roaring. Jerked Adem back in the chair. His arms over his head.

The white man in the back started yelling, "Wait! The van! Wait for the van! We need the other guy!"

The driver said, "We have to go! Leave it!"

"Wait for them!"

Adem lifted his eyes enough to peek in the rearview. The blue shirts by the van were firing their rifles, one taken down by pistol fire. Iles's guards swarmed the van, forced the other blue shirt to the ground.

The white man was watching too. "Shit! Shit! No! He was—I needed—Shit!" He reached into the front seat and grabbed a handful of Adem's suit, jerked him hard. "Say he did it! Come on! Your friend, Jibriil! Say it!"

His dad had latched on to the man's arms, trying to break him from Adem. "That wasn't him! I swear! That wasn't Jibriil!"

Adem a rag doll between them. The driver was barely in control of the Rover. Every corner felt like an imminent rollover, but he somehow righted it with a violent shake and kept on at warp speed, the two cops still clinging to the sides.

Adem tried to get a word in, the coat tight against his throat. "It's not...not Jibriil. I swear, please. It's not!"

Dad: "It wasn't him!"

Adem: "It wasn't him!"

The look in his eyes. Revenge. The only thing that mattered. Adem knew then this was the woman cop's husband or boyfriend or something. Had to be. Why else would his blood boil like that?

Dad finally got the man's arms free. "Ray, no, Ray, it wasn't him. Calm down!"

The driver slowed, said, "We're safe now. But we lost Wiil and Ali." Hard breaths. Then, "What have we done?"

His dad reached both arms around Adem's seat, embraced him as best he could. "We were all willing to sacrifice. And we got him. Praise God, we got him."

Adem couldn't help but smile. He reached for his father's hand, gave it a hard squeeze. "Thank you. Oh God, thank you."

TWENTY-FOUR

The African teenager coming out of the hotel wore a summer shirt, a fedora, and was already running at a good clip when the two cousins posing as police stopped him. Mustafa said, "He's the one that was with Adem just now."

That was all it took. Bleeker climbed out of the Rover while Mustafa tried to pull him back in. Had to be Jibriil. Had to be. Single-minded. Bleeker got to him as he tried to shamble away from the cousins and gave him a vicious crack on the head with the butt of his pistol. He went down. Bleeker straddled him, turned him over, and punched the living shit out of him. Nose, teeth, eye, jaw. Rained down his right fist over and over. The cousins stood back, had no idea what to do. Same with the doorman and Iles's guards. The media cameras immediately swung around, red lights blazing on all of them. The cousins lifted their guns, shouted at the cameramen and the journalists, scattered them back into the hotel or out into the streets while Bleeker kept punching, finally dragged off the kid by Mustafa, dragged back to the Rover. The cousins lifted the teenager by his armpits. He was woozy, dripping blood. They led him to the van that had met them on the way to the hotel.

Warfaa had gone inside, undercover as an Interpol agent, with two fake cops. These two had stayed outside. Another couple of cousins were somewhere else in the city, preparing for the next step. The whole plan was simply to get Adem and Jibriil into the vehicles and get out of there before anyone realized what had happened. But seeing the arrogant bastard trying to escape, Bleeker had to...well, had to do *something*. The cousins were more than capable of handling it, but Bleeker didn't want to watch anymore. He'd heard of Jibriil shooting Cindy secondhand. He'd heard about the recruitment of the Minneapolis Somalis. He'd seen Adem on a laptop screen negotiating for pirates. He was tired of letting others handle what should have been *his*.

So yeah, it was his turn.

Then Warfaa came out with Adem, got him into the Rover. Then Iles figured it out and started a firefight. Then Warfaa and his cousins got the Rover away, but the van had remained. And Bleeker watched his chance at revenge fade behind them.

Until Adem and Mustafa told him the boy he'd beaten so severely wasn't Jibriil anyway.

Later, after dumping the Rover and making their way to a warehouse where the cousins had set up a temporary rest stop, Adem explained who Garaad was, why he was in the picture. Explained how Jibriil was now an officer with the ragtag army in Mogadishu.

But it wasn't Bleeker's party. Mustafa and Adem, a big embrace as soon as they could all take a moment to breathe again, the kid asking about his mom, other family and friends, Mustafa making fun of the suit, the shaved head. Bleeker didn't think Adem seemed the murdering type. Definitely not the soldiering type. He waited at the door, looking out into the dark, listening to the small talk. He finally shook his head and let out the breath he was holding. He marched up to Adem.

"You were in the car that night in New Pheasant Run. You swear you didn't fire a shot? Not a single shot?"

Adem raised his palms. Eyes wide. "I didn't even touch a gun, I promise! I didn't know he had a gun! I pleaded with him to let it go, to leave the police alone. But I couldn't stop him. I wanted to, but he didn't listen. I'm sorry. The poor woman. I'm so sorry."

Bleeker cut him off with a growl. "Why? Why did you come here? What's all this about?"

A shrug. He'd seen the same shrug from many Somali teenagers. Hell, he'd seen it from plenty of Hispanic, Nepalese, and white teenagers, too. As if the only answer to any question anymore was *I don't know*.

Adem said, "He was my friend. I...it was something new. I needed to know if it was real."

Mustafa said, "So how about it?"

Adem shook his head. "It's not like they're wrong about everything. But they're doing it the wrong way. That's the hardest thing to get your head around. Why would they do what they do to other people? Every little thing. Killers and sadists telling people how to live or something terrible will happen to them."

Bleeker snorted. "Whole fucking religion."

Adem turned to Bleeker, finding some energy. "No, it's not. Not at all. It's...like, Sufia. I met this girl, see? She was great. I thought she was, anyway. I don't know. She's brilliant. She went to school in London, and she knows English and Arabic and Somali like me, but also French and

Portuguese. And she's strong, you know? Sort of like a feminist, something like that, but she's a believer. And she's loyal. And she wants them, those boys in the army, her whole family, she wants them to be better."

"That's not going to happen."

"Not in a *week*. Not in a year. Maybe not ten years. But, who knows, right?"

Bleeker grinned. "Sounds to me like you want to get laid."

Mustafa backhanded Bleeker's shoulder. Not hard, but enough. "Don't."

Nothing else to say for a long moment. Dark in the warehouse except for a couple of small kerosene lamps floating around the vehicles as the remaining cousins checked for bullet holes. Warfaa was on the phone. Bleeker couldn't pick up the entire conversation, but the tone and the tears told him he was letting his family know that they had lost two men. Mustafa's cousins, but probably Warfaa's brother, uncle, or nephew. All to help Mustafa, a man Warfaa hadn't spoken to in decades. It left Bleeker feeling tired, like all his vengeance wasn't worth the price these others were paying.

Mustafa said, "Adem, is the girl in town? Is she going to be alright?"

"Gone." Cleared his throat. "I think Jibriil's men took her back. Or she left on her own. I don't know. That's the worst part."

Bleeker said, "You'll meet a good one back home. Have some fun first, don't get so serious."

"You think love is about fun? Is that why I feel like my stomach is full of bile? Because it's fun?" Adem, in Bleeker's face. Surprised him. He shoved his hands in his pockets and let the kid go on. "She's special. She's good. I have to know if we had a chance together."

"You're talking about going back to Mogadishu?"

"If she's there, you know. All I need to do is ask."

Mustafa said, "No way. No, we're not going there. They already tried to cut your head off once."

"You'll be with me this time"

"Who said?"

"That's why you're here, right? You want to help me?"

Mustafa got in Adem's face, reached up and loosened the fancy tie that complemented the fancy suit. He spoke softly, but hard. "I am here. To take. You. Home. Period."

Adem blinked. More. Then said, "What about Jibriil?"

"He made his choice. We should go."

Adem stepped back, rolled his shoulders and fixed his suit, slipped his tie flush to his collar. "I'm going to find Sufia. You can go home without me."

Bleeker heard Mustafa's breathing, growing louder. His back muscles tightened through the shirt, relaxed. "Ungrateful. What was about to happen back there at the hotel? Who was that shadowing you, the one Ray beat up? Should I take you back, drop you off with Derrick Iles?"

"I'm *grateful*, don't you see? I am. I am so happy to see you. But it's not that easy. I can't leave her. And, and, Jibriil, you can't leave him. It's not—"

Mustafa didn't even let him finish before unleashing, full volume: "I can and I will!" Waited for Adem to shut up. "We're driving out of here tonight and flying home tomorrow. We'll find an American Embassy and sort out your passport. That's the way it is. I will *not* tell your mother that I had you, saved you, and then let you go, like some fish or something."

"I'm not leaving!"

"You fucking well are!"

Bleeker said, "Adem?"

He turned. Maybe a lot of bluster in the kid, but he was scared.

Bleeker said, "I'll go with you. Back to Mogadishu."

"Just you?"

Shrug. "I want to talk to your friend. So I'll go with you."

Mustafa stepped between Bleeker and Adem, leaning in close, whispering to the cop, "What are you doing? You can't."

"I told you when I signed up. I've got to. Same as he's got to find this woman."

"You want me to fly home empty handed?"

Bleeker tried to grin. Not much to it. "I don't want you to go home at all. Not yet."

Mustafa turned his head, looked at Adem over his shoulder. Then back to Bleeker. "You're white. Very white."

"I thought we were done with that."

"I didn't mean your skin."

Mustafa walked off, began speaking Somali to his cousin Warfaa. It got loud. It got animated, hands waving, stabbing the air. Mustafa angrier and angrier, but in the end it seemed he won out over Warfaa, who stalked off, talked to the cousins. Solemn nods. Time to pack up.

But Bleeker heard Adem sigh. He turned to the kid. "What?"

Adem laughed. "Dad told him we're going to Mogadishu."

TWENTY-FIVE

"Bring him out." The guard waved his hand as he said it. He looked young, maybe nineteen, but ancient compared to the boys around him. Some hadn't even reached puberty. They all handled their guns as if they'd been trained from birth.

It had taken them four days to get here, finally, to the outskirts of Mogadishu. Plenty of trouble along the way—flat tire, questions about the white man (told some he was a holy man from Turkey, others he was a reporter, still others he was a prisoner being escorted to his beheading), sickness, lack of water. They had guns, at least one apiece. Had to hide them carefully in order to avoid the soldiers taking them. They had money, had to have money, in order to pay off so many men along the way. They had gas. Lost some of it to bandits, others who stopped the Rover, searched it, never telling them exactly what it was the men found worth seeking. Humiliated, tired, dirty, irate with each other, but here they were.

The guard said it again. Then in English, as if they hadn't heard him. Bleeker sat in the back between Mustafa and Warfaa. Mustafa opened his door, slid out, and took Bleeker by the arm. Pulled him. Bleeker fought back, but Warfaa yelled at him, pushed his head. Kept saying, "Out! Out! Out!"

One more push and Bleeker fell to the ground. The boys with guns laughed. Warfaa kicked him. "Up! Up!"

Mustafa helped Bleeker to his feet. The guards looked at him the same way they looked at camels. They recognized Adem, sitting in-between the cousins up front. They clamored around, calling out for "Mr. Mohammed", like he was a TV star. Some of the young men climbed onto the hood of the Rover. "It's him! Look, it really is."

They hadn't expected that. But once it happened, they played it up, Adem smiling for the soldiers, talking to them. Had to have seen him on TV, or online. The negotiator who stood up to the Americans! Well, the

Canadians, anyway. And he was hauled off in handcuffs, only to escape in a firefight with American mercenaries! Yes! A folk hero in the making.

Soldiers put their hands on the windows, and Adem pressed his palms against the opposite side. Three, four, five, six times.

The guard examining Bleeker didn't have a reason to do it. He just wanted to. Bleeker knew by the way this guy circled him, sniffed him. Bullshit stuff.

Mustafa finally said, "He's from the Canadian ship. Mr. Mohammed has brought back a prize for the men."

The teenage leader smiled. "Okay. You leave him here?"

"We take him. He goes to Jibriil."

"No, is okay. We take him to Jibriil. You leave him here."

Mustafa had a blade at the kid's throat before he had a chance to make a threat. All the others, starstruck by Adem, slowly took notice, turned to watch. The guard and Mustafa, eye to eye, tip of the knife at the guard's throat.

"You want credit, get your own prisoner, jackass." Mustafa, unwavering.

The guard's eyes were wide, unblinking. A few moments passed, Mustafa smiled, laughed. Let his arm droop. The guard knocked the blade down with a weak elbow, embarrassed but defiant. "Go on, go on."

Warfaa manhandled Bleeker into the backseat again. They got in on both sides of him. The young soldiers clambered off the truck but stood close around it, mesmerized, making it difficult for the driver to navigate. But he steered through, back onto the road. Desert finally gave way to modern buildings, pavement, greenery, and smoke that carried both the smell of death and spices.

They drove slowly, not wanting any more attention than they'd already attracted. Nearly there. Only a vague idea what to do once they arrived.

"We'd better hurry," Bleeker said. "Those guys are going to blow our cover. I know it."

Chuckles around the rover. Mustafa was the one who said, "They've known almost since we started. All the bribe money? Soon as we had driven away, they were on their mobiles, telling Jibriil where we were."

"So we never had a chance?"

"I don't think he knows I'm here, and he sure as hell doesn't know what to make of you. So all these boys could tell him is that Adem is returning with a carload of protection and a white guy."

"Will they be waiting for us?"

"They think we're coming from the previous checkpoint. But we're going to circle the city, try sneaking in. That won't buy much time, but enough."

"Enough for what?"

Mustafa put his finger to his lips. That was that.

The driver took a sudden left and sped up on a vacant road leading back into the wild.

*

When they stopped again, hours later, it was behind a building miles from the soldiers' camp. Adem wasn't sure he would be able to navigate from here, a part of the city he'd never seen before. It took a pair of binoculars and twenty minutes to find some landmarks and build a map in his head. He should've been scared out of his mind, he knew, but was instead excited. Thoughts of Sufia, waiting for him to come and take her away. They could hit Cairo later. First, Minneapolis. She would enjoy the lakes, the woods, the art. It sure as hell wasn't Somalia, but the expatriates somehow made it work, Little Mogadishu in much better shape than the real thing.

They were all out of the Rover, sunset coming fast, beginning to pick up eyes watching from alleys and windows. Adem buttoned his suit coat, straightened the knot on his tie, and cleared his throat. The men turned to him. He didn't exactly know what to say, but this was all about him. Him and Bleeker. And they would all die for what these two wanted if they had to.

"I'm going to find Sufia. I'll go alone. Jibriil is looking for me, so if he finds me, I don't want to hold you up."

His dad shook his head. "I have to come with you. I can't let you out of my sight."

"What good is this if you come? He catches you, he'll kill you. He'll know what's going on."

"Then why are we even here? What's the point?"

"Just...I didn't think about that. But you can't...I want Sufia out of this. That's all."

"Then tell me what she looks like. I'll go find her."

"I can't take that chance. You don't know her. I have to be the one to ask her. It's complicated."

Dad looked at Warfaa. Both nodded one time. Warfaa stepped over to Adem and took him by the arm. "Back in the truck."

Adem snatched his arm free. "What are you talking about?"

"You have to stay here. You can't go in there alone, and we've got work to do."

Warfaa took Adem's arm again, pulled him towards the Rover. Adem tried to snatch it back again but Warfaa had a better grip. Adem said, "No!" Then louder and louder. Then he planted his feet, tried to loosen the grip with his free hand. Went limp. Went spastic. Shouting, crying. On the ground. Warfaa leaned over and slapped him on the face. Again and again until Adem got it together. Warfaa helped him to his feet, then to the back of the Rover. Helped him inside. Closed the door.

Dad opened the opposite door, leaned inside. "Listen, okay? Listen to me. I can't let you go. I came all this way because of this shit you pulled. I'm not going to let you die here. You're going home."

Adem stared straight ahead, sniffing.

"If I can find your girl, I will, I promise. But if not, we've got to leave. We have to get Jibriil and leave."

No response.

"For fuck's sake, boy, I'm willing to die for you! That white cop with me is willing to die for you! Jibriil killed his woman, and he's still here for you."

Adem swallowed hard. Turned his head away.

"I've got to go." Dad grabbed his shoulder, gave it a squeeze. Adem stared out the opposite window, sniffing.

Dad closed the door. Blinked away tears. Swallowed anger. Warfaa told the driver to watch Adem, and to drive the hell out of there if anyone got too close, especially the soldiers. Drive for the border, clear across the desert, and get the kid on a plane. The other men huddled, talked it out.

"You and Ray." Dad lifted his chin at Warfaa. "Go find Jibriil. He won't know you like he does me. And Ray, cover your face or something. You're target practice here. Dawit and I will go talk to some women, see if they know Sufia. As soon as you get Jibriil, call us and we're done. That's all there is to it. Back to the truck."

Dawit spit on the ground, licked his teeth, and said, "Shouldn't we pray first?"

Warfaa turned to Adem's dad. His decision.

He said, "No."

And started walking into town.

*

Warfaa let Bleeker use his headscarf to cover his face. Helped him fashion it the way the soldiers wore it. Eyes only. Then they split from Mustafa and Dawit and made their way through the streets like they belonged there. Burned out buildings, people in the streets covered in dust, as if they'd been digging in the ruins, trying to rescue their belongings. Some stalls were still open, some storefronts intact but worse for wear.

Adem had given them a general direction to follow, but once in the streets they lost their sense of direction—the sights and smells and random pops of gunfire overwhelming, especially contrasted against the deep blue sky. Above, a painting. Below, a morgue.

Warfaa led them through streets, then through alleys, trying to keep out of sight. They came across a news crew at one point, surprised they were in the city. BBC, it looked like. Doing hit and run spot pieces, avoiding the boys with guns. All Bleeker had heard led him to believe the capital was a wasteland, but hey, look, *life* all over. They either chose not to leave, couldn't leave, or showed up to see for themselves. But they were the exceptions. No reason to ask himself "Why Minneapolis?" anymore. After living through something that did this sort of damage to the city, of course they'd want someplace cold. Someplace serene. Frozen in place.

Warfaa rounded the next corner, then whiplashed into Bleeker, stepping on his feet. Seethed, "Get back! Get back!" Bleeker retreated, flat against the wall. Warfaa too.

"Soldiers. Ten or more. Backtrack."

Down the alley again, not even getting to the end before hearing the unafraid, barking laughter of more teenage soldiers. Shit. Looking right at them. A handful. Two in full camo garb with their faces covered by the trademark red-and-white checkered scarf. Another shirtless. The others in everyday shirts you could pick up at Wal Mart back home. They stopped, stared.

Warfaa spoke up. Something about Jibriil. And "prisoner". So much easier to understand the language in New Pheasant Run when he asked them to repeat it and they peppered sentences with English phrases.

One of the covered faces waved his hand towards Bleeker. "But he's got a gun."

Of course. He knew that phrase. The one time it would've been better not to...

Warfaa said something else. Bleeker was guessing at this point. What would make the most sense? *It's not loaded. He's Mr. Mohammed's prisoner. The gun is just a disguise.*

Or something.

The soldiers weren't looking anymore convinced. The shirtless one lifted his rifle to his shoulder.

Right before he fired, he said something in Somali that Bleeker thought sounded an awful lot like, "Bullshit."

TWENTY-SIX

Fifteen minutes. Twenty. Twenty-five. Adem climbed out of the Rover.

"Where are you going? You're staying here."

Adem shut the door. "I'm going to find Sufia."

"No, wait." His cousin had been sprawled across the front seat, barely awake. Now he scrambled, got his rifle, climbed out and wobbled, fell down.

Adem thought about taking a gun, but then decided it didn't matter. They knew who he was around here. Why not flaunt it? He started towards the city. Then his cousin began shouting at his back, "Stop! Stop, don't! I'll shoot you! I fucking will!"

Adem turned. Smiling. Yeah, the guy really had his rifle ready. "Why would you shoot me? You know that my father flew from America to get me. A really long way. And you helped rescue me! So why would you be stupid enough to shoot me? What are you thinking?"

"I'll shoot you in the leg. Then you won't go anywhere."

Adem stopped, started back towards his cousin. "Which knee? The left here? The right? Which one is my stronger knee? And how will you stop the bleeding? Can you guarantee I won't bleed out? How will you explain it?"

Adem's cousin did not respond. He was shaking a little, the rifle barrel wavering. He wasn't going to kill anyone. But Adem could tell that he was dying to pop off a shot. A nick. Maybe a toe. Anything. No joy in doing it to Adem, but he'd come all this way.

Adem said, "Are you coming?"

"What?"

"You've got to come with me. You have to keep an eye on me, make sure I don't do anything stupid. Better than sitting here all day."

The rifle dropped a couple of inches, enough for Adem to see both the man's eyes. "I'm not going in there."

"I guess you don't have to. But I am. Better if you do."

This guy, he was really afraid. Would he have been if Dad had chosen him over Dawit? Was there some reason he hadn't? Did they know he wasn't up to it?

The cousin—Adem didn't know the name of his own cousin. "What's your name?"

"You don't know?"

"I've known you for a day and I don't know. Tell me."

"Chi. I'm Chi."

Adem smiled. It meant *God*. "Well, look at us, God and the First Man. Absolutely. We're more than family."

"You're one of them." Louder. Stressed.

Adem's brow tightened. "One of who?"

"One of the soldiers. The kids with the guns. You work for them. This is all some, some sort of, ah, it's a trick." He raised the rifle, settled it against his shoulder. "That's what I'll tell them, too. You tried to escape. Tried calling for help."

It was as if the man was trying to convince himself. Grasping, holding on to any shred, all on faith. Adem hadn't really thought about it. He was still one of them. He hadn't made up his mind, had he? Being rescued from a bad situation—from pirates, for God's sake—convincing his dad to come back here, none of that made him *free* yet, did it? Finding Sufia, taking off together, only the two of them, that was freedom. What was waiting for him if he found Jibriil? Or if he flew back to Minnesota? What was there, really?

He didn't hesitate. Walked right up to Chi, slapped the barrel aside and grabbed the gun, gave it a hard yank. Chi held on. Adem yanked it again. Chi let go. He didn't step away, though. His nostrils flared. His left eye blinked over and over.

Adem stayed close. Eyes to eyes, except Chi was blinking and looking down, anything to avoid looking right at Adem.

"You stay here, then. I'll go, you know, rejoin my brothers."

He backed up, turned, let the rifle dangle in one hand. He'd probably get rid of it as soon as he could. Same with the suitcoat. Ridiculous. They all knew who he was, all the anonymous warriors in their checkered headscarves. He could always rejoin their ranks, cover his face, march in formation. There was a peace in that, the feeling of being part of a cause so much larger than himself. God said, and thus you do it. It was comforting. He wouldn't have to compete for grades anymore. He wouldn't have to work so hard to make inroads with the white kids in a Midwestern farm town who pretty much thought he was Muslim already anyway. Why not stick it out awhile, see where this led? He still had plenty of questions, plenty of doubts, but he wouldn't get any answers by running back home.

Then again, there was Sufia. The exception to the rule. The wrench in the works. Someone so beautiful, smart, able, and she chose to come back in spite of what sort of life awaited her here. She fought him tooth and nail until that last moment, asking to go to Cairo.

He had to find her. He had to see if she'd meant it.

He looked over his shoulder, expecting Chi to catch up. But his cousin had already sat on the hardscrabble ground, his back against the Rover, eyes closed. Adem thought about calling to him, waving him over. But then he heard himself sigh and say, "Fuck it," and he kept on like he was bulletproof.

*

The BBC. Really? What sort of masochists were these reporters? They followed "Mr. Mohammed" for a couple of blocks, asking breathless questions, fending off the people on the street who recognized the pirate negotiator from the stories they'd heard from soldiers or read on the internet with their smartphones.

"No, you have me confused with someone else."

"But you heard about the raid? The ship sinking? The pirate leader escaped. Did you know he had rigged the ship with explosives?"

Adem wanted to ask questions, find out more. Mahmood blew up the ship? And Adem hadn't even known that part of the plan. He wanted to ask if the crew was lost. What about Derrick Iles?

The reporter kept on in that terribly same voice they all had, chipper but serious. "Weren't you arrested? How are you out? Why do you have a rifle?"

"I told you—" He stopped. The cameraman stopped too, moved even closer. The reporter, arms crossed, expecting an answer. Adem shook his head. "I don't know what you're talking about. I'm not this Mr. Mohammed you think I am. Sorry."

Adem tried to brush past the cameraman, who said, "Don't touch the camera!" So Adem lifted his rifle and butted the stock into it. Let the audience chew on that. The cameraman said, "Hey! You stay away!"

Adem kept walking. A man joined him, tried to hand him a cup of water. Told him he was praying for him. Adem wasn't sure if he should drink the water. Poisoned, maybe? Why were these people so nice to him? They hated the soldiers, hated those who had come into their city, attacked it, reduced it to rubble, and then forced them all to live under an increasingly severe set of Sharia rules. So why was Mr. Mohammed such a folk hero to both sides?

The man read Adem's mind. Said, "See?" He took a sip himself, then handed it to Adem. "Drink, drink."

Adem thanked him. He drank the cool water, which only made him thirsty for more. None of that. He didn't need distractions. He gave the cup back, thanked the man again, and kept on. A faster clip. He wanted to outrun the reporters, the well-wishers, the soldiers, all of them. He didn't care.

Soldiers on the corner, watching. Starstruck as if he was a soccer star. A couple of them already on their mobiles, leaving Adem alone. If anything, at least now someone knew he was coming. Alone, armed, and angry.

*

He began going over to the soldiers he saw. Most of them knew him, both as Adem and Mr. Mohammed. They acted as if they were all friends— asked about Bosaso, about the pirates, about being on TV, about the food, the beds. Laughed. They asked to see the scar on his neck.

Adem played along, sure. Anything to get on their good side. He asked about Sufia, described her, if anyone had seen her. He didn't come up with much. Some of them had seen her on TV in the background when Adem had been speaking. They said she was an angel. Then they said she was like, who was it, you know—Halle Berry. Yes. Like her.

For some reason, Adem began drifting towards the sea. He knew the way to the hospital, or whatever it had been before they turned it into one. The smell of the sea, the salt, leading him along. Smiling and waving now. Jibriil had to know, right? Phones were ringing all over town. Maybe Jibriil would be waiting for him. He couldn't send Adem back to Bosaso now. Every block showed him that, more people now, like they were coming out specifically to see him. No, he couldn't go back. He was too important for....what? Morale? What sort of guy could appeal to both sides? Hell, they might have to make him President. Not that he'd have any true power, but the people would look up to him. It made Adem unkillable. Invincible! Necessary!

Sufia could be at his side while he ruled, right? If she didn't want to leave a fugitive, maybe she'd be okay leaving on diplomatic missions. Adem and Sufia, President and First Lady, jetting all over the world to extend a hand of diplomacy as they tried to stabilize the motherland. Spend most of each year on the road in the best hotels, chauffeured cars, first class flights, Michelin-starred restaurants. All paid for by pirate money.

If that's the way it was, then who was he to say it was wrong? Let the boys enjoy their playground in country. They *needed* someone like Adem out there in the upper echelons to legitimize the killing. A calm voice, a good suit, and a politician's handshake. For the cause, of course.

Closer still. He could hear waves now. He had lost the coat, rolled up the sleeves of his white dress shirt, soaked with sweat and stuck to his skin. The last time he was on this street, he could barely walk. The soldiers were embarrassed by him, having been saved from a proper death and coddled here. His leg cramped a little. A phantom pain, had to be. He hadn't felt any cramps in weeks. Muscle memory, maybe. If he were to go left instead of right, he would end up on the beach, where they found him and changed his life. No matter what had happened along the way, he no longer thought coming to Somalia had been a mistake. It had taken until this moment—right as he came to the front of the building, people crowding around now, waiting for him to go inside—to understand that it had all been baptism by fire. Burned away everything about Adem that had held him back. Scorching, painful, but in the end he had come out the other side a new man.

A man who was going to walk inside, find the woman he loved, and win her over.

He dropped the rifle. He didn't need it. The guards at the front door weren't trying to keep him out. One even opened the door for him.

He thanked the guard and walked inside.

*

The third floor. His home for months, at first a prison before becoming his sanctuary. Some patients were scattered around in beds, quiet in the heat of the day. The guards continued to watch him with goofy grins on their faces, calling their friends, "Yes, yes, he's here! He's right here!" Nurses. They looked at him but wouldn't acknowledge him.

Where was she? Was she tending a patient? On a different floor? Or had he been wrong? The whole thing some misguided leap of faith to believe they'd let her live, let alone come back here. Mosquito nets. Buzzing. The smell of unwashed patients.

Adem saw a nurse he remembered from before, an older woman. He'd never spoken to her, but every day there she had been. Still here, still doing her duty.

"Ma'am, is she here? I've come a long way for her."

The woman closed her eyes, shook her head. "You shouldn't have come. They said you would, but you should not have."

"I don't understand." Was it a trap? He looked around at the guards. They weren't making a move. Goofy grins. Mobiles pressed to ears.

The woman took his hand. "Please leave. Please, go with God."

"I won't go until I know where she is. Can you help me?"

She continued to protest, but he caught her eyes flicking to the left. Back among the beds. One covered with more than just netting. A thick sheet, red and faded, splotchy, draped around a bed like a tent.

The woman said, "They said you would come. They said you'd tell me what happened. You'd explain why. But I don't even want to know why anymore. I don't care."

He squeezed the woman's hands, let them go, and headed for the tent. Behind him, the woman began wailing. Adem heard a guard say to her, "Not now, you hag." She kept wailing. No one said another word.

Adem wanted to throw up. He began coughing. Shaking. What was waiting there for him? All of it, the whole walk, it had all been set up for him. Maybe instead of being celebrated, all of the people were glad to see him so they could finally see the prank through to the end. Snapshots in his mind, what might possibly be behind the sheet. He shut them down as soon as they developed. Sufia dead—no. Jibriil dead—no. Dad—no no no, how could that be? They couldn't have found him already.

Trembling. He needed to pee. Badly. A catch in his throat. Almost there. Someone was sitting on the bed. A shadow appearing through the sheet. Living, breathing. Whoever it was moved, subtly. Adem swallowed, relieved. Let out a hard breath. He pulled back the sheet to find a woman sitting there, her back to him. But he recognized the *hijab*, one of her favorites. She loved purple.

"Sufia?"

Nothing.

"It's me. I'm sorry. I'm here for you."

"Go away."

It was her voice, yes, but it was defanged and scratchy.

"Please, I can't do that." He was so happy to see her. He wasn't going to let her talk her way out of it this time. "We need to talk. Whatever happened back in Bosaso, we need to get past it. I have an idea."

"Adem, no—"

"I'm serious. It's a good plan." He stepped closer, put his hand on her shoulder. "Look at me."

She turned around.

TWENTY-SEVEN

The only reason to take Bleeker as a hostage was because he was white and they could make demands, get attention, before doing unspeakable things to him. Some while alive. Most after he was dead.

He didn't know if Warfaa was alive or dead, limp like a scarecrow between two soldiers. They'd been walking a half hour, it felt like. But the sun was too bright for him to place it in the sky and follow it. All he could do was look down and try to create enough saliva to keep from drying out. He was determined not to ask these bastards for water. Sand in his boots, his socks. Grinding against his skin, creating blisters, then grinding into the blisters.

It didn't matter what shape he was in when he got to his destination. All he wanted was a chance at Jibriil. He'd hidden the blade. A stiletto. He'd taken off the handle, wrapped the bottom in electrical tape. Enough so he could grip it without slicing all his fingers at once. Flat. Taped to his shin.

Fuck Mustafa. Fuck Adem. Fuck justice. This was exactly what he'd wanted.

The streets were thicker with soldiers now, much closer to home, Bleeker guessed. Some of the boys were ignoring him, on their cell phones. Excited. Others stared at him as if he was a zoo exhibit. Chants. More of that inane laughter that made his skin crawl like he was cold in spite of the broiling heat. He could feel the sweat on his skin boil away.

The army had taken over the neighborhood. Buildings were teeming with soldiers, looking more like some kind of orphanage than an HQ, all the kids running around. A few women, the only ones who seemed to being doing any work, carrying supplies for dinner. Guns everywhere. A group of children on his left, looking up at him, all dragging rifles in the dirt.

Then there were the tents past the buildings, all made of rough tarp, held up on tall poles with heavy rope. Heading for one of those. The man in front swept open the flap and held it for the two men carrying Warfaa.

Then it fell in Bleeker's face. He pushed through in time to see Warfaa being dropped to the floor. Warfaa screamed. Alive, good, alive. How much pain? How much life left?

Bleeker went to him, turned him onto his back. He'd been shot twice. Both on his left side. His shirt was gummy with blood, his breathing like a train on bad tracks. Bleeker looked back. What was Somali for "Doctor"? His Somalis all said "Doc-tar" but that was English, right? He tried it: "Doc-tar. He needs a doc-tar."

The first man came over, looked over Bleeker's shoulder at the blood. "Doctor, yes. No. No doctor."

Bleeker pointed at the blood. "Yes, Doctor! Come on." Bleeker found where the bullet had made a hole in the fabric, stuck his finger in. Warfaa gritted his teeth and whined. Bleeker ripped the shirt open wide. Rifle bullets. Full jackets. In and out, no massive exit wounds. The shirt had helped soak up the blood, hold it close to the wound. Now there was more blood flowing. Bleeker freaked, pulled the scarf from around his neck and shoved it against the wounds. More screaming. More shouting, "Doctor! Doctor! Goddamn it, get a doctor!"

One of the men mocked him, trying on a Minnesota accent: "Dok-tor! Dok-tor!" His buddies laughed.

Bleeker stood, ready to grab the man closest to him. "Listen, you—"

Rifle stock to the gut. Put him to the floor. The soldier lifted his boot, pressed it against Bleeker's face. Pushed his nose to the side, pushed until Bleeker's face was touching dirt. Then a last, dismissive shove that tore the skin under Bleeker's eye.

The soldier knelt beside Bleeker, said, "You lose head, American. You will beg for mecry."

"Fuck that right now. What about him?"

The soldier spit onto the ground by Warfaa's feet. "Hang him in tree, let him bleed."

Two other soldiers got up, each grabbing one of Warfaa's feet, and dragged him out of the tent. Bleeker scrambled to get up, to latch onto Warfaa's arm. More screams. More soldiers using their rifles as clubs to beat Bleeker back. He had Warfaa's wrist. Bleeker's hand covered in blood. Slipping. Slipping. A couple of whacks to the back of Bleeker's head. Slipped.

Warfaa was gone. Out of the tent flap, his screams loud then less so then faint.

The soldier kneeling by Bleeker smiled. "You're next."

He left the tent. Bleeker heard him shout a couple of names. Moments later, a handful of gun-wielding teenagers swarmed inside, took up posts all around the tent. One of them held up a knife. Nasty looking thing. Pointed it at Bleeker.

"Your neck. Mine. It's mine."

Bleeker sat up and pulled his knees to his face, wrapped his arms around. They weren't going to cut his fucking head off, not these kids. If he was going to go, he'd be fighting. A bullet. Not by fucking knife in front of a camera.

Or if it had to be like that, he'd demand that Jibriil do it. The only way. Jibriil had to be man enough to do it himself. And Bleeker would sure as shit bite the hand that held the blade.

TWENTY-EIGHT

Her eyes, behind those librarian's glasses, were as clear and honest as before. Her forehead, nose, most of her cheeks, all smooth and rich as before. But her lips and chin and throat belonged to a zombie. Cracked, eaten through, white. A bandage around her neck, but Adem saw that the burns, bright with petroleum jelly, ran down beneath them. This wasn't one of those hit-and-run acid attacks he'd seen in the streets. The sick fuck had taken his time. Tied her hands so she couldn't wipe it away. Targeted her mouth, her vocal cords—that would teach her to say whatever came to mind. From now on, the perpetrator must have assumed, she would have to hide her face behind the hijab, show only her lovely eyes, and not say a word.

"Who did this?"

Sufia said, "I told you. Go away. This is what I deserved."

"You don't mean that." It was hard to look at her. He forced himself. The teeth like those on a skull, lips reduced to nearly nothing but blisters. This was his fault. He had to look. Strips of skin under her chin tight, like rubber bands nearly stretched to their snapping points. "Let's show the people what they've done to you. They're all outside right now. We...we can find the reporter. I saw one back there. We...we can...show..."

Sufia had looked away, not even listening to him. Clearing her throat. Coughing. When she finally turned back, she said, "I'm not going anywhere with you."

The others were watching. The noise from the old nurse had died down. The guards were huddled together, watching. Other women had stopped what they were doing, cautiously peeking over.

Slink away defeated or do something...bold. Scratch the first. Never again, not after his walk through town. So, that left option two.

He stepped forward grabbed Sufia's hand and pulled her to her feet. He thought about kissing her, but feared doing so would hurt her even more than she was already. So he stood eye to eye, concentrating on all of her that wasn't scarred. Finally pecked her forehead. Then, "We're leaving."

Hand in hand, Adem a few steps ahead. It wasn't that she was fighting him, but she wasn't keeping up either. The guards did nothing. The nurses did nothing. Watched them like it was TV.

Sufia said, "I'm not leaving."

"Stop it, okay? Stop with the pride already. If you don't want me, fine. If you don't want me to find someone to help you, you're nuts."

She planted her feet and Adem nearly pulled her to the ground. They were right there, right at the door. Only the stairs between them and the outside world. He didn't let go of her hand.

"You'll thank me later," he said.

"I will not! You...you think you're always right, but you are not. I am sick of this. You've *ruined* me. Until you, I was happy, and look at me." Shouting, phlegmy and painful. Words scratching up her throat, full of *K-k-k-k-k-k*.

"I offered you better! They ruined you!"

"Please, go, before it gets worse. You don't know what they've got planned for you."

"We're going, you and me, outside and to the nearest foreign camera."

One more pull. She wasn't budging. Harder. Yanked her a foot closer. Harder still. She stumbled, fell. Crying now. He pulled again, sliding her across the floor, outside the threshold. She caught the railing at the top of the stairs.

"Come on!"

"Please, no, please, no, no, Adem, no, please."

"You're insane! I'm saving you!"

Sufia held tight, lifted her head back, opened her jaw wide and let out a banshee yell. Ululating. Rasping. Her bandages spotted with blood. And more blood from the blisters around her lips, under her chin, pooling into her lap. She ululated while she cried, like gargling gravel.

Adem let go. He watched another minute, shouting right back at her in English, "No! God, Sufia, I love you! I love you so bad! Don't do this! Don't! *Don't! I love you, I love you, love you, so much, Sufia!*"

She took a tortured breath and kept on with the wailing, finally turning her head to him. Staring him down as she ululated. Holding her blood-soaked palm out towards him, not for him to take, but for him to *see*. To remember.

He huffed. Took three stairs down. Turned and watched. She sat in the same position making the same noise. Guards now crowded behind her. The old nurse came to her side, a towel in her hand, wiping Sufia's blood from her hands. She didn't stop wailing. Adem took a few more steps. Turned again. The nurse was trying to silence her, but she brushed away the woman's help, took another ragged breath and kept on with the awful, awful noise.

Another few steps and Adem could only see Sufia's head. He wiped water from his eyes. The pain was like being stepped on. But he had to let go. He had no choice. It was either that or give his life for her. But something had clicked inside his head. Why give your life for someone who didn't want it. What sort of self-satisfaction was that? What sort of righteousness? He could've died to stay beside her, and all she would've done was kick his body and leave him in her past. What a dumbass thing to do. The anger of love assaulted his brain. The bitch. The *dabo dhiibato*. The *bitch*. She couldn't save herself. She didn't want to. All she wanted was someone to blame.

He kicked the wall on his way downstairs. Jammed his toes. Screamed. Just made him angrier. More afraid. He had left the cell phone in his pocket. He had to get back to the Rover. Limping on aching toes. Or maybe back to the BBC reporter. An exclusive interview, if only he would give him shelter, security, some goddamned aspirin, even.

He gritted his teeth, curled his bruised toes, and headed outside.

All the guns were pointed directly at his head. Ten soldiers, maybe more. And in the center of it all, not smiling, stood Jibriil.

"Welcome back, my nigga."

TWENTY-NINE

Twenty minutes, maybe. Without a watch, it felt like longer, even if it felt like no time at all. Bleeker at the center of the tent, like a sweat lodge. One of the guards had said something Bleeker thought meant "I've got to take a shit." So only three guards, bored. Talking to each other as if he wasn't there. The heat, Jesus, the heat. Sweat stinking of whatever spices had been in the food. Gurgling in the pit of his stomach. Chills. Was he getting sick?

Rocking back and forth. Arms tight around his knees. He could take three guards, right? He had to distract one. Had to get them closer. He'd been trained to stay patient in situations like this, look for opportunity, take it when it presented itself. Not yet. Not yet. And Jibriil hadn't shown up yet. Not yet. Not yet.

The guard who took the bathroom break came back. Well, maybe it was him. He'd had his face covered by the checkered scarf, wearing vague camouflage fatigues, so it could've been anyone. He had another guard with him, bigger and taller, carrying a bag. The first one said something to two of the others. Again, Bleeker only got a little of it. Something like, "You leave. We're here." And then Jibriil's name popped up. Another couple of words Bleeker knew were names.

The guards on duty talked it over—"You want to go?" "I'm fine here." "I could use a nap." "Sure, I can go." Two of them lowered their rifles, left the tent. The big new guard opened the bag, pulled out a slab of flatbread. He threw it at Bleeker. Growled something like "Ass" or "Dirt Ass", fuck, Bleeker wasn't even listening anymore. Making up his own translations now. Could've called him "Sir" for all he knew.

He picked up the bread, ate some of the damp, cardboard-like stuff without thinking. Had already swallowed half before it occurred to him: poison? Or maybe they had pissed all over it and left it out in the sun. Probably not, because the big guy handed another slab to his buddy, who then tore it in two, offered some to the third guard. He stepped over, reached out for it.

The big guard grabbed his arm, wound it up, while the smaller guard clamped down a palm on the man's mouth, sliced his throat. Arterial blood shot far then pulsed then calmed down. A curtain of it across the guard's chest, down his legs. The other guard held on waiting, waiting, not yet, not yet, until the guard went slack. Dumped him onto the ground.

The taller guard pushed the scarf off his head, let it hang loose around his neck. Mustafa, breathing hard.

"Holy shit." Bleeker couldn't help but laugh.

Mustafa, lips curled, knelt by Bleeker and slapped him across the face. Damned hard. He pointed towards the flap. "You let them do that to Warfaa! Why isn't it you out there? What did you say?"

"I tried. I tried to get him a doctor. They shot him, and we walked. Walked a long way, and then I wanted a doctor, and they said no and dragged him out. What did they do? What?"

"We followed the blood. But..." Mustafa stopped, took in a long breath through his nose. "It's not fair. He gave up everything to help us, not even his fight."

"What did they do?"

Dawit pulled his scarf off. "They cut him like a pig."

Mustafa wrapped his hand around Bleeker's arm, pulled him to his feet and drug him to the tent flap. Pushed on through—sudden sun. Bleeker squeezed his eyes shut.

"Open your eyes! Look at him! Look!"

"I can't see."

"Then open your eyes!" He felt Mustafa's fingers gripping his chin, pointing his face. "Look!"

Bleeker squinted, saw shadows. Clearer, clearer, then, the shadows maybe thirty yards away. A tree, a naked black man strung up by his feet, arms touching the ground. His sternum had been opened, guts falling earthward, obscuring his face. Dark blood beneath him already soaking into the ground.

"Oh god."

"See it?"

"Oh god, I see, I see." He squeezed his eyes shut again. Fingers off his chin, a push back through the flap, stumbling onto his side, the wind *oofing* out of him.

Mustafa, still raging. "Why isn't it you out there? What did they say? What did you tell them?"

"Please, he doesn't know," Dawit said.

"Of course he knows."

"I told them to get a doctor. I tried, goddamn it, I *fucking tried*."

Mustafa shook his head, paced the tent. "What have I done? Shit, shit,

shit."

Bleeker rubbed his eyes with the heels of his hands. Full of water. He smeared it away, blinked until he could see again. "Think about it. He was gone. There wasn't anything they could do. It was an easy choice. Me, a white man? An American? Can you even imagine what they've got planned for me?"

Dawit stepped over, helped Bleeker to his feet again. "Don't worry about it. We're here."

"Did you find the girl?"

"We found you first. We saw them taking you both. We followed."

"So..." He reached down, took the rifle off the dead guard, shook the blood off. Still plenty all over. Bleeker thought of Malaria, AIDS, Ebola, other nasty African bugs. Fuck it. He made sure the gun was cocked and ready. "You go find her. I'll hunt down Jibriil."

Mustafa shook his head. "We're not splitting up again."

"Well, then let's go kill him together and go get the girl and get out of here."

"It's not a video game."

"I know that! Fuck, you think...I know, alright?" Bleeker stared at the dead guard. Eyes bulging, mouth open. Then he took Warfaa's scarf off, started wrapping it around his head so that only his eyes were exposed. He looked at his hands. "Should've brought gloves. Why didn't we think of gloves?"

He grinned. Held up his hands. "Stupid, huh?"

They couldn't help but laugh, lightly, trying to hide it. Dawit held up his hands, too. A little louder. "Stupid white man!"

Bleeker let it roll. Full on smiling. "Funny as shit. And this dead guy, the thing with the bread, that was pretty badass."

Mustafa shrugged. "Told you I was a gangsta."

They got quiet.

Mustafa said, "I don't know what to do next. I'm sorry."

"I don't either."

They stood around the dead guard, already gathering flies. The smell—the shit in the guard's pants, the hot blood, the spicy sweat—made them cough.

Mustafa cleared his throat. "Let's go out there and figure it out."

He turned and walked out of the tent. Bleeker and Dawit followed, just in time to hear a huge cheer go up from soldiers all over the place.

THIRTY

Jibriil, laughing, stepped forward and embraced Adem. A giant, back-pounding hug. A truly-happy-to-see-you hug. Adem's arms were paralyzed at his sides. Didn't faze Jibriil at all. He looked rougher, beard a little longer, a stronger odor than when they were last in close quarters. Surrounded by all these men who turned their guns to the ground as soon as Jibriil took Adem into his grasp. Jibriil stepped back, grabbed his friend by the shoulders, big smile.

"Look at you! Excellent! Glad you're back. Now I can forgive you. We can start over again. I'm sorry I was angry last time we spoke. Really."

Adem realized he couldn't hear Sufia anymore. He wanted to go back inside, see if she was okay, but what would that help? Maybe in the days to come, once she calmed down. There he went, thinking about a future here. Even after seeing her like that, he had forgotten the escape clause, his dad and the cop who wanted to kill Jibriil. Almost as if that had been a dream. He woke up when he saw Sufia's face.

"Sufia," he said. "Did you...why?"

Jibriil shook his head sadly. "She was going to sell you out. She had no plans of going away with you. I don't care how loyal she was to our cause. She wanted to do you harm, and *that*, son, I couldn't let happen. I didn't realize...I should've kept you close to me all along."

"Who did it? Who sat there and poured acid on her like that?"

Jibriil averted his eyes. Looked at the men behind him, the building behind Adem. The sky. "Someone had to. Someone who would take it seriously."

"What are you saying?"

Jibriil wrapped an arm around Adem's shoulders, guided him towards the line of men with guns. "You'll never guess where these guys are from. You know, once they promoted me, I put my own crew together. All these soldiers, they're from the Cities."

The soldiers nodded or lifted their guns one-armed into the sky, shot off rounds. Smiled.

Jibriil: "I put out the call. They told me some are dead, some already on their way home, some lost out there, no idea where they went. The rest, my own private squad. How's that? Tell your dad about that, me with my own gang."

He couldn't know, could he? Yes, all those checkpoints, all those soldiers calling ahead, but he couldn't have figured it out, right? It was too crazy.

"Yeah, I know," Jibriil said. "Garaad told me about what happened. Right before he died. He was hit, several times, when they were taking you away. He made it through the night, that was it. Blood in his lungs."

He let go of Adem, put his hands behind his back like some Kung-fu master, all the movies they'd watch on DVD as kids. He walked in front of his line of soldiers. "It wasn't hard to put it together. I used to look up to Mustafa, you know. He was always dissing me, but I always came back. I kept trying to impress him. Then he went and showed what a pussy he really was, like, telling the Killahs to keep away from me, and working that shit job. Like he was better than all that because he was earning a paycheck all the sudden. Like he got a discount at Target, yeah. All because of you."

"I don't know what you're talking about."

Ignored him, kept on. "If I had to guess, I'd say the white man's some cop. I killed that girl cop, so I'm sure he's going to try and arrest me, some shit like that."

"That's crazy. Why would they...you're all paranoid now."

Jibriil marched back to his friend, teeth hard on his bottom lip, and grabbed Adem behind the neck, vice-grip. Adem hunched his shoulders.

"Don't make me do something. Boy, I'm giving you the benefit of the doubt right now. And that bitch in there..." He stabbed a finger at the hospital. "She couldn't wait to sell you out. Wanted to go back in your place, do your job. Right, like they're gonna listen to some educated bitch, white men or pirates. All they'd want to do is fuck her."

Adem, muscles on the edge of spasming: "You're crazy."

"I did it for *you*. Sat by her bedside, arms and legs and head strapped down, and I listened to her *scream*. You think that was fun? Think I got off on that? Shit, man, it broke my heart. But I was thinking about you the whole time. Then I hear you're trying to bring me down?"

Adem went to his knees, trying to escape the grip, but Jibriil held on tight. Still talking. "Calling in Big Bad Bahdoon to deal with me? What, you want to wear this uniform? You want what I got?"

He finally let go, and Adem fell back onto his ass. Most of the Minneapolis soldiers—"the disappeared", they were called back home—couldn't even watch. Adem's muscles hitched back and forth, kept his shoulders up.

Jibriil, back to pacing *a la* kung-fu master, said, "I mean, if you're back because you're with me, *really* with me, then we're cool. That's alright with me. But first we're going to drive over to camp, have a feast for you, and wait for your Daddy to come for you so we can take his fucking head off."

He spun on his heels. Weird all over his face. "And you're the one who's going to be holding the knife."

*

Back into Jibriil's truck, the Minneapolis soldiers in the back, Jibriil, Adem, and a driver in the cab. A long hot drive back to camp. Jibriil jabbered the whole way, Adem still hearing Sufia's screeching in the back of his mind, not letting him concentrate. But he picked up that it was about battles—the Ethiopians again, the African Union, some UN bluehats who wandered too far from base. About how people were starting to give them more respect. "They talk about us in the States now. They actually know who we are! That's something, I'm telling you."

Ragtag army grows up, becomes an international terrorist organization. Just like the big dogs in Afghanistan, how they started out. One country at a time. One strike at a time. That's how Sharia was going to win in the end. The Christians, the Infidels, The Democracies, all of them, would grow too tired to fight anymore. Adem closed his eyes. Even if it took decades, centuries, there would always be someone to take the place of the fallen. More and more from America, even. If only to be on the side of the winners. Adem tried to imagine it. America? Under Sharia law? The whole reason there hadn't been uprisings in the States was because of all this freedom and tolerance the Muslim warriors seemed determined to extinguish. American Muslims had it made, right? All the conveniences of the modern world, the protection of secular law, while still free to dress up in the *hijab* or grow their beards or even not to touch the pork if they worked at Wal Mart. In America, Islamic women didn't have to fear acid attacks or public stonings because they happened to be in a car with a men who weren't their husbands, not to mention adultery.

Like a tennis match in his head—America, Somalia, America, Somalia. He buried his head in his hands. Felt Jibriil's hand on his back.

"Don't worry. It's going to be alright. We'll get you back to doing what you're good at. We'll get some food in you. You can have any girl you want. Marry her tonight, get rid of her tomorrow if you like. It's going to be okay. Your own room, your own bed, whatever you want."

Adem almost said *I want to go home*. But he didn't, not really. Not yet. He wanted to go...somewhere else. Anywhere nice.

He heard the cheering over the noise of the engine. Lifted his head, saw they were on the edge of the camp. Lots of dust kicked up. Lots of bullets fired into the air. Lots of smiling soldiers. Mobs in the streets.

The driver slid to a stop. Soldiers surrounded the truck. The Minneapolis brigade climbed out. Jibriil pushed the door open, stepped out and started shouting, "Calm down! What's going on? Somebody tell me."

Several of the teenage soldiers gathered around, all talking at once. Adem stepped out of the truck. Lots of eyes on him. None of them wanting to kill him this time. A relief.

Jibriil was smiling again, nodding at the stories he was being told. Adem picked up, "Killed him. Stabbed him! And, and, then, we found a white man, too."

A white man?

Adem leaned in. "What was that?"

Jibriil spoke close to his ear, spittle flying. "One of our brothers, in Belgium. He killed a writer, a novelist, a blasphemer."

"Really?"

"Stabbed him at a book signing! Cut his throat, too. He wrote terrible shit about the Prophet, lots of lies. One of ours did it! Killed him!"

"What did he say about capturing a white man?"

Jibriil raised his eyebrows. "Come on, let's go see for ourselves."

*

As they walked through camp, the chanting, singing, and gunfire grew louder. It reminded Adem of celebrations in the streets of Minneapolis when the Timberwolves or Vikings won a playoff, except for the guns.

Jibriil soaked it in, stopping to pat soldiers on the back or raise his arms like a beloved leader. To embrace other officers. Imams. Kids who didn't really know why they were celebrating. Many of them recognized Adem—"Mr. Mohammed"—and embraced him, too. Snapped pictures with their phones. Tried to ask him questions about what it was like on the pirate ships, but he was propelled forward, unable to answer, on to the next crowd, same questions. When he heard ululating, he thought of Sufia and turned every which way—was she following him? Pointing her finger at him? But it was some of the other women in camp. It didn't make Adem's stomach feel any less nervous.

Onward to the tents, the wind kicking up the hanging edges like flags. Cloth walls bulged inward. Sand blowing all over. It was getting worse.

They approached a tent of orange, mottled fabric, nobody guarding it. Adem looked around, shielded his eyes against the sand, and saw an animal hanging from a tree. Didn't register at first. A pig? A camel? Then the features made sudden horrible sense in his mind, and his eyes went wide. A man. Upside down, slit from crotch to neck, his intestines piled in front of his face.

He gagged. Grabbed the back of Jibriil's shirt. Pointed. Gagged again. He couldn't look, no, no he couldn't. What sort of day was this? To see the worst things he'd ever seen, one after the other, his trip through Hell led by Jibriil, of all people?

Jibriil glanced over. Solemn. Nodded. "I'm sure he deserved it. I hope."

Into the tent. Adem followed, along with two other soldiers. Before even getting a look, the smell overwhelmed him. He turned, ready to run outside. The two soldiers got in his way, wouldn't let him past.

Jibriil shouted, in English, "Fuck!"

Adem looked over his shoulder. A shocked soldier, his neck a jagged, sticky chasm, was lying in his own goo. Hundreds of flies, buzzing all at once, all over the wound and the ground. Thick in the air, a dark cloud. The side of the tent facing the sandstorm was filled, a hard bubble, the sound of sand hitting it like sleet against windows back in the Cities.

"Fuck!" Jibriil got in one of the soldier's faces. "Find someone who knows what happened here! Now!"

The solider ran from the tent. Jibriil didn't even bother with the flap. He lifted the nearest wall, tossed it over his shoulder as he ducked under. Adem was right behind. He took in a huge gulp of air. Sand in his mouth. He coughed and spit and hacked until Jibriil handed him a bottle of water. Adem drank it down, sand in his teeth, sand down his throat. Grating his esophagus.

Jibriil was shouting over the wind. "We've got an escaped prisoner! Don't let him out of camp! He's a white man! An American!"

He wrapped his scarf over his mouth and nose. Adem tried to keep the sand out with his shirttail lifted to his nose, but then the sand slapped his exposed torso.

Jibriil turned back to him, shouted for a soldier to get Adem a scarf, then said, "Come on, let's go hunting."

Off into the wild. Soldiers who were celebrating before were now chanting "Death to the American!" Rifles. Bigger rifles. Even bigger machine guns.

Adem hoped he got to Bleeker before any of the others did. And where the hell was his dad?

THIRTY-ONE

The sandstorm at full strength, they ducked under an empty tent, half reeds and sticks, half a torn sheet, enough holes in it to keep it from filling like a sail. Huddled together, trying to hide Bleeker from the others. They'd already made a sling from the dead guard's scarf in order to hide one of his hands. He'd shoved the other in his pocket, slung the rifle over his shoulder.

The celebration gave them good cover, Mustafa asking what it was all about, translating for Bleeker. A dead novelist. Criticize Islam in public too much, and you're a target. Say something about the Prophet, draw a picture of him, and that's reason enough to die. It pissed Bleeker off. Some fucking wannabe Bin Laden gunned down Cindy and that was justifiable, but should Bleeker ever say something un-PC about lunatic Muslims on TV, then mobs of thousands all over the world believed he was the worst of the worst. Fuck culture, fuck tolerance. When he got back to Minnesota, he was going to retire and retreat up north, the woods, and hope never to see another Muslim for as long as he lived.

"What now?"

Mustafa glanced around, a pained expression. "If you want to find Jibriil, we need to ask around, find out if anyone's seen him. If that's what you still want."

Mustafa looked at him. Blank. Whatever it took. But Bleeker knew. Whatever it took now that he'd found Adem. As long as he was safe. Bleeker thought about Warfaa, shot and gutted for helping them. About the others who had lost their lives up in Bosaso. What was more important in the long run?

Maybe one day he would journey back to this shithole on his time. Plenty of time once he retired. He'd find the son of a bitch then, take the time to plan a proper assassination. Cold blooded instead of warm. A long-range hunting rifle instead of up-close, the way Jibriil shot a pregnant woman in the face. Jibriil would never see it coming. Bleeker would live to enjoy it instead of being cut down by the fanatics.

Cold. Just the way he liked it.

"Let's get out of here," he told Mustafa. "We've got Adem. This was a mistake. I'm done."

"You sure?"

Bleeker let out a deep breath. Next year. Take time to prepare. Cold. He nodded.

He could tell that Mustafa was relieved. Like he shrunk three inches, all the tension held in his muscles flowing out, carried away by the wind. Mustafa pulled out his cell phone, called Chi. He covered his mouth with his hand, pressed the phone tight against his ear. He still had to shout. Bleeker watched. All he had to do was give the guy a landmark, maybe half a mile away, tell him to come pick them up. But Mustafa's voice was growing even louder. Louder still. Bleeker couldn't make it out against the gunfire and shouting and the sand. Outside, he heard the celebrations turn into one uniform Arabic chant: "Death to the American!"

Had to be him.

Mustafa was yelling now. He stood, hunched over in the tent. Cursing in Somali. Bleeker knew those words well. Heard them every weekend in New Pheasant Run from the kids.

Mustafa took the phone from his ear, cut the call. Stared at the ground. "Adem's gone. He left."

"Where'd he—"

"Looking for her. Off looking for her. Chi couldn't shoot him. Shit. It's my fault."

Nothing to say. The chanting outside began to thunder. Mustafa caught onto what they were saying. "No."

"We knew they'd figure it out."

"Not now. How do we know they mean you?"

"You saw how they treated Adem. Guy's a star."

Dawit shook his head. "But a star who makes a mistake…" A finger sliced across the neck.

Mustafa flexed his fingers on both hands. "Shit! Goddamnit!"

Death to the American!

Death to the American!

Bleeker stood. "Let's go march with them."

"What?"

"It looks better than hiding out here. We go out, march, chant, what are they going to do?"

"You stick out like a sore dick."

"There are a few white guys here, right? Like they'll know."

Outside, boots, all marching the same direction. A few faces looked their way. A few more would follow suit. They had to get out of there, the only way.

Bleeker unslung his rifle, held it up high, and shouted in Arabic, "Death to the American! Death to the American! Islam forever!"

He headed out into the crowd, the intensity of the sand surprising him. Carried along with the flow. "Death to the American!"

He turned his head as far as he could. Mustafa and Dawit finally emerged from the tent, struggled to catch up. Bleeker looked ahead again, no idea where he was going, but chanting for his own death the whole way as he blinked sand out of his eyes.

THIRTY-TWO

Jibriil, jubilant outside of the tent. As if he hadn't blown his cool two minutes before. Big smile, chanting—no, not that. *Leading* the chant. When he moved, the swarm moved, the way clouds of birds did in a split second. Adem was out of sync, bumping into soldiers, stepping on boots, having to grab Jibriil to keep up. The leader took deliberate steps, guiding an army on feel alone. Adem remembered the last mob he was at the center of, and he was desperate to keep Jibriil in view.

The sand, thick in the air. Hard to see beyond ten, twelve, fifteen soldiers on all sides, but Adem could hear them. They were out there, chanting and singing and shooting into the air. How did this help them find the cop? Would he surrender because the odds were against him? Would they pin him under a bush and stomp the infidel out of him?

This was what it had come to. Adem wasn't leaving Somalia. He was going to be Jibriil's puppet, the celebrity face of this ragtag army after all, but without Sufia by his side. She'd always be there, somewhere in the camp, ready to be put on display for Adem whenever he steered off the path set out for him. The sharpest reminder of all, besides the raised scar on his neck.

"Death to the American!"

For a moment he forgot about the white cop. *He* was the American. So was Jibriil. And it could turn on them like that, couldn't it?

*

When Mustafa caught up to Bleeker, landing a heavy hand on the man's shoulder, the cop thought he'd been found out. A moment of panic, Bleeker seeing himself shooting his way out of the crowd, only to be filled with so much lead that he'd be a statue of himself.

But then Mustafa's voice at his ear: "Easy. Don't give yourself away."

How long until Chi got there with the Rover? They needed to find their way out of the crowd, a safe place on the edge where they could wait. But the sandstorm had gotten worse and the mob was swirling and they didn't know how far they had circled around the camp.

Mustafa pushed Bleeker to the left, the slightest force, to begin threading towards freedom. Dawit shouldered his way ahead of Bleeker. Couldn't be too obvious about what they were doing. It was a trigger-happy crowd. Didn't matter if it was an American they killed or not. Someone had to die now.

Like a dance, shuffling ahead, hop, shuffling ahead, hop. *Death to the American! Death to the American!*

Shuffle, shuffle. Hop. Shuffle, shuffle. Hop.

Bleeker tripped on his own boots. Going down. Crashed into Dawit and the soldiers ahead. They parted like the Red Sea, and Bleeker kept falling. Mustafa was right there, hands under his arms, lifting up, up, up, but getting nowhere. A shove from behind. Mustafa shouted for Dawit, who was fighting his way back against the tide of soldiers. More soldiers behind shoving, kicking, losing the rhythm of the chant, the shuffle, descending into chaos. Dawit, finally there, kneeling to help Bleeker. Other soldiers closing the part, trampling Bleeker's fingers, Dawit's legs, and some of the soldiers were now stopping to help, making it worse. Lifting Bleeker to his feet, pointing at his white hands, looking into his eyes, the white skin peeking through. They tugged at his scarf, Mustafa slapping hands away.

The scarf revealed more and more skin. More shouting, more pointing, hands reaching, Mustafa slapping them away, putting his back against Bleeker's, waving his gun. Fifteen hands on Mustafa's rifle, stripped from his grip before he could get off one shot. He looked over his shoulder. Dawit, also defenseless. Looked to the ground. Bleeker's rifle, off in the dust, picked up by one of the teenagers.

Someone gouged Bleeker's eye. He jerked away before they did any real damage. Someone tried to pull his scalp off. Someone shouted something about his crotch. Bleeker guessed it was someone holding a machete. All three of them, he could feel in the air, in the sand in his eyes and nose and mouth, in the chants hurting his ears, yes, all three of them were going to be ripped apart limb from limb by all these hands.

The only thing he could do was wait for it.

*

Like watching the skies for tornados, something about the crowd changed. Louder, more intense, the rhythm set by Jibriil thrown off by something up ahead, the effect rippling through the mass. Adem lifted his head, tip-toed, trying to find it. A clogged artery, stopping the flow of soldiers. Hands in the air, fingers pointing towards the center of the jam.

"They found the American! They found him!"

Adem heard it coming from all around, louder as more soldiers picked it up, carried on until all of the men surrounding him and Jibriil were telling them "They found the American!"

The smile of Jibriil's face faded. Staring ahead. Lips parted. Adem had never seen his friend like this before. As if power could somehow create new expressions, new personalities overnight. "Let me see."

"Jibriil wants to see! Let him through!"

It rippled back across the crowd, and a path opened through the men, always about five steps worth, closing again as soon as Jibriil and Adem passed by. The message still traveling forward: "Jibriil wants to see! Let him through!"

Adem thought about where he'd seen men walk the way Jibriil was walking right now—deliberately, reaching for outstretched hands, waving as if blessing the surrounding pilgrims. Like Castro, like Saddam Hussein, like Mugabe. The Pope. Those sorts of men. Jibriil had it down. He was a natural.

The opening ahead swelled wide. A handful of soldiers surrounding three men, holding their arms and legs while they fought. Their scarves had been stripped. When he saw Jibriil, Adem's dad let out a primal yell and lunged forward, breaking the grip of his captors. Dropped like dead weight when cracked on the back of the head with a rifle butt. Not out cold, but writhing. Bleeding.

The guy with the rifle was leaning over to take another whack.

Adem hit Jibriil on the shoulder, about to shout *Stop him!*

But Jibriil beat him, already wailing above the sandstorm howl. The rifle butt jerked to a halt in mid-swing.

Jibriil took slow, important-man steps towards Adem's dad, kneeled beside him. Adem stood over his shoulder. His dad's wound was caked with sand. He pushed himself up, got his knees under him. A string of blood and spit rolled to the ground.

Jibriil grabbed his chin, forced his dad to look into his eyes.

Said, "You'll never be part of my gang, son."

He dropped the chin, stood, and walked off, shouting orders in Somali. Guards grabbed Dawit, Bleeker, and Adem's dad, pushed them after Jibriil. Adem was left standing there, his fists balled up, no one to hit.

THIRTY-THREE

Jibriil led them to the tree where Warfaa's body swung in the wind. The longer he was dead, the more horrified the look on his face. Impossible, but Bleeker would've sworn to it. Jibrill had pointed and barked orders, and soldiers threw ropes over branches, one uncomfortably close to Warfaa. Three ropes. Who was getting the reprieve? Adem? Was he a traitor after all?

Adem had followed a few minutes after the rest of them were forced along behind Jibriil. He had stayed quiet while that thug beat up on Mustafa. He wasn't tied up. He seemed to fit cozily back into his old spot at Jibriil's side. Made Bleeker rethink all that talk about Cindy's murder being Jibriil's idea alone. Like it mattered anymore. He wouldn't get within five feet of Jibriil before they strung all of them from the tree, sliced balls to throat.

Soldiers forced Dawit, Mustafa, and Bleeker to their knees. Adem watched from over Jibriil's shoulder.

How was this going to happen? Shot then gutted? Or gutted first, then strung up, or strung up first, then gutted?

Jibriil raised his arms high. The chanting, babbling, and laughing from his army came to a gradual stop, only the wind and the sand left to speak over.

Some sort of speech. Bleeker would've preferred they go straight to the gutting.

Jibriil raised his voice, in English. Another of his soldiers translated for him. "Glorious day! We have reached across the desert to Europe, and struck a blow! And on the same day, America has come to us! Stumbled in, as it usually does, trying to be the hero. But look at them! They are fools! Pathetic, bleeding, and easy to slaughter! And our own Mr. Mohammed has brought them to us on a silver platter!"

No longer the smug teenager Mustafa had told him about. No, this

Jibriil sounded like a leader. Damn near a god to these kids. Fewer than a handful of months in the war zone had changed him into this. Must have been lurking under the surface his whole life, waiting for a chance to rise. All it took was a lot of killing. A whole lot of murder without consequence.

"Where's the camera?" Jibriil searched the crowd. Always someone videotaping it all. A couple of soldiers with cameras nudged out of the crowd. Jibriil told one to circle the captives, linger on their faces individually. The other stood back, the wider shot, the whole scene in panorama.

He had the camera turned to him. "So let's show the world what we're capable of. Let's—"

"That's enough!" Adem's voice, drowning out Jibriil. Almost a howl. He stepped up to his friend, pushed the camera out of the way. "That's enough of the show. You can't kill them."

Jibriil's chest swelled. "I can do anything I want. What, you want a *favor*, now? I've saved you so many times already."

"No, forget saving me. Forget all of it. You're not going to kill him or that cop. We all know that. I'm tired of all this. It's not a game."

"Yeah it is." Smile. "It's a game all right. It's the only game we've got. And, goddamn, son, we're winning!"

Bleeker strained to hear. The cameraman was getting in his face again, zooming in, out, in. Adem kept on, "We're not winning anything. It's the same every day. You don't want to win, you just want to play."

"Fuck off." He pushed Adem, sent him back a few steps. Adem stepped up.

Louder. "If this is what you want, fine, but let them take me back to the States. This isn't for me. I can't do it, man. I'm done! Let them take me home."

Bleeker felt as the boys fit a loop of rope around his ankles. He looked over. Dawit and Mustafa hadn't been fitted with theirs yet. They were running out of time. Bleeker could do it. He could get out of this. He could make a run. But then the others would be left behind. How far could he get? One ranger against all these guys, trigger-happy, bloodthirsty. Bored.

What if he killed Jibriil? Then the attention of the mob would be focused on him. Mustafa could grab Adem, lose himself in the crowd until the Rover came for them.

That's what he had to do. Shit. They'd tear him apart. But that's what he had to do. He wobbled, got one knee off the ground and set his foot in front of him. The boys yelled. They cinched the rope around his other ankle, tried to pull him down. He stood, turned on them. Hopping on one leg. He reached for the rope, held on tight, pulled it right through the hands of his captors.

He had slack enough to get the loop off his ankle when he was hit by a truck. No, not a truck. A brick wall. A giant fist made of iron. God himself. His back. He reached behind him, grabbed hold. Hurt more when he grabbed it. Fell forward. His hand was wet and sticky. His head was still overloaded with the shock of impact.

Mustafa at his side. "Shit, Ray, shit, stay still. Shit, don't move."

"I've gotta. I can't…you know. Jesus Christ. What…what…?"

"Don't move, I swear, man, don't move."

A peek over his shoulder. Every muscle in him screamed not to do it, not to look.

Jibriil. Holding his pistol. Grim but satisfied.

Bleeker rolled his eyes. Of course. Fuck that guy.

THIRTY-FOUR

Adem felt like a stickman. All bones. Unable to move. His dad knelt by Bleeker, bleeding from his lower back where Jibriil had shot him. Still moving, though. Fighting. Dawit pushed away the soldiers trying to get at the fallen cop. They finally gave up, stood off a few feet, watching the man bleed.

Jibriil, same look on his face as when he killed that woman back home. An entire family, gunned down by Jibriil, on two different continents. Then he turned to Adem, lifted his eyebrows, and started singing. The first music Adem had heard in the country. The army had banned all Somali music. All of it. But their leader was singing. And then some of his followers joined in. And then more. And then more. They knew the song. Every last one of them.

He knew it, too. American. All the soldiers scat singing a familar rhythm: DAH da da, da, doh DAH DAH /DHA da da da, doh DOH DOH...

An old Michael Jackson tune. "Wanna Be Startin'" or something like that. Had he taught this song to all these soldiers? Or did they all just know it because everybody all over the world knew Michael Jackson songs?

Adem glanced at Bleeker again, trying to get upright while his dad tried to keep him still. He'd rolled over and was sitting, wincing, one hand on his back, the other gripping Dad's as tight as two men could hold on.

Jibriil's voice wasn't exactly the same as it was in high school. It was more raw, tempered by the sand. When he and Adem both sang in the choral group, Jibriil was the more talented one. He got the solos. He had an ear for the melody. But he was embarrassed to be that good when all of his friends and all the gangstas wanted to be rappers. If only he'd realized that the rappers needed people like him for the choruses—Cee Lo, D'Angelo, Anthony Hamilton—then maybe he wouldn't have wanted to join Dad's gang. Maybe he wouldn't have wanted to prove himself in more primitive ways.

They sang the opening lines, over and over.

Then Jibriil on his own in the verses. It was good. Jibriil could still hit the high notes. Impressive.

Jibriil ignored him, played to the crowd. So Adem shielded his eyes from the sand and walked over to Mustafa and Bleeker. "How is he?"

"He was shot in the kidney. How do you think he is?"

"I mean, is he going to make it?"

Dad let out a long sigh. Closed his eyes. "Make what? None of us are going to get out of here alive." He waved Adem closer, lowered his voice. "You, stay alive. Get in good with him. If that means you've got to let us go, you do it. Get in good with him until there's a chance to escape."

"No, don't, he'll listen to me. It's going to be alright."

"He won't. Promise me you'll do what it takes to stay alive."

"Don't!" Bleeker, through his teeth. He grabbed Adem by the collar. "Listen to me. Are you going to stand with him or die with us?"

"Hey!" Dad said.

Got a smile from the cop. "Just saying. That guy's led you around by your balls all this time."

"I'm not telling my own son to die."

"Good, let him decide on his own." He lifted his hand to Adem. "Help me up. I want to face this on my feet."

Dad on one side, Bleeker's arm draped over his shoulder, and Adem on the other.

Jibriil finally saw, letting the boys sing on while he lifted the gun and fired without aiming. Bullets sliced over their heads.

"What's this? Helping him to his death, Adem?" Jibriil waved the gun, loose in his grip. "That's it. You always were a gentleman. Help him over here and I'll finish him off."

Adem thought, *Yeah, yeah.*

"Us or them?" Bleeker, lips resting on Adem's shoulder, mumbling. "Us or them?"

Again, Yeah, yeah.

Adem took a step towards Jibriil.

Yeah, yeah.

Dad seething, "No, man, not like this!"

Yeah, yeah.

Adem took another step. Bleeker followed, forcing Dad to come along.

Jibriil laughing, whooping, to the delight of the army. "Yes, my brother! Yes, you bring that sack of bones on over. He was doomed from the start, yes indeed!"

They made it to Jibriil's feet. Adem unburdened himself from Bleeker. The man fell to one knee.

Adem said, "You killed his woman back home. Let me take this one."

Dad reached out and grabbed Adem by the back of the neck, squeezed hard. Adem hunched his shoulders. Jibriil shoved his gun barrel in Dad's face. Poked him in the eye, banged against his teeth. Dad let go. A couple of soldiers rambled over and restrained his arms.

Jibriil held out his pistol to Adem. "Here, then. Go on."

Adem shook his head. "Give me a machete."

"Really? Again?"

"I'm ready this time. Get one."

There's the grin. The smile. The head bob. There it was. Jibriil held up a hand and shouted, "Bring him a blade."

A twelve-year-old boy stepped forward, already with a scar starting at his scalp, tracing across his eye, nose, and lips. He lifted the machete two-handed. Eager to please Mr. Mohammed. Lifting it another inch.

Adem took the handle. A clean blade. It hadn't been used recently. Sharp, he could tell from the way it cut the air. *Swosh*. What a sound. Nothing else like it anywhere. He'd heard it right before his would-be assassin settled in and put the blade to his throat. The tip slicing in when word came—the Imam wants him alive! You can't kill him! He's protected!

A favor for Jibriil. Seemed there was always someone there to do a favor for Jibriil.

Adem bit his bottom lip, arcing the blade across the air, showing off, the crowd on edge. Blood. More Blood.

Adem place the edge of the machete on the back of Bleeker's neck.

Bleeker said, "Do it already."

Adem pulled back the machete.

Yeah, yeah.

And he sliced Jibriil's gun hand clean off with one stroke.

*

There should've been more outrage. But it all went quiet except for Jibriil cursing at top volume, holding his stump while it poured blood, calling Adem every vile name a man had ever thought to call another man.

"You bleeding cunt goddamned motherfucking...aaaahhhhhWWWWWWLLLL!"

Lost all the words, twisted them into noise. The boys watched on, not sure whether to be happy or pissed or what. The blood was hypnotic, shooting out at first like a cartoon before pulsing, pulsing. One of the soldiers ran to Jibriil's side, wrapped a scarf around what was left of his commander's forearm, tourniquet tight. Jibriil grabbed the AK-47 on the soldier's shoulder. Pulled and pulled, cursed the guy for helping him, and he awkwardly got a handle on the rifle. Lifted it towards Adem, nostrils flared.

The barrel wavered wildly. Adem flinched, waiting for the sound, the impact. The pain.

But nothing. Jibriil kept adjusting the gun, stone cold eyes on Adem, but then he blinked and the gun wobbled and he had to start all over.

Bleeker gripped Adem's belt, pulled himself standing. He leaned on Adem's shoulder. "He's not going to shoot you. Finish the job."

Adem tried to answer. Words had to push through thorns in his throat, it felt like. "I can't. Can't."

"I get it. Don't worry about it. You did alright, kid. That'll be enough. We can take it to our grave." Laughed a little. Weak, coughing, but still a laugh.

Adem fought it, but couldn't help it. Laughing and crying. Sniffing. Jibriil, helpless, unable to pull the trigger. Then he dropped the rifle. Walked in little circles. Then nearly fell. The closest soldier helped him to sit on the ground. Cross legged, still looking up at Adem with wrinkled anger and saying, "You motherfucker. You fucking...mother*fucker*, you."

A faint noise. Shifting gears. Whining engine. Adem turned, trying to find where it was coming from. Then his dad's phone rang.

A bunch of guns came up, aimed at his dad. He held up one hand, surrender palm, slipped the other in his pocket and pulled out the phone. Slid it open, held it to his ear. "Yeah?"

Listened. Listened. *Mm hm. Mm hm.* Then, "Yeah, you found us. That's us."

Adem saw it at the back of the mob, a dust cloud rising. Engine whine, louder. The ruckus from the crowd rising. Bursts of automatic rifle fire. Soldiers scattering. Then the grill appearing as the crowd cleared. The Rover. Chi behind the wheel. And he had help—at least six, seven, maybe eight men, all with rifles, hanging off the runners, the back bumper. Older men, business owners and fathers and grandfathers, all of whom hadn't left, sick of what the boys were doing to their city. Anyone who tried to pull them off got shot. Chi waved wildly. *Get in! Get in!*

Revved the engine. The soldiers kept a careful distance but they were starting to get antsy. A few fired back, shattered a window, put holes in the side, felled a man. Chi hunched, kept waving.

Dad took up Bleeker again, still leaning on Adem. Started towards the Rover, Dawit covering them, then going ahead, opened the back door for them. More potshots. No one ready to massacre them. Maybe because they still weren't sure where Mr. Mohammed stood. He brought down Jibriil but didn't kill him. Was he taking over? Was he against them?

Bleeker stopped mid-stride. Shook his head. "No, go on. Just go on."

"Into the truck, Ray."

"No, you guys need to go. Let me go. Really, let me go."

"Not gonna happen."

"Goddamn it, *let me go.*" He pushed off Dad, let go of Adem, stood on his own. He took a step backwards. Wobbly, but he didn't fall. He made a face and reached for his back, arched it. Pain all over his face. Trembling. But Bleeker let out a breath and looked at Adem.

Pointed at Jibriil's hand in the dirt. "Get me that gun."

Adem didn't move. The fighting by the Rover was getting worse, and Dawit was yelling at them. Dad yelled back. Chi waving madly now. Bulletholes in every window.

"Come on. The pistol. Give it to me." Bleeker, his hand out.

Adem didn't move. "What do you want with it? What are you doing?"

It took a few more labored breaths for Bleeker to say it. "I'm…listen, I'm giving them a reason not to follow you, okay? I'll keep them busy."

"You can't hold off the whole army."

A wink. "I don't plan on it. Get me that gun."

Adem walked over to the hand, lifted the gun by the barrel. The fingers didn't come loose. Adem tried to pry them off. It took a little effort. The fingers already felt fake, like a Halloween prop. But he finally got them off, carefully pulling the index finger from the trigger guard, the thumb off the opposite side. Ducked and ran back to Bleeker, put it in his hand.

Bleeker hefted it, dropped the clip into his other hand, checked that it still had some ammo. Then he slid it back, not hard, pressed until it clicked. Grinned at Adem as he did it.

Said, "Now get the hell out of here. Keep your dad alive. He deserves a parade for what he's done for you."

Silly to talk him out of it. Adem knew what was next. As much as he wanted to tell him not to, they were all way beyond that. Jibriil had made his choice. Made it a long time ago. How was saving his life going to make anything better ever again?

"Can you walk?"

Bleeker nodded. "I've got a few steps left in me. Go on, dumbass, get in the car."

He backed away, needing to say *Thank you* but it didn't feel right. Not at all. Still eye to eye until Bleeker turned and began walking towards Jibriil, still sitting on the ground. Jibriil lifted his face to Bleeker. Other soldiers noticed. Began yelling. The helper stepped between Jibriil and Bleeker. The cop shot him in the chest three times, pushed him to the side before he fell. Now inches from Jibriil. Gun in his face, lingering. The same pose Jibriil was in before he shot that woman, watching her on the ground before taking her life. Jibriil, eyes up, mouth open just so, shrugged.

Bleeker shot him. Jibriil recoiled. A piece of his skull flew off. Blood, brain. Fell onto his back, his legs still crossed in front of him.

His dad grabbed Adem from behind. Drug him to the Rover, covering him with his bulk as the gunfire ramped up. "Into the truck! Now! Get in!"

Dawit, already in, grabbed Adem, held his head down at Dawit's knees. He had the window down, firing at the soldiers. Another two volunteers had fallen. Dad crunched inside with them, slammed the door. "Go! Go! Go!"

Chi threw it into gear and spun the tires. They caught, and he rocketed away, a hail of bullets following.

Adem lifted his head so he could see out. Saw Bleeker still standing there, smiling, as the horde overtook him from all directions.

Faster, faster. Farther and farther from the crowd. Harder to tell where Bleeker was in all of that. All of them except Chi watching through the back windows. The chase died down. The bullets stopped plinging against the back of the Rover. Dad rubbed his hand across the top of Adem's scalp.

Adem couldn't help but tremble. He was too stunned to cry. As the dust clouds kicked up by the Rover grew thicker, harder to see through, Adem righted himself in his seat, fell against his father, and noticed that Chi's shoulder was bleeding. His face had been peppered with glass and was running blood. He wiped it with his sleeve and said, "I'm fine. We'll be fine. We're going to be fine."

Hundreds of miles to go before they were safe. Plenty of patrols to outrun. Borders to cross. Lies to tell. But despite all of that, Adem believed him. Yeah, they were all going to be just fine.

THIRTY-FIVE

The shrug. He didn't get that. Was the bastard just resigned to it? Thought he deserved it? All out of fight? Or had he lost too much blood? Why only a shrug?

He didn't have much time to think about it, though. Once he shot the guard, he knew it had to go quickly. So Jibriil shrugged and Bleeker blew his brains out and it was done. The kid and Mustafa were in the Rover, on their way out of camp. Maybe some of the soldiers would mount up in a truck and chase them, but Bleeker hoped he would prove to be too irresistible a target—a white American to string up. Their mighty leader's assassin, even. The perfect star for their little movies.

He saw the truck hightailing it out of camp. Adem peeking through the window at him. He felt pretty good. And then they attacked. Pulled both arms out of socket. Hit him with rocks and rifle butts and fists and boots. Grabbed his hair. Knives sliced him all over. One slit right across his eye. His lips. Blood in his mouth. By the time one held his forehead and ripped the blade across his throat, he was mostly beyond feeling. He smelled the body odor around him, his own blood, felt the heat, and saw an army of hands all wanting to take their turn with him, but none of it hurt. Knew his lips were curled into a grin. It was natural, dying and grinning. They went hand in hand. But Bleeker knew it was more than that. He had beat them. No matter what they did to him next, he wasn't feeling it anyway.

They carried him to the tree while he choked on his blood. They strung the rope around his ankles. They pulled him up. How much longer was he going to have to watch this from one good eye? Swung back and forth. Chanting. Angry men in scarves wielding machetes.

And then, well, look at that. A girl in her Sunday best. A toddler. Her mother behind her, hair like silk falling over her shoulders, urging the girl forward. *Go to Daddy. Walk to him. You can do it.*

He held his arms out to her. Pudgy little girl. Yellow and white dress, stained purple from her juicebox. Inching forward. Giggling, burbling. *Come on, baby. Walk to Daddy.*

Wasn't she the cutest thing you had ever seen?

EPILOGUE

The Buick hauled the ice shack out onto the lake. Hard ice this year. January not as cold as the old days, everyone said, but not as crazy as the year before with the blizzards, one after the other. Just good clear air, colder than death.

Dad parked the car, got out. He unhooked the shack while Adem climbed out of the passenger's seat and walked around to take the wheel. He was finally free of courts, debriefings, jail, threats of being taken to secret prisons overseas.

They held him for three months. He made a deal with the Feds, and it helped that Dad spent most of his cash on the best lawyer he could afford. Pretty much everything he'd stashed away from his gang days went into Adem's defense team. And it worked. Adem was free, the records about this whole ordeal sealed for a handful of years, and he was able to pick up where he left off at school.

Dad unhitched the rig and retracted the wheels on the trailer, easing the shack onto the ice. Adem pulled the Buick away, circled back and parked by the shack, left to Dad in a handwritten will Bleeker must have made right before they left for Africa. It wasn't official, and it didn't supercede the one he'd put together with Trish years before, back when they weren't exactly happy in the marriage but still had the good sense to know it needed to be done.

Trish didn't want the ice house or the car. So she called Dad, told him what the new will said, and "If you want to do it, it's all yours. I'm done."

Adem got out, looked around. "Not exactly Lake Superior."

"Better than nothing."

Adem let out a stream of breath that floated in front of him like cigar smoke. He'd missed this. His first time to really enjoy the cold again after being indoors most of the past year. Definitely more to his blood's liking than Somalia. If he never saw a desert again, he'd be plenty happy.

Dad called out, "Didn't want to help, did you?"

A shrug. "You were doing fine."

"Just...come on. Let's do it."

Adem reached into the backseat, grabbed a plastic box, and closed the door. He walked over to the ice house, stepped inside.

They hadn't bothered to clean out the empty rum and coke bottles yet, leaving sticky spots on the floor and a sweet-and-sour smell all over. Adem opened the window to air it out. Dad picked up the folding chairs, set them around the hole in the floor. He knelt down, uncovered it, and started to work with a hand drill. Adem had told him to buy an electric one, but Dad said, "If we like it this once, we'll buy one for next time."

The will had also stated that Ray Bleeker had decided to have his ashes spread into his favorite ice fishing spot like Forrest's had been. He hadn't said that Dad should be the one to do it. In fact, he wanted Trish to be the one. God knew why, because she sure didn't. When Dad picked up the Roadmaster and ice house, she showed him the letter. Then handed him the box. "I had already moved on a long time ago. He's confusing me with the woman who loved him."

Dad said he would be honored to follow through. Trish *hmphed* and brushed him off. "Suit yourself."

Some UN workers had found the body several months after Dad and Adem returned home. It had been castrated, burned in places, probably while he was still alive, gutted like Warfaa, then beheaded. Left in a shallow grave with a few other victims, the desert had managed to cover them with enough sand to keep them in somewhat decent shape, enough to ID Bleeker's head from a photo. They shipped him back home, handed the remains over to Trish, since there was no one else remotely like family, and let her cremate them. Not even a ceremony, a memorial, not even witnesses. Trish signed some papers, wrote a check, and picked up the plastic box the next day, which she'd left in her garage until Dad came by.

Adem took his turn on the drill, churning up ice, his hands tiring a lot faster than he had expected, but he didn't give up. He was determined to start working out, build up his body and his strength. He never wanted to feel helpless like he had at the hands of that mob who nearly took his head clean off. He had been the one pushing for this more than his father. He had heard Bleeker's last words before they drove away. Turning himself into bait. Hard to shake that sort of thing, hearing a man's last words.

When they finally got the drill through to the water—ice looked like five or six inches thick this year—they stood side-by-side above the hole, Adem holding the plastic box Trish had handed over, full of Bleeker's ashes, a few bits of bone.

Dad said, "Do you want to, like, *say* anything? A prayer, something like that?"

Adem thought about it. His experience, instead of turning him off to religion, made him explore Islam more. Were the crazies right? Or were they way off? He was learning a lot. He began adhering to the tenets of the faith, just to see how it felt. Daily prayers, a new diet, a beard. Could be it brought him some peace. Could be it helped clear his mind of the hate and fear he'd carried home, nightmares every night for months, loud noises making him flinch and sweat. He hadn't decided yet if he really believed it, but it felt good to try.

Adem shook his head. "I don't think he would've wanted us to."

"Yeah, that's what I thought."

Adem knelt on one knee. Popped the top off the box, and aimed a corner towards the hole in the ice. He carefully shook the ashes into the water, nice and slow, until there was nothing left but the residue clinging to the plastic. He sat the box aside, stood again.

Dad was standing, head bowed and eyes closed. Adem knew he wasn't praying. Dad had come back from Somalia and abandoned his faith. It didn't mean anything to him anymore after seeing what it did to those soldiers, to Jibriil, and to his own son. He talked to his wife about his choice, and it turned out she'd been leaning in the same direction, just afraid to disappoint him. So whatever Dad was doing now, it had nothing to do with Allah. He was drinking again, quite a lot most nights, but he hadn't turned back to crime. He fought hard to get his job back at Target, convinced his boss. Even got a couple of pay raises. Not the best life, not the worst either. He was making do.

The water under the hole was clear again as the ashes swirled away. Still nothing from Dad. Adem wondered if he was asleep.

"Okay."

Dad blinked open his eyes, sniffed. "Okay."

Another long quiet moment.

Dad said, "Do you want to try it? See if we can catch something?"

Sitting around a hole in the ice in sub-zero temps, hoping to catch a fish. A year ago, it would not have been Adem's idea of a good time. But if it meant another couple of hours with his dad, who hadn't spoken to him as much as Adem had hoped he would after coming back home, then fine. He hoped over time things would get back to normal. In the meantime, take a seat, fish in the winter.

They drilled another hole, the first one now kind of sacred. They set up a line. They sat, waited.

His dad said, "Do you still think about her?"

Sufia. The kind nurse who helped him back to his feet. The fiercely intelligent woman who fought him every step of the way as he negotiated for pirates. The wretched, pitiable thing on the stairs of the hospital, wailing and bleeding through acid-scarred skin.

Yes. Every day.

Adem said, "Not much, no. Try not to."

Dad said, "Hm."

And that was it until they gave up a couple of hours later after no bites. Dad hooked the rig up, drove them back to New Pheasant Run, let Adem out. A handshake. A good long one. Then he dragged the ice shack back to the Cities.

He put it on Craigslist a few days later, sold it the same afternoon.

But he kept the Buick. It was a fine car.

***

ALSO BY ANTHONY NEIL SMITH

Novels

Choke On Your Lies
Hogdoggin'
Yellow Medicine
The Drummer
Psychosomatic

Novellas

To the Devil, My Regards (with Victor Gischler)
Colder than Hell: Dead Man #16 (with Lee Goldberg and William Rabkin)